The Trouble with Rose

is Amita Murray's debut novel. Having lived in and around London, Delhi and California, Amita loves writing about the comedy and tragedy of cultural encounters. In 2016, Amita won the SI Leeds Literary prize for her short story collection *Marmite and Mango Chutney*. Amita lives in London, and teaches creative writing and yoga workshops when she can be dragged away from the characters in her head.

The Trouble with Rose

Amita Murray

HarperCollins*Publishers*

HarperCollins*Publishers* Ltd
1 London Bridge Street,
London SE1 9GF

www.harpercollins.co.uk

First published by HarperCollins*Publishers* 2019
1

A catalogue record for this book is available from the British Library

ISBN: 978-0-00-829124-2
ISBN: 978-000-832770-5 (IN-only)

This novel is entirely a work of fiction.
The names, characters and incidents portrayed in it are
the work of the author's imagination. Any resemblance to
actual persons, living or dead, events or localities is
entirely coincidental.

Typeset in Berling LT Std by Palimpsest Book Production Ltd,
Falkirk, Stirlingshire

Printed and bound in the UK by CPI Group (UK) Ltd, Croydon CR0 4YY

MIX
Paper from
responsible sources
FSC™ C007454

This book is produced from independently certified FSC™ paper to ensure
responsible forest management.

For more information visit: www.harpercollins.co.uk/green

anisha
first reader, best sister
s.l.a
because everything is about you

1

Wedding Day

In the natural course of things, by the afternoon of her wedding, a bride is thinking ahead to all the things life will have in store for her. Love, joy, romance, silly little spats with her soul-mate that will be sorted out – hopefully in bed, nibbling on toes – and the endless harmony, the never-ending fun and the countless hours she will spend doing nothing much at all in the arms of the love of her life. She imagines that from now on things will be perfect, she will be happy, and gone forever will be anxiety, irritability, chin hair and a generalized tendency towards narkiness. In short, she will become a better, more grown-up version of herself.

She knows that all of this wonderfulness will start with an enormous slice of cake followed by a steamy night in bed, hopefully in a remote tropical island where none of her extended family will be able to call her, text her, tweet her, or otherwise be able to find her. In the normal course of things, on the afternoon of her wedding, a bride is not behind the bars of the local prison waiting for her lawyer to bail her out or for her extended family to tell her all the things that have gone wrong in her life. I'm not saying that this has never happened in the history of weddings. I'm just saying that it is rare.

Before I tell you about my wedding day, I should make a note here – actually it's more of a disclaimer – about my enormous extended family (mentioned above). Is this story about them, you ask? Well, no. Are they always there, do they have an opinion about everything, and can't you just ignore them?

Well. Yes, yes, and no.

I have so many cousins, aunties and uncles that live in London that I have to look at every Indian man or woman passing by just to make sure they aren't one of them. The thing with my relatives is that they tend to feel insulted pretty easily. You should know this before I go on with my story. They keep score of who gives them regular updates about their life and grovels for advice, who invites them to what, and who sends them a box of champagne truffles for Diwali and not just a regular Indian sweet box with plain *laddu* in it. They also like to write notes.

Dear Rilla,

I hope you enjoy the hundred-and-fifty-piece NutriBullet I sent you. It is a superior brand to the plain three-piece blender sent by Auntie Parul. Thank you for the champagne truffles. I don't drink (as you know), so I have given them to my cleaner. I know you are too busy to visit us (have you got a job yet?) but I thought that I would remind you that our home is your home. Don't forget your family.

Best wishes.

Yours truly, etc.

All in all, it is better to turn and stare at every Indian person walking by, just to make sure it isn't one of the GIF (Great Indian Family) in case you accidentally ignore them. Or, in my case, so you can make a quick getaway. Of course, since every other person you see in London looks more or less Indian, this can make you see monsters lurking around every corner, and turn you into a neurotic mess.

My GIF forms the backdrop of just about everything. They are the wallpaper and the furniture, the muzak, the Thames, London traffic, pollution and global warming rolled into one. They are always there and generally in the way. And no matter how much you think you can deal with them, the truth is you can't.

Let's go back now to the matter at hand, the story of the bride who got arrested on her wedding day. I'll tell you the story the way it happened. Or at least, I'll tell it to you *almost* the way it happened. Which is nearly as good.

*

The setting for the wedding is Bloomington House, a country estate near Cambridge, its rambling red-brick walls charmingly cocooned in a wood of crab-apple and ash. Today, cloud shadows play hide-and-seek on the lawns, and the trees that are waking up in the half-light of spring shiver naked in the breeze, their reflections playing leapfrog with the koi in the pond. Next to the pond is a Japanese meditation garden, where someone has clearly been thinking about alien invasions because there are crop circles ranging all the way from one side to the other in order of size.

In this romantic scene, a large number of cars have recently pulled up and evacuated my numerous relatives in all their colourful glory, tucking in sari trains, sprucing maroon lipstick, jingling bracelets, chattering non-stop. I watch this from a window in the back room in which I am waiting. How long before all of them head into the barn for the wedding ceremony? I scan the grounds. There are too many of them, this is the problem. They keep stopping, gesturing and exclaiming at the view, the manor, the gardens, the weather, each other's clothes, jewellery, complexion, hair, manicures, the works. Just looking at them is exhausting. I turn and pace the room, my hands on my waist. Why is this dress so tight? I fidget with the buttons at the back but the snug bodice won't let me stretch my arms far enough.

This will be over soon. *This will be over soon.* What is the matter with this place? Why is it so hot in here? I fan myself with my hands but it makes no difference.

I look around me. Unlike the garden that is lit up with lanterns, and the hall for the wedding breakfast that is covered at my request in all sorts of roses – red, pink, Cabbage, yellow, white, Hot Cocoa, the lot – the back room in which I'm waiting is white-washed and uninspiring. There are rolled-up yoga mats at one end, chairs piled one on top of the other, a hatch in the wall with a view into the newly painted kitchen, a headless Spiderman on the counter, no doubt forgotten by a child. On the cork board, there are notices for yoga classes, an advert for the local florist, a dog walker whose 'best friend has always been a dog' since she was three, a request for clothes for the Salvation Army, a phone number to call if someone spots a missing person and another for people with gonorrhoea.

I stare at them and my breathing gets short and heavy. I look out of the window again. The flock of relatives is thinning but a few linger outside the barn. *Come on, come on, come on*, I whisper. I stare at them, willing them to go faster, and give me some space in which to think. And maybe to breathe.

My reflection stares back at me, the little bronze hoops in my ears and the band of dark pink and orange flowers pinned all around my head suddenly looking out of place, like they belong to someone else. My silver dress is fuzzy in the window. What made me choose silver? It is washing out my complexion, making me look pasty. My black hair is bundled up on top of my head but already coiled strands are making a getaway. There is a look in my eyes, a maniacal look. Do I always frown like this? I try to relax my forehead, but almost at once the brows knit back together. I rub hard at my forehead.

There is so little air in this room that I am finding it hard to breathe. I take gasping breaths. Finally, every last one of my relatives disappears into the barn, through the wisteria that hangs over the barn door like the tail of a bejewelled pony getting ready for dressage. It's now or never. I struggle with the window latch. It is jammed shut, having recently been painted over with thick white paint. I push against the window, try to budge the latch. I take off my shoe and pound it, I claw at it with my fingers, rubbing my knuckles raw, but the window doesn't budge. Not a smidge. I need a wedge, something that will slide under the window, splinter the new paint that has glued it shut. I look all around me. There's nothing. *Nothing!* There is a knock at the door. A relative? My fiancé? A summons? I stare at the door then, heart pounding, I walk slowly to open it. Standing outside is a policeman.

'You need to step this way, miss,' he says.

I look frantically behind him towards the inner door of the barn. I am supposed to walk through it any moment now. I look at the police officer. His ginger hair has been hastily brushed and there are two croissant crumbs clinging to his enormous moustache. The man was clearly in the middle of his breakfast when he was sent out on this mission.

I take a deep breath and hold out my hands, keeping a wary eye on the barn door.

'That's okay, miss,' the man says. 'If you cooperate, there's no need for handcuffs.'

The man is so relaxed his hands are lolling in his pockets. What is the matter with this man? He is smiling and bored at the same time. I am now starting to feel a little faint. Or maybe like I'm going to explode. I am going to burst out of this dress. The tiny buttons at the back are going to ping-ping-ping off me like bullets. I flap my hands to cool myself. I look desperately at the man.

'Please, please, I—'

'Now, miss, steady now—'

'You don't understand—'

'Calm down, you need to calm down—'

This is when I scream. My scream rents the air and the man looks startled.

I'm good at screaming. When I was seven, a drama teacher spent a month with my sister and me, basically teaching us how to scream. There's not a lot I remember about my education – through most of it I was busy trying to show everyone that I was unteachable, bunking lessons, running away from school, sitting morosely with my hands in my pockets and not saying a word when asked a question, getting into endless debates with teachers about the conformist nature of the school system – but I have learnt how to scream.

The man holds out his hands to me. 'Now, now, miss, there's no need to be like that about it.' He still sees no need for restraints, not really. This is all in a day's work for him. I feel a little affronted that I rank so low on his list of important criminals to track down.

I tear the gerberas off from my head, and the rest of my hair comes bundling down. I stamp on the flowers a few times and scream again. The inner door to the barn bangs open and a small horde of people come crashing through it. Behind them, I can hear a buzzing, like the busy hum of a beehive that can turn into thunder at any moment.

My parents, my fiancé and his parents all try to push into the back room, all at the same time, with my Auntie PK and Auntie Dharma.

My mother, Renu Kumar, first through the door, makes straight for me and grabs my shoulders. Her forehead is deeply furrowed, her pink lipstick indifferently applied and now a little smudged, her purple silk sari with its green border tucked in a little too high at her waist so that you can see her ankles.

'What's happening? Who is this man? What's happening?' She sounds a little frantic. She stares into my eyes.

Then Simon crashes into the room. His grey suit and tailored burgundy waistcoat with the blue paisley tie tucked in looks good on him but he has already managed to undo the top button of his shirt.

'I saw a policeman walking up the driveway! What's wrong?'

'Nothing! Nothing at all. I—'

'What are you doing here?' Simon is staring at the policeman, looking completely confused.

'Now, sir, there's no need to panic. I just need to speak to Miss Kumar here, that's all. At the police station, that is.'

'You know you're not supposed to see her!' My fiancé's mother waves a hand about, tries in vain to get Simon out of the room. She is wearing a steel-blue skirt, with a long coat and hat to match. She looks as neatly put together as always, but her cheeks are a little red and her pearl necklace slightly askew, giving her a jaunty Camilla Parker Bowles look. Marie Langton has obviously been hitting the gin a little early today.

'What is all this about, Officer?' my father Manoj Kumar intones, smoothing back his salt-and-pepper hair that has been styled to such perfection that parallel comb-streaks can still be seen in it. He pats the collar of his Indian *sherwani* coat – long, gold and white, and too tight for him – that the GIF has made him wear today. 'Surely, there's been a mistake. We can get it cleared up in a jiff.'

There's something about uniforms and official people that makes my father use his posh English, the one from which all trace of an Indian accent has been wiped. His disinfected accent does have its uses in some situations. Not in this one though.

'Miss,' the officer says, totally ignoring him, 'if you come with me quietly, there's no need for a display.' He's looking significantly at me. The man actually wants me to go quietly, he doesn't want to make a fuss and that's not out of laziness, I can see that. He is trying to protect my feelings. If he doesn't have to say what he's arresting me for in front of my family and in-laws, he won't.

Everyone is staring at me. There is a sea of unblinking eyes, all waiting for me to speak.

'The thing is,' I look from face to face, 'here's the thing. See? I'm being arrested for shoplifting. You see what I'm saying?' I say it with the air of someone about to choreograph a song to the theme. If this were a musical, I would be singing it. *The thing is, the thing is, folks, be-ware! I am being arrested because I am wild as a hare! A hare, you say? A hare, I say! A hare? A hare! A hare? Be-ware!* I think I'm going to pass out. I stare frantically from face to face. *Get me out of here, get me out of here*, I want to say, but nothing comes out.

'That's piffle,' my father says to the police officer. 'Rilla is a good girl. She would never do such a thing.' He looks genuinely confused. It's like my teenage years have left no impression on his memory.

My mother's chin is trembling though. She's pulling out a hanky that she has tucked into the sleeve of her sari blouse. My mother has the tendency to burst into tears. In family pictures she can be seen in the background with a hanky covering her eyes. Of course, since every family picture is crammed with the GIF, you would have to really be searching – a Where's-Wally-scale search – to find her.

Now my father is patting her on her back and making shush-shush noises. It's my wedding day, I'm getting arrested, and it's just been revealed to everyone that I am a kleptomaniac. But no, my father is comforting my mother. Everything is upside down.

'Darling, what's going on?' Simon asks. He has tucked a Hot Cocoa rose in the lapel of his new grey suit just for me, and his eyes, his eyes are even now looking lovingly

10

at me. I swallow painfully. I don't want to hurt him, but I know I'm going to. He places a hand on my shoulder. He is medium height, though this still makes him a good few inches taller than me. His dark hair falls over his forehead just the way I like it. 'This is just a mistake, isn't it? We should really get on with it. There's a crowd of people waiting.'

The thing with Simon is he always thinks the best of me (and he hates to keep people waiting). He's loyal, doesn't worry a lot about little things and he rarely has any problems with other people. Which basically makes him the opposite of me.

'I did something stupid. I'm so sorry.' Suddenly my shoulders are slumped and there is a crack in my voice. I hate this kind of thing in myself. You think you are dealing with a situation in one way and then your body betrays you and it turns out you are not dealing with it at all. I realize that right about now I could do with a hug, but no one is offering me one.

'This won't take long, sir,' the police officer says to Simon. 'Now if you just—'

'We're about to get married though.' Simon frowns. 'You can't just take her away. What's your proof anyway?'

'I am not at liberty to discuss the details, sir.' The officer smoothens his moustache.

'Can't you wait till they're married?' My mother's hands are clasped, beseeching. 'At least wait till they're married. Please, you have to!'

My mother – the only one in this room who really

knows me, besides my sister Rose – has always said that no one will want to marry me. I'm just too rude, clumsy, stupid, standoffish, unfeminine and ungroomed. At the moment she just wants to make sure that I get married quickly, before Simon finds out what I'm really like. The one thing she is sure would never happen is now actually starting to look like it never will. There is an ominous twitch in her cheek.

One of the aunties, Auntie Dharma, is counting her beads. 'I told you not to fix a date when Mercury was retrograde. *Shani* is in the house of marriage.' She is wearing a *salwar*-suit, her *chunni* placidly on her head, and a long thin white plait lying mousily on her back. She is skinny, her face as wrinkled as a prune, and her large eyes goggle from behind thick black spectacles. She calls herself a spiritual healer and works in a local meditation centre. She believes luck in marriage comes from your karma in a past life.

The other auntie, Auntie PK – the journalist who only ever wears *khadi* cotton, only ever in shades of beige, and doesn't pluck her eyebrows or wax her upper lip or armpits – is looking cross and saying that someone will pay for this. She means some man somewhere in an air-conditioned office drinking a macchiato before changing for his tennis game. Her short spiky hair is standing up all around her head.

I breathe deeply. I can get through this, I've been through worse. And this isn't the first time I've been arrested. But the walls of the white room are closing in on me. There are too many people between me and the door. I look hopelessly at the window. This is when Rose steps in.

Rose. My beautiful sister Rose, in her long silver dress – silver is really her colour, not mine, her beautiful hair blacker than black, her eyes dark as coal, her rosebud mouth, a glow all around her body, walks up to me and gives me a hug. I swallow painfully. A tear escapes but it disappears in Rose's hair – or she brushes it away for me, knowing I hate people seeing me cry. It is just like Rose, she knew I needed a hug. No one else did. But she did.

She pulls back now and looks into my eyes. 'It'll be all right. Okay? *Okay?*'

I swallow and nod. I try to take deep breaths.

She cups my cheek in her hand. 'This is not a big deal. You're bigger than this.'

'We'll get a lawyer,' Simon's father John Langton cuts in. He is short and broad-boned, his hair cut neatly so that all the strands are exactly the same length. His eyes are a pale grey, so that they seem to look through you, not like Simon and his mother's dark blue.

'You *are* a lawyer,' Simon reminds him.

'We'll get a lawyer,' his father says.

At the police station, things happen quickly. Since what I have stolen costs less than two hundred pounds, I am told that I will be turned away with a police caution. Though, if I accept these terms, this will still count as a conviction and I will have a criminal record. (It's true I've been arrested before but, since I was underage at the time, I didn't get a criminal record.) When the officer interrogating me suggests the caution, I say, 'I will take this under advisement.' I have been waiting all my life to say these words. I confer with my lawyer, and I take the caution and the criminal record that comes with it. When we come out, my lawyer (organized by my nearly-father-in-law), a middle-aged woman called Gudrun, who is built like a Rottweiler, tells me to get a grip on my life.

'Grow up. Get therapy. Next time, you'll get fined or do time. And it'll get really difficult to get a job. Kosher?'

Various members of my family are standing about outside the police station, waiting to pick me up. Simon is pacing up and down, ignoring everyone. The moment he sees me, he rushes up to me and engulfs me in a hug. He holds me tight and I stand rigid, not feeling like I can touch him right now, though I can feel the thudding of his heart.

He pulls back finally and searches my eyes. 'Rilla, we can still do this. They didn't want to give us another slot, but they did in the end. Let's do it now. Okay?' He's still looking at me like I'm the most important person in the world. He has taken his jacket and tie off and he probably has no idea where they are. I love this about him. I love that he doesn't care where half his clothes are.

'Simon,' I whisper, 'I shoplifted. Don't you see? That's not normal.'

'You're under a lot of stress. The wedding, and the warning about not completing your MA. It happened. It happens to a lot of people.' He looks firm. 'If you just put one foot in front of another, it'll be over soon. Then we can deal with the rest of it.'

'Don't you see?' my voice cracks. 'I can't do this. I'm – not ready.'

'You want to postpone the wedding? Okay, okay, look, we can do that. We'll do whatever you want. Whatever you need.' He is scanning my face, trying to sound re-assuring, though I can see none of this is making sense to him, none of it is really sinking in.

I look at him wordlessly. How can I explain it to him? How can I find words for something that I can't fully understand myself?

I mutely shake my head. 'The thing is, Simon,' I blurt out finally, 'I can't go through with it. None of this is working.'

'I told you,' says my mother, tears pouring down her cheeks.

Somehow I escape everyone. I think it is because I scream, 'Leave me alone!' and disappear down into the under-ground before anyone can stop me. I enter a train at random, staring down anyone who dares to look at me, standing there holding on for dear life, still in my silver wedding dress. After a few random stations have whizzed by, I get off. I run out of the tube station and I end up on a park bench, bent double, face in hands, taking gasping breaths.

I say I escaped everyone, but I didn't, because Rose is here with me.

I sit up. 'I made such a mess of it. I always make a mess of it. Rose, why can't I get one thing right?' The tears that have been threatening all morning now start to pour down my face.

She takes my hand. She sits quietly, just holding my hand. Sometimes I think it's uncanny how she knows just what I need her to do. When you've grown up with someone, maybe you get so used to each other that you know what every movement means. Every gesture comes with its code, every mood, each slump of the shoulders, every turning away. My sister knows the code. She can sense it before I can.

The fit of crying passes after a while and I sit there, my nose red, sniffles catching in my throat.

'I guess you knew I was going to break up with him?' I say now. I don't look at her. I don't need to, I know the look on her face. She doesn't respond.

I stare blankly around me, where life seems to be carrying on as normal. A swan sits regally on the edge of a duck pond, its mate doing laps in the water. A chunky peanut-butter Kit-Kat wrapper sits next to an overfull bin that is starting to smell of dead rat in the sunshine. The bench I am sitting on has been dedicated to Lady Cornelia North, who donated it to the council in 1986. Red buses line the park, parents with dark circles under their eyes determinedly push buggies, a jogger talks to herself as she fast-walks past. I shut my eyes tight.

'I guess I knew,' Rose says.

'I'm hopeless.' I place my face in my hands again. 'I wreck everything.'

'Why this though, Rilla? I thought Simon was the one.'

I jerk my head. 'He barely knows me. He thinks I'm perfect. I'm the opposite of perfect. *You* know! It wouldn't have worked. How could it ever have worked?'

'*What if I make you the most beautiful garland in the world, Princess Multan, my* phool, *my Queen of Roses, Princess of Hearts?*' Rose's voice becomes rounder, louder. Like she's talking in a theatre, her voice ricocheting off moonbeams.

I speak through my tears. '*Then perhaps I will marry you, Rup. Is that really your name?*'

Rose gently blots away my tears, then she bows ironically. '*Of course, my princess. It is I, Rup Singh. I was a prince once. A sorceress turned me into a commoner. I wait for the love of a true princess to change me back into the real me.*' Rose switches back to her normal voice. She speaks as if seeing this scene in her mind's eye, from a long time ago. 'And now you sit on the balcony waiting for the garland. You comb your beautiful black hair. Roses bloom in your cheeks. Your delicate hands cradle your heart. Your voice, like a nightingale's, sings to your lover. To me.'

'My lover with swarthy brown cheeks and coarse hands,' I say. 'But I love you anyway. And you come back with the most beautiful garland in the world, made of roses and marigolds, jasmine and hot-house zinnias. And in the centre, forming the heart pendant, a moth orchid. The most precious flower in the world for the most beautiful princess. You scurry up the trellis outside my window like a monkey. You give me the garland. I give you a kiss and promise to marry you.'

'And I turn into a girl,' Rose says.

We both laugh. My laugh has a catch in it, but it's a laugh nonetheless.

'I turn into a little brown nut of a girl,' my sister says. 'Ugly and scrawny, shifty and sly. Because the witch that transformed me did so not from a prince, but a princess. Now I am back. I am not Rup, but Rupa Singh.'

'*Oh well,*' I say softly, looking at her face now, shimmering in front of my eyes, '*I promised to marry you, so I will.*'

'*You will take me for your partner?*' Rose says. '*Even though I am a woman?*'

'*No one is perfect,*' I say.

We laugh. Laugh at this script that we know better than anything we've ever said. Because we've rehearsed it a thousand times, performed it a hundred. When I was seven, and Rose was nine.

'Rose,' I whisper. 'Rose.'

We sit together, neither saying a word. I am scared to break the silence, scared that this moment will disappear.

'I don't think I know how,' I finally say. The words well up. 'Don't you see? I don't know how to make it work. I don't know how to be with someone. I have never known.' I look desperately in front of me, searching for something that isn't there. Rose doesn't say anything.

'That is where I have to go back, isn't it?' I say it softly.

'I have to go back to that. To Princess Multan and Rup Singh. To those living rooms in Tooting and Wembley and Harrow and Hampstead. That's where I have to go.'

Rose doesn't answer. She doesn't need to. She knows as well as I that to make love work, you have to go back to where you learnt how to love.

2

Spot the Difference

Hold up two illustrations and spot the differences between them.

So I told you a story, the story of my wedding day. As I told you, it was almost the story of my wedding day. Actually, in all important details, it was *the* story.

But if you hold up the two pictures, one real, one almost-real, you'll spot ten differences. Let's go through the list.

One. I told you that the back room in which I was waiting, the one with the yoga mats and chairs, the back room of the main building of Bloomington House, an estate in Cambridgeshire, was white-washed. In actual fact, I think it was eggshell blue.

Two. I said that the name of the estate was Bloomington House, but in fact it is Bloomington Manor.

Three. Auntie PK, the feminist, was not wearing unrelieved beige. Thinking back, I can see in my mind's eye that she had actually taken the trouble to wear an oxblood scarf. Auntie PK was either trying to make an effort – a bit of colour for a wedding – or making a statement.

'You are Indian,' I can imagine her saying, 'yet getting married in a silver dress. Shouldn't you be wearing red? What are you, white?'

Or, who knows, she could have been wearing it under threat from whichever auntie had knitted it for her.

Four. My mother's hanky was not tucked into her sleeve today. She had pinned it to the green train or *pallu* of her sari for the occasion. *She* had made an effort, even if she had been certain the wedding would come to nothing, she would tell me later.

Five. There wasn't a slump in my shoulders when I was facing Simon and my family. If I look carefully at the actual picture, the real one, not the almost-real one, my shoulders are riding up. It's my defensive look, the one my mother is always quick to point out. 'It isn't attractive, Rilla, and no one will want to marry you.'

Six. I told you that Auntie Dharma said that Mercury was in my fifth house. But for all I know about this, she could have said that the Savannah Bird Girl was making sweet love to a humpback whale in the garden. I have no idea what she said, but it was definitely something about a planet in our solar system messing up whichever one of my houses deals with marriage.

Seven. When Simon's father said we should get a lawyer and Simon reminded him that he is a lawyer, Simon's father stage-whispered, 'I'm not going to be dragged into one of your messes. If you had any sense, you wouldn't be either.' Simon's father doesn't hate me. But for him, someone who has been arrested doesn't belong in the Langton family; they besmirch the family name. Well no, I don't think he cares about the family name. It's more that carelessness – the kind that gets you arrested, the kind that shows a disregard for morality or at least decorum – makes him feel physically ill. It's the way mortgage brokers feel about people with poor Experian scores. That is how Simon's father feels about my record. Simon shouldn't have told him that I had been arrested in the past, you say? Well, he didn't. I did. The first time I met him, which was two months ago. Which was four months after I met Simon. Your eyebrows are rising now. A bit hasty to be calling the banns, you say? Well, you could just be right, and we will come back to this, I promise.

Eight. Simon is too nice to remind me that my MA committee has warned that if I don't make any progress in my thesis, then I am out. Out, out, out. Forever. He is too nice, and also I haven't told him about that yet. I would have gotten round to it, but I hadn't yet. So he couldn't have reminded me even if he had wanted to.

Nine. You've probably already noticed this one, it's quite glaring. I'm sure you spotted it right away. I'm the small brown nut. My sister Rose is the princess, tall, beautiful, fair, her skin bathing in permanent blossoms. So, in that little sketch we re-enacted on the park bench, of course Rose is Princess Multan, who weighs as much as a flower, whose every word pours out of her like birdsong, whose beauty is shielded by groves so dense that no one but the most daring prince could get through. Beautiful and kind, soulful and lyrical, that's my sister. I am Rup Singh, her suitor, a walnut, hoping that my skill in making garlands will help her overlook the fact that I am ugly and that I am a girl. In the play we enacted as children, Rose was the princess, I was the suitor. I changed this around in that scene on the park bench.

Ten. Rose of course wasn't at the wedding at all or on the park bench. The last time I saw her was seventeen years ago. Still, that doesn't mean that she isn't the one person in the world who knows me best. And that she wouldn't have said and done exactly those things if she had been there.

3

The Morning After

The next morning, I wake up from a dream that I can't remember. I panic because I don't know where I am. I stare all around me blindly, then things in my room slowly start to come into focus. The thick wooden beams that divide the attic room into bedroom and bathroom solidify, and the fairy lights, strung up on the wall above my bed, draw into focus. A blue Massive Attack poster that reads 'Unfinished Symphony' stares down at the bed, and next to it a dog finds a ladder to the moon in a Miro print. Through the large window on the opposite wall, I see the park lined with trees, two children playing hopscotch in the playground, a man blowing leaves around and a Joker sitting on a bench, beer bottle in hand, his exaggerated red lips smudged and his purple coat a little the worse for wear. He is leering into the distance, seemingly straight at me.

I spring out of bed and pull the blackout curtains shut,

not letting a single file of light into the room. My head pressed hard on my fisted hands, I keep a firm hold on the curtains, just in case they spring open again. I turn around, keeping my eyes half closed.

What else is waiting to attack me? On the slouchy sofa-chair with red stripes that I dragged home from a car boot some weeks ago and that Simon and I pushed and pulled up three flights of stairs lies my discarded wedding dress. It looks like it's never been worn, like it has quickly got rid of any memory of me. Not a billow or a crease, not a broken button to remind me of how it might have been if Simon had slipped it off me last night.

I shove it under the bed, but now the sofa-chair is staring at me accusingly. It seems to murmur, *Why did you do it, Rilla, why did you do it?* I run to my bed, drag my duvet off it and fling it on the sofa-chair, but I can still see its shape. I fling myself face down on the bed. I am safer now, now that I can't see the things in my room, but the dream starts to come back in threads and there's that choking feeling in my throat again. There is Simon in my dream wearing an orange t-shirt that says 'Go Bahamas'. I'm wearing pretty much what I'm wearing now, a tank top and floral pyjama bottoms. I don't know what I have said to the dream-Simon, or what I have done, but he looks stubborn. He has that look on his face that he gets when we argue, the jaw clenched, the ocean-blue eyes remote and unreachable. He will never forgive me. He *should* never forgive me. My mother is standing behind him, her arms crossed over her chest. *You always do this*, she says, *you always push people away. I told you. I told you!* And then it comes back to me. There had been someone else in my dream, standing behind my mother, looking at me with sad eyes. A dog. Mine and Rose's dog, Gus-Gus. I gasp for breath as the memory of the dream hits me. Gus-Gus, when was the last time I dreamed of Gus-Gus?

The dream-memory threatens to choke me so I jump off the bed, push my hair to the top of my head, stick a hairclip into it and start cleaning. I have to clean. I have to do something with my hands or I'll go mad. There is stuff everywhere. There should be boxes, ready to go to the flat Simon and I are – were – moving into, in Crystal Palace. But there aren't because I hadn't got that far yet. I had only got to the point of pulling things out of closets and drawers and staring at them. I start folding. Picking up, folding, placing in drawers. This is a good task to do, I can do it for hours. I can do it for the rest of my life.

I'm halfway through the first drawer when my phone rings. It is my mother. I close my eyes, willing her to go away. My parents are possibly the last people I want to talk to right now, but she keeps ringing. After the seventh missed call, I tap the green button.

'Rilla,' my mother says without so much as a hello, 'what are you doing?' She doesn't mean right now, in my room at this particular moment, but generally, with my life. 'Why do you have to ruin everything?'

'I don't want to talk about it,' I mutter. I stab viciously at strands of my hair that are trying to escape the hairclip.

'What are you trying to do, show Simon that you're thoughtless, selfish? Rilla, he'll find out what you're really like, don't you see, and then what will happen?' Her voice has a panicky note in it, a twang of desperation. 'You're twenty-five. When are you going to grow up? Are you there? Are you listening? You can't treat people like they're nothing, you just can't!'

'Really?' I grind my teeth. 'You've always said I'm really good at it.' I whack at a t-shirt to get it into shape and fling it into a drawer, holding the phone between my ear and shoulder.

'Do you think Simon will take you back after what you did? How will we face him again?'

We?

'Did I say I want him to take me back?' I mime thwacking the phone on the floor a few times. 'Did I say that?'

'We just want you to be happy. What is wrong with that? Tell me, what is wrong with that?'

'You want me to be happy?' I say slowly. 'Now that's too much, Mum. I would have said that's the one thing you've never wanted me to be.'

My mother is breathing hard now, I can hear her. I squeeze my eyes tightly shut but the familiar guilt is starting to creep up. My father takes the phone, and in the background I hear my mother say, 'I don't know what he sees in her, Manoj, I really don't!'

'Rilla, why have you upset your mother? Can you have one conversation that doesn't end like that?' Dad says. He doesn't sound annoyed, he just sounds like my dad – tired and resigned. I picture him sticking a finger and thumb in his eyes and rubbing wearily.

'Well, Dad, why don't you tell me?'

'Rilla, *beta*—'

'Sorry,' I mutter. 'I'm going now. Sorry, okay? Just – don't call me, please, okay?' When I put down the phone, I notice missed calls from Simon, some from last night, others from this morning when my phone was on silent. There is also a text message: *Please call me. Just let me know you're okay.*

Tears threaten to rise but I push them down. *Not now, Rilla. This is not the time.* I stab at my face with the back of my hand and carry on tidying.

I clean obsessively. I can't think about Simon. I can't think about Simon and I can't think about my mother. And I definitely can't think about Gus-Gus.

After an hour, I give up trying to sort my room out and walk slowly downstairs to the living room. My flatmate Federico is sitting in the middle of the floor in child's pose, looking in through the window of a miniature Victorian house.

The flat Federico and I share is part of a three-flat house in Lewisham. When I started my MA three years ago, I came across a pamphlet on a notice board at university, advertising for a flatmate. It gave details of the flat, and then ended with the words, 'Even if you hate everyone else, you'll love me!' We met on campus and had a long chat about American politics, Simon Cowell and Lucozade (and how much we couldn't stand any of those things). I told him about my favourite Mexican restaurant – La Choza in Brighton – and he told me he would make me nachos (all made from scratch) once a fortnight if I lived with him. I moved in the following week.

As I step into the living room, a floorboard creaks under my weight, and the four walls of Federico's model house collapse. Down comes the sloping roof.

'Oof,' Federico says, sitting up. His springy curls are standing up all around his head, his hands are now on his small-boy hips. He is wearing his red tracky bottoms that say 'Ho Ho Hoe'. A joint sits next to him in an ashtray and there's some Tibetan chanting emerging in wafts out of his phone. 'Do you have to come crashing in here like a water buffalo?'

Federico has discovered a passion for model villages and he is trying to build the San Francisco of the 1900s. So far he has built two Victorian houses, one pink, one lilac, a few lamp posts, a post box, and a road – at the moment they look like a post-apocalyptic San Francisco, craggy angles, buildings falling everywhere, everything grey and smudged, all rather steampunk.

'If you can figure out how to build them so they actually look like something real, that would make a difference,' I say irritably.

'Regretting it now?' he asks, bending down again, trying to get the structure back up, one wall at a time, holding his pinky fingers out for balance. His stare is so dark and intense that his eyes look like they are lined with eyeliner.

I flop down on the window sill. 'No,' I say. 'No, I am not.'

'Okay, then,' Federico says. 'I'm glad you're happy with your decision. It must be a good feeling.'

Federico is from Mexico. He is short and wiry, and has a mass of curly hair that comes out of his head like an explosion. He is on a post-graduate scholarship to study music at Trinity. He had been accepted by Columbia, but he decided to move to London instead as a protest against the divisionary politics of the American government. (Also he didn't get a visa.) When he is being sarcastic he talks in exactly the same tone as when he's not, so sometimes it's difficult to know if he's being serious. At the moment, though, his meaning is crystal clear. I glare at him. After a few minutes, I finally think of a good comeback.

'And anyway, you think you're better at relationships?' Ha, take that, Federico.

He rolls his eyes. 'Is that the best you can do? I never said I am good at relationships. But chucking someone at the altar, that would be a first, even for me. Still, as long as you are happy . . .' He peers at one of the walls of the model house. He holds it straight up, then upside down, then sideways. He abstractedly scratches the C and D tattoo on his right shoulder, then grunts and rummages in his petite toolbox.

'Happiness is overrated.' I examine my hands, my customary clipped nails buffed and polished with transparent nail polish by an auntie for the wedding. 'Can you think of times in your life when you've been truly happy?'

'Are you saying you can't?' Federico says, shovelling through the toolbox, picking up and discarding tools. 'That is truly tragic, *chica*.'

A vision arises in my mind. A vision of being chased up and down the house by my sister Rose. Giggling helplessly, hiding in cupboards, behind curtains, under chairs and tables, getting tickled till I was upside down and inside out. The helpless giggles, the cries of 'Rose, stop! Rose, *stop*!' ringing in my ears. Rose's face, leaning in, checking to see if I was okay, if I really wanted her to stop. I never did, not really. And she would go at it again, and I would run shrieking through the house. Yes, I want to say, yes, I can remember a time in my life when I was truly happy. I can still feel it in my body so it must have been real. It's just that it was a long time ago and I was a different person then. I pick up a cushion and try to push it into my eyes. These are unnecessary memories. I don't need them and I don't want them. I *can't* have them.

'Everyone has the capacity for happiness,' Federico says. 'Now take what you did to Simon—'

'Can we talk about something else?' I say through the cushion.

Why can't people talk about something, anything, else? I close my eyes but Simon's face seems to be imprinted on the insides of my eyelids because I can see him even when I shut them tight. And he doesn't look stubborn like he did in my dream. He looks something else, something I'd never seen until yesterday, until the afternoon of our wedding when I told him I couldn't be with him any more.

31

He had looked like he couldn't understand what I was saying. He had looked lost.

'Bad karma to leave someone at the altar. And if you've done it, at least tell him why.'

'Seriously, Federico, drop it.'

'Avoidance helps no one, *chica*.'

I emerge from my cushion and snap. 'I know you like playing the therapist. But how come we never talk about you? Why don't you look at why your relationships don't work? What are *you* afraid of?'

Federico has gone through four boyfriends in the last year. He is with someone he cares about now, but they always seem to be at odds. If I can change the subject, throw it back in his face, maybe he'll leave me alone. Maybe I'll feel like I'm not the only broken one.

He shrugs, picks a buff he likes and starts shaving the wall to even it out. 'I don't push people away. *I'm* not intentionally cruel.'

I grind my teeth. 'I am *not* – maybe your boyfriends don't like that you act like you're straight,' I snap.

There is silence. Not much changes in Federico's face. There's a slight shift, a clicking of his jaw, but not much else.

I want to claw my tongue out. I want to sit up and slap my face a few times. What is the matter with me? It's like words spring out of my mouth and I have no control over them.

'Sorry. Okay? Sorry. I shouldn't have said that.' I have the stupid impulse to ask, *Do you still like me? Please say you still like me*. But I never say things like that, and I don't say it now. Even though I could do with some people liking me right about now.

Finally, after many suspended moments, Federico moves, he reaches out a hand. The four walls of Federico's model house are standing up together. He takes one down and starts cutting out a square shape to make a window. He can't quite get the four sides to be the same length, so the window is getting bigger and bigger. I watch him at this task for a while. He is no longer talking to me. In fact, he's acting like I'm not here. I sigh and leave him to it.

Outside our house there is a lonely patio on which people rarely sit. Sitting there bears the risk of being sociable, so everyone avoids it, and this works perfectly for me. Sometimes I leave a pair of smelly socks there to drive the point home. I go down to it now and sit down heavily on the swing, hugging my knees to myself. I can't tell if I never want to see Simon's face again or if all I want is for him to come walking up to the house right now. A tinny twang-twang-twang is coming from the ground-floor flat. Our downstairs neighbour Phil (who is a teacher in training) wants to join a mariachi band and Federico is teaching him the vihuela. I clamp my hands over my ears. There are workmen digging outside the park across the road. They've been there for weeks, and the local residents are complaining to the council about how the noise is bad for their children. This has to be the noisiest street in the world. I stare into the distance.

My neighbour Earl rides past on his mobility scooter. Earl's mobility scooter is the Cecil Turtle of vehicles. It is so slow that I can say hello, pop inside, put the kettle on, make my vanilla Rooibos *chai*, pop back out, drink the entire mugful and say goodbye to him as he rides out of sight. When he sees me this morning he does a double-take. Yup, I'm still here. I'm not on my way to my blissful new life with Simon.

'To get somewhere, you have to leave the house, Rilla!' Earl calls as he slo-mos past.

I curl my mouth. 'I've always been better at staying put, Earl. That's the problem.'

His snowy shock of hair blows gently in the breeze as he glides past.

That's when I notice that I have a text message. *20 mins*, it says.

For a moment, I'm paralysed. I stare at it like I can't understand the words.

It is from my cousin Jharna. It was sent eighteen minutes ago. This means I have two minutes before the GIF arrives. I run inside and fling myself up the stairs and all the way up to my room in the attic. I barricade myself, I wedge the dresser inside the closed door, I place a dozen or so books on top of the dresser. I sit down on the stripy sofa-chair, cover myself with the duvet and squeeze my eyes shut. The GIF is on its way.

4

Luncheoning

Two minutes after I disappear inside my room, my parents, an auntie and an uncle, and Jharna turn up. Federico lets them in. I can hear them downstairs in the living room. Well, that's just fine. They can sit and chat with Federico for as long as they like. There's absolutely no reason I need to leave my room. I will read a book. I pick one up from on top of my dresser and stare at the words. It is one of my books for my MA thesis: Roland Barthes saying something about love, something about how we meet millions of people in our life, but out of these we only truly love one. I snap the book shut. One out of millions! His arithmetic is clearly all wrong, that's the problem with Barthes. How can anyone find love if faced with such odds? The man is a kook!

I look at the clock on the wall. I spring up off the chair, crouch on the floor and put my ear down to it. The odd thing is that the GIF has been there for a quarter of an hour but no one has bothered to even come up and knock at my door. Well, that suits me perfectly. What I need is exercise, I'm so restless I feel like I'm going to break things. I pace up and down, do some push-ups against the wall, and jog around the room. The buzzer rings. At once, I'm on the floor again, my ear pressed to it. I can't hear anything for a few minutes. Someone, probably Federico, has walked all the way down to the front door, and then walked up again, slower this time. There are some exclamations, followed by silence. Then there it is. The sure waft of cheesy dough. The wily bastards have ordered pizza! I jump up and look out of my window. In the distance I see the delivery man. He's from our local and they do really good pizzas. There's the usual pepperoni and chicken sausage and farmhouse, but they also do goats cheese and caramelized onion, butternut squash and spicy bacon. My tummy moans, long and slowly. All of a sudden, I desperately want pizza. I've eaten nothing but Federico's kale chips and tonic water since yesterday, my stomach turning at the thought of food after what I did to Simon, but now I can smell it. I can smell the pizza. In fact, I'm pretty sure I can hear them chewing. I pace around the room for another five minutes. Argh! I hate them so much!

I give in to the inevitable and walk slowly downstairs where a small army seems to be crammed into my living room.

'Talk some sense into her, men don't like it if you take them for granted,' my Auntie Pinky says as soon as she sees me. She is munching pepperoni pizza.

I leap at a random pizza box and inhale half a slice in

two bites. I close my eyes. It's the tastiest thing I've ever eaten. Spicy sausage. I shudder it's so good.

I turn around to look at the assembled company. 'Hey Auntie Pinky, Uncle Jat,' I give them a wave. I munch up the rest of my slice and grab another one.

Of course my Uncle Jatinder – my mother's brother – and Auntie Pinky are here. They are always here. They are self-appointed custodians of everything. Everything that anyone in the GIF does or wants to do has to go through them. If you're getting a job, a haircut, a mortgage, a pet, a manicure, a degree, a marriage license, a wax, it has to be discussed with Uncle Jat and Auntie Pinky so that they can tell you the best way to go about it.

Auntie Pinky is short and plump, her hair is uncoloured with two white wings (we call them the East Wing and the West Wing) that make her look like a zebra crossing. Uncle Jat has soft curves, he wears glasses with a gold chain attached and his hands gesture softly when he talks. He wears *kohlapuri* slippers even in the dead of winter and sneezes soundlessly by squeezing his nose. He doesn't look it, but he is very good at all things finance. They own a catering business, an empire really, that supplies Indian restaurants with dessert.

'Let's not heckle the girl, Pinky,' he says.

'Thanks, Uncle Jat.' I munch on the crust. Even the crust is good. Crunchy and skinny and cheesy, just the way I like it. 'I ate frogs' legs on pizza once,' I say to no one in particular.

My parents, Uncle Jat and Auntie Pinky are all jammed

into the one sofa in the room. It isn't a large living room and the GIF is making it leak at the seams. Federico is sitting on the cane rocking chair. I have nowhere to sit, so I stand leaning against a wall.

Suddenly Auntie Pinky slaps her head with a hand. She gets up, walks to a large shopping bag that is sitting in the corner of the room, brings out an enormous plastic box and starts laying homemade cupcakes onto a tray, since apparently several boxes of pizza are not enough to feed our small GIF army.

'I came prepared,' Auntie Pinky says, holding up the tray, 'with Rilla not having a tray.' She turns to look at me. 'What do you do when you have guests anyway, Rilla, please tell me?'

'I don't,' I say.

'Well, you have Simon. I expect he comes around all the time,' Auntie Pinky says. 'What?' she says, turning around and looking at everyone – even though no one has said anything. 'I'm a liberal. They were nearly married. You think I don't know that he comes around all the time? Anyway, you should own a tray, Rilla. A man likes to know he's appreciated.'

'And I need a tray for that?' I goggle at her.

'How do you bring him a cup of tea?' Auntie Pinky says, raising her eyebrows. She forgets the cupcakes for a second to fixate on this fresh disaster. 'Seriously?'

'*He* brings *me* – used to bring me – a beer out of the fridge,' I respond.

'Oye, what are we living in? An episode of *Friends*?' Auntie Pinky says.

'Anyway,' Uncle Jat says, opening his eyes wide and looking at us significantly, 'let us not make a mountain out of a tray.' He chuckles at his own joke. 'Look, Rilla, we will take care of everything.' He wipes his fingers on a tissue. 'We'll get the criminal record dropped first, then we'll talk to Simon. People make mistakes all the time. I spoke to his father on the phone this morning . . .'

'You did what?' I shriek. I unpeel from the wall like someone whipping off a plaster – in one quick definite motion.

Uncle Jat is unperturbed. 'We are in a precarious position, after what you did. But I called him and I said let us not cry over spilt milk. I said, in my humble opinion, the girl is afraid of – you know – the hanky-panky business. Indian girls are shy like that.'

I groan. 'I want to die.' I slump against the wall again and close my eyes.

'I said maybe we can settle the matter over a drink.'

'And what did he say?'

'He was most amenable. Very reasonable man. He said he wouldn't dream of inconveniencing me like that. And of course the wedding would be back on, there was no negotiation necessary. White people know how to be rational, I have always said that.'

'It is all right, Rilla. We have your back,' Auntie Pinky says. 'I will make chicken tikka masala if necessary. And we will serve the finest scotch. Nothing is too good for you.' She smooths her sari. 'And also the situation is desperate.'

My mother's family were well-off when she was growing up, but Uncle Jat has taken 'well-off' to a new level. His dessert empire keeps going from strength to strength, providing desserts not only for Indian weddings and parties, but increasingly for big events like Wimbledon and Royal Ascot. Instead of distancing him from the rest of the family, this wealth has made him feel like he owns everyone. No, that is a mean thing to think. It's more that he feels he has to take care of everyone, make sure that they are living their life correctly. He is of the mind that there is no problem that can't be solved if you have money to throw at it. Uncle Jat and Auntie Pinky like to tell you where you are going wrong, and then be the ones to fix it.

My mother Renu is crammed into a corner of the sofa, perched in about two inches of space. She is accusing me with her eyes. As far as she is concerned, if things have gone wrong in my life, it is no one's fault but my own. She is wearing a plain navy sari today, probably to express that this is a sad, sombre day. An African Bee-Eater brooch holds her sari in place, given to her by one of her Ugandan students. She teaches Life in the UK classes, telling her students that people in this country eat with a knife and fork, that they don't squat on toilet seats, that mince pies have no meat in them, and that Henry VIII beheaded his wives because divorce was not allowed back then. She tells them that the first fish and chip shop was opened in 1860 by a Jewish immigrant.

Her chin is trembling and she's doing her hand-flapping thing. 'If you only thought of other people for once. What will happen now, what will become of you? What will Simon's family think of us?'

I incline my head to look at her. 'That hand-flapping makes you look like a geisha.'

She stops abruptly. Dad gives me a *really, why?* kind of look. He is back in his customary check shirt today, tucked neatly into his jeans, his brown belt tied a little too tight. His hair has been ruthlessly combed so that no stray strands can spring up. He is looking apprehensively at Mum. For someone who has written a book on Indian street theatre called *Nautanki and Other North Indian Curiosities*, who loves melodrama on the stage and on the page, he shies away from all forms of it in real life. My father, the great pacifier, the one who steps in as soon as he smells a storm brewing. The one who will do anything to keep at bay a painful truth.

My mum has no such hang-ups. 'Why did you do it? Why, Rilla, why? After everything we do for you, this is how you repay us. It is like a slap in the face.'

'Yes,' I start, 'yes, it is definitely all about you—'

Dad gives me a warning shake of the head. I roll my eyes, and slide down to the floor. Dad pats my mother's arm.

'The thing is, it doesn't matter why she did it.' Uncle Jat folds his hands together. 'Let sleeping waters lie, I say. What we want to think about is how to fix it.'

'We can invite them to dinner.' Auntie Pinky has her plotting face on. 'Rilla can cook for them, say sorry to them—'

'I can offer Simon's father shares in my company,' Uncle Jat says.

'All she needs to do is call Simon.' My father looks from person to person, nodding his head. 'He is a sensible boy, it can all be sorted out. If she calls Simon—'

'If she says it is all her fault, that she is a stupid girl who has no more sense than a newborn sparrow, he will listen.' Auntie Pinky slowly nods her head.

'I *am* here, you know,' I say mildly.

'And while we're at it,' she looks sternly at me, 'I'd like to know why you didn't wear the earrings, bangles and two necklaces I gave you for the wedding. Not one bit of gold – what kind of bride wears *bronze* hoops? They will think we are paupers. With no respect.'

I close my eyes for a second. The GIF seems to be here to make me feel bad. Well, most of the party is here for that reason. I look over at where my cousin Jharna is sitting. She is definitely only here to be on social media. And when I say *here*, I don't mean in my flat, but on this earth. She is eighteen years old. She only ever looks at me with one eye. The other is reading her tweets, darting left and right, gobbling up news bites, 140-character morsels that tell her important items of news, like which one of her favourite celeb-crushes is just chillin' in their PJs y'all and which is taking their hipster poodle out for a doggie manicure. Still, I can't forget her text message warning me that the GIF was on its way, cavalry and all, and that I could run if I wanted to; I didn't even know she cared. She is now stabbing at her phone, sitting on the floor with her knees tucked up under her chin. The position startles me. It reminds me of me, and then it reminds me suddenly and forcefully of my sister Rose. It catches me unawares, and a sharp pain hits me in the chest. *Don't you see*, I want to say to everyone, *my life has gone completely wrong, doesn't anyone see?* I look around for help, but no one is looking at me. They're all tucking in to the cupcakes. I slump back against the wall.

'Can't you get your ass out of that phone?' Auntie Pinky complains to her daughter after a while. She stands up, tugs at Jharna's crop top for a second in a vain effort to make it longer, then starts tidying the flat. She picks up old tissue off the floor, wine glasses from a few days ago from behind the sofa. She tidies cushions (after she gives them a wary sniff), gets the dustpan and brush from the kitchen and starts clearing away wood dust. She drags the model village carefully under the rustic coffee table in the corner. Federico and I look sideways at each other but neither of us tries to stop her. It's the first clean the living room has had in weeks. He makes a face, I shrug. Does this mean he has forgiven me for what I said to him earlier about his relationships?

'How will you get a job, *beta*, if you're always on your phone?' Uncle Jat says to Jharna.

'You didn't have such a problem with it last week,' Jharna responds.

'I was looking for an old school friend from Delhi,' Auntie Pinky expands, panting a little with the strain of

43

bending and straightening, bending and straightening. 'Jharna tracked her down. The girl can find a needle in a haystack as long as the haystack is on the WWW.'

'Whatevs Muvs,' Jharna says.

Since her vocabulary is better than most people I know, I'm guessing she's doing the teen lingo just to annoy her parents. She goes back to her phone, works furiously with her thumbs, and blows an enormous bubblegum bubble that nearly smothers her nose ring. She is wearing a crop top that says 'Everybody Should Be a Feminist', a pair of loose boyfriend jeans and a military-print hairband knotted in her hair.

'How can you live like this?' Auntie Pinky complains. 'If you take these posters off the wall, Federico, I could give it a proper spring clean. Look at the cobwebs.'

Federico looks like he wants to go and stand in front of his precious posters. Greenpeace, Janis Joplin, yin-and-yang, an *X-Files* 'I Want to Believe', an embossed Om. But he also doesn't want Auntie Pinky to stop cleaning. I throw a cushion at him.

'Oye, why are you hitting the poor boy?' Auntie Pinky demands.

'Spider,' I mumble.

'Where?' Auntie Pinky shrieks.

'It's—' I clear my throat, 'disappeared under the sofa.'

Auntie Pinky marches over to the sofa, stares for a second, then goes into a crouching position, armed with a patent leather pump. But she doesn't stop there. She keeps sliding until she is lying flat on the floor and peering under the sofa, holding her phone in the gap between the sofa and floor for light.

'Hold your horses,' Auntie Pinky says. 'I see it, I see it!'

Federico and I are staring at her. I glance at him. On a normal day, he would be enjoying this pantomime, and also basking in the sight of someone actually cleaning our flat for once. But he is avoiding my eyes. *Has* he forgiven me?

'Anyway, why did you dump him?' Jharna says.

It takes me a few seconds to realize that she is talking to me. I wince. I didn't dump Simon, that is an ugly word. Dump. Definition: a) Drop heavily or suddenly, b) Knock down in a prize fight, c) Another word for tip – an area for dropping your rubbish, and d) Slang for doing a shit. Clearly none of these apply here.

'Dump? Is that what Hannah Montana would say?' I say wickedly.

'What are you, twelve?' She gives me a look of disgust before going back to whatever she is doing – probably unfriending me on Facebook.

'Why *did* you do it?' my father asks.

I blow air out of my mouth like a kettle on the boil. 'We shouldn't have got engaged in the first place. It was a mistake.'

'And it took you till the wedding day to figure this out?' my mother says.

'I thought I could go through with it. Okay?' I spread my hands out to emphasize that this should be obvious to everyone. I take a deep breath. 'I thought – I thought if I could just get through it, it would be okay after-wards—'

'Look, Rilla,' my father says, carefully wiping his hands on the toilet paper thoughtfully provided by Federico, 'let's think rationally about this.'

'I'm done thinking rationally.'

'When do you ever think rationally?' my mother says.

'Why are you all here?' I snap.

The doorbell rings. Federico runs down the stairs and brings up my Auntie Menaka. No way. No way. I groan.

'Oye hoye,' she says, 'look at these young people, so cool, so cute.' She gives me and Jharna a wave. She is wearing a strapless long *kurta* today, black, embroidered in red, with aqua blue trousers. Her hair has obviously been done this morning, and her make-up is flawless. She stands next to Federico. Now she is running her fingers through his hair. Auntie Menaka knows that Federico is gay but she is the most non-judgemental person I know. She will flirt with anyone. Well, any man at any rate. 'What's up? How's studies?'

Federico shrugs. 'Boring.'

'Oh, so sad,' she says, and puts his head on her large breasts and strokes his hair with her fingers. 'So, what are we going to do about Simon?' she says to the room at large. 'Such a lovely boy. Have you seen those dreamy eyes?'

'We were just talking to her about that,' Auntie Pinky says. 'Trying to talk some sense into the girl. You know what happens to spinsters? Even ones with careers?'

Auntie Pinky doesn't have time to elaborate because Federico helpfully chips in. 'Career, what career? She's been thrown out of her MA programme.'

I choke on my pizza crust. The man has not forgiven me at all! There are tears in my eyes. I'm still choking but no one is even thumping me on my back.

When I stop there is complete silence in the room. There is a moment when everything is suspended. Nothing moves. But then the *nagara*-drum is boiling, Mum's tears are flowing and the air is crackling. Not only have I broken up with my fiancé but I am also being thrown out of my MA. No one in the history of the Kumar family has ever failed in their studies before. The word failure does not occur in the Kumar family dictionary. The Kumars and the Kapoors, my mum's family, complete things. We conquer, we cruise through our studies, we appear at the other end complacent in our excellence.

'They did what?!' Uncle Jat sits forward on the sofa. 'It's atrocious. Do they know who we are? I will talk to your supervisor. What is his phone number? Just a name will do.'

Auntie Pinky is patting my mother with one hand, holding the dustpan with the other. 'It'll be all right,' she is saying. 'It's all right. There is no saying why these things happen to us. But it will pass. It will pass. God, oh God, why are you doing this to us!'

5

Family Melodrama

The doorbell rings again, and Federico runs down to answer. For heaven's sake, who is it this time? Up he comes, bringing with him the Unmarried Ones. Auntie PK, Auntie Dharma and my father's sister Auntie Promilla enter the living room. My parents and relatives give each other sombre hugs, not unsuited to a funeral.

The three aunties hold me until I'm ready to scream. I glare at my father. Since he is the least likely to have had anything to do with this ambush, he is the one I'm most irritated at. *Why didn't you do something to stop this onslaught?* my eyes ask. *Why didn't you stop it?*

As if anyone ever listens to me, his shoulders answer.

The Unmarried Ones are the bogie man of the GIF. When young girls of the GIF behave badly – shriek, yell, fight, drop and break things, eat in such a messy way that they get covered head to toe in melting chocolate, point out everything their parents are doing wrong with their lives, that kind of thing – a helpful GIF member reminds them that if they carry on behaving this way, no one will marry them, and they will turn out like one of the Unmarried Ones.

It is unfair to club them together, really. Auntie Dharma, the spiritual healer, was married briefly, a long time ago, until her husband died. She doesn't say *out loud* that it was the best thing that ever happened to her, but the implication is that her loss was the spiritual realm's gain.

Auntie PK, the feminist journalist, has a 'friend' she lives with, who is a lawyer named Zeze. Now and again when one of the GIF invites people over for dinner, they'll say to Auntie PK, 'Why don't you bring your special friend along, Parminder?' But apparently Zeze is always busy and rarely able to attend GIF social occasions. This could be true, Zeze is a very important human rights lawyer. But it could also be that the only time she encountered the GIF some years ago, Uncle Jat tried to get her to work for him, and Auntie Pinky suggested she meet some nice Indian men who were great 'marriage material' and who would like that Zeze was half-white and half-black.

Auntie Promilla is single because – well, because Auntie Promilla is an animal charity. That's right. She doesn't *work* at an animal charity, she *is* an animal charity. She collects animals like burs. She rarely speaks to humans, she has nothing to say to us and she looks over our shoulder when compelled to say something. But with animals – the more disabled and abused the better – she is a fairy godmother.

The Unmarried Ones are all crammed into the tiny living room. And now they are all talking about me again.

'Wait till *shani* has moved on,' Auntie Dharma says. 'Then let me set a date.'

'Living without a man isn't the end of the world,' Auntie PK chips in, but no one pays any attention.

'Her chart says she might have problems in the romance department,' Auntie Dharma says thoughtfully.

'I say, get a haircut.' Auntie Menaka takes a tiny nibble of a pizza slice that she has been eyeing for a while, then places the rest down on a plate. 'Any man problem can be solved if you get a haircut.'

'Look, we can kill two birds with one stone—' Uncle Jat starts.

His wife takes up the thread. 'Yes, yes, throw a party, call everyone, her friends and supervisor and Simon and his parents!' Her eyes are dancing at the idea.

They volley ideas back and forth. People are nodding their heads, starting to look excited. Federico actually has the grace to look a little sheepish at this fresh attack. He glances at me, but I avoid his gaze.

'Plain talking is the best way, I find,' Auntie PK says. 'No games.'

'What's the point?' Mum interjects. She has been sitting silently for a while, but now this question bursts from her. 'What's the point? Nothing can change what has happened!'

'Mum—'

'I knew this would happen! Didn't I tell you, Manoj? I knew!'

'How could you possibly know, Mum—'

'You ruin everything! That's how I knew!'

'Now, Renu—'

I stand up abruptly. 'What? What do I ruin? Go on, tell me!'

Mum's tears are flowing now. 'You alienate everyone. You're selfish!'

'And – and what else! Don't stop there, Mum!'

'You don't call us, you don't visit, you never even say thank you for anything anyone does. You – you killed that budgie Auntie Promilla gave you!'

Everyone turns to stare at me. I clench my fists at this list that my mum has come up with, the list of all the things I do wrong. I am so mad I can't even see her properly. Mad at my mum, at my dad for letting her say these things, at all of them, sitting here in my flat, passing judgement. Even Auntie Promilla, who rarely says anything, is looking at me with sad eyes.

'You said the budgie flew away,' she says, a tremor in her voice.

My mouth tightens. My dream from this morning hits me square in my chest, and suddenly I can't breathe. I look at all of them, not daring to say what is on the tip of my tongue, yet knowing I'm going to blurt it out. I stare at Auntie Promilla, who has given the GIF various family pets over the years, some beloved and others hated. But the first pet that she ever gave us, gave me and Rose, was Gus-Gus.

'Talking of Auntie Promilla's pets,' I say breathlessly,

talking quickly so I can't change my mind, 'I've been meaning to ask you for years. Whatever happened to Gus-Gus?'

The silence in the room can be cut with a knife. For many moments, nothing happens. No one speaks and nothing moves. People look blankly into space, at their shoes, at the wall, at anything but each other. Jharna is the only one who has no idea something cataclysmic has been said. Jharna, and Federico, whose hair is standing on end in the face of all these arrows aimed straight at my heart by my family.

My mother looks down at her trainers, my father at the shiny laminate floor. Auntie Pinky and Uncle Jat finally look at each other, then away, then each other, then away. Auntie Menaka is looking absorbedly at her long manicured yellow fingernails.

Auntie Promilla doesn't say anything, not one word, but she flinches. Yes, Auntie Promilla remembers the Irish wolfhound.

In the silence that follows my question about Gus-Gus, I can hear the thumping of my heart and it sounds suspiciously like a time bomb.

Uncle Jat clears his throat, finally breaking the silence. He turns to Auntie Promilla.

'So are you doing anything important at the moment?' Uncle Jat disapproves of Auntie Promilla's obsession with animals. 'I can get you a job, you know. All these animals-shanimals, they are okay as a hobby, but they are hardly a profession. We could send them to a charity—'

Auntie Promilla shakes her head, shrugs, nods her head. This covers every possible answer. She is looking nervously at me.

'I'm so lucky I don't have to work,' Auntie Menaka cuts in, sitting on the arm of a sofa. 'Or look after animals.'

'Do you remember the hamster?' my father asks.

Everyone laughs nervously. They avoid my eyes. They discuss various other pets that the GIF has had over the years. There's nervous fidgeting all around.

'I once saw a spider monkey in our back garden,' Federico says. 'Its long arms and legs were crossed. I tell you, it was meditating! I swear it even had its eyes closed.' Federico thinks we are talking about pets. Jharna is looking at me, though, with a slight frown on her brow.

Everyone else is smiling and nodding now. We can move on from the awkwardness brought on by my unfortunate mention of Gus-Gus, who disappeared at the same time as my sister.

'There was a time I thought I would take up silent meditation. For the rest of my life.' Auntie Pinky laughs nervously.

'You, silent!' Uncle Jat makes a sound like *upph*.

'Hard to imagine,' Dad agrees. Apparently we can move on.

But then he glances sideways at me. Just for a fraction of a second, so that it's hardly there at all. But I know they all remember what I've said. I know they can hardly breathe in case they blurt out the wrong thing. In case words are spoken that can't be taken back.

'This is how we're going to play it, is it?' I say softly.

Jharna looks up from her phone, her eyebrows raised. Everyone else is quiet.

My father rubs his face. He looks suddenly old. His face is pinched and there is so much grey in his hair. He looks shrunken. 'This is all my fault.'

I roll my eyes. 'Enough, okay? Enough with the drama.'

'No, *beta*,' Dad says. 'That's for us to say. Enough. You need to come and live at home if you can't cope with day-to-day life like a normal adult. We've tried and tried with you—'

'Damn you,' I whisper. 'Damn you all.' *They've* tried and tried? When have they ever tried?

Then I find I can't speak. There are words I want to say that I have never been allowed to say, words that even now are stuck in my throat. Words that hurt too much to say out loud.

'Please just go,' I say finally. I want it to come out angry but instead there is a crack in my voice and I can't meet anyone's eyes. I suddenly have no fight left. I can't even look at them any more. I shake my head, holding back tears, and leave the room. I walk up the stairs to my room, close the door behind me. I slide down to the floor, squeeze my eyes shut with my hands and try not to think about anything at all. Not my family, not the mess I seem to be making of my life, not Gus-Gus. And certainly not my sister Rose.

6

Back to Normal

The next day, a Monday, I resolve to go back to my normal life. I've found that in times of stress over the years, having a regular and predictable routine is the one thing that I've been able to depend on. In the last six months with Simon, I let my routine slide a little, let it get scruffy around the edges, but now it's time to put my life back on track.

As I walk out of my house, I take a deep breath to brace myself for the day. But I needn't have worried, because the city looks like it is determined to help me in my resolve. On the train to New Cross Gate, to get to campus, I easily get a seat. On my walk to Goldsmiths, a little girl with a cheerful pigtail on top of her head waves shyly at me. As I make my way across campus to get to my department, the March sun plays peek-a-boo on the common, and candyfloss pollen floats on the breeze. I turn my face up to the warmth.

Maybe, just maybe, I can go back to who I was before

I met Simon. If I can do that, if I can let go of the image Simon created of me – a tempting picture of someone who knows who they are, for whom something vital didn't get left behind a long time ago – then maybe things will be okay.

I walk into my department building, humming along to someone who is listening to 'Cake by the Ocean' on their phone, determined to make this the first day of the rest of my life.

My optimism is severely tested as I walk through the double-doors.

'Ohhhhh,' says an undergrad who I tutor, making a sad face when she sees me. 'What happened?'

'Oh,' I say, staring at her. She is wearing dark red lipstick and thick black eyeliner, a pair of harem trousers and a sports bra. 'Yes. It's all fine.' I smile brightly and give her a thumbs-up.

I keep my eyes focused ahead of me as I walk quickly past the student towards the stairs that lead up to my office. I can do this. This still makes sense. Of course people are going to want to know what happened, and why I'm not on my honeymoon. But as news stories go, I'm sure I'm not the most important of the day. And, in any case, I am not going to let an eighteen-year-old who thinks underwear is suitable to wear around campus ruin my day.

'Rilla!' another voice says, as I place one foot on the stairs. I slowly turn around. It is one of my professors. Professor Maxine is French, she teaches phenomenology, and she tells her students: *Talk with your body, yes? Your heart, she is the same as your crotch, yes?* 'What happened? Why are you here?' she says to me now, her face a picture of deep distress. 'Come here!' She embraces me. 'Cry, *ma petite*! Cry!'

I shake myself like a dog when she lets go of me. 'Professor Maxine,' I say, though there is a breathlessness to my voice now, 'really, it's all fine.'

I run up the stairs before she can say anything else. I look left and right, and pass by a meeting room in which a few of the admin staff are having a meeting. It is glass-fronted, and I resist the urge to hide my face behind a book as I pass by. The department administrator pauses in the act of giving a PowerPoint presentation whose title reads, *What does* your *work allocation say about* you? and does a double-take. *No way!* she mouths, her face aghast.

Now I'm running. I can't get to my office fast enough. Why on earth did I think it was a good idea to come to university today? Of course I'm the scandal of the week, and I should have known I would be! I run inside my office, slam the door shut and press my back against it. I look frantically around at the broom cupboard that is my office: the grey cabinet, the posters of philosophy conferences that other grad students have left on the walls, my work desk and chair, my old department-issue desktop, the thick leaves of the aloe plant that a student gave to me as a present.

And then I realize it. I'm alone here, I'm alone in my office. No flatmate, no GIF, no students or professors. Yes, I am alone here and that's a good thing. I am still feeling the weight of the onslaught, but perspective slowly starts to return. I can stay in here and I can work. I put my bag down, take off my jacket and scan my workspace. I move things around. I place my water bottle and a chocolate-and-orange cereal bar next to my computer, fiddle with the height of my chair, place my spring jacket on the back of it. There, the room looks familiar now. I feel safer, I can breathe.

I automatically reach out to the desk calendar to change the date. And there it is. Monday, March 13th.

I have neatly crossed out the words 'Office Hours' and instead written 'First Day of Honeymoon'. My hand snaps back like I've been stung. I stand staring at the words, feeling trickles of something crawling up my spine.

Why, why not even one exclamation point, I think irrelevantly. Why not more excitement at the thought of spending ten days with Simon in Hawaii? Tears prick my eyes and I turn blindly around.

Why am I here? I had woken up with the idea that if I could just carry on as normal, then maybe all this would go away. But what is normal now? What is normal for me? In the time I've been with Simon, my 'normal' seems to have morphed into something I no longer recognize. I stand with my back to my desk, a hand on my mouth, eyes tightly shut. I'm unable to move, unable even to think clearly.

After many minutes, I slowly open my eyes. And there is a thought in my head, a clear one. Focus, I need to focus. I turn slowly around, refusing to look at my calendar. I turn on the computer, I slowly sit on my chair, tentatively now, not daring to move too fast. I open a file I've been ignoring for too long – the file in which I have made notes for my MA thesis.

Just as I click on the file, there is a knock at my door that nearly makes me jump out of my skin. I creep to the door, open it a notch and sneak a peek. What looks like the entire undergraduate population of the philosophy department is standing outside my office. I slam my door shut. Another invasion. First the GIF, now this.

I have something of a reputation for saying it like it is, for not being nice, but getting straight to the heart of the problem. And not just about undergraduate papers, but also undergraduate lives, so my office hours (held twice a week on Mondays and Thursdays) are usually full with back-to-back tutorials. I'm employed as my supervisor Professor Grundy's teaching assistant, so I assist in classes, mark essays and give feedback to students on their coursework. But today, two days after my non-wedding, there is already a line snaking its way out of my office and down the corridor to the common room. Popular or not, my office hours have never been this well attended.

There is a knock behind me again. I close my eyes, willing the student to go away, but the knock is repeated. I open the door an inch, heave a shuddering sigh, then reluctantly gesture in the first student.

'Oh no, what happened?' It is Sara, a redhead with Britney Spears pigtails.

I purse my lips. 'I thought I'd cancelled my office hours.'

Her green eyes are wide. 'Yes, but then we saw you were in. You look so sad!' She reaches out a hand.

I stop myself from springing back. 'I'm fine,' I mutter. 'Now, what did you want to talk about?'

I gesture her to the 'student chair'. Sara settles into it like she's here for a picnic. She seems to have no questions about her essay or about my feedback, but it still takes me fifteen minutes to get rid of her.

The next student comes in. 'Oh no, what happened?' Mimi gasps, as soon as she walks in. 'I am so sorry for you! Did you literally leave him at the altar? In front of all the guests? At the very last minute?'

My heart is pounding, and I can hear a busy hum from outside the door, the swarm of locusts is expanding further. I decide that my best strategy is to attack.

'You need to think about whether this is what you want to do with your life, Mimi,' I tell her, finding her paper on my desktop and clicking on the file. 'Look at this paper – it's so awful I don't even want to use it as a coaster!'

She peers closely at the computer. 'Well, you can't,' she points out. 'It isn't printed out.'

'Totally not my point,' I say sternly. 'How much time did you spend writing it? Half an hour?'

This strategy works. I use this form of address with each student as they filter in.

'Tell your girlfriend how you really feel,' I say to Jacob. 'Don't be a douche-bag.' He looks mildly hurt at my words, but his natural laziness kicks in and the hurt vanishes. He lounges back in the chair, the front legs of the chair come off the ground and now he is almost horizontal. 'She's, like, you don't talk, and I'm like, whaaaa?'

Several more students come in. Each one asks me what happened, and why I look so awful (one actually uses the word *decaying*) but I am like an Olympic ping-pong champion, I thrust the ball right back at them.

I have been at it for almost two hours, and am starting to feel more like myself, when Wu Li comes in. She gives me the standard sad face and question. I prepare myself for attack. It is harder to do with Wu Li, though, because she is one of the top undergraduates in the department, and her personal life seems spotless as well, not riddled with broken relationships, binge-drinking, flatmate crises or chlamydia scares like everyone else's. I search her paper frantically for any of my comments that don't read, *Excellent! Great point! Wow, never thought of it that way! Have you thought of doing a PhD (talk to me about this!).*

She's looking at me seriously for what feels like minutes on end, her eyes unblinking beneath curly eyelashes. 'Maybe you're like Nietzsche,' she says at last. 'You can only talk about love, but not practise it.'

My stomach clenches. I stare at my computer.

'But it's okay,' she adds sympathetically. 'Some people are just not cut out for love.'

I stumble blindly up from my chair. 'I need to make a phone call,' I say to her, holding the door open, my voice sounding strangled and choked. She gives me a sympathetic, knowing glance on her way out. I slam the door shut for the third time this morning. I need to get out of here!

But my options are limited. I can either leave through the door and face the fifteen or so shiny young faces that are still waiting on the other side of it, or I can climb down through the tiny twelve-inch-square window in my office, adopt my father's way of dealing with confrontation – i.e., avoiding it like the plague.

My friend Tyra walks in as I stand there, hands tangled in my hair. She stares at me aghast. Tyra was invited to my wedding, so she doesn't need to ask, *Oh no, what happened?* She quickly closes the door shut behind her.

'Rilla—' she says. 'You look terrible. Your hair, your skin, your shirt is buttoned all wrong and' – she looks down at my feet – 'you're wearing mismatched socks!'

I look at her, panic clear on my face. 'I shouldn't have come today—'

She walks over to me and places her hands on my shoulders. 'Rilla. For crying out loud, get yourself together! Who cares what anyone thinks?' She quickly buttons my shirt right, pats my hair, and squeezes my cheeks to get some colour back into them.

I collapse on my chair and lift my head to stare up at the ceiling. 'I never want to see anyone again.'

Tyra perches herself on my desk and swings her legs, stylish in her orange jumpsuit and platform sandals. She is watching me, her caramel skin beautifully offset by an emerald scarf and enormous silver hoops.

'Rilla, what's going on?'

'With what?'

'You know what. All of it!'

I shrug defensively. 'I couldn't go through with it, okay? Why is everyone staring at me like I've lost a limb? I made a mistake getting engaged in the first place.'

She nods slowly. 'Well, I could have told you that.'

I look at her sharply. This is the first time since I left Simon at the altar that anyone has expressed this opinion. Everyone else in my life is convinced that I'm a terrible person, that I hurt Simon and I ruined my life. I narrow my eyes at her. I want to ask her what the hell she's talking about but, characteristically, her rapid-fire brain is already moving on to the next thing. She's looking at my computer screen where she can see the notes I've made for my MA thesis.

'Any progress?' she asks, trying to read what I've written.

Federico was wrong about what he said to my family. I have not been thrown out of my MA, I've only been given a warning. I need to produce more work, have more to show for the last three years. I'm doing an MA in philosophy, writing a thesis on multicultural perspectives on love. I want to know, I genuinely want to understand how some people are so good at love and others aren't. Yet the more I study it, the less I seem to know.

I shake my head. 'Nope, no progress.'

She inclines her head to study me. 'You're good at this stuff. I don't get it. What's stopping you from writing something, anything? You can do it in your sleep.'

I cluck impatiently. 'And act like I know about love?'

She raises a stylish shoulder. It was Tyra, my best friend during the three years of my undergraduate degree, who convinced me to apply for a scholarship to do an MA at Goldsmiths. She's writing an MA thesis on sex in black feminist literature. Soon she'll be moving on to a PhD. *She's* nearly done and I don't even have a clue where I'm headed.

'Do it, finish it. What's stopping you?' she asks.

This is a really good question. I have pages and pages of notes, hundreds of pages. Yet, I am no closer to finding a thesis topic.

The years of my degree, a BA in English Literature, weren't easy. I was haunted by a recurrent unease with my life, maybe even with being in my own skin. I felt restless and unsure with just about everything. But I was able to focus on one thing – the degree itself. On the books we read and the papers we wrote. Once I completed my degree, though, I had no idea what I wanted to do with my life. I felt like I had no anchor, that even the relative grounding that my degree had given me had been stripped away from me. What were my skills? What was I good at? What did I want to do? I'd never been in love with any job I'd had over the years – teaching chocolate-making workshops, selling vintage clothes, working in a pub. So when the scholarship was offered to me, I had said yes. It felt like a lifeline.

'I can't write anything at all. I feel like I'm pretending I know things that . . . I've never known.'

'Why does everything need to be perfect? This is the

problem with you. Either something is perfect, or it's total shit.' Tyra raises an eyebrow.

I shake my head. 'That's not true.'

'It so is. Take your MA, for instance. It could be about, say, Jane Austen's perspective on love. That would do. But no, the woman has to find out *everything* on love that's ever been written anywhere in the world. Compartmentalize, Rilla. Write the thesis. It doesn't have to be perfect!'

'Maybe.'

She's looking at me now, not saying anything.

I frown, determined to give her the silent treatment, but then I give up. 'Fine, just tell me. What did I do wrong with Simon?'

She widens her eyes, looks about the room, seemingly looking for an answer to my question. 'You got engaged three months after you met. You were getting married three months after that. I mean, duh, you don't need to look far for what went wrong! Anyway, look, what's the big deal? We all make mistakes. Love and marriage and all that, it's not for everyone. I mean, look at me!'

'Love and marriage and all that,' I repeat stupidly.

'Come out with me Friday. We'll pick up some blokes, go on, say yes!'

This is Tyra's answer to any problem. I don't say anything. She jumps off the desk, gives me a kiss and knocks on my forehead with a bony knuckle. She waves her fingers, mouths *Friday* and disappears out of the door, leaving me staring blankly at my computer screen.

I should appreciate everything she just said. Tyra is the

one person who doesn't believe I'm the worst person in the world after what I did to Simon. Yet, the voice in my head is saying: *It's Tyra, she's supportive, she cares, but she also tends to wash her hands of sticky situations, to fix things and move on quickly.* She likes to think she knows what people should be doing with their lives. Come to think of it, not so unlike my GIF. A minute after she leaves, she sends me a text message and I expect it will reiterate what she has already said to me. But it doesn't. It says, *Prof on prowl.* She means Professor Grundy, my supervisor. If Professor Grundy finds me in university today, she will not let me go without an interrogation, an interrogation that will make my undergraduates' sad questions seem like a birthday party. In fact, it would be safe to say that her cross-examination wouldn't be out of place in a prison camp.

I squeeze my eyes shut for a second, then stand up, picking up my bag and my coat. I feel exhausted, weary to the bone. *Some people are just not cut out for love.* This seems to be the consensus today. And I'm really not sure they're wrong.

7

Not Romance

When Simon and I first met it wasn't at all romantic. We met at the police station, that was the scene of our first meeting. Wait, I know what you're thinking. You're saying to yourself, *Ah, another one of those times*. But it wasn't one of those times, because I wasn't the one in handcuffs, Simon was. I was only there because my fellow philosophy students had decided to volunteer some time with underage kids in custody. I was the first one frisked and I was waiting for the others to finish their turn and join me. Into the waiting area came a constable, leading a man in handcuffs. You guessed it, it was Simon. The constable was trying to establish what to do with him, so there was a lot of waiting about. No one could figure out what to do with the man and everyone had a different point of view about it.

I was leaning against the wall, looking at the floor. There is no point looking a hardened criminal in the eye, even a dead sexy one, so I was determined not to look at him.

Nicely fitted jeans, a shirt the colour of mushroom soup, those deep blue eyes and hair that fell onto his forehead. No, it would definitely be a mistake to look at him.

'I'm completely innocent, I promise,' he said.

I smiled politely. He gave me a charming smile, so I quickly looked away again.

'I can see you don't believe me. But you see, the thing is, I just happened to be at the wrong taco stall at the wrong time.' He made a face. 'It just goes to show.'

I looked up after ten seconds. I couldn't help it, there was something about those eyes.

'Goes to show what?'

He smiled again. 'That just because a man makes the best fish tacos in London, it doesn't mean he isn't a crook. The man was handing me a bag of tacos, my mouth was watering, my heart was racing. I had been waiting for that bag all morning. No, wait, all my life. And then guess what happened?'

I couldn't not ask. 'What?'

'A copper turns up out of nowhere. The fish taco man – Paolo – who I thought was my friend, I really did, handed me another bag. Free nachos, I thought. On the house, made in the house, this day can't get any better. Though at the time, of course I didn't know I was going to meet you.'

I gave him a crooked smile and, to save my life, I couldn't stop myself from twirling my hair behind my ear and placing a foot jauntily behind me on the wall. What was the matter with me? I was going to end this day in a body bag at this rate.

'But the bag wasn't full of nachos. Nope. It was – you guessed it – a bag of coke.'

'Coca cola?' (I'm not proud of it, but I said it. So there it is.)

He stared at me. 'Cocaine.'

'That makes a lot more sense.'

'That is the only reason I'm in here and Paolo isn't. Anyway my lawyer is going to come and get me out any time. And then I can take you to dinner.'

I smiled.

'I'm Simon, by the way.'

'Rilla,' I said reluctantly. He was a very charming drug dealer; he must be very good at his job. I really should be careful not to talk to him, or even look at him. Anyone whose arms look so sexy and muscly with folded-up shirt-sleeves deserves to be behind bars, I thought sternly. We were standing in a bland corridor, with police officers walking to and fro and there was still no sign of my fellow students. I pretended to look at my mobile.

'What are your three worst things in the world?' Simon asked.

His hands in handcuffs, he was now leaning against the wall opposite to me. His hair fell all the way to his eyebrows and his eyes were deeply set.

I thought about it. 'Vomit. Slug slime. People who smile all the time for no reason.' I meant the last one to be pointed and cruel but he didn't take it personally.

'Mine are snot, religion, bigots and One Direction,' he said.

'That's four things! Anyway . . . what's wrong with One Direction?'

He stared at me with round eyes. 'I knew you couldn't be perfect. *What is wrong with One Direction?* Where would you like me to start? What is wrong with them is exactly the same as what is wrong with the world. For instance, have you ever looked at their—'

At that moment, the door opened and the constable basically dragged Simon through it. 'I'll wait for you,' he called as he disappeared.

The next two hours are better forgotten. Three of us led a workshop in 'Using Philosophy to Make Better Life Choices' or some such bullshit. The youth offenders who had been bullied, coerced or bribed into being there mostly ignored us, sent an occasional paper aeroplane our way, munched endlessly on gum, and didn't hesitate to laugh in our faces. One of them farted throughout the whole thing. Only it turned out that he hadn't been farting, but had in fact done a crap in his pants. The smell was unbearable, especially since it had leaked through his clothes onto the chair he was sitting on. This led to our workshop coming to an early finish, but then the room had to be locked down – with all of us still in it – until the matter was cleared up. Those were two hours of my life I was never going to get back and no one could convince me that I had made a jot of difference in the lives of these damaged young people. Never again, I was telling myself, never again.

I walked out of the police station filled with rage and

loathing for all young things. Someone peeled themselves off the wall outside and I screamed. It took me several moments to recognize him. Yes, beautiful as his eyes were, I had forgotten all about Simon. A body bag, for sure, I thought now. That is how this day is going to end.

How, then, we actually ended up with my legs wrapped around his hips against the toilet wall of an Ethiopian restaurant in Kentish Town later that night, I have no idea. Probably because when he saw me come out of the station, he handed me a tissue. I hadn't realized I had tears in my eyes. Tears of rage because the young gentleman of the doing-a-shit-in-your-pants fame had, as we were about to leave the room, come up to me and written an X on my notebook. With excrement.

If Simon had been nice, given me a platitude about how though it was difficult to work with young offenders, it would change their lives, I probably would have walked away. But he said, 'The little shits. The only thing we can hope for is that they'll kill each other in prison.'

That really is the only way I can explain it.

There is something about Simon – there *was* something about Simon! Simon is no longer in my life – I have to get this straight in my head! There *was* something about him, something assured, something sure of its place that I have never had. For example when I walk into an unfamiliar room, with unfamiliar people in it, I scan it. Is there anyone there I know? Are there groups of people who all know each other who won't want to talk to me? People who maybe have known each other for years, people who went to school together, who have common references? People who seem to know what to say and how to say it, people who can talk about anything or nothing and it makes sense to them. I wonder, will someone come up to me, an older woman probably, talk to me kindly and extra clearly because – given my brown skin – I'm probably a foreigner? And yet if there is a group of Indian people in the room, they will think I'm not Indian enough. These are the thoughts that go through my head when I enter a room.

But Simon, he's probably thinking, what's on the menu, is there anything more substantial than salmon and horse-radish canapés? He could talk to people about anything really, but he didn't seek people out either. He was comfortable in his own skin.

There are two kinds of people in the world. Room-scanners like me, and people like Simon, who never worry about things like that.

For a while, with Simon, it had started to seem like I could be more carefree too. Less troubled by my place in the world, by the rivulets in my past that refused to find a home. Less troubled, more assured, more able to navigate the world.

Yes, it had seemed like that for a short while.

8

Living a Lie. Oh, Sorry, I Mean Living a Life

As psychologist Alison Gopnik reminds us, in a child's
universe, parents are like stars – fixed and stable. But siblings
are more like comets that sweep into our lives, lighting us up
but sometimes scalding us.

Rilla's notes

On Thursday, three days later, still desperate to get a sense
of normality back into my life, I try going to university
again. And this time, it isn't as bad, maybe people do have
short memories when it comes to scandal. I hold my
normal office hours, I attend a seminar, and I even type
up some notes. I am still getting missed calls from Simon
every day, but I have switched off the notifications and
so I only have to look at his name on my phone log briefly
before I go to bed. Slowly, slowly, I can start to get my
life back on track.

Late on Thursday afternoon, on the train back from

university, I am hanging on for dear life. It is rush hour and the train is packed. People are standing in sweat-smelling distance, and I am trying to hold my breath. The people in my immediate vicinity must be acrobats because they all seem to perform complicated tasks while trying to stay upright on a moving train. A woman with a Chihuahua in her straw handbag is fanning herself with a receipt with one hand and feeding the miniature dog chicken wings with the other. A man with soft long curls and a borg-collar bomber jacket is reading Issue 97 of *The Walking Dead*. An attractive young man with red hair is teaching the woman next to him how to YOK2, which is apparently knitting jargon and not something to do with missiles. And an Indian man is having a phone conversation while also writing notes on his hand.

'I said give me your CV,' he says, 'and she was like, I already told them my qualifications. I said to her what have you done in your life? How can I recommend you? I can't put my name to this. And she started crying, man. I was like, what are you, a bloody *nautanki*?'

And just as quick as that, I can't breathe. I grope blindly, I clutch at people. 'I want to stop the train,' I gasp. 'I have to stop the train.'

People around me are staring. They look like they are going to arm-wrestle me to the floor if I say this again. They will do anything not to have to stop the train. Someone creates a bit of room, drags me down to a sitting position, puts my head in between my legs – I have no idea if this is so I can get breath back in my body or to make sure I can't reach the emergency lever. I fight them, flailing, punching, kicking, but nothing works because I am surrounded by a savannah of legs. Jean-clad ones, nude pantyhose, varicose veins, and then there is a face. It's a little girl.

'More,' she says in her baby voice, and hands me a wad of gummy tissue with mushy banana in it. At the next stop, someone practically throws me off the train. I run all the way down the platform, all the way up the stairs, and I stand outside in Lewisham next to a florist. I bend over double and gasp for breath.

My father disappeared into his study to write a book on Indian street theatre or *nautanki* when I was eight years old, soon after Rose disappeared. Before then, as far as I know, he had no ambitions of writing a book. When I was little, he taught drama in a college and he used to tell me – Rose and me – all about *nautanki*.

Rose and me. Yes, I suppose it's time to talk about that now. To talk about Rose and me. Though it is also the hardest thing I can think to do right now.

That's how it was for the first seven years of my life. It was always Rose and me. Rose and me did this or that, Rose and me are going out, Rose and me got into a fight. Rose and me are hungry, thirsty, tired, back from school, too awake to go to bed.

It was difficult, maybe impossible, to talk about myself without also talking about Rose. And Rose – she hardly knew what it was to exist without me either.

Our night-time stories were not the same as other children's.

We knew about *Pippi Longstocking*, the *Wishing-Chair* and *The Bobbsey Twins* from school. But my father didn't read these stories to us. He read us the notes he made about Indian street theatre, gathered from books written in the Sanskrit script that would take him weeks and months to decipher. We would sit on rugs, the two of us in our pyjamas, the kind that had a matching top and bottom, and the top had a collar. I can see us now, all I have to do is close my eyes.

Me in my purple pyjamas, with the moon and stars dotted all over them. Rose in her lemon yellow top and bottom, printed with a dancing Popeye.

We would sit holding one blanket around us, skinny beans crouching together for warmth, and we would share a cup of hot chocolate. Or at least, our mother told us it was hot chocolate, but looking back it was mostly milk with the tiniest pinch, a smidge of brown in it, hardly there.

'That looks like me,' Rose would say, staring into the steaming milk. 'Make it like Rilla, Mummy, please, please, Mummy!' And our mother would. She would add another pinch to the cup and the brown would swirl and aria till it mixed with the milk. We would sit under our blanket, drink our hot chocolate, and listen to Dad tell us about *nautanki*.

'Melodrama – you have to have melodrama in a *nautanki*. Without it, there is nothing. When you cry, you cry like you will die of sadness. You cry so loud, aliens on another planet can hear you and their hearts melt. When you are angry, you are full of rage. So much rage that if you tried to, you could swallow the sky whole. There's no point feeling unless you feel big, see? And the *nagara* – the kettledrum – heightens the drama. Only when it reaches fever pitch is there an explosion. Get it? Try it. Show me.'

I would laugh, a shrill, high-pitched, over-the-top, machine-gun kind of laugh. But Rose would cry. And when she cried, she didn't scream or sniffle. Her face turned inwards, her eyes swam and silent tears poured down her face in two long streams.

There was something about Rose's eyes. They searched, they were always alert. She was always looking for things to go wrong, always on the lookout for trouble, something that could hurt her, and maybe me too. Yes, that's true. She was always alert for anything that could hurt her or me. When she cried it was as if the world was coming to an end. It wasn't the kind of melodrama that Dad was telling us about, but there was something about Rose's tears. They broke your heart. Even our puppy was reduced to a pitiful moaning.

Gus-Gus. Yes, it is time to talk about Gus-Gus too.

When I turned seven, the same day that my sister Rose turned nine, Auntie Promilla's Irish wolfhound Gus-Gus came to live with us and he was enormous. All he had to do was come and stand next to you – not lean on you or jump on you – but just stand next to you for you to fall over. Rose and I were in hysterics. He was easily, hands down, the best thing that had ever happened to us. I loved Gus-Gus. There was only one problem. He loved Rose more than he loved me. I was always giving him treats and throwing things for him to fetch. Smiling at him, singing, *She'll be wearing pink pyjamas when she comes* (his favourite song), generally grovelling at his feet. But if Rose came into the room, quietly with hardly a whisper, as was her way, he would instantly drop what he was doing and go to her. Given the choice of going out for a run (his other favourite thing) with me or sitting under Rose's feet, he would always choose the latter. In fact, I was sure that when we were playing he kept one ear pricked for the sound of Rose. If Rose was out and she was on her way back, even before she had come anywhere near our house, the other ear would prick up and his hair would coil tighter. He would start doing laps – front door, living room, dining room, kitchen, pantry, through the bathroom, back to the front door, living room, dining room, kitchen, pantry, and so on, until she entered the house. Rose often had that effect on people.

'Rose hasn't washed her hands,' I would complain. 'And she's putting her hand in the liquorice allsorts.'

'Wash your hands, Rose,' my mother would say. But with that indulgent voice she saved for her first daughter.

'She's giving the dog a sweetie!' I would cry.

My mother would walk up to Rose and take the allsorts from her hand. Then she would turn to me.

'Have you seen how dirty your frock is? Go and change, right now! Stop bothering Rose. If you don't have any manners, you can stop going to school and stay at home and clean the house!'

I would glare at Rose, pinch her as I passed by her on my way to the bedroom. I knew my mother was bluffing. Of course I knew! No one would keep their child at home and get them to clean the house instead of going to school. Yet what a thing to say to your child! To someone you were supposed to automatically love!

'Take your shoes off before you go upstairs, how many times!' my mother would shout.

This was before my mother started teaching adult education classes. That didn't come till much later. If you looked at my mother in those days you would think that we were always late for something. We never did things quickly enough for her.

'Hurry up, Rose! Come on, we're getting late. Can you drag your feet any more than you are, Rilla, for god's sake? Wash your hands! Clean your teeth! You're late for bed! You're so slow, what's the matter with you girls?'

She was tired. Two demanding young girls with itchy feet must have been exhausting work. Add to that my father who was good at telling us stories but not at helping with our homework, cleaning our school uniforms, shopping for groceries, or any of those things that fell to my mother. I guess there were other reasons as well, but kids aren't conscious of these things. On top of everything else, an enormous dog had arrived for her to look after. All because my father had wanted a horse for his play, for our play, all because he was a failed actor. And this brings us full circle to the *nautanki*, our foray into street theatre, Rose's and mine.

But I'll have to come back to that later. To say some things, you have to work up the words.

For many minutes, after practically being thrown off the train where I had a panic attack, I sit outside the train station in Lewisham. The florist who has been watching over me says now, 'You have to take care in these lurching trains, luv!'

I have the impulse to grab his arm and say, 'Do I look mad to you?' Not in accusation, but as a real question.

A week ago my life seemed like it was more or less on track. It was true I needed to work harder at my MA, I needed to show more discipline and focus, but I was getting married, moving to a new flat, becoming an adult, putting the past behind me.

Now, merely a few days later, the past seems to be chasing me. The faster I run, the harder it seems to run after me.

The thing is, I don't want to go back to the past, I don't even want to unravel it. I'm not pushing for answers that I don't have the courage to face. All I'm asking for is a version of my life that makes sense, a narrative that people can agree on, or even one that I can agree with myself about. I want to find a few missing pieces of the jigsaw.

Yet, whether I resist or not, the memories are trying to claw their way back up through the canyon now, knocking at the door. And their Gollum neediness is starting to gnaw at my insides.

I thank the florist for his patience with me, I don't ask

him if he thinks I am mad. Instead, I pick up my bag and the water bottle handed to me by a stranger, and slowly through the streets of Lewisham, I start walking back towards my flat.

9

An Incoherent Narrative

The Sufi poet Rumi says it isn't for us to run after love, but
instead to look within, to see what is stopping us from loving.
He says that our task in life is to find all the obstacles we
place around us, the shields we build that keep us from love.

Rilla's notes

'A coherent narrative, Rilla,' my supervisor said a month
ago when she gave me the warning about my MA. 'That
is what you need, and that is what you don't have yet,
not after three whole years here.' Professor Grundy sat
behind her desk, looking thoughtfully at me, tapping her
fingers. 'The thing is, I do like you. You're a good teaching
assistant, the students respect you. They like your honest
feedback about their work.'

She looked around her like she was searching for something more to say. We were sitting in her office, her walls
covered with old invites for conferences, framed certificates,

pictures of her receiving awards from important-looking people. On her desk there was a statue of Michel Foucault wearing a turtle-neck and a pair of seventies-style trousers, his head an egg, his lower lip cheeky but sensual, his hands crossed behind his back. She looked at him for many moments before she spoke again.

'You don't really like people, do you,' she said finally.

I flinched. 'That's a little harsh.'

'Oh, it's not meant to be. I am the same way. To be a philosopher, you have to be a little removed.'

My breath caught in my throat. Not liking people was one thing, but being like Professor Grundy, that was too much. She once made a student wait for six months to hear if he had passed a re-sit of his dissertation. She had known all along that she would pass him; I later saw a dated confirmation of this. But she didn't tell the student. She made him wait, she made him cry, she turned him into a shadow of his former self. And all because she didn't like him. 'He needs to learn respect,' she said at the time.

And she thought I was like her. This made me die inside.

'You are making no progress in your work.' Professor Grundy was caressing Foucault, her thumb slowly stroking his egg-head back and forth.

'I like this stuff,' I muttered. 'I want to make sense of it.'

'Rilla. Are you going to complete your MA? *Can* you? Do you even want to?' She sat back in her chair and looked at me.

I didn't know what to say.

*

83

When I applied for an MA, with Tyra's encouragement, I wanted to explore the connections between what a culture thinks about love and what it thinks about other things like life, work, and war. I had imagined finding a kernel that was at the heart of a culture, its most basic beliefs around which everything else was organized. I had thought at the time that it was a good, concrete idea, that it was something I could focus on and develop for three years. But recently the idea seems to have evaporated.

The more I read about what other people have said about love, all I can think about is how little I know about it myself. How there is a blankness in my brain where there should be an understanding of love.

Why do we form an attachment to another? Who attracts us? How do we form the bonds of love? And when love is lost, then what happens, how do we go on living?

After three years doing an MA, I am nowhere near answering these questions, and in fact I am further away than I was when I started writing my thesis.

Well, I say *writing* my thesis, but at the moment I am *reading* it more than I am writing it. I do a lot of reading and I make a lot of notes. But that's what you are meant to do, isn't it? You're meant to read what everyone else has written on your subject before you can say what you want to say. If there's nothing else I've learned from my father, surely I've learned the art and craft of methodical application. Having grown up in a family of artists and academics in Bombay, he should know how it's done.

The only thing is there is a heck of a lot written on the

subject of love. Every poet, philosopher, mathematician, mother, baker of treacle tarts, damaged teenager turned death-row inmate – everyone seems to have said something about love. Until I've read it all, how am I supposed to know what my take on it is? How do I know when I've learnt enough about love?

Federico says love is the same as breath, that as humans we are programmed to go after it, the same way we have to go on breathing to be alive. 'And such a basic thing, it is not something one can analyse, is it? Why don't you do something else?'

Do something else, says Federico-the-fixer. But what else can I do? I have no other skills.

Tyra helped me deal with the aimlessness I felt after university. She didn't know about Rose, of course she didn't, but that's the thing with Tyra. She doesn't push, she doesn't try to draw out anything about you that you don't want to tell. She saved me. She got me out of my room and into the world, she got me out of myself, and she pointed me in a direction. Now, three years later, I don't know if it is the right direction or not. But it is a direction, the direction of the books that have saved me in the past.

And I need a direction right now.

'I can do it. I know I can,' I told Professor Grundy.

I tried to keep at bay the trickle of panic that was trying to climb up my skin. I couldn't go back to having no direction. I couldn't.

'Hmm,' Professor Grundy said. 'The thing is, we ask you to do a report on something you've read, you can do that. You can do a critique. When pushed, you can deliver a summary, a decent one. But we ask you to develop your own writing on the subject, and, well, how much of that have we seen so far?'

'Not enough?'

'No, Rilla. We haven't seen anything. Not a page, not a word. We can't have you be a student here for life. You can't just be here in this programme so you can take notes. You have to make a choice. Either write something or leave. You're not a romantic, you know how things work. Which is it going to be, Rilla? Sink or swim?'

You're not a romantic.

My professor says I'm not a romantic, and Tyra says I'm too much of one. So, which is it? You know, I just don't know.

10

Romancing the Chickpea

For Slavoj Žižek, the *falling* in love is important. He makes love an event or an encounter. It isn't just a *being* in love, but the moment of falling in love that matters, it changes the rest of your life. It is such an important event that not only is it a catalyst for everything that will follow in your life, but it feels like everything in your life has been leading up to that moment.

Rilla's notes

The day after we met, I really thought I would never see Simon again. Maybe that was the unromantic side of me. I had had such a good evening that first night when he took me out to dinner, but I had convinced myself that it must have been a one-off, something not real. We had talked nonsense for three hours over our shared platter of *injera* (Simon had wanted to know if it made him a cannibal that he liked bread that felt so much like human skin), *shiro*, yellow split peas, red lentils and the house speciality, lamb stew. Over the enormous platter we discussed – well, everything. Victorian pocket-watches. Fondue and Simon's complete abhorrence for liquid cheese. Rye crackers and how they were really hyped-up cardboard. Whether or not Liv Tyler looked like a Disney princess version of Steven Tyler. Whether or not the Steps reunion would reveal that members of that band had frozen their bodies back in the nineties and they had now re-emerged from the freezer. If concept art was actually art or just something produced by people who couldn't paint. And whether Theresa May looked like Arrietty's mum in the Studio Ghibli version of *The Borrowers*.

We played a game where each of us said something about ourselves and the other had to guess if it was true or false. If you guessed wrong you would have to take a gulp of your prosecco and if you guessed right, the other would have to take a drink. The scale of this game varied from Simon saying he didn't vote in the last election and that he nearly joined the army, to me saying that I had a girlfriend in college. We moved on from there – after several glasses of prosecco – to talking about our families. I was holding a hand up at this point and looking through the keyhole made by my fingers to see if Simon looked any bigger if I looked at him through a telescope. It was possibly time to lay off the sparkly.

I bit my lip and eyed him. 'I have an enormous family where everyone has a say about everything you're doing,' I said. I don't know what it was that made me start talking about my family. Maybe I wanted to lay it all out there, get the worst over with. Maybe I wanted to test if it would put him off me. Or maybe I just couldn't stop picking at scabs. 'There's no polite reticence about giving advice. It's all, *Why aren't you doing this in your life*, and, *Why are you doing that*. Like why don't I have a real job, when am I finishing my MA, why am I doing a pointless MA in the first place. When am I getting married to a nice Indian boy, and having two children, one boy and one girl.' I shut one eye. 'You do look bigger, I'm sure of it.' I put the other hand up to the other eye – would binoculars have the same effect? But then I started speaking again. It felt like now that I had started talking about the GIF, I couldn't stop. What was this, a confession? 'There are so many of them. Don't ask how they're all related to us – because the thing is they're probably not – but everyone is family.'

I gave up trying to focus through my binoculars – the telescope had worked better – and tried instead to spear one yellow split pea with my fork. It kept slipping away, but finally I had it. 'Ah ha!'

'That's nothing,' Simon said. 'If you can get the tiny red lentils, then I'll be impressed.'

We both tried this fruitlessly for several minutes.

'Dad is working on a book,' I told him, spearing him a chickpea since he was having no luck with the red lentils, and popping it in his mouth with my fork. 'So he can't talk about anything but indexes and references and tables and things at the moment. But if you do talk about those

89

things, he can go on for hours. He comes from a very academic family. Research oozes out of his pores.'

'Did he train to be an academic?'

'Dad studied history at university. Mum and Dad both did. They both love it in their own way – Dad with his obsession for studying the same thing for years, and Mum picking at morsels like a bird. Dad comes from a family of academics but Mum's the first teacher in her family – her family is made of businessmen, so everyone thinks of her and Dad as starving academics. Mum—' I fiddled with a piece of *injera*.

'Your mum?' he prodded.

It was ridiculous that at the age of twenty-five I still found it difficult to talk about my mother. But how to explain to him the strained relationship we'd always had, a strain that you couldn't even pinpoint, that was hardly visible to anyone else – except perhaps my father.

I sat back in my chair. The restaurant was decorated in red and brown and orange striped curtains, little cane stools and chairs, and there were metal ornaments everywhere – silver glasses and curly jugs, platters and bells and little lyres. A man walked into the room, lifted a mike up onto a raised section in the corner, sat down on a stool and started playing the lute. We listened to him for a few moments. I drew circles on the rim of my glass. Talking about the GIF, this was new territory for me. But there was something about Simon. Something that made me want him to see the real me – or at least something of the real me.

'I don't know. I can irritate her pretty easily.' I tried to think back to when I was a child. '*I love this bunny rabbit*, I said once to her at a jumble sale. *I love it so much, I love it so much, Mummy, can we please get it, Mummy please, I'll die if we don't!* And she got it for me. It was this patch-work thing, all floppy, with enormous ears, one blue, one pink. But then on the way back home its ear – the pink one – started falling apart. *I hate this bunny rabbit*, I cried, *I hate it, it's so ugly, I hate it!* I actually started wailing and beating my fists about.' I shook my head ruefully. 'It was like the end of the world. I was five.'

'Ears are kind of important,' Simon said, taking a sip of his prosecco. 'What did your mum say?'

'She got really cross about how my feelings were always going from one extreme to another. She wanted me to be level about things. We used to get into spats like that all the time, over just about everything. She found my feelings unnerving, that's the only way I can explain it. If I was crying, it would make her anxious. *Stop crying, Rilla*, she would say, *please, just stop making such a scene, can't you ever think about other people, you're so selfish!* Anyway, that time she took the bunny rabbit and threw it out of the car window. I cried about it for a week. I imagined it being squashed under cars and dying slowly and painfully, and it was all my fault for making such a fuss about its ear. Mum said it *was* my fault. But it was like the harder I tried to please her, the more impossible I found it to keep my feelings level. I know it sounds stupid.'

I abruptly stopped talking. I *felt* stupid. Why was I talking so much about my family? But Simon was looking at me like he wanted to hear what I was saying, like he wanted to know – everything. I felt self-conscious all of a sudden. Yet I couldn't look away from him either.

'Do you still do that?' he asked suddenly, softly.

I looked at him in surprise. 'Try to keep my feelings under control? Around people, I guess, sometimes,' I said defensively. 'Doesn't everyone?'

'Oh, totally. I try my best to show my dad I don't care about anything at all.' He grinned. 'God, he's so uptight. He hates me making jokes about everything, so I do it even more.'

'That's funny. I didn't think you'd react to what he thinks. Or even care what he thinks, come to that.'

He was playing with the cork of our bottle. He looked up at me and gave me that lazy sideways smile. 'I care what you think.'

I gazed back into his eyes. I had had too much to drink. I stared at his dark hair, the way it fell onto his forehead, the ear with the scar he had got when he fell off his bike as a boy because he was carrying a rescued mouse in one hand, the eyebrows that made him look slightly concerned about something, his way of looking up at you with a direct gaze.

'You are way too cocky to care what I think.'

'Too cocky, makes too many jokes, doesn't care what anyone thinks. That sounds annoying.'

I looked at those ocean eyes. 'It's . . .' I couldn't find the right words 'reassuring,' I said finally. 'And kind of sexy.'

That's when we ended up in the toilet of that particular restaurant, with my arms and legs wrapped around him, my back pressed to the green tiles, his hands tangled in my hair, kissing to the lute of the man on the stool outside. Now I remember.

11

The Birth of the Theatre

The story of Indian theatre goes thus.

Many thousands of years ago, the gods realized that reading and literature were pastimes for the upper classes; these were not recreations that were available to the poor. The gods asked Brahma to create a recreation that could be enjoyed by all. Brahma, having thought long and hard, took one skill each from the four Vedas – these were recitation of words (*pathya*), singing (*gita*), emotion (*rasa*), and gestures and acting (*abhinaya*) – to create a fifth Veda: theatre.

There are many folk theatre forms in India, and one of them is North Indian street theatre, or *nautanki*.

Manoj Kumar's book, *Nautanki and Other North Indian*
Curiosities (working title)

Our *nautanki* – Rose's and mine – started small. My father had the idea that all his research into North Indian street theatre was going to waste. What is the point of it all if no one will ever learn about it, he would ask. So he decided to try and write a play, direct it as a *nautanki*, and show people what it was all about.

At first it was just the two of us enacting, in the most amateurish way possible, the story of Princess Multan and Rup Singh at family gatherings. I was seven at the time and Rose nine. The hallmarks of *nautanki* were there from the start – a love story, obstacles standing in the way, comedy, song-and-dance, pathos and melodrama – but the story my father had written and directed grew over the course of a few months. From a little sketch performed for close family and friends, it took on a different life altogether, one that none of us could ever have anticipated.

At first I was actually supposed to be a man. I was Rup Singh, trying to woo the beautiful Princess Multan – Rose. But then one night when we were performing it for some family friends, my trousers got caught in a nail in one of the floorboards and dropped down to my ankles. The audience laughed until there were tears pouring from their eyes. If there were tears pouring from mine – and Rose's in sympathy – then they went unnoticed and my father realized the potential of this last gender-bending master stroke. From then on, I was secretly Rupa Singh, in love with Princess Multan but unable to tell her that I was really a girl. My life was a conundrum, perhaps even a tragedy. There was a witch who had cursed me. I could only tell someone I was a girl if they fell in love with me. Yet, if I told them who I was, could they still love me?

To everyone's surprise, but especially my mother's,

everyone who watched the play loved it. By the end of the performance, people would be crying they were laughing so much. So Dad became more ambitious, he pulled Uncle Jat into the mix, and they started advertising publicly, putting up flyers in Tooting and Southall, and we started getting asked to do shows.

The performance also became more complex. Dad hired a drummer and a sitar player, and for some performances a clarinet joined them. For the very special occasions, like a Diwali party in the temple or a wedding party, Dad hired an Odissi dancer to do a short introduction. Those were special nights. Rose and I would stare open-mouthed at the Odissi dancer – Sapna, her name was – as she did her make-up in the mirror. Vermillion lipstick, her face framed in white jewels, an enormous bun at the back of her head, around it a garland of flowers. Her sari, orange with green pleats that feathered open and shut, open and shut as she rippled from one hip to another, was cinched in around her pelvis with coils of glass crystals. Her hands and feet were lined in red, the colour of a betel nut. She stood lopsided on stage, a hip and the opposite knee thrust out, a heel rising, beating, flowing like water. Rose and I practised endlessly in the mirror, trying to dance like Sapna. On those special nights, the musicians set the mood, then Sapna performed a short piece, usually about Lord Krishna, and then Dad came onto the stage. Only after he'd chatted with the audience, got them warmed up, was it Rose's and my turn.

So what started with friends and family quickly escalated.

Soon we were available for hire for kitty parties and tambola nights, engagement parties and *sangeets*, temple nights and Holi celebrations, birthdays and anniversaries. The audience started the evening sipping their G&Ts, their *jal jeera* and their Dirty Martinis, exclaiming at the familiar-yet-distant strum of India that recalled lives and loves better forgotten. And then it was Rose and me, and they would end the evening crying tears of laughter. As the weeks went on, Rose became more and more beautiful, more serene, her eyes became more soulful, her hair darker, her skin lighter. And my part became funnier and funnier.

'Trip over!' my father called at a rehearsal, his hair standing on end, sweat spreading shadows in his armpits. We were in our living room, which was not a large room in the first place and it was crammed with furniture, but my father thought we should be able to do the show anywhere, adapt it to small and large spaces. 'No, no, you have to make it realistic, Rilla! See over there, you're on the donkey. Look, Gus-Gus is doing it perfectly. And you ride in, you get off, and here you fall off. Catch yourself in the stirrup or something. Don't make it look premeditated! Like you know it's going to happen!'

'Maybe his turban could fall forward onto his face!' Uncle Jat was so excited he was pacing up and down, up and down. If my father was the artistic director of the enterprise, Uncle Jat was the tour manager. He got us the business, and since he was good at all things entrepreneurial, he could get our weekends booked up weeks in advance.

'Brilliant!' Dad called excitedly. 'Can you do that Rilla, make your turban fall forward? Jog it with your arm on your way down!'

I fell off Gus-Gus. I lay there for a moment winded, then slowly stood up, looking dazed and confused. Then, with perfect timing, I sneezed so that I tripped over my own feet and this time landed splayed on top of Gus-Gus who took off and started running laps around the living room. This bit was my idea. What can I say, I was good at it. When I was finally on my feet again, I walked up to the makeshift balcony and serenaded my sister and sang to her about my love.

But love is complicated.

Afterwards, Uncle Jat gathered us together for what he called the debrief. He had studied psychology and economics at Durham. Here was a job where he could use both of his skills at once. It was, like it was for my father, a dream job for him. He was born to be an agent, a manager, a therapist, a trainer. Unlike my father and his sister, my Auntie Promilla, who grew up in Bombay, my mother and Uncle Jat grew up in London. Uncle Jat is a Londoner through and through, there is no doubt about it. The nine-to-five office job isn't for him; he has to invent, expand and create. And here was an outlet for his entrepreneurial skills.

'Now, girls,' he said, clapping his hands, 'come, come, come, how was it? Good? Bad? What?'

'Can I maybe speak some more words? I don't get to say anything, Daddy,' Rose said.

'And you missed your cue when you did have your line about the garland,' I said. 'Didn't she, Daddy?'

'She did.' Dad nodded, consulting his notes.

'Maybe learn your lines better.' I looked to Rose. 'I told her so last night, Daddy, but she was reading *The Famous Five* instead!'

Like I said, love is complicated.

12

The Beating of the Heart

The day after we met, Simon called me.

I saw his name turn up on my phone, I closed my eyes for a beat or two, my heart doing a funny fluttery thing in my chest, then took the call. He asked me how I was, what I was doing, in that already-familiar voice of his. I told him I was on my way to campus.

Perhaps he heard something in my voice, my very own neurotic mixture of longing and fear, because he paused for a second. Then he said, 'There's this great Thai place I know. Could we go there for dinner? Though remind me to avoid the papaya salad. Have you noticed there's something a little slug-like about papaya?'

'Sorry, can't do dinner.' I tapped my fingernail on the phone, keeping my voice as expressionless as I could. 'I have plans.'

'How about lunch then? I could probably swing it if I promise my boss I'll work all night.'

I mumbled something about tutorials.

'Okay, then. Call you tomorrow.'

And he did. He called me to make plans for dinner four days in a row, and I kept saying no.

'Why do you keep saying no?' Federico asked me, when he overheard my latest conversation with Simon. He was fiddling with two hollow carrots and half a hollowed-out turnip, trying to incorporate a vegetable orchestra into his thesis project.

'Because. I'm not over Jeremiah yet,' I said. We were sitting in the living room, Federico on the rocking chair, me in my favourite spot, the window seat, watching *Ellen*.

Federico made a noise that sounded like *hmph*.

Almost a year before I met Simon, I had briefly dated Jeremiah before he moved back to the States. He was an American political science post-doc doing an internship in Westminster, who had been certain he would become the American president one day. He was tall, intense-looking, talked almost non-stop and really fast. Everything Jeremiah did was fast – he talked fast, he ate his double cheeseburgers like the cow was still alive and might spring out of his mouth if he didn't chew fast enough. Sex was a competition – who could come up with the craziest positions, who could come the quickest (I mean, who thought up that one?), who could make the most noise. Every day we were together, we had to plan out and do at least five things (lunch out with friends, an anti-Trump rally, a lecture titled *Triceratops Is the New T-Rex*, dinner in the Sky Garden, drinks by the Thames) or else it was a boring day. He would start planning things the minute he woke up. He was exhausting. Though I guess at least he knew what to do, he was never short of ideas, he always seemed to know where he was going. There was something exciting about that, about that much drive.

'Well I'm not over him, so there,' I said to Federico. 'You don't like him because he was always trying to set you up on blind dates.'

'He was a douche-bag. Even you weren't sure you liked him at the time,' Federico said. 'Didn't you say there was no romance, it was all a little scripted? So, I get it, you like him now he's on the other side of the planet. But just go out with this Simon guy, put him out of his misery.'

'Why?' I said, frowning.

'Because you like him.'

I tried to think of a suitable retort to this huge assumption, but for some reason, I couldn't think of one. After several minutes, I mumbled, 'You don't know me,' but Federico didn't even bother to grace this with a mildly sarcastic eyebrow.

The next day Simon called again. 'Okay, it's clear to me that you don't like eating dinner. So I have another idea. How about you come for a walk along the Southbank and I buy you candyfloss?'

I snorted but I agreed to go out with him.

It was a weekday and I met him after work. There were people everywhere, walking in the sunshine of an early autumn evening, a barely-there marbled slice of moon hovering patiently above the skyline, waiting for the day to be over. We stood on the Golden Jubilee Bridge looking across at the London Eye with a merry-go-round at its feet, the odd inquisitive seagull pecking at our toes. Down on the bank, children tiptoed closer to a table with a severed head on it and then ran away shrieking when it moved. An entertainer blew bubbles that floated across the river, some making it only a few feet before a child jumped up and popped them, others floating all the way to the opposite bank, perhaps making their way towards St Paul's, or smashing against the windows of the Oxo Tower.

Simon pulled out a paper bag of sweet roasted peanuts that he had bought from a woman on the bank and offered me some. I absently put one in my mouth, but then gasped because the taste reminded me suddenly, searingly, of the time Rose and I had gone to Brighton with our parents when I was six. Tastes and smells sometimes did that to me, brought Rose suddenly and horribly to mind, but often I was prepared, knowing the taste of a Twix would do that, or Christmas pudding with custard the way Rose liked it, or a slice of not-quite-ripe green apple, and I knew to avoid those things. But the peanut caught me unawares.

I didn't say anything, I just carried on staring at the river, trying to blink away the sudden, unexpected tears. And then I felt it, Simon's fingers casually slipping under mine, interlacing, holding my hand. He took my hand to his lips, kissed it and then held it to his chest. Maybe no one else on the bridge noticed that anything had happened but, for some reason, a knot that had formed in my heart eased and dissolved. And I found I could breathe again.

13

Dinner for Sixty, Please

The GIF used to have monthly dinners when we were little, and that is how the *nautanki* took birth. The venue of the dinners varied. The idea was that each family would take their turn to host the dinner, and someone had come up with the idea that we should go clockwise around London. That way you always knew if it was your turn next and there would be no waiting around to decide who was going to play host. This still led to occasional problems of course. It was the GIF, there were always problems. Like, when going up from Paddington to Hampstead, on the way, what comes first – Willesden or South Hampstead? When looking at places like Wembley, as compared to, say, Hammersmith, would we look at the tube map or an actual map of London to sort out where Wembley is? These kinds of questions could take weeks, if not months, to sort out. There was a lot of, *No, you must come to us first*, and, *Listen, ji, let us not have open warfare. It is our turn, there are no two ways about it, and anyway you hosted the New Year's party last year, so it is our turn this year. And while we are at it, I must tell you that the microwave you gave us last Diwali stopped working after a month. I didn't want to say at the time.* But all in all it was a suitable method of making our way around London. On any given day, there could be anything up to thirty or forty people at these dinners, they were no small affair.

The evening usually started with games. Tug of war in the garden if it was summer, splashes in the swimming pool at Uncle Terry's house, hide-and-seek inside if it was winter, charades, Taboo, board games if nothing else was available. The adults drank scotch and Kingfisher beer, the children drank pink milk with Rooh Afza in it. Then it would be time for dinner – and of course there was competition to see who could do the best Mughal dinner, the best continental, the gourmet pizza buffet, the most authentic Indian-Chinese. There had to be at least five different kinds of dessert. Usually involving a tubful of ice-cream and chocolate sauce, chocolate fudge cake, buckets of *gulab-jamun*, truck-loads of sweet *kheer* and *phirni*.

At some stage, it evolved so that the people hosting the dinner would also hire entertainment. The first such event had a two-person Gipsy Kings tribute band that everyone went crazy over. There was lots of boozy dancing (though most Indian events end with a lot of boozy dancing, it has to be said). It was such a success that the next house to host the dinner decided to go one up. They hired an Indian-jazz fusion band with a guitar and *tabla*. People were talking about it for ages, calling each other on the phone to rave about it, doing research on jazz and Indian classical music and dropping names like Miles Davis, Dizzy Gillespie, Nusrat Fateh Ali Khan and Zakir Hussain into conversations. 'So cool, *ji*, so cool,' was the general consensus. The next family did a Bollywood band complete with a singer, and someone else hired a dancer. But Dad had to do it his way. When it was our turn to host, he got Rose and me to put on the *nautanki* he had been secretly working on.

I remember that night like it was yesterday. I don't remember all of our shows, of course; there were too many and they tend to blur. But I remember the first. Rose dressed in Mum's purple *lehenga*, the long skirt trailing all the way behind her, the filmy *chunni* delicately covering the back of her head. She had flowers in her hair and delicate little clip-on earrings. Me – I don't remember what I wore. My mother had taken two hours to sort Rose out, but me – as Rose's suitor Rup Singh – I could wear just about anything, it didn't really matter. So I had sat around watching Mum dressing Rose. I kept on tripping over things, dropping a box of hairpins all over the floor, pinching Rose, generally getting in the way. *Rilla, I know you're doing it on purpose*, Mum kept saying, *can't you just sit down?* But I was sulking and complaining and generally making it hard for them to do anything.

We lived in a pink Victorian terrace house in Balham at this time, with a small living room. Things in the house – furniture and ornaments – were always changing places. My mother, who had grown up in London, wanted Indian things in the house, cane furniture, colourful wooden cabinets, dancing *natrajas*, and my father, who had grown up in Bombay, wanted only Victorian antiques, curly-legged tables, heavily patterned William Morris wallpaper, blue-and-white china, floral upholstered sofas. But neither had negotiated over this. They kept moving things around, hiding some things, bringing others out, putting their things in front and moving the other's to the back. So the house was shifting and changeable, depending on who had been in the mood to decorate.

There were too many people to fit into the small living room, but the garden was long and narrow, so that's where all the guests sat when it was our turn to host the monthly dinner. On that night, the night of our *nautanki*, after dinner, people were jammed in the garden swing, sprawled on chairs, and sitting on the lawn. Various cousins were running in and out amongst the adults, jumping on our rickety second-hand trampoline and squirting each other with water.

Everyone was analysing the dinner. The chicken was under-salted, the roast potatoes good but not as good as the more traditional *jeera aloo*. The *saag paneer* was bland. But everyone was raving about the samosas. 'They're almost as good as Ambala, Renu,' Auntie Dharma said to my mother. 'So tasty.'

'Oh my God, why go to Ambala when you can eat these at home!' Auntie Pinky reached a hand out to the platters that lay scattered about and grabbed another samosa.

My mother smiled graciously. The samosas were of

course from Ambala Sweets but the GIF didn't need to know that.

'Who cares if they're from Ambala or if you made them?' Dad had said earlier when my mother was crying over how hard it was to get the dinner right and how everyone would judge her. Mum was convinced that her relatives pitied them for not having as much money as they did and she always worked herself up about the dinners.

So the samosas came from Ambala and everyone thought they were almost as good. During the post-dinner analysis, my father announced that there was something special he wanted to share with the family. It was time for the evening's entertainment. Out of the house came Rose and I shyly, tripping over our clothes, and we did our thing. It was finished pretty quickly and I was stumbling through most of my lines – and they were probably drowned out by the shrieks of the younger cousins who had been banished to the back of the garden. But it was a bigger hit than anything that had been done before by any of the other relatives.

'You know you can sell this? You know that, don't you?' Uncle Jat's eyes were shining. He followed Dad around – one of the little children had nearly set fire to Rose's train with one of the *diyas*, so Dad had been instructed to douse them as quickly as possible when the show was over. 'Let me ask some questions. Let me see the interest. See what I can do.'

'Ever the man of business, Jat,' Dad said, bending down, getting the wicks out of the oil and dunking them in water.

'We should think about this,' Mum said, handing out iced drinks – beer, lemonade and spicy *jal jeera*. 'Let's not rush into anything.'

'Nothing will come of it, Renu, don't worry,' Dad said.

For me the applause at the end of the show was something completely unanticipated, something thrilling. But it was even before then that the magic began. It was when I spoke my lines, when I projected out to the family on the lawn. I can still feel the thrill. I became a different person when I acted. It wasn't me, Rilla, but someone else who took over my body. Someone more interesting, more confident, less nervy. That night I was sure I wanted to grow up and be an actress. I posed in front of mirrors for weeks afterwards.

That's what I remember of that night. Most of the time. Sometimes other memories hit me.

'My god, *ji*, Rose is so beautiful. I've never seen a girl so beautiful.'

'I have a prediction. Tall, beautiful, fair, that is how she is going to turn out. I'll put money on it. She could go into modelling, she could marry Prince William.'

'You'll have a handful, I can tell you. Boys lining up. So pretty, so fair, so graceful at such a young age.'

It was true. There was something about Rose, but it wasn't just the hair and the face. It was something about her. Even now I can't put my finger on it. There was a sadness to her, a longing, like she could see what was really going on underneath everything, like nothing was hidden from her, like she couldn't hide from anything.

'She could be Miss World, so beautiful, so tall,' they said.

Out of the blue, words like that come unbidden to my mind. There's no warning. It's not like I'm thinking about that night, or about anything to do with our *nautanki*. Yet something from that night, something overheard, will come at me in the dark. I'll try to ward it off, sometimes with a raised hand, often with a quick shake of the head. This works most of the time, though not when I remember Dad's words. 'Don't worry, okay? Don't mind them,' he said seriously to me afterwards, when he was putting us to bed, after everyone had left around midnight, after our make-up had been wiped. 'Brains are so much more important.'

And Mum the next day, 'She's tall and very pretty. She will be noticed. You'll have to get used to it.'

I was playing with a cricket bat at the time, and when she said that, I started whacking it on the ground, over and over. I didn't say anything.

'Everyone can see you don't like it, Rilla. Try not to be so obvious,' Mum said.

I don't know why this bothers me now. Enough boyfriends have found me beautiful, so who cares?

I really don't know. My brain hurts from trying not to care.

I got hold of the purple *lehenga* later on and managed to tear the hem quite badly, knowing that it would get Rose into trouble with Mum. Or at least hoping that it would.

14

A Cat with Nine Lives

A week after my failed wedding, I am sitting on my porch, looking through my notes. Tyra tells me that I can do this, that I can write something. She thinks I can do it in my sleep. So I am looking through my notes, hoping that some grain of understanding, a flame of meaning will ignite something in my brain and I will know what I want to say about love. At the moment, my MA is all I have. If I get kicked out, I have nothing left. Nothing to show for the last three years, and nothing to hold me now that everything else seems to be crumbling.

So I sit down, I open my laptop. I can do this. I know I can! It's true that so far whenever I've tried to get some words on the page I've shut my computer down in panic, feeling sick and stupid from anxiety. But I can crack this. I click on my notes.

This is when I realize I've left my phone inside the flat. I am outside and my phone is inside. How am I supposed to concentrate on Barthes – who is going on interminably about how we fall in love not with a person but with a scene, the scene of our first meeting or some such madness – when something like this happens? Of course I can't be working on my MA. The only thing I can do right now is to get up and search for my phone. It could be anywhere, this is the nature of phones.

I stand up, dropping everything, pen, Barthes, laptop.

And now it turns out I can only find one of my slippers. Why is this happening to me? I look under my rocking chair, under the swing, behind the flower pot, *in* the flower pot.

'What's the crack, Rilla?'

It's Earl. I wave abstractedly. My entire life is falling apart. First my phone, then my slipper. It's like the universe is trying to tell me something.

'What are you looking for in the plant pot?' Earl calls. He has now reached a quarter of the way past the house.

'My slipper!' I call, without turning around.

'Were you standing in the plant pot?'

'What? No!'

'You won't find something by looking where it never was!' says Earl.

I now have my slipper (it was under the blanket next to where I was sitting on the rocking chair) and my phone (it took half an hour to find – it was on top of the toilet roll, under yesterday's *Metro*, and there was yet another missed call from Simon, but that's neither here nor there).

I feel better now, more in control of things. Now all I have to do is start again. Maybe working outside isn't a good idea. Perhaps, instead I can sit at the little desk in my bedroom. It will only take an hour or two to clear it of books, papers and clothes. Once it is clear of all those things, I will be able to work.

Our doorbell rings. I walk down the stairs to answer it.

'Auntie Promilla!' I say. 'Has someone died?' I blurt this out before I think better of it. That's how rare it is to see Auntie Promilla at mine by herself, without any social occasion or anyone else from the GIF to accompany her.

Her round face looks strained, her hennaed hair is standing up all around her head, her eyes are looking anywhere but into mine. She keeps glancing over her shoulder. She is carrying a large object under a blanket, which she carefully places on the porch.

'You have to keep him,' she says shiftily. 'Okay? Don't say no. They'll kill him.'

I glance at the object. Given how Auntie Promilla is behaving, I am expecting to see some body parts, cut up into small bits. Auntie Promilla lifts one side of the blanket, then puts it hurriedly back in its place. I have a second in which to see that under the blanket is a cat box with a cat in it. Are there people following Auntie Promilla who are trying to kill her cat?

'Lord Basingstoke. He's had a stroke. The other cats in my house can't stand him. The cats and the dogs and even the guinea pigs, they're going to kill him. You have to keep him here till I can find someone who wants him.'

These are probably the most words I've ever heard Auntie Promilla speak in my life, all put together. She is flapping her hands about, fanning herself. Either carrying the cat box is heavy work or she is imitating my mother. She grimaces, or perhaps she smiles, but it's such a foreign thing for her that it looks painful.

'You have to take him.'

I spring back. 'No way. Why me? I don't want him.'

'You – well, you have time. You don't have a regular job, and you're not getting married.' It is hurting her to speak, I can see it. It's like using these parts of her mouth, her vocal cords, is so alien, she's not sure what is happening to her.

'No one else will have him.'

I screw up my eyes. 'Do you mean that you asked all the others first and they refused, or that you know they won't want him so you haven't asked?'

She doesn't answer. 'I'll call back when I find someone to adopt him.'

And she's gone, just like that.

There is definitely something not right with Lord Basingstoke. He's grey-blue, has no neck and he walks sideways. He bumps into anything there is in the same room as him – even things that are not in his way. Federico and I stare at him. When we put food next to him, he starts wailing and scratching like he's trying to get to it but he can't figure out how.

'This shit is crazy,' Federico says. His hair is tied back

114

with a red bandana today and he has a little silver hoop in one ear. His t-shirt is tie-dye, with an Om in the centre of his chest.

Jharna is here too. She is suddenly spending a lot of time at my flat, I'm not sure why. It's possible that the GIF has appointed her custodian. They're keeping watch on me after my runaway bride fiasco. It's hard to say what they're watching out for, but it's the kind of thing they would do.

Or she could be here because – no, I'm out of reasons.

Lord Basingstoke is the first thing that has made Jharna look away from her phone. I mean, she is actually not looking at it. It's still in her hand but she doesn't have one eye on it all the time. This has never happened before.

Jharna has long hair that she wears on top of her head in a bun. I've never seen her in anything but torn jeans and tank tops. Occasionally she wears eyeliner. She believes that marijuana should be legal and all kids should learn code in primary school. If she were Prime Minister, she says, those would be her first priorities. I have no idea what that means – learn code. But she thinks it should be the political manifesto for the world. That it is more important than dealing with plagues like climate change, the Middle-East crisis and Donald Trump.

Last night Federico rolled a joint and offered it to Jharna and me, an eyebrow raised. 'The situation warrants it, *chica*,' he said, knowing I wasn't always game.

'Oh, what the hell,' I said. 'Life sucks right about now,' and took a long drag.

Federico and Jharna talked all night, Federico talking like he was floating through space and Jharna like someone had hit the fast-forward button. I was staring at my thumbs for a long time, and then for no reason at all tears were streaming down my cheeks. I was murmuring things that made Jharna and Federico nod sympathetically, but now I can't remember what I was saying.

The two of them were having this crazy conversation. It started with Federico explaining what kind of music he wants to make.

'It's like technology reaching into your soul and making love, you know? With your organs? Like if you breathe through your spleen, it'll sound like this, it'll be the ambient noise of your digestive tract, the soundtrack to your blood. It's ambient life sound.'

'That's so cool, man,' was Jharna's contribution.

'You sound American, Fountain,' Federico said. (*Jharna* means fountain.)

'I'm a citizen of the world, Feds,' Jharna said. (She's started referring to Federico as the FBI.) 'Drink sangria, sing to the world, you know what I'm saying? Love has no boundaries.'

'That's so post-modern I can't even smell it,' Federico said, shaking his head, trying to hold the smoke in his lungs.

They went on and on like that all night. We all ended up singing along to Snoop Dogg's 'Gin and Juice'.

But even as I was singing, I had a picture, a memory. Of Rose, age six probably, of her trying to teach me to slide down the banister. That's how I felt last night, like I was free-falling, sliding down the banister, shrieking, jumping into her arms at the bottom, completely safe in the knowledge that she would catch me, or that I would fall onto one of the twenty or so enormous cushions she had lined up around the stairs. Every cell in my body remembers how her body felt as I collided with it, both of us collapsing on the cushions, giggling helplessly but also knowing that we were on borrowed time, that Mum would tick us off as soon as she realized what we were up to.

Today, we're all subdued. There are dark circles under our eyes. I've had the near-loss of my phone to deal with and Jharna and Federico have been out to buy us some lunch, but have come back empty-handed. The words 'Borrowed Time' are tattooed on my brain. We're watching Lord Basingstoke miss his cat bowl by a mile.

'What is wrong with that cat?' Federico asks.

'It's so rad,' Jharna says. 'See how he's walking to the bamboo in that pot there? I think he actually thinks that's where the food is. It's awesome.'

I scratch my chin. 'He had a stroke. What if he can't sense space?' This is exactly the kind of problem I like, this is the kind of problem I can deal with.

'That's it!' Federico says. 'He thinks he's moving towards the cat bowl, but he's moving in a completely different direction. Ouch, not the plant pot again. All the head bumps will not be helping.'

'We have to teach it to walk in an arc,' Jharna says.

I frown. 'How do we teach him to walk in an arc?'

'We have to calculate the parabola – where he is to where the bowl is.' Federico is holding up his hands, apparently measuring things in the air.

'But the bowl is right next to him,' I point out.

'Yes, but he doesn't see it that way. He sees it as if it is some distance away. So, how about we put it some distance away, and then find a way for him to walk towards it in an arc? See how he is leaning right? That's what we have to work with.'

'That's a great idea!' I roll up my metaphorical sleeves. 'Let's do this! No matter how much time it takes, it's totally worth it!'

Federico and Jharna turn to look at me in surprise. 'Wow, I've literally never seen you so enthusiastic about anything. Like, anything,' Jharna says.

Federico is looking at me knowingly.

I shrug. 'What?'

'You don't have any other things you need to be doing?' he asks casually.

I cross my arms. 'Like what?'

'I'm only saying – don't you have any writing to do, or people you need to have a conversation with?'

I purse my mouth. The cat gives a pitiful meow. 'He's hungry,' I say. 'Can you see anything more important than that?'

So now that's what we're doing. We are trying to teach Lord Basingstoke to walk in parabolas.

15

High and Dry

Bhang: One cup yogurt. Green cardamom, black peppercorns, sweet palm *jaggery*. For a gourmet taste, a hair of saffron, a pinch of nutmeg and cinnamon. A dollop of cream if you're in the mood. Blend it with some edible cannabis and you're good to go.

I don't think that I've ever had as much anxiety as I did at university. It wasn't about anything in particular, at least I don't think so. I had somehow thought that as soon as I moved to university, left my parents' home, left behind our strained relationship that was so full of unspeakable memories, that things would get better, that I would turn into a new person perhaps. But instead, soon after moving out from my parents', I started getting the worst anxiety I've ever got.

In my final year of university, I was a wreck. It was so bad towards the end that I only felt okay as long as I was reading, my nose buried in a book. But ask me to come out of the book and my heart would start pounding, my palms sweating, my throat would go dry and I would start seeing floating bubbles in front of my eyes.

In the final year of my degree, when I was at my lowest ebb, when everything looked bleak and dark, and I was having panic attacks, I did something I had never done before. I googled our *nautanki*. I don't know what I had thought I would find, I did it unthinkingly, like my body was doing something that my brain had no control over. At the same time I had no clue why I hadn't done it before.

To my surprise a few archived newspaper clippings had come up. There was an article in a local newspaper reporting our success at a Holi party and another about a community event in Southall. An article on Indian culture in London had a fleeting reference to us and another on a local MP briefly mentioned us too. And then my heart nearly stopped because there was a picture, taken at a Diwali *mela* in Brick Lane. I had not been expecting it. Yet when I saw it, it was like the photo had been waiting there all along, waiting for me to find it.

Now a few days after my failed wedding, feeling like I'd rather be anyone but me, like I'd rather have someone else's life and someone else's memories, I pull out the print I had taken of it three years ago. I have a hunger sometimes to see Rose's face, and almost always when I have this hunger, this hollow feeling in the pit of my stomach, I dream of her.

Often, I dream of the time she built us a doll's house because our parents had told us they couldn't afford to buy us a big one, and they didn't want Uncle Jat to find out we wanted one. So, Rose sat down and made one. I remember she was completely absorbed in the details. She used cardboard boxes to make the walls, boxes wrapped carefully in wrapping paper.

'This can be the wallpaper,' she'd said, dividing levels with flat pieces of cardboard cut neatly, cut to exact measurements. It took weeks, and I loved it more than anything in the world. But now, thinking back to it, it was so tatty I'm surprised we spent more than two minutes working on it or playing with it. But we did, we had it for a long time. I never had the focus for that kind of thing, and I was also the kind of person to scream and complain about how tight our parents were, but Rose wasn't. She was good at finding a way through problems.

After Rose disappeared, I would sit staring at the doll's house for hours at a time until, one day, my mother threw it out when I was at school. *I hate you, I hate you,* I screamed at her when I found out, and she said, *Well, why don't you leave too?*

Anyway, that's neither here nor there. And it's too painful to think about. What I'm saying is that when I am starving for a glimpse of Rose's face, for the feel of her gentle hands combing my bushy hair, for her soft laugh, then my dreams give her to me, like a gift. I know I only have to wait.

But I'm going through a drought at the moment. I've

either been sleeping so deeply that I can't remember any of my dreams or my dreams have been of Simon. No Rose. Not for weeks. So I have to look at her. I have to see her face. I pull out the picture I found a few years ago, the picture of us that I had printed and then pushed to the back of the eaves in my room. I stare at it. I take deep gulping breaths.

It's black-and-white. It was taken right after we did a show. And now as I look at it I remember that Rose was wearing a yellow skirt and gold top that was stuck to her with safety pins. I remember it like she's standing in front of me right now. Dad, Uncle Jat and Gus-Gus were there too on the stage. This was one of the few times we did our show outdoors and on an actual, though temporary, stage. Usually it was cordoned-off areas in community halls or a room in a house, but that night we had a small stage, a rickety one that shivered with every step we took. And someone had the bright idea to try to cram the four of us on it with an Irish wolfhound the size of a Shetland, just to take a picture. Rose was next to my father, Uncle Jat and Gus-Gus, and right at the end, I was teetering on the edge of the stage, nearly falling off.

'If you move, move along!' the cameraman shouted. 'We can get you all in. Move another couple of inches, love, there's a poppet!'

Rose had her arm around me so I didn't fall off, holding me onto the stage by sheer force of will as I scowled and squirmed.

'Get your arm off me!' I hissed.

'You'll fall off!' Rose whispered. 'It'll be finished in a second, Rilla, can't you stop wriggling?'

I shrugged her arm off as soon as the cameraman gave us a thumbs-up. 'You're not Mum, stop acting like you are.'

'Stop being a baby!' Rose said. 'You're such a baby.' There were already tears in her eyes. She had no stomach for confrontation. But then I had enough for the two of us.

'Keep your hands off me, okay?' I stormed off as soon as the picture was taken, flinging off my waistcoat and turban on the floor. I knew I would get into trouble for this. It was up to Mum to keep our costumes clean and ironed, and because they were delicate, made of satin or silk, with sparkling gold *zari* at their borders, little appliquéd mirrors, dancing elephants and parading peacocks turning this way and that, she had to handwash them, not toss them in the washing machine. But I didn't care. Or maybe I threw them on the floor because I wanted to get into trouble.

'You're so funny, sweetie!' someone called. It was a woman who I remembered seeing in the audience, right in the front row, tears of laughter running down her face. 'Can I take a picture with you? Is that okay? I can check with your parents. Being a minor and all that.'

'You want one with my sister,' I scowled. 'She's back there.' People always wanted pictures with Rose, with the band of red roses in her hair.

'No, with you,' she insisted. She looked down at her camera.

'Leave me alone!'

'Just one picture, that wouldn't be so bad?' She was smiling hopefully.

I screamed. 'Can't you leave me alone!'

The woman looked utterly shocked.

I ran off. I stood for a second looking at my relatives cleaning up after us, making sure we didn't forget any of our paraphernalia. Uncle Jat was chatting with the musicians, being their best friend so that they wouldn't mind working for 'artistic excellence, for nostalgia, for the great Indian revival!' as he said. For free, is what he meant. Mum was collecting costumes and props. Dad was somewhere around, I couldn't see him. I stood there at the periphery between inside and outside, and then I ran.

It was dark. I have no idea if it was seven in the evening or eleven. There were lights everywhere, flashing shop names, Masala, Chili, Spicy Curry. Wonder Woman was spray-painted on a wall, graffitied faces with splayed lips, teapots with decaying teeth, elephants wearing top hats and doing the polka, a cow whose t-shirt read 'Che', the artwork of Brick Lane.

The street was full of people following the smells of frying fish and gram flour, jerk chicken and hot waffles. I ran and ran, my trousers, loose and heavily pleated, getting caught between my legs.

When I stopped running, I was panting and I had no idea where I was. I turned around but I could no longer see the stage where we had done our show. I don't remember being scared. I wanted to get lost, wanted someone to find me, drag me off by the ear and tell me off. I was looking for trouble. I joined a parade of people. A *dhol*-drum player was leading it, and behind him was a troupe of dancers in Indian costumes, yellow loose tunics and blue trousers. The men in turbans and yellow tunics started doing a kind of crazy dancing that I had never seen before – they were doing *bhangra*, a Punjabi dance from the farms in the North of India. Their legs were bent and they were moving forward, beating their chests. A few got onto the shoulders of their partners and then back-flipped off them, others were doing cartwheels and somersaults. I started dancing like a maniac, beating my chest, looking up at the sky, closing my eyes and shaking my shoulders. My sweat was flying and my clothes were drenched.

The routine was repeated a few times but eventually the troupe ended up at a café and I slipped in with them. Some of the dancers sat right down on the floor, others leaned against the walls. Orders were placed for chilli fish and steamed rice. Glasses of something went around. I grabbed one before someone could stop me. It was a thin yogurt with a lot of sugar in it, sweet and sour at the same time. If I close my eyes now I can still taste it. Someone grabbed my empty glass.

'Oye, *ladki*, don't tell me you drank that!' It was a young woman, one of the dancers, her cheeks made up with big round red spots, her eyebrows lined with sparkling *bindis*. 'Shit, man, you're not going to like this.'

I smiled at her. I couldn't stop smiling. Her hair was almost down to her knees in one long plait. Her lips had lost most of their lipstick and there was just an outline of dark red now framing her mouth. She smelt like Rose and I smelt after we had done a show, of costume and make-up and sweat.

'You're so nice,' I said.

And it was the strangest thing I had ever said, because I said it really slow and it took a long time to get the words out. I giggled, my mouth feathery, like a velvety ladybird's back.

'Here, put your head down in my lap,' the woman said.

A group of hippies came in and joined the ever-expanding table. There was a woman with dirty-blonde dreadlocks and a couple of men in cotton shirts. They had musical instruments, a ukulele, a mouth organ, castanets, and clave and now they were singing 'Us and Them', the hippies and the *bhangra* troupe.

'Will you adopt me?' I shouted to the woman.

'You're whispering,' she said, kissing me on the head. 'Speak up, girl, what's your name?'

'Rose. You'll adopt me?'

'I definitely will. I'll buy you off your parents if they don't give you to me.'

'I have a sister.'

'I'll buy her too.'

'No, no don't buy her.'

And then I knew I was going to throw up. I stood up suddenly and tried to run out of the café. But I was wading in treacle. I finally made it out, gasping for air, and was sick in the corner of the street.

'You're so stupid, Rilla, you know that? Do you know how long I've been looking for you?'

It was Rose.

Of course she had followed me. She wouldn't let me go by myself. She held me by the shoulders. There were tears in her eyes. This hadn't been my own adventure, after all.

'Why do you always have to follow me?' I scowled.

'Because you don't know how to look after yourself! Come on.' She was dragging me by the arm.

I pulled a face at her, flailed my arms about to hit her. I slapped her in the jaw like a wet fish.

'Stop hitting me! Come on!' Her chin was trembling. She was looking all around her.

'You're scared of being out here,' I said smugly. 'Poor Rose is a scaredy-cat,' I sang. And it didn't even occur to me that she had followed me out here to look after me, even though she was scared. Those kinds of things never occurred to me then.

All I could think about were all the people in the audience, going on about how beautiful, how unusual, how poised she was. Everyone always loved Rose so much. She was irresistible, I get it. I get it now, and I got it then. How could anyone not love her? How could anyone look at me when she was in the room?

'I don't want you here!' I screamed.

Her chin trembled but she said, 'I'm not going to leave you.'

'Go away!' I screamed.

Then I needed to throw up again. And Rose was behind me, stroking my back, making cooing noises. 'Poor Rilla, poor thing, go on, throw it all up.'

Rose gently held me by the shoulders and helped me stand up. I was shaking, and there was a burning in my stomach. I cried into her shoulder as she walked me back to our stage, where people were still clearing up and eating dinner.

But it wasn't over yet, because our mother was waiting for us.

'Rose, go out to the car. I need to talk to Rilla.'

She wore a long skirt and an embroidered top whose back had sweat creases. She looked tired, her hair dishevelled.

'I want to stay,' Rose said. But Mum wasn't listening.

'What is it with you?' she said to me. 'Do you know how worried I was?'

I could see Rose's face. She wanted to say it was her that ran away, but she was too honest. 'I ran too,' was the best she could manage.

But Mum wasn't paying any attention. 'Why do you do it?' she said to me. 'Thoughtless, you're completely thoughtless. I've never known you think of anyone but yourself. You're dumb and stupid. Rotten girl!'

I stared at her, my chin shaking uncontrollably. I couldn't speak, because I knew it would come out like a horrible croaking and I wouldn't let Mum see that about me.

'Are you going to say anything? Or are we just going

to have more drama, more tears, more screaming? Do you think anyone falls for that trick?'

Why are you horrible to me, that's what I wanted to ask. *Why don't you love me like you love Rose.* But I couldn't open my mouth. I couldn't let her see how I felt. And I was afraid I would start screaming and yelling at her. I couldn't do that either, I couldn't do that and prove her right about me.

Now, as I stare at the photograph, as I look at us lined up on that stage, the memories hit me. And they aren't just memories, I can see them and be in them like I'm still there, doing our show with Rose, running off, getting caught, stuck there, reliving that scene over and over.

And perhaps I am.

16

Walking in Straight Parabolas

Auntie Promilla calls the next day to check up on the progress of Lord Basingstoke. What can I say except that our progress is slow, very slow. We cannot get that cat to aim for anything.

'Someone wants to take him.' She is whispering down the phone, like she doesn't want this conversation to be overheard.

'Great.' I want nothing but to be rid of that grey-blue hair-shedder. My enthusiasm to train him to walk and eat properly has died an early demise. His hair is everywhere. In my clothes, on our furniture, in my armpits, my unopened pots of Yoplait, inside my socks, it is coming out of my nostrils and my pores. The thing yowls all the time because he's hungry. This can't go on, there's no room in my life for a cat. I have to focus on my thesis and this damn cat is taking up all my time. Professor Grundy has already sent me three emails since I last saw her to ask if I have anything ready to send her.

Even Federico and Jharna have given up doing anything but trying to teach the cat to aim for stuff. It's just as well someone wants to take him.

'You have told this person about the weeing and the not walking straight and banging into things? He keeps on trying to go to the toilet on the kitchen table.'

'It's a nice chap,' Auntie Promilla says, ignoring my question. 'He wants to pop over.'

'To take him?' It can't be too soon as far as I'm concerned.

'Oh no.' Auntie Promilla sounds horrified. 'No, just to bond. We have to let them bond, and to see that this man is the right person to take Lord Basingstoke.'

'When?'

'Today.'

'Today?' This sounds really soon. Then I catch myself, I shake my head. I have to get rid of that cat. 'Good,' I say to Auntie Promilla. 'That's a good thing.'

I get off the phone and grab some popcorn and a beer from the kitchen. Then I head to the living room where Federico is talking on the phone to his boyfriend and Jharna is dangling a red soft mouse for Lord Basingstoke. He keeps batting at something, but whatever it is, it isn't the mouse, or anywhere in the vicinity of the mouse. I sit down and play at this with her for some time. Federico doesn't let us make fun of the creature. He's busy giving his boyfriend monosyllabic responses, but he isn't exactly out of hearing range so we're snorting with suppressed laughter.

'Do you have a boyfriend?' I ask casually.

'I'm not the type boys go for. Not like you.'

I stare at her. Has she had a mini-stroke too, like the damn cat? 'You're gorgeous.'

'Ask me something,' she says. 'Anything.'

Wow. That's the most difficult thing anyone has ever asked me to do. I look around for inspiration.

'Do you think Federico looks gay?'

'There's no such thing as "looking gay". There's only the way we're taught someone should look. Identity categories are socially conditioned. They are clouded by social expectations, as are our perceptions. See?' She is sitting on the floor, in denim shorts and a tank top. She has large hoops dangling from her ears and eyeliner on today.

'No,' I say slowly.

'I always give a serious answer to questions like that. Boys don't like that kind of thing.'

'Oh, I don't know. You'll meet someone. I mean, look at you. And there are all kinds of boys. Some like serious philosophical chat.'

'Hard to imagine.'

She throws the mouse at Lord Basingstoke this time. It hits him square on the nose. He looks startled, his hair stands on end and he hisses into the distance at something only he can see, then he sits down and starts licking his paws. We've put butter on them because that's the only way we can get him to eat anything.

I stare at the bubbles in my drink. I'm no good at things like this. Rose, what would Rose say to Jharna? Rose, who can feel everyone's feelings, who can block nothing out. Her voice, the one that lives in my head, says, *You'll do just fine, Jharna*. That's what I need to say.

'No shit,' I say. It's close enough.

'I don't even know how to talk to boys in any way that's not like a "friend". They all give me hugs and thump me on the back.'

'It just takes practice. Ask questions, show an interest. It's not that hard.'

Looking back, I really wish I hadn't said that.

'It's hard for me,' she says.

We gossip about various relatives. An auntie who keeps sending Jharna's parents pictures of 'nice Indian boys', an uncle who is looking up American grad schools for her in case she wants to do a PhD in the States, someone else who keeps asking her if she will do computer science at university.

'Tell them no,' I say. 'Just to get them to worry a little bit.' I get up off the floor and go and sit on the window seat with my popcorn and beer bottle.

Jharna laughs. 'Good idea. Except then they'll call me every day instead of every other.' She's quiet for a moment. 'What's happening with you?' she says finally.

I shrug. 'Not much.'

'I mean, with Simon.'

'Oh.' I don't know what else to say. 'I have things to work out.'

'Like about your sister?' Jharna says.

I splutter on my Bass. I can't say anything, and I can't look at her. My heart is pounding, I can hear it, the blood gushing through my body.

'Sorry,' she mutters. 'It's just – the other day when you mentioned Gus-Gus – I asked my parents about it. They made such a song-and-dance about not wanting to talk about it and trying to distract me that I – obviously there's something up. I don't really get how I didn't know that you had a sister.' She's quiet again. 'How did she die?'

It's an obvious thing to think.

I shake my head. The rock that has lodged itself in my throat won't budge, but I have to say it, deny it, because if I don't deny it, then I'm admitting that it could be true, and I can't do that.

'She's not dead,' I croak. 'At least, I don't think she is.'

The question rises in my mind, like it does sometimes when I can't keep it at bay, like it had on the morning of my wedding: what if she is dead? What if my sister is gone forever? That's the question I had woken up with that day. What if something happened to her? What if she's dead and I'll never know for sure?

'Where is she then?' Jharna says. She moves her feet out of the way of the cat who's chasing something invisible. Her feet are bare, the toenails clipped and unpolished, the same as nine of her fingernails – one pinky has a flaky multi-coloured pattern on it, and at the moment, I can't stop staring at it. I'd rather look at Jharna's fingernail than at anything else. Especially her face.

I shake my head. 'I don't know.' I clear my throat. 'Maybe adopted. Or sent away somewhere. Something like that.'

She looks disbelieving, though she's nodding her head. 'Sure, sure.'

This is what I had thought when I was a child, this story is what I had told myself. But as I've grown older, though the cloud that covers Rose's disappearance has only become more dense and impenetrable, still, it has over the years started to dawn on me that my story doesn't add up. It doesn't add up that someone adopted Rose. But then what? What the bloody hell happened to her and where is she now?

'I know it doesn't make sense,' I mutter.

Jharna doesn't talk for a while. She gets a text, and fiddles with her phone for a minute.

'Sorry,' she says, but I can tell she sees nothing wrong in text messaging at the same time as having a conversation with me. She finally gets off the phone and looks at me again. 'I could look her up,' she says. She says it so casually it takes me a few moments to understand what she's saying.

I am startled. 'No!' I shake my head. 'No, there's nothing to find. I've looked her up. There's nothing there. She was sent away, to – to keep her away from me.' I stop abruptly. I take a deep breath. 'There's nothing about her, just some old news stories about this street theatre sketch thing we used to do.'

She looks incredulous. 'To keep her away from *you*?'

I shake my head. 'I don't know. It's just – just something I've always wondered about.'

She makes a face but something in *my* face obviously

tells her not to go down that road. She thinks for a moment.

'If she was adopted she might not be Rose Kumar any more.' She still looks like she doesn't believe in this story, but she's willing to play along, humour me, because she thinks there is only one explanation, that Rose is dead. I don't believe in my story either, but I have no other. The story is all I have. 'She might have a different name,' Jharna says.

I want this conversation to stop because we're talking details, and I can't, I can't talk about the details. 'There's – nothing to do.'

I can see she's hesitating, she wants to say something. 'It's just – the other night when you were high, you were talking about sisters.'

I stare at her. 'I was what?'

'Not about her specifically. Just about how nice it would be to have a sister, something like that. And you kept on rocking back and forth and saying if you hurt a sister, she goes away.' She makes a face. 'I don't know. A lot of it was nonsense.'

My breathing is shallow and I'm finding it hard to get enough air, like the oxygen in the room has shrunk, is oozing out from under the windows and the door, leaving me bereft. I stare blankly at my feet, then at the window ledge, then out of the window but I can't see anything, everything appears to be out of focus, blurry.

'Could she have died and they didn't want to tell you?' Jharna can't help saying it after all. She says it like she would to a child, softly, patiently.

'No!' I stand up. My bottle crashes to the floor. 'No, okay? That's not possible.' I crouch down on my hands and knees, using tissue to try to mop up the spilt beer. 'Look, there's nothing to do, okay?' I stand up again, sopping wet tissue in my hands, trailing streaks of beer all over my legs. 'I should head to my room. Should get some work done.'

I start to walk out of the room, but she quickly gets up, stops me with a hand on my arm, her face serious. 'Sorry. I shouldn't have said anything.'

Her kindness hurts and I can't meet her eyes. 'I know it sounds crazy. But the thing is she's alive. I would know if she's not. She's – she's like my limb or something. I can't explain it, but I know she's alive.'

'That's weird shit.' She twists her mouth. Jharna's an only child. I know she can't possibly understand. But that's how it feels even now, after all these years.

'I have to go. Okay? I'll – see you around.'

17

Running but Staying in the Same Place

I sit in my office marking papers, waiting for a tutorial with Professor Grundy about my thesis. Someone has had the bright idea to furnish all the offices with wall clocks that go tick-tick-tick and for some reason, today, the clock seems to mirror the pounding of my heart. What have I to show Professor Grundy? What can I write about when my experience of love seems to be wrapped around a tight little nugget of guilt? No, not about Rose, I tell myself, closing my eyes shut, the guilt can't be about Rose, because somewhere, in some place, Rose is okay. I know it in my heart. So the guilt *cannot* be about her. That is what I tell myself. It must be about Simon. Though this thought hardly feels better. Can you love without a conscience? Can too much of a conscience get in the way of love? I clutch my head in my hands. *I don't know!*

Okay, just breathe Rilla, take a pause. Think! I have

twenty minutes until my meeting with Professor Grundy. I need to get something of my own down. Maybe I can work with this. I wonder if my own conscience is over- or under-developed. My fingers hover over the keyboard.

My conscience is over-developed, I think, because I feel guilty for just about everything. I feel guilty not only when I say something hurtful to someone, but also when they say something hurtful to me. I feel guilty about human trafficking and sexism and racism and also religious violence. Actually the entire human race should feel guilty about that one, not just me. We're all responsible. We all need to grow up. The only problem is that religious violence thrives on guilt and fear. So feeling guilty about it may be a bit of a moral loop-a-loop. It's like eating red meat to cure constipation; you're just contributing to the problem.

But then again maybe my conscience is under-developed, because given the chance to own up to my guilt, I never take it. Take, for example, my near inability to speak to Simon after my runaway bride act. I take my hands away from the keyboard and rub my face. I shake my head to clear it. I look at the blank document and try to focus.

Is conscience about *feeling* guilt or owning up to guilt? And is the owning up to it its undoing?

For the feeling of guilt, I get eleven out of ten points. For the owning up to it, I probably get half a point.

But what happens if you can't express your guilt, what happens when guilt becomes a part of you? What if it jams up your heart? What if my feelings for Rose – the love, the guilt, the terrible pervading weight of loss – what if they are the blueprint, a map of love that I must follow for the rest of my life?

Now my heart is pounding. In my head is an incessant record. I'm sorry, I'm so sorry. I'm sorry, I'm so sorry. It's stuck and I can't switch it off. It's like when you fall asleep to Jeremy Vine on Radio 2. You're in that liminal state where you think you're sleeping but you can hear every word the man is saying. Come to think about it, if I do have a conscience, it has Jeremy Vine's voice. It's annoying but almost always right. So now Jeremy is telling me: *Rilla, do you think you need to talk to someone? Rilla, do you think it's time to talk to Simon?*

I growl at Jeremy.

I walk over for my tutorial with Professor Grundy. I sit across from her, my hands folded contritely in my lap, knowing I haven't done enough, not nearly enough on my thesis. *This isn't about her, this is about me*, I try to tell myself. But it doesn't help. I still feel like a criminal in the dock, waiting for judgement to be passed. She is wearing an olive blazer this morning, a cream turtle-neck underneath and a chequered pair of trousers. She looks over my notes. She frowns. She's trying to help me, I can see that.

'We could work with this,' she says, pointing to my notes about Lacan and Žižek. 'Wanting something that's always around the next corner. We can work with that. Maybe you need something – a novel – to analyse. That will make it more concrete. Didn't you do an undergraduate thesis on *The Importance of Being Earnest* and how the cynic is hiding a romantic, or was it the other way round?'

I stare at the computer blankly. The words I had typed in that document just a few weeks ago don't make sense any more. Analyse – what does analyse mean? Sign, symbol, language – I look at the words I've written, but I have no idea what they mean.

'What's going on with you?' Professor Grundy asks, sitting back in her chair. There is a hint of impatience in her voice, but mostly she's curious. Her analytical mind wants to solve the problem. 'I've given you time. In fact, you've had nothing but time on your side. You know the consequences if you don't produce more. But I don't feel like I'm getting through to you. What's going on, Rilla?'

'Brain fog.'

She looks at me thoughtfully for some time. 'Don't let this wedding fiasco break you into pieces.'

Wedding fiasco are the words I should focus on here, but instead I want to say, 'I broke into pieces a long time ago. I glued them back together, but the glue is melting now. I should have used something stronger.' But I don't say this. I nod thoughtfully and say, 'Yes, I should be able to do it. I *want* to do it, Prof, I want to finish it.'

She doesn't look convinced and I'm not surprised. *I'm* not convinced either. This world – university, thesis, my job – this is what I have. This can ground me and hold me. Yet somehow, for some reason, books and words are no longer working. At the end of the tutorial, I leave

Professor Grundy's office, I walk automatically to my office, pick up my things and walk out.

Throughout the walk to the train station and the train ride back home, my heart starts to fill. Not with hope, certainly not with love, but with despair. Even when I was doing my degree, locked in a terrible cycle of indecision and anxiety, books helped me, brought me a sense of normalcy, made me feel like me. But now even the *me* I thought I knew feels splintered. And no books, friends, work – not even Simon – can heal those cracks.

I get off the train and stand long after the train has pulled out of the station. I stare at the train tracks. A worried-looking guard in a fluorescent jacket comes and virtually pulls me away from the edge. I shrug away. 'I wasn't going to jump, if that's what you're thinking.'

I start to quickly walk away. Of course I wasn't going to jump. But just sometimes the thought of it, the thought of doing something drastic, something irrevocable, draws across my mind like a whisper. What if, my mind says at these times, what if that is the only way I can be with Rose again?

18

Punched

Back at home, feeling like a big, fat failure, I flop face down on my bed. How do I get out of this state and move on? There has to be a way forward. There has to be a way to clear the mess I've made of my life and start again.

The doorbell rings. *Go away, for heaven's sake, just go away.* I stay on my bed, I don't move, not a muscle. I don't want to see anyone, talk to anyone, buy anything, donate money that I don't have. I don't want to open my front door and be a normal person.

But whoever it is won't go away. The doorbell keeps on ringing. I get off my bed, mainly out of annoyance, and stomp downstairs. Why can't people leave me alone?

And then my rage evaporates, because standing at the door is Simon.

I feel like I've been punched in the stomach. It is ten days since our non-wedding, and this is something I've been anticipating, dreading. Seeing his face is too much

143

for me. The blue t-shirt, the jeans, the clenched jaw, lifted a little in that stubborn way of his, his eyes searching mine.

'Simon.' At least I try to say 'Simon', but it comes out as 'Khaaakhakikh'.

'Rilla.'

'I'm so sorry.' The words stumble out at the same time as he says, 'I don't understand what happened.' His hands are in his pockets and he's still staring at me.

I am trying hard to breathe, but my breath seems to be stuck in my chest. I don't know what to say. I've run downstairs in my t-shirt and as I look at Simon, standing at my door, I start to shiver. What, what am I supposed to say now, what am I supposed to do? I can't bear it, I can't bear looking at him. Then I blurt out something that I don't even know I've been thinking.

'Why did you ask me to marry you?'

Simon takes his hands out of his pockets. I can see I've surprised him. I've certainly surprised myself. Now we're both silent, and there are noises in sharp relief – the manic tweeting of sparrows, cars driving past, the sound of a pneumatic drill somewhere, the plinky-plonk of the vihuela from the ground-floor flat – and there are noises within noises. Suddenly I can hear everything, noises from far away, airplanes, voices, trains, dogs, whispers, shudders, the breeze. The beating of my heart. Or it could be Simon's.

'I felt you backing off. Slipping away,' he says. He takes a deep breath, closes his eyes for a second, then opens them and looks up at the sky. I see the stubble on his jaw now, the unusual paleness of his face, the tiredness around his eyes.

I cross my arms over my chest. 'I don't know what you mean.'

'You were taking longer to answer my texts, you were busy when I asked you to come out. It's hard to pinpoint exactly. I could feel you pulling back so I asked you to marry me. I panicked.' He lifts his head. 'I panicked, okay?'

And now Simon has surprised me. Whatever answer I expected, I hadn't expected this.

We had been staring at rock pools in Bexhill that fateful day, counting sea anemones to see who could find the most, me counting the ones that were open, their tentacles shivering and reaching into the sea air, and Simon counting ones that were closed, barely visible, globular like mushrooms. The rocks were slimy and slippery with moss and seaweed, and it was raining and neither one of us had a raincoat with us. We'd spent the morning walking through the town, getting coffee, looking at books in Oxfam. He had been asking for us to have a day out for a couple of weeks, and I had kept saying no, saying I had too many assessments to work on, but then I had given in.

Tiring of sea anemones, I had wiped the rain from my eyes, bent down to collect cracked sea-shells and pebbles of all colours. A red one, a mustard, a sea-salt, a black, all kinds of pebbles that I kept handing to Simon to store for me. I straightened after I picked one up and slipped and fell into Simon's arms. I held my arms out, not even trying to save myself from falling straight into the rocks or the sea water lapping between them. I kept my eyes closed, arms still out, smiling like an idiot.

'Let's get married,' he whispered, his cheek pressed to mine.

For some moments I said nothing, then whispered, 'Okay,' my eyes still closed.

We clasped each other tightly for a second, just for a second, heartbeats colliding against each other, but that was it. There was no other acknowledgement that something momentous had just happened.

'Maybe I was wrong, maybe I imagined it,' Simon says now.

But I have to be truthful, I owe him that. I shake my head. 'No, you didn't imagine it.'

I come out of the doorway, walk over to the swing, and sit down heavily. I poke at a chink in the wood. I chip away at it, dropping flakes on the ground. I don't talk for some time and neither does Simon. He leans against the railing of the porch.

'I can't – I shouldn't have said yes. I – there's a lot going on,' I say finally.

'I see,' Simon says. 'That is possibly the lamest thing I've ever heard anyone say.'

'I have to figure things out, okay?' I make an impatient noise. 'I can't just – I can't do this. Don't you see? Even trying to explain things to you – explain things that I don't even understand – I can't do it. It makes it all somehow – less. I can't explain it, you just have to take my word for it.'

'I could help you with whatever it is.' He's looking at me now but I can't look at him. He's not close enough, but it's like I can smell his skin under the smell of the briar bush that is just outside the porch, under the smell of his aftershave, under the smell of the damp leaves on the ground. And it's too much.

I close my eyes with my fingertips. 'I don't want your help. I don't even know—'

Something wells up in me. Words – *my sister, Rose, I have a sister, I don't know where she is.* They arise and then they get stuck in my throat. I stand up suddenly. Words ring in my ears. My father's. *We can't talk about this any more, you see that, don't you, Rilla? Do you see it? It's important that you understand what could happen. What could have happened. Please, you have to understand.* My father's voice, desperate, begging me to be quiet. And there's the familiar panic, the constriction in my stomach, the knowledge that I damage and break things that shouldn't be touched.

'I have to go inside,' I say now, feeling dizzy. I shake my head to clear it. 'I'm sorry. I know I hurt you, and I'm sorry, but there's nothing more I can say.'

I have to get away. The need to get away is so strong I have to will myself not to run. I don't know what Simon is going to do. I don't know if he is going to leave, or if he will sit there for some time, alone, on the swing, but I can't think about him. He pulls away from the railing. As I walk towards the front door, out of the corner of my eye I see a little mouse, nibbling at something, seeing us, freezing for a second, then scuttling away. I am not usually the one that notices little things like that, it's Simon that notices mice and rabbits in the field and unusual leaves and flowers. I don't point out the mouse to him. I turn and unlock the door into the house and rush inside. I close the door, and stand leaning with my back to it, my eyes tightly closed. I half expect him to knock at any second, but he doesn't. I slowly walk up the stairs to my flat, so numb that I can't even feel my regret, my guilt, or my sorrow. Not much, anyway.

19

Running but Paralysed

For Nietzsche, love is greedy, it seeks, it wants to possess. Instead of being opposite, these feelings of love and greed are intertwined, perhaps even interchangeable. Love isn't about the greater good, but instead about ego, about the biological drive to own. Love goes towards, and fear avoids, retreats, withdraws.

Yet, what if in your poor little human brain, love and fear have become twinned? What if you can't feel one without evoking the other? What will win? The love, the desire for possession, or the fear? Will you go towards, or will you run away?

Rilla's notes

When the GIF met Simon for the first time, they had this to say about him:

He's so informal
He's sho shweet
Very good boy

No pampering-wampering required, no?
No *lafrda* (like, no complications)
He's not proud
He's normal

What they meant was this:

He's so informal (even though he's white)
He's so sweet (even though he's white)
He is such a good boy (even though he's white)
No pampering-wampering required, no? (even though
  he's white?)
No *lafrda* (even though he's white)
He's not proud (even though he's white)
He's normal (even though he's white)

Not that there was *nothing* wrong with him. One thing wrong with him was that he was a children's party entertainer by profession. (Actually that's not strictly true. He works in a charity for the disabled, that's his profession, and the party entertaining is a hobby. But working in a charity doesn't pay all that much and party entertaining does, so you tell me which one is the profession and which the hobby.)

According to GIF laws there are four acceptable professions. You can be a doctor, a lawyer, an engineer, or be in finance. Nothing else counts. The only reason the GIF has good things to say about Simon is because white people are not held to the same standards as people with more melanin in their skin. White people do crazy, unnatural things, like work freelance jobs, or jobs they love but that don't pay a lot. And in any case, since none of the GIF thought that I would ever get married, Simon could be forgiven all things. He had the most desirable quality of all: he wanted to marry me.

Now everyone is sure I've ruined my life.

I am sure I will not see Simon for some time. There's a voice at the back of my mind, reminding me that I may never see him again, but I can't pay attention to that right now, because never is a very long time. I don't have room in my life for never. I have to learn to put one foot in front of the other first, to get through each minute.

But the next day, as I am hanging up laundry on a clothes rack, the doorbell rings. I walk down to open the door, cross at having been interrupted just as I'm thinking of doing some work, and Simon's back again. He's standing on the porch.

'What?' I ask irritably.

'I'm here to bond with my cat,' he says.

I stare open-mouthed at him. 'Bond with your cat?' I say stupidly. It takes me a few moments to realize he means Lord Basingstoke. He can't possibly mean Auntie Promilla's cat? I gawk at him. A master stroke, one I didn't see coming. 'You can't come in here.' I can't think of what else to say. I hold the door tight, in case he's planning to push in.

'I thought you wanted to get rid of the cat. Auntie Promilla told me.' He's not trying to push in, he is just

151

standing there casually, hands in his pockets, looking entirely reasonable.

'She's not your auntie,' I say, my nostrils flaring.

'She asked me to call her Auntie. She's very nice. We have some riveting conversations. Hidden depths, has Auntie Promilla.' His face is expressionless. I don't know if he's annoyed at me, or what. It's a familiar look, the set jaw, the direct eyes that are unreadable at the moment.

'I've grown quite attached to Lord Basingstoke actually. I might think about keeping it. Him.' I am watching him like a hawk.

'Your landlord doesn't allow pets.'

'She's changed her mind about that policy.'

'Regardless, Auntie Promilla said I could visit the cat. What you decide to do is between you and her.'

I grit my teeth. I teeter for several moments, then I push the door open for him with a flourish. 'After you,' I say.

He steps through the door, then abruptly turns around so my nose is practically in his chest. I reel back. 'What is the matter with you?' I yell.

'That wasn't the only reason,' he says, his head slightly inclined.

I frown at him. The man has lost his mind.

'It wasn't just panic that made me ask you to marry me. I knew we were meant to be together. I figured we could work everything else out.'

I glare at him. Bloody man.

'Shit!' Federico calls down the stairs. 'It's done a pee again, in your shoes!'

152

I roar. 'I'm going to kill that freakin' cat!' I push past Simon and storm upstairs. Simon follows me.

I spend the next hour trying to clean out the smell of death coming from my best – and only – pair of trainers. The cat can't see the dining table before banging its head on it, but it recognizes the most expensive thing I own. In the meantime, Federico and Jharna have explained the cat's special needs to Simon, and so now the three of them are trying to calculate arching trajectories. They're sitting on the floor around the rustic coffee table, making charts.

'What if we put food all the way to the food bowl, in an arc?' Simon says. 'He'll eat it along the way, and finally arrive at the cat bowl. Then we can gradually eliminate some of the food, but it will learn to walk in an arc.'

This is tried. Now there is wet cat food all along the floor. The smell of cat pee and wet Whiskas is going to kill me. They are all in a conspiracy to kill me, especially my Auntie Promilla, who I will never trust again.

Federico, Jharna and Simon are now discussing Spotify, and whether or not indie musicians should use that digital platform. They go on to discussing American politics while planting bits of fishy goop on the floor. Jharna usually has a lot of opinions on politics.

She says now, 'What we need to do is to send around an invite to all the world's male politicians for a Masons' meeting. And then send them off on a spaceship that keeps orbiting the earth forever.'

Then she does something, she makes a strange choky sound. She's giggling, and pushing the strands of hair that are coming loose from her bun behind her ear. She is wearing a shaggy oversized cardigan, green and orange, threaded with silver, that is falling off both shoulders and her collar bones are springing out in dainty shards. I stare at her. This is the first time I've heard her give a stupid answer in a serious conversation about politics. Usually she gives you percentages and facts and quotes from news analysis, but not today.

'So where did you grow up, Simon?' she is now asking.

'Right in the centre of town. Flat near Hyde Park. Sorry, Dad is a lawyer. They moved to Woldingham a few years ago.'

'Did you have any pets growing up?' Jharna asks.

'A budgie, a snake that used to shed its skin every time you moved a muscle, a series of clumsy puppies, a lunatic hamster.' He is shading one part of a chart, possibly to point out Lord Basingstoke's blind spots.

'What is it like to be a high-flying lawyer's son?' Jharna has given up on the charts and plans and is twiddling a ribbon from her cardigan.

The cow is fluttering her eyelashes at Simon. That's the end of my short career trying to be supportive of damaged young things. I stab my trainer with the brush I'm cleaning it with and blow viciously at the suds.

'Can't stand it. He assumed I would want to be a lawyer too. I am a big fat disappointment.'

Simon rolls a soft ball towards Lord Basingstoke in an arc. The cat inclines its head. Its whiskers twitch every time the ball comes close. I focus on my cleaning. The man is telling Jharna things, all kinds of things that only I am supposed to know. When he told me those things, he had assured me he never talked about them with other people. Now, mere months, perhaps only weeks later, he is telling Jharna. Jharna is fiddling with her razor-cut hair and looking at him from underneath her long eyelashes.

'How did you get into party entertaining?' Jharna's voice sounded funny and unnatural when she started with this interrogation but now she's warming up. The chit is better at this flirting business than she knows. She moves to the sofa. She sits cross-legged, looking all spiky and young, her skin clearer than a sky on a summer's day, her hair shiny. Does she not have a home to go to? Why is she always at mine?

She and Federico are getting way too close as well. Yesterday, she asked him about his boyfriend, Pip, and he confided it wasn't going so great. Pip says Federico doesn't pay him enough attention, that Federico doesn't really care, that the relationship isn't important to him. Jharna thought for a minute about this and said, 'Well if you want to show you care, you can do little things. If they don't come naturally to you, let's make a list and you can just do them one at a time. Then you won't have to think about it or feel awkward doing it.' And Federico, who can't stand any interference from anyone, especially not me, instantly picked up the notepad in which he makes diagrams for his model houses and started making a list. 'Call him for no reason,' Jharna said. 'Remember something he told you and ask about it. Touch him when he's talking about something important, so that he can see that you're really there with him.' They made a long list. Federico never lets me give him any advice about relationships, or about anything else, but there he was making lists with Jharna who has informed me that she is no good at dating and relationships!

Now she is fingering the choker she is wearing around her long slender neck and inclining her head at my ex-fiancé.

'I learned circus tricks when I was little,' Simon says. 'There was this kids' circus we used to go to in Hyde Park, you know, with a red-and-white stripy tent, hippos in skirts, people juggling fire, that kind of thing. They used to get kids involved. I learned juggling, unicycling, tightrope walking, stilt walking.'

'That is rad!' Jharna exclaims. 'Can I come and watch you at one of your parties? Is that allowed?'

'Sure, come and watch. You can be my assistant. That way you get free cake.'

Jharna is beaming. 'Wow, that's cool. I'm there!'

Okay, I have never seen Simon do his circus tricks. I didn't know it was on the table to go to one of his birthday parties. I mean, who does that? That would be like Simon asking if he could come and sit in one of my classes, or someone asking a surgeon if they can come and take pictures when she removes someone's appendix. You just don't do that. You don't go to someone's workplace and watch them.

Jharna's phone rings. She looks down at it in surprise.

She hasn't looked at it in so long she doesn't know what is making the sound. It takes her a moment to find it, wedged as it is between the cushions on the sofa. She walks out of the room to take the call. Federico is in his room having some kind of long drawn-out argument with Pip again. Ha, I think, the list doesn't seem to be working after all.

'You want to come to this party?' Simon asks casually.

'No thanks.' I stab at my trainer. 'I wouldn't want to spoil the fun.'

'Why did you say yes?' he says suddenly, and I don't have to ask him what he's talking about.

I can't say anything for a few moments. I finally blurt out, 'I – I thought if we could get it over with quickly I would just have to deal with it.'

'That hard, was it?' he says. Then he turns away and starts looking at the charts drawn up for Lord Basingstoke.

I didn't mean it like that, I want to say, but actually there is nothing to say.

The day after we got engaged we had been sitting on the tube, on our way to meeting some friends, holding hands, not saying anything, stupidly grinning. If embers of panic were starting to claw their way up my stomach and into my throat, I was mostly ignoring them, pushing them back down.

I could get through this, I kept telling myself. If I married Simon, Simon who didn't worry about things, who soothed my anxieties, then this other thing, this unexplainable thing in my life, my missing sister Rose, maybe I could move on from that too, I could leave it behind. Maybe the clawing fear – the certainty that everyone I cared about would always leave me – would go away.

A woman with curling hair and a soft expanding body had got on the tube and, seeing her creased face and grey hair, Simon had offered her a seat. She sat next to me and grinned and nodded at us. She asked us our names, and how long we had been together and Simon said, 'We're getting married.' He liked saying that out loud.

She beamed. 'How nice to embrace people of other cultures.' She looked from me to Simon. 'How will you decide what to eat? How will you decide if your children will be Christian or—?' She nodded at me.

When we got off the tube at Victoria, we walked past Buckingham Palace, across the park, and past the Royal Academy. It was a Saturday afternoon, we were going to meet some friends for lunch. There were people every-where, eating doughnuts, taking pictures, kissing, holding hands, mowing their children into a straight line. I was silent for some time. The words the woman had said on the tube, the questions she had asked were still ringing in my mind. There was a tight little black knot in my stomach. I felt a familiar sense of loss, a loss of self, a splintering. The woman had been so sure that the colours of our skin were weighted with meaning. But what could I have said to her, how could I have explained myself? Could I say to her, *I'm British*? But that label didn't seem to capture everything I am. Could I say, *I'm Indian*? The word British lacked something, but the word Indian said too much. The truth is I never knew how to explain myself to people, to face their silent assumptions and questions. To colour the components of my otherness in a way that someone else would understand.

'Do you ever think about things like that?' I had said suddenly.

He was holding my hand. He gave it a little squeeze. 'What the woman said? Never occurred to me.'

I knew this was true. It had never occurred to me either that we were in any way bridging a cultural divide, because as far as I was concerned there *was* no cultural divide. About food, we thought the same: the more of it the better. About religion, we were of the same mind: the less of it, the better the world would be for it. Chocolate: always good. Caviar: couldn't see what the fuss was about, though could eat sushi every day for the rest of our lives. Box-sets: the bedrocks of a solid relationship. LOL versus ha ha ha: *always* ha ha ha. 'Thunder' or 'Radioactive' by Imagine Dragons: 'Thunder', definitely 'Thunder'. Favourite couple of all time: Mike and Eleven.

'My feeling is,' he said slowly, like he was about to say something profound, 'the woman was bonkers.'

I gripped his hand. I realized that it was in being with Simon – Simon who never asked me to explain myself, define who I was, who never made easy assumptions about me – it was in being with him that I could forget the questions everyone else asked. It was in being with him that I could just be me. I could just be.

Now looking at him sitting in my living room plotting trajectories for Lord Basingstoke, I realize all of a sudden that I might never have that in my life again. The sense that Simon gave me, of calm and safety, the feeling he gave me that I was okay.

20

Wining and Dining

In *nautanki* it is practically impossible for in-laws to get along, the relationship doesn't allow for accord. It is possible for the relationship to start with both sides of the family praising one another, giving each other gifts, hugs, and sweets but this initial accord often leads to open warfare. In some cases, there is open warfare from the start. So much so that the boy and girl are told that they will be disinherited if they marry, disinherited, dismembered, killed, something along those lines, something final and irrevocable. There has to be conflict in a good story, and in a *nautanki*, in-laws are pretty good at *being* the conflict.

Manoj Kumar's book, *Nautanki and Other North Indian Curiosities* (working title)

The first time I met Simon's parents was four months after I met him, it was after we had got engaged. I had wanted to keep the GIF out of it, out of our relationship, for as long as possible and Simon hadn't been in any hurry to get the two sides to meet up either. We were happy just to be the two of us for as long as we could get away with it. But we did finally tell our respective families that we were engaged.

At Simon's end, when his father heard the news he'd said, 'Bit soon, don't you think? You want me to run checks on this girl? What is her credit rating? Will you be able to get a mortgage? What does she do for a living?'

I told my parents awkwardly on the phone.

'Engaged!' shrieked my mother. 'Engaged!'

'That's what I said.'

'Well, well, *beta*, how splendid,' Dad said in the background.

'Engaged!'

'Okay, then, Mum, nice talking and all—'

'Rilla, are you sure?' she asked, with a quiver in her voice.

I rolled my eyes.

'Oh, Rilla, I had given up hope! Rilla! This is the best thing—'

Dad took the phone, cutting her short in his excitement. 'Is it Simon?'

'Of course it's Simon. Who else would it be?' I said irritably. They knew about Simon but I hadn't had the courage to bring them together yet. What was I afraid of? I suppose that Mum would tie him to a chair and never let him out of her sight, that Dad would discuss cultural relativity with him, man-to-man – Indians say *champi*, the

British say shampoo, Indians can get very private about their stuff and the British have their stiff upper lip, how we're all the same underneath, blah, blah, blah. And Simon? What would he make of them?

Mum grabbed the phone again. 'Rilla,' she said, a little tremor in her voice, 'darling, don't do – you won't do anything to ruin it, will you?'

'How about I just behave myself until the wedding?'

'Yes, yes, that would be sensible,' my mother said, my sarcasm lost on her.

Though, in retrospect, I suppose I should have promised to behave until *after* the wedding.

But it wasn't just my parents I had to deal with once we were engaged, that would be too much to expect. The GIF took over in a matter of minutes. The news went around London quicker than a YouTube video of toddlers falling off things goes viral. They're all chatting constantly on Facebook, that's probably how the news travelled that quickly, but I was telling my mother on the phone one minute and the next they – all of them – had already organized what they were calling an engagement party. It was record speed, even for them.

'What's an engagement party?' Simon understandably asked when I told him what was happening through my rage and despair and all the other things the GIF makes me feel.

'It's mainly an exchange of rings. Then you eat lots of food and take pictures. Anyway, I'll take care of it. There's no way we're doing one.'

And I did try. I called Uncle Jat, then Auntie Pinky on her mobile, even Auntie PK, but they were already designing invitations, making email lists for e-vites, calling caterers for samples. They sent me a list of dates to check with the Langtons, and they asked me to find out how many of the Langton family were planning to be there.

'Twenty? Fifty?' Uncle Jat asked.

'Two? Three, if you include Simon?'

Uncle Jat laughed like this was a very funny joke.

Nothing I could say would put them off the idea, so the only thing to do was to try and keep it small.

'No more than five people, Mum, please!' I beseeched.

'That's impossible, Rilla, and you know it. Anyway, you're talking as if I have any control over it.'

I got Dad involved and this was probably why we didn't have a hundred people attending. It was finally decided that the party would include my parents, Uncle Jat, Auntie Pinky, Auntie Dharma, Auntie Promilla, Auntie PK, and Uncle Promod and Auntie Menaka. There were also two cousins and their toddlers. Really, quite a respectable size. On the other side, there was Simon and his parents.

'I'm so sorry about this,' I said to Simon a few times a day as the party drew nearer.

'Don't be crazy. It sounds great!' He was actually enthusiastic. Mind you, this was before he had met everyone.

Though the event had started as Uncle Jat's idea, it ended up being held at the Langtons' home just outside London, in Woldingham. I have no idea how this happened. Uncle Jat was saying, *Great, that is indeed wonderful*, but he found it insulting that the whole thing wasn't taking place at his and Auntie Pinky's, which, in his mind, is the rightful venue for events of any importance. If he had it his way, the Queen's garden party would be at their house in Hampstead. My panic grew as the day drew nearer. I kept telling myself: how bad can it be? It can't be that bad. How bad can it be? It can't possibly, *possibly* be as bad as I'm imagining.

The evening of the party swung around all too quickly, and we all landed at the Langtons' place. They lived in a bungalow with charming grounds around it, logs piled up in picturesque woodsheds, smoke coming out of the chimney. There was a light sprinkling of snow on the grass. Auntie Pinky looked shocked when she saw me. 'What is the matter with you?' she said, looking me up and down. She unbuttoned my coat and stared at me. 'A strapless black dress for an engagement party? Very sexy, I'm sure, but not a bit of bling! That won't work.' She leaned into their BMW and pulled out a gold embroidered long skirt and blouse from the car, along with what looked like my weight in gold jewellery, a *chunni* to cover my head, earrings that would hang down to my navel, sparkly pink stilettos and a little clutch bag that was supposed to hold, what exactly? A Lego-person's head?

'Are you mad?' I hissed. I quickly buttoned my coat back up – it was clear we weren't quite ready to go in. 'Have you looked at this stuff? Who in their right mind would think I would wear this?'

'You can't get engaged in that!' Auntie Pinky swiped

her hand up and down in the air. 'They will think we are paupers. They will be all dressed up in their Sunday best.' Auntie Pinky grew up in a flat above a shop in Leicester. She is in awe of large country houses and the people she imagines live in them. 'Come now, *beta*. Leave this kind of thing to the grown-ups.'

Auntie Pinky was wearing a heavy magenta sari, arranged impeccably around her soft, plump frame and she'd been to the parlour to have her hair back-combed in the 1960s style and made into an enormous bun at the back.

Auntie Menaka and her husband Uncle Promod pulled up as we were arguing. Don't ask how they're related to my parents. They probably aren't, is the answer. Uncle Promod was wearing a suit, and a tie that was trying to strangle him. Auntie Menaka was wearing a sparkling blue long dress with gold *pyjama*, her face and arms had been waxed to within an inch of her life and her hair had a gravity-defying wave in it.

'Oh, look at you!' she said, placing her hands on my shoulders. She gave the air next to my cheeks kisses. 'Leave her, *na*, Pinky. These kids will do things their own way. Let's not be old fuddy-duddies.' I could see she was just happy that I wasn't going to outshine her.

'A *chunni* for her head at least, a couple of necklaces, earrings, that's all I ask.' Auntie Pinky was nearly in tears.

'She looks nice, in any case,' Auntie Menaka said.

'She has her days,' my mother responded. 'Just do it, *na*, Rilla! Get it over with!' She was a jangle of nerves. Oh dear. This was not a promising start.

Uncle Jat and Uncle Promod were discussing the prices of various shares. 'Actually Jat, it's good I have a chance to talk to you. I have a little scheme I want to run by you,' Uncle Promod was saying. Uncle Promod markets himself as a shares consultant. He likes to come up with schemes for people to invest in.

'No way,' Uncle Jat said, used to Uncle Promod's ways. 'I'm not even getting into this, Promod.'

My dad had been parking the car, and now he ran up, rubbing his hands. 'Great, great, let's go.'

Just as we rang the doorbell and the door opened, Auntie Pinky pushed a sparkly *chunni* around my neck.

'Stop it!' I hissed.

'Wow, blinding,' said Simon giving me a kiss. 'You should have reminded me to put my sunglasses on.' He grinned.

'Fuck you,' I said.

Those were the first words Simon's parents – John and Marie Langton – heard me utter. Luckily, they had no time to dwell on it because my entire family – the rest of them had arrived by this point – pushed into the house. They were like a herd of excited water buffalo, there was a lot of stamping and shrieking and exclaiming. My cousin Sulekha and her husband Benji were there, with their three toddler boys. They're not all toddlers, they range in age from three to seven, but the family still calls them the Toddlers. They ran into the house and instantly started running in circles.

'Auntie Rilla, what are you wearing?'

'Auntie Rilla-Tarantula, why doesn't your dress have any sleeves?'

'Auntie Rilla, aren't you cold?'

'Auntie Rilla, where is the toilet?'

'It's lovely to finally meet you, dear,' Marie said to me, staring at the boys who were running all over her sparkling real-wood floor. She was wearing a beige skirt, nude tights, a lavender cashmere cardigan, a string of pearls, her blonde hair cut neatly into a bob and styled. It was difficult to see her amidst the dazzling colours and gold jewellery that my lot were wearing. She kissed me on both cheeks. 'You should have told us you were bringing children,' she said looking bemused, like someone might ask for a warning when you were bringing your pet rattlesnake to a party. 'What do they eat?' She looked genuinely scared. In my mind, though, that was the right reaction to the Toddlers.

'Rilla,' John said, shaking my hand. 'How good to meet you, at last.'

'Jolly good to meet you,' Dad said, shaking John's hand. 'A neat little estate you have here, what?' He sounded like Mr Bean.

'Don't worry about the children,' Mum said. 'They're really no trouble at all.'

'Get off the bloody sofas!' I hissed. I grabbed a scruffy curly head as it ran past me.

'No bloody trouble! No bloody trouble!' a Toddler shouted.

People stood around awkwardly for a few seconds.

'Please, please do make yourselves comfortable,' Marie said.

Drinks went around. Auntie Menaka immediately got

her hands on the largest G&T money could buy. Sulekha and Benji picked up drinks off the tray, sat themselves down in the corner of the room and closed their eyes. I swear Benji was snoring within seconds. In their defence, they looked like they hadn't slept for seven years.

'So gorgeous, exquisite,' Auntie Menaka said to Marie, fingering Marie's necklace, running fingers down Marie's throat. It made Marie go red in the face. 'I know real pearls when I see them.'

'Oh,' Marie said, 'yes, they are, how clever of you. My one extravagance. And I did buy them on a five-per-cent-off sale. Who can afford real pearls these days? Percy, my jeweller, always emails me when there is a sale on.'

Mum had brought samosas with her. 'I hope you don't mind,' she said apologetically to Marie, handing her a hot-case. 'We don't have to eat them if they are not suitable.'

'Oh, how wonderful!' Marie instantly broke off a corner to taste it. It was a bird-sized bite but I thought it was nice of her. 'Oh, delicious. You must tell me the recipe.'

'A family secret,' Mum said. 'But people say they're almost as good as Ambala's,' she said modestly.

'Oh, we're practically family now,' Marie said. 'You'll give me the recipe, won't you, Rilla?' She smiled at me.

'I don't know the second thing about cooking,' I said. 'Or the first.'

'Oh, you're so modest. All Indian girls know how to cook,' Marie said, waving her hand.

There was a sound of shrill laughter from the other end

of the room. It was Auntie Menaka. She was flinging her head back and laughing at something John was saying. 'That is SO funny,' she said. 'Such a hoot. You're SO funny.'

'You're SO funny!' shouted one of the Toddlers.

'You are LITERALLY so funny!' said another one.

'Mind the vase!' I screamed, grabbing the vase that was in one of the Toddlers' hands and about to be flung across the room.

Marie quickly took it from me and placed it safely out of reach. 'It's Belgian,' she said apologetically. 'A tad on the expensive side.'

'Have a samosa,' Mum said quickly, passing around the plate.

'I won't have one,' Auntie Dharma said. 'It's my yoga fast. I can only eat things that don't contain onions, and only made with gram flour.' She broke off a corner of a samosa and nibbled at it. 'Deep-fried foods play havoc with my *vata*.'

'Oh,' Marie said. 'I do wish I had known that. I would have done something for you.' She looked dismayed.

'Really, don't worry,' Mum said.

Auntie Dharma was digging into her copious handbag. 'I bring food with me, in any case.' She brought out a large bundle of oily paper napkins and started handing around gram-flour pancakes.

'How lovely,' Marie said, lifting one and letting it dangle from her fingers.

'What a beautiful rug!' Mum said, looking like she was fraying at the edges.

On the floor was a plush rug. Crimson, with a white swirly pattern and large black spiky flowers. The rest of the long living room was decorated in shades of ivory, with mushroom-coloured sofas and curtains, so the rug was quite dramatic in comparison.

'Oh, it's my one extravagance,' Marie said. 'Bashish, this lovely Persian dealer, brings them over from the East. He tells such wonderful stories of the Orient. I get a special discount.'

John was still talking to Auntie Menaka, who kept laughing and going, 'Oh, how funny!'

I could see Marie looking over at them. I don't know what it is about Auntie Menaka. She's a bit of a family joke, but at the same time men can't seem to resist her. I looked over to see John wiping his upper lip with his hanky. He was a little red in the face.

'You do yoga?' Marie asked Auntie Dharma nervously. She kept glancing over at her husband.

'Well, you can't actually *do* yoga. Yoga is a way of life.'

'Ah, ha ha ha,' Auntie Menaka went at the other end of the room. 'Stop!'

'Come on, *beta*,' Auntie Pinky hissed at me, 'find something to do. Pass around the shrimp tempura. This will be your house soon.' She tried to lasso me with a large necklace.

'Oh, for god's sake.' I scowled. 'Keep your hands off me.'

Then there was one of those silences. And in it we all heard the story that Auntie Menaka loves to tell. The story is about her younger brother Archie who at the age of nine found packets of balloons while on a school trip. He and his friends filled these up with water and walked around with them all day.

'And they turned out to be condoms, would you believe it!' was the line we heard in the silence.

John was spluttering on his drink. Simon was making faces at me. Marie said, 'Excuse me,' and walked over to John and whispered something in his ear.

I took a deep breath. It would be over soon. It would be over very soon. I grabbed a passing Toddler by the hair, 'Oye, stop it. Put down that knife, do you hear?'

'Mummy, Mummy, Auntie Rilla grabbed me by the hair. Mummy, Mummy, Auntie Rilla is trying to kill me!'

The Toddler was yanked away by Auntie PK. 'Silly spoilt children,' she said indulgently. 'Come over here, I'll tell you a story. Stop trying to wake your parents up.'

'Drink this,' Simon whispered, walking over to me and handing me a neat scotch, 'bottoms-up.'

I downed the scotch in one go. 'More, please. More, okay? In fact, for the rest of the evening, just keep filling my glass up every time you walk by me.'

'Sorry, I know they're embarrassing.'

I looked at him incredulously. 'Your parents? Are you crazy?'

He slipped an arm around me and gave my ear a peck. 'It'll be okay. Just ignore everyone.'

'Footsteps aren't made on the sands of time,' I heard Uncle Jat say. 'Let's get this engagement party on the road! Where are the rings?'

The engagement ceremony was over quickly. But then there were lots of excruciating pictures taken. Mum kept on nudging me, 'Smile, smile, Rilla, for god's sake. You're scowling. How do you think that will look? Smile!'

Auntie Pinky kept on trying to put more sparkly things on me. 'At least for the pictures, *beta*, just for the pictures, at least.'

'Stop it!' I kept hissing.

There was a box of *laddu* passed around. There had to be pictures taken of Dad putting a *laddu* in Marie's mouth, Mum in John's mouth, Marie in Mum's mouth. Anyway, you get the picture. It took forever. And everyone – in my family at least – seemed to find it extremely funny. Simon was smiling, but even he was starting to wilt under the pressure of the photographs. He was wearing a cream shirt with a light blue paisley pattern on it, a pair of tailored trousers. He never put anything in his hair, so after thirty or so pictures, and a lot of hugging and patting from the GIF, his hair was starting to stick up all around his head.

I felt a pang of sympathy and walked up to him. 'I like the hedgehog look,' I whispered. He was eating one of my mother's samosas. 'You don't have to eat all the samosas, though,' I said, patting his stomach, taking the one he was eating out of his hands and taking a large bite. 'And if you smile any more at my relatives, the wind will change and your face will be stuck forever.'

I caught my mother's eye. She was frowning and shaking her head at me. *What*, I mouthed irritably.

Simon patted my bottom. 'I'm sure there are things you

can do to unstick my mouth,' he whispered, as he walked off to rescue the Toddlers from Marie.

Someone put on some Indian music, and Auntie Menaka started dancing to it. She dragged John over to her and they started this funny, 'no touching' dancing. The Toddlers instantly ran over to the centre of the room and started imitating the adults, a hand on the hip, one in the air, closing their eyes. '*Hai, hai*, so cute!' one of them kept saying, in an imitation of Auntie PK, in the thickest Punjabi accent he could cook up.

'Oh supersonic cute, *ji*, supernova spectacular Harry Potter cute!' said another.

'Oye, oye, oye,' they shouted.

Someone was discussing Brexit in the corner. I looked over. It was my father and Marie.

'We like immigrants. What's wrong with immigrants?' she was saying. She kept on gesturing around the room at the entire immigrant population of London that seemed to be in her house that night.

Auntie Menaka was now teaching John a dance move. 'Screw in the lightbulb, go on, like that, like that!'

'What the fuck,' I muttered, looking at them.

'What the *fuck* are you talking about, what the *fuck*!' said one of the Toddlers.

Of course everyone heard them. Marie looked like she was going to have a heart attack. Dad, making a soothing gesture at me, walked over to John, and teased him away from Auntie Menaka.

'Have you heard this story?' I heard him say to John.

'It is often used in Indian street theatre. It is about Lord Harishchandra who was the King of Ayodhya.' John was listening. Maybe it would be okay for a while. I walked over to the buffet table. I steadied myself and looked at the wall clock. How soon was it okay to leave?

John walked up to me when Dad's story was over. He looked around the table, picking a mushroom puff.

'Families,' he said. 'Can't live with or without them. I'm ravenous. Are you?'

'Oh, I can easily live without mine.' I picked up an oyster and put it in my mouth before I realized what it was. Who on earth would serve oysters at an engagement party? I bet it was Marie, who got them at a discount. I bit my lip at the mean thought. I put a hand on my mouth. I hate oysters. But with John watching me, I didn't feel like I could spit it out. It slid down my throat in a slimy swoosh.

'So, what is it that you do, Rilla?' John said, loading his plate. John ignored the canapés and went straight for the dessert that Auntie Pinky had brought with her.

'I am doing a master's in philosophy.' I was starting to feel queasy. I imagined the oyster sitting in a slimy puddle in my belly. I hiccoughed. I eyed the *barfi* and *laddu*, all made with sweet thickened milk, and wondered if it would make me feel better or worse if I ate some. I hiccoughed again. Worse, definitely worse.

'And what do you hope to do with that?' John asked.

'I'm reading philosophy so that I can be qualified to read more philosophy.' That was my standard joke, but John wasn't impressed.

.'And does that pay?'

'Er, sorry, I haven't really given it much thought.'

'Simon seems to be inclined the same way. This is the trouble when you young people have everything you want growing up. You grow up without a tether. Simon with his party tricks and charities. I'd like him to grow up and get a real job.'

'Simon likes what he does,' I said with some heat. I burped oyster.

Uncle Promod walked up to us and spoke to John. 'You know, I would love to tell you about this scheme I have in mind.'

I groaned. I dug my fingers into my tummy.

Marie came up to me. 'Do let me refill your glass,' she said. 'So Rilla, I never asked Simon, do you have any siblings?'

The question came at me like a shot with no preparation, no lead up at all. I had no way to defend myself. I opened my mouth but no words came out and I gaped like a fish.

'No, no, Rilla's an only lonely,' Mum said, walking up to us.

I threw up all over Marie's Persian rug.

Marie shrieked before she could stop herself. John looked like he was going to have apoplexy, that's how hard he was trying not to say something.

Simon walked over quickly. 'Come on, let's get you cleaned up.' He started steering me towards the door.

I looked down at myself. There were vomited-up bits of food on my dress. Auntie Pinky ran up and covered me

in a red embroidered stole. 'Put this on,' she said triumphantly.

'Will you get away from me!' I shouted, and ran out of
the room without turning to see the shocked faces that I
left behind me.

21

Oh, But I Bet You Didn't Know That

Simon took me to a guest bedroom at the back of the bungalow. By this time I was crying hopelessly. 'I can't go back there, please don't make me!'

He helped me out of my dress. I gasped and cried to him to not let the vomit touch my face when he was pulling it off over my head. Once I was in my bra and knickers, he took a step closer and held me, his hands warm on my back. I placed my forehead on his shoulder. I thought he was going to say something soothing, that would be like Simon, but then I realized he was laughing into my hair. I pushed him away. He was laughing so hard there were tears in his eyes.

'You should have seen the look on Dad's face when you threw up. I've been trying to get him to look like that for years, and you achieve it in one night.'

I stared at him. 'Are you mad?'

'I wish I'd taken a picture of it!'

'What is it with you and your dad?' This was an insane reaction to what had just happened. Surely rage – *my* most common reaction to the GIF – would be more appropriate! Certainly not laughter.

Simon lived in a studio flat near Waterloo but he had spent the previous night at his parents' to help out for the party. He had some clothes in a backpack and he now rummaged in it and pulled out a shirt for me.

'We're just too different. We had a rough time when I was a teenager, couldn't see eye to eye on anything. He likes schedules and lists and organization and living your life the right way. Can't stand it if you're late for things, or if you forget to pay your bills, or you don't have a job that you spend twelve-hour days in. Things need to be regimented, there need to be rules and people need to live by them. I barely saw him when I was growing up. He was away a lot on work, and when he wasn't away he worked long hours.'

'That sounds tough,' I muttered.

He shrugged. 'I don't know. I guess it was. It was hard on my mum.' He made a face. 'Shopping and drinking aren't great substitutes for a husband.'

I grimaced. He made it sound like it was okay, but I could hear something else in his voice, a tightness that wasn't often there.

'You were there,' I tried to say. 'For her.'

He shook his head quickly. 'Not really. Not enough. I was too annoyed with my dad to stick around much. Look, never mind all that, try this shirt, see if it works.'

179

I slipped into his shirt, feeling a sick empty fluttering in my tummy.

He pulled me towards him, his hand slipping in through the buttons of his shirt. 'I think you should only wear my shirts from now on.' He kissed me, first on the nose, then on my mouth.

I pulled away. I searched his face. 'There's so much we don't know about each other.'

'Don't be silly.' He pulled me to him again.

'Simon,' I said, feeling a little faint, 'don't you see? There are still so many missing pieces. What if – what if things don't work out?' I looked into his eyes a little desperately.

'That's stupid. Of course it'll work out. Forget about it, let's get out of here.'

He started packing his things, putting shirts and socks and a shaver back into his backpack.

But I didn't move. 'Simon, can't you listen to me for once?' I begged. 'You have this image of me, all in your head. It's like you don't want to see the real me.'

He turned towards me. His face was set. 'I don't know why we have to talk about this.' He turned away and kept on packing up. 'Anyway, I've seen the real you from the moment I saw you. Have I ever asked you to explain yourself to me?'

He never had. And I desperately wanted to believe what he was saying, all of it. But I couldn't let myself, not quite.

'What if – what if we just depend on each other so much because we're not close to our families? What if that's all there is to it?' Then another thought struck me. 'What if you like me because I shake your dad up?'

Simon's jaw was tight. He didn't turn around. Now he was making the bed. 'It's a hell of a lot more than that, and you know it.'

'You don't actually know a lot about me, Simon.'

'I know everything I need to know about you. Neither one of us has ever been in a serious relationship before. Neither one of us has ever met anyone we wanted to be with for the rest of our lives. That's not nothing.'

'Simon—'

He made an impatient sound. He dropped the duvet he was folding and turned to look at me, his eyes remote. 'There's nothing to talk about.'

I ground my teeth. 'You want life to be a children's party.'

'And what do you want it to be, Rilla? All a bunch of theory, so that nothing real ever happens and no one ever gets hurt? Is that it?'

Simon threw the backpack on the floor. We didn't say anything for some minutes. I stood there in his shirt, shaking a little.

'Let's just get out of here,' he said.

'Simon—'

'Let's get out of here, okay?'

'We need to talk about this!'

'First, let's get out of here.'

I took a shuddering breath. 'Can we do that?'

'Let me pop down and get our coats. We'll get out the

back way. I'll tell Dad.' Then he walked up to me and quickly kissed my forehead. 'You have to trust me. It'll be okay. All of it. Nothing's going to go wrong.'

He disappeared. I waited for ages, lying on the bed in the spare room. I stared up at the ceiling. It was painted with some oblong black lines and I felt like I was sinking into them, then pulling out, sinking in, then pulling out. I listened to Leftfield on my phone. I felt an urgency for Simon to understand what I was trying to say. I wanted him to see me, the real me, the one that hid all the time, the one whose past he knew nothing of. The urgency was spiralling into a wild panic. What was keeping Simon? I pulled the earphones out of my ears and wandered out of the bedroom. Before I got to the living room, I heard Simon and John talking behind a half-closed door. 'The man was actually asking me for money. For some half-baked scheme to do with toilet seats. Can you believe that?' I heard John say.

'Sure, crazy. Okay if we go now though? You can take it from here, can't you?'

'Are you sure about this girl?' John said. 'She's pretty and all. But that's not the only thing that's important. And she swears a lot, you know how your mum feels about people swearing. It makes her feel ill. And don't get me started with those boys! Have they not been taught any manners? I've never seen children like that. And her auntie is crazy, the dancing one who has an inch of make-up all around her face. And what's wrong with the other uncle who's always talking like the oracle of Delphi?'

'Lighten up, Dad,' I heard Simon say. His voice was clipped. I swallowed painfully. This was my fault.

'I'm not saying there's anything specifically wrong with the girl. But you marry into the family, you know that. And they seem like a handful, to say the least. Even if she is nice and normal, she won't be able to protect you from the rest of them.'

I screwed up my eyes. He was judging my entire family on the basis of one night! I get it, they could be maddening, but who was he to judge them! I walked into the room.

'I don't know about nice and normal. I did get arrested when I was fourteen. I'm surprised they let it drop really, considering all the previous cautions I had for drinking and smoking and missing school and helping this girl run away with our music teacher. But our police, they're too lenient. Strange, don't you think?'

22

Model Villages

One evening, Jharna and I are moving things around in Federico's model village. He is out, playing a gig with his vegetable orchestra. We have dragged his village out from under the table – he'd moved it there to keep it away from Lord Basingstoke. We swap some of the walls around, so that the houses are all rickety, none of the walls fitting together any more. The houses are barely standing up once we're done with it. Jharna giggles. I am still trying to stand a wall up so that Federico won't immediately know that something is wrong, but it keeps falling over.

'Stop giggling!' I hiss. 'You're going to make it collapse. Don't breathe! Here, give me!'

I hold a hand out for Jharna's bubblegum. I stand the wall up using the sticky pink wad. Jharna stands up in an exaggerated slow motion so that nothing can move, not a whisper can make my bubblegummed wall collapse. But then she snorts and spit comes flying out of her mouth all over the model village. The chit is giggling so hard, she is bent double. She picks up Federico's precious glue from his kit, takes it to the toilet, empties it out, then fills the bottle with shampoo. She comes back, giggling. I place the bottle carefully back with Federico's tools. I glance at Jharna for a second. This is new for us, teasing Federico, messing with his head. I mean, I get the general principle, Federico is fun to mess with, he gets so serious and it takes him a while to figure out what's going on, but I can't help thinking there's something more going on in what we're doing. Jharna, the only child, and me – what am I? A soul craving a lost sister? But Jharna? I desperately need a sister, but a Rose-substitute? No, my head says, no, I can't do that! That's not what I need! I sit down hard on the sofa.

'I'm starving!' Jharna says.

A friend, maybe a friend is what I need, what I can handle. I order Chinese food.

The noodles and dumplings arrive thirty minutes later, the delivery man loaded with sachets of extra-chilli sauce and an impossibly large grin. I sit down, cradling my noodles close to my chest, and pop a chunk of garlic chicken in my mouth with my chopsticks. I flick through television channels.

'*Gogglebox*?' I untangle a spring onion from my noodles and place it gingerly at the edge of my plate. '*Frasier*?'

Jharna is staring at me.

'What?' I say defensively. 'It's a funny sitcom. Very slapstick. People who've never watched it don't really get it.'

She screws up her mouth, inclines her head like a sparrow. 'Okay, here's the thing, Sis. I *know* you told me not to, okay?'

I shake my head. 'What?' I say, through a mouthful of noodles.

She comes and sits down on the sofa next to me, picks up her box of dumplings. 'I kind of had a poke around to see what I could find on Rose.'

I slowly put down the remote control. I can't say anything for a few moments. 'I did tell you not to,' I say slowly, finally. 'I said not to.'

'Look, just hear me out. I can't find a heck of a lot. There are really only a few little things from when you were kids and doing that show. I can only think that Kumar might not be her last name any more, otherwise I bet I would be able to find something, any little detail about her as an adult. See, even *you* come up in searches and you don't do anything special.'

I'm too stunned by what she is saying to be offended by this. She's speaking quickly, in case I stop her.

'You have your profile page as a teaching assistant at uni, and there are a couple of other little things. So she has probably changed her name, which would make sense if she was adopted by someone, like you'd wondered about.' I can see she's decided to play along with this story – for now. 'We need her last name. If we had that we could look up medical records, old school records, credit scores, that kind of thing.'

'There is no we,' I snap. I turn to her and look at her

desperately. How can I make her understand? I blow out a breath that I don't know I'm holding. 'Jharna, I can't do this. Please, you have to listen to me.'

She places her box of dumplings on the floor next to the sofa. 'I won't if you really don't want me to. All I'm saying is, I can do this better if we had a last name. Your parents would know it, wouldn't they?'

Yes, perhaps they would know, or at least they *should*. But I can't ask them, I can't talk to them about this. Yet, this thing that Jharna says, I can't completely ignore it either.

'Do you want me to hack into your mum's email address?' Jharna says.

I stare at the silent television screen on which a banana in a top hat is holding a cane and singing a song. I can't say it, I can't say anything. I am quiet for many minutes.

'Please don't do anything, okay?' I say finally.

She sits back on her sofa. She picks her dumplings up again. She doesn't eat them. She just keeps dipping one in the soy sauce. She glances sideways at me, but then looks away.

'Okay, so let's give *Frasier* a try.'

I stare at the television screen. It takes me a long time before I can say anything.

'So,' I say finally, 'did you go to that party in the end?'

'Oh, Simon's thing? That's not for a few days. But we're rehearsing for it so I know what to do. It's really fun. You don't mind, do you?'

I look at her out of the corners of my eyes. The woman

is invading my life. The GIF has set her on me, I know it. She's prying and prying. And the question is: what will she find if she keeps digging?

In this silence that my parents and I share around Rose there is a co-dependency, a habit that can't be broken. If we talk about it now, it's as if all the years that we have stuffed it, stifled it, eaten it, suppressed and repressed it will have been a waste.

Rose with a different last name. I want Jharna to go away, to stop prying, yet I can't stop thinking about it. Is this the answer? Is this why I can't find anything about her other than our *nautanki* when I look online? Because she is no longer Rose Kumar? The thought is frightening and shocking, but it also makes sense. Would my parents know if she had changed her last name? I just don't know.

When Tyra calls the next morning, a Saturday, to see if I want to go out later, I say, 'I will. But not yet.'

'Come on, Rilla, enough moping around, time to get back on the horse!'

'You should get that put on a t-shirt.'

'Seriously, think about it. It'll take your mind off the wedding.'

I stare into space. I don't want to take my mind off things. I want to sit in my room and imagine what it would be like to look through my mum's email, to find something, anything, a nugget of truth.

'I'll talk to you later, okay?' I say to Tyra, and then stay sitting on my bed, unable to move.

What if what I'm searching for is there in Mum's inbox, waiting for me? What if all I have to do is look? What if that's all I've ever had to do? I think of all the years I lived with my parents, all the years after Rose, and before I left for university. What if – in all that time – all I had to do was turn on Mum's laptop?

I lie down on the bed. Mum, Rose, me. Images of the three of us start flicking through my head. Mum, with two girls, just two years apart in age, but quite different in temperament, different in the way they approach the world. I fight it for a few seconds, the flood of memories, but then I close my eyes, and I let the images come.

When I was six and Rose eight, Mum decided that we would have a weekly date after school, just the three of us. I remember going to three things: Camden Market, Kensington Gardens and, once, an art gallery in Walthamstow. Mum would still be a bit frazzled on these trips, worrying about the commute, getting back, getting dinner on, making sure our uniforms were ready for the morning, but there were moments now and again when she would relax.

At Camden Market, one time, it was late afternoon and the food vendors were going for the hard sell to make sure they shifted as much as they could. 'One pound noodles, one pound, one pound!' one vendor was calling. 'Best hotdog money can buy! The top dawg!' another one yelled. 'Eat this!' said one sternly, thrusting a wrap of some kind in Mum's face. At first, typically, Mum was worrying about what food to get for us, what we should eat, what would be healthy and clean and hygienic. But I suddenly said, 'Eat this! Eat this now, stupid girl!' sternly in Rose's face, in imitation of a vendor.

Suddenly all three of us were bent double, laughing hysterically. We laughed so much and for so long that we had to sit down on a bench until we were able to get our breath back.

It was on days like that that I felt like I could *see* Mum. Like the layers of defence that were so much a part of her personality would peel back for a moment, and I would be allowed in. She would for some moments forget that she had to sort me out, correct me, make me a better version of myself, make sure I didn't ruin things just by virtue of being me.

But those moments were few and far between. Soon after we started going out on this 'date', I joined a drama club in school. Mostly the society was for older kids, but the teacher had specially asked my parents if I could join in. *She has a way with words*, my teacher had said. The drama club timetable clashed with our Thursday afternoon trips, so Mum and Rose kept on going by themselves, heading out after school and not coming back until dinner time. I knew Rose felt guilty about this and her time spent alone with Mum. She asked her to change the day but my mum just stuck with Thursdays. Rose would try to make it sound like the trips weren't that good, not nearly as fun without me. She would always bring me back things to eat or little toys – but when she gave me a sweet I would often 'forget' to eat it, and if there was a toy I would thrust it into the darkest depths of the toy cupboard.

When Rose was nine, and my parents told me that she had been invited on a holiday to the Lake District, I thought it was more of the same – Rose getting to do fun things and me not getting to do them. She was going away for a week with a friend, that's what they told me, my parents.

Where is she, Mummy, where is she, please you have to tell me.

When did I start asking that question? How many times did I ask?

I remember once after the crying and screaming, standing in the middle of the kitchen, throwing every single plate and cup my parents owned onto the floor, making sure each one was breakable first.

Where is Rose, where is she, you have to tell me!

And my mother crying, my father turning to comfort her.

But I can't think about that right now. Because when I think back to that time in my childhood my blood pounds in my head. When I think about Rose, about her absence, there is a blackness, there is a slow kind of death.

23

A Sticky Kind of Glue

In *nautanki*, parental love is extreme. Grown men cry at their mothers' feet. Daughters are obedient and beautiful. And parents sacrifice themselves for their children. There is only one thing that can get in the way of the parent-child bond. And that is romance. The child's first love. In *nautanki*, romance shakes the Great Wall of China that is the love between parent and child. It is the parents' job to remind the child of the dangers of the great love story. It is for them to explain that love can lead to disaster.

Manoj Kumar's book, *Nautanki and Other North Indian Curiosities* (working title)

Ever since Jharna spoke to me about Mum's email, it's like there is an incessant ticking in my brain. Every morning when I wake up and every night before I go to bed, I find myself picturing in great detail a trip to my parents' place. I imagine finding an excuse to turn my mum's laptop on.

I imagine finding her inbox open and I picture scrolling through it, looking for some clue. Yet, the thought of going there, now, after my failed wedding, with the spectre of Simon's name haunting our every word and every look, I don't know if I could bear it.

The last time I went to their house in Belsize Park was a couple of months ago, soon after Simon and I got engaged. I had imagined that the afternoon would be horribly uncomfortable, no one saying much, my parents going over the top trying to make Simon feel welcome. But the afternoon turned out to be – well, surprising. Just for that afternoon, we seemed to have a good time, the four of us, we seemed able to relax and laugh. It was so unexpected, this hint of a possibility that my parents and I could spend an easy afternoon together with Simon there. It seemed so significant at the time.

My parents had both dressed with care for our lunch, Dad wearing a tie, Mum in a sparkling turquoise sari with fat red roses all the way down the *pallu* and along the border. They'd gone to the trouble of making a lavish Indian meal – chicken curry, three kinds of vegetables, chickpeas, biryani, naan. And the afternoon *had* started stiff and awkward, my mother whispering to me to fix my hair, to clean my trainers, to wear sun-screen so I wouldn't go quite so brown, or what would Simon think. But Simon was soon raving about the food, the prints on the wall, the garden, and it helped all of us relax. We ate lots, and then we sat around the dining table, sipping cup after cup of tea. I was still watching my parents like a hawk but, despite myself, despite our history, a tiny corner of my heart had opened a hopeful eye.

'So, Simon,' Dad said, 'when did you know that Rilla was the one?'

I rolled my eyes. 'Dad, let's not do that.'

'As soon as I saw her.' Simon grinned at me. He had taken the trouble to wear a shirt that day, a fitted dark green shirt with dots all over it, and trousers rather than his standard jeans. Even his hair was more or less behaving itself.

I shook my head. 'No way.'

'I did. You were standing there, back to the wall in your orange skirt and black top, the one you wear to formal things, ignoring everyone, looking through your phone, pretending you hadn't seen me.'

I stared at him. 'How can you possibly remember what I wore? That is bullshit, a total lie.' I gave his ear a tug. Mum frowned at me and shook her head slightly but I pretended I hadn't noticed. I wasn't actually sure which part of me or my behaviour she was taking an objection to anyway.

Dad beamed. 'Exactly, exactly like that when I met your mother.'

I looked incredulously at Simon and my dad. 'How can you possibly know as soon as you see someone? That's just fiction.'

Dad and Simon were nodding at each other and Simon shrugged, 'You just know.'

'Yes, yes,' Dad said enthusiastically.

My mother didn't say anything. 'I guess you can't imagine why anyone would think that about me,' I said to her, I couldn't help it. My parents were silent. Simon briefly put a hand on my back, then went back to picking on pomegranate seeds that were still lingering in a bowl. I felt stupid. I stood up, walked to the kitchen to get more tea.

'How did you two meet?' I heard Simon ask my parents.

'She asked me to buy her a packet of fags when I was waiting for the Number 10 bus to Hammersmith,' Dad said.

'Romantic.' I walked back to the dining table. I couldn't help a glance at the clock.

'She called me Mister. I thought to myself, here's the woman I'm going to marry. She was wearing red cords and this folky kind of blouse and big earrings. And she had a British accent, not like my kind of clipped correct English, learned from teachers who had correct grammar but whose pronunciation was hopelessly phonetic. *Eat all-monds on a Ved-nes-day, Manoj*, they used to say, *To save your rupees, save your penis.*' Dad laughed. Mum smiled. Simon was grinning. I couldn't help staring at them. I had pictured an uncomfortable lunch and a quick getaway and this camaraderie was – well – strange.

'She had this haircut – what do they call it?' Dad continued.

'A pixie cut.' Mum smiled into her *chai*.

'I put on my black sunglasses, I lifted the collar on my

leather jacket and said, "Hey you, is it me you're looking for?"'

I groaned. 'You *did* not.'

Simon was shaking his head, a warm hand on my back.

'Did too,' Dad said. 'She nearly died, she was laughing so hard. And her little friend—?'

'Janet.'

'Oh my god, Janet, she was wearing this cowboy hat, wasn't she? And boots?'

'She used to live in those things. She was a fan of The Cure. What was that song?' Mum paused a second, before launching into a somewhat hesitant rendition of 'Boys Don't Cry'. After a second Dad joined in.

They were both grinning. I looked covertly at Mum. A young Renu, someone hopeful and funny, did I recognize this picture?

We were all silent for some moments, but this was a different kind of silence from those that I usually faced with my parents. It was almost – comfortable.

'You grew up in India?' Simon asked my dad, after a while.

'Bombay,' Dad replied. 'When I was in college in Bombay, I tried doing Shakespearean plays in local theatres. I was pretty good too. I made a smashing Hamlet, but Romeo was my special role, I was very good at it.'

I suddenly realized that Dad sounded like he did when Rose and I were little. I got up slowly and walked over to the French windows, sipping my tea, but I could still hear him. Hear Rose's father telling his stories. I hadn't heard

Rose's father's voice in so many years. Sudden tears blinded me but I ferociously blinked them away.

'I thought to be an actor on stage, where better than London? Over the years, of course, as you know, I realized I wanted to teach acting, not be an actor.'

I turned around. 'You mean you couldn't make a success of it.' I couldn't help it. I couldn't stop myself from saying those words. Maybe it was habit, or maybe it was my father, sounding so normal, sounding like he did when we were kids, sounding like everything was okay.

My mother frowned.

'She's right,' Dad said quickly. 'Rilla's right. It's funny. When you're in India and you grow up reading English literature, it's like you think you're really an Englishman. You think the values in Hardy and Austen and Dickens, of honesty and integrity and loyalty, and all that, that is being an Englishman, that is being a man. You come here and no one talks in refined English. They use an exaggerated cockney and they get boozy and drunk and pick fights over football and everyone has spiky hair that stands up against the force of gravity. And no one thinks you're an Englishman at all, even though you're always dressed in a suit and tie and your hair is neatly combed and your shoes shining and you say things like 'Hark!' And then you realize that you are a character in a book, not a real person.' He shook his head.

'Were you disappointed, coming here?' Simon asked.

'Not exactly that.' Dad thought about it. 'You have to re-focus your lenses, that's all.'

Mum brought out clotted cream and strawberries, Indian sweets and mango ice-cream. When I walked slowly back to the dining table, Simon was dipping shards of *jalebi* in the ice-cream.

Dad continued. 'I remember going to an audition for Hamlet once, in Covent Garden. Covent Garden was much the same as it is now. You know they used to have a shoe repair shop and a snuff shop and various dairies? Anyway, so this audition, I was so good at it in Bombay I thought I'll only need to give them a speech and they'll get over the colour of my skin. So at this thing, the director talked to his assistant throughout, and I knew I wasn't going to get the part. I had had just about as much as I could take of auditions back then. But then at the end he said they were doing a TV show, and needed an Indian doctor. They asked if I'd like to play that, although they added I'd have to make my accent more Indian.' Dad chuckled. 'I said, "I surely will, Sahib, thanking you very much, mention not, please to be." He had the grace to laugh. And he did get me a couple of roles. But they were always "Indian doctor," "Indian shopkeeper," once an "Indian neighbour" who was always cooking "curry" and bringing it around.'

Simon nodded thoughtfully. 'I think actors still complain of that. It isn't easy.'

Dad shrugged. 'Maybe I should have stuck with it.'

'Why didn't you?' I couldn't help asking. I was curious. These weren't things that Dad talked about often – certainly not with me.

'When I met Renu, we decided to get married pretty quickly. Once you have bills to pay, it's different.'

My parents were silent for a moment, and I remembered my childhood, I remembered Dad expressing regret about his failed acting career, I remembered that he had always thought that my mother had been against it. I looked from one to the other, but they didn't say anything more about it. I glanced over at Simon. He raised his eyebrows slightly but didn't say anything.

'What I wasn't prepared for was her family,' Dad continued. 'It was like the royal family. Promilla and me, it was just the two of us. But Renu came with half the population of London. Can you imagine? Jat offered me a job within two seconds of meeting me. *No man is an island,* he said. *Fortune favours the bold.*'

I snorted. I couldn't help it. Dad sounded exactly like Uncle Jat. I had forgotten that Dad was funny when he got going. I glanced at my mother, but she was not looking at me.

'Everyone was always in your face. *When are you getting married? Just tell us, and we'll organize it. Don't wait too long. What are you waiting for? And this acting-shacting, when are you getting a real job? Come and live with us. We have a ten-bedroom estate in Surrey. You can have your own bathroom, just like in India. We had it in-built, ensuite, by our own personal architect. We have lots of room. You just say the word. Here's the train routes out of Woking. You can be in London in a minute. Or we can get you your own personal car.*'

Suddenly, despite myself, I was spluttering on my tea and Simon was grinning. 'I have to meet these people,' he said.

'Believe me, you don't.' I shook my head.

'Have to know where you come from,' he said, teasing me.

I punched him on his arm, getting another warning look from my mother. I frowned. What was wrong with her?

'Dress like this, speak like that.' Dad leaned back in his chair, a reminiscing look in his eyes. 'It isn't Ly-ces-ter and Glou-ces-ter, it's Lester and Gloster. Etc, etc. And they organized the whole wedding. It was huge too. It had to be, just to accommodate the family, and not just the London lot but people from India, Australia, America, they're bloody everywhere, your mother's family. On my side, there were my two parents from India – my father a poet, and my mother an amateur painter, who'd made a living out of staying away from other people – and Promilla. There were about two hundred people from your mother's side. And then of course, as soon as we were married, other questions started. When were we going to have kids, what were we waiting for. *So, when are you giving us some good news,* hain ji, *what do you say? Some good news for some nice* laddu?'

'That's what they said to you,' Mum said. 'To me they were suggesting hormone injections and they were always giving me things to eat that are supposed to boost your fertility. They were telling me to eat vegetables, avoid meat, drink a lot of milk with turmeric in it. *Mung daal*, banana, and *lassi* – that's what I would be fed whenever I met anyone for lunch.'

I stared at my mother in surprise. I had no idea they had had any problems having children before Rose came along, that there had been years of unhappiness, maybe even desperation, that they were not talking about right now. Simon must have sensed something, because he clasped my hand.

'You're lucky, Renu,' Dad said. 'They were telling me to wear loose underpants, avoid heat, eat broccoli and drink Medjool date milkshakes with black cumin. Avoid drinking alcohol, that was the mantra.'

Abruptly both of them stopped talking. Of course the obvious thing to say then was that Rose came along and put a stop to all that. But there was just silence. I stared from one to the other. Simon, of course, didn't know about Rose. But she was there, she was in all our minds. There had been moments like that throughout the years, those moments of complete silence in which my parents and I were acutely aware that we were all thinking about Rose. And right then, sitting around my parents' dining table, I knew with stark clarity that there was one person in the room who didn't know what we were thinking about. My fiancé Simon didn't have any idea about my sister Rose. I knew this, of course I did, yet it hit me just then. And I almost choked on my tea.

'More tea?' Simon said and this broke the silence. There was a protest from my mother about Simon being a guest in the house, but he just said, 'Let me do it.' He walked to the kitchen. I saw him drink a glass of water, put the kettle on, open cupboards to find tea bags. I splintered the *jalebi* on my plate. This was my moment to say something, to say something about the child they had waited for, for so long. But of course I didn't. So I didn't say anything at all.

24

Lost

For C.S. Lewis, affection is nine-tenths responsible for everything that is stable and durable in this world. I suppose without affection, without parental love, the world would stop working.

Rilla's notes

Thoughts of Mum's email account take over everything. I walk around the flat, not seeing things, not noticing Federico, or Lord Basingstoke, or chores I need to do. Every waking moment, I daydream about her inbox, I imagine it in great detail, I picture the setup of the page, the trail of emails and responses. I imagine going through them, further and further into the past, skimming some and reading others in painstaking detail. In my mind's eye, I sift through the rubble of emails from family and colleagues and come up with something, one precious email, from someone important that tells me everything I need to know.

I've always been good at daydreaming, and not just idle daydreaming, but getting completely lost, disorientated, in the vision. Just as I've buried myself in books over the years, daydreaming has saved me from myself. I've daydreamed about many things: love, sex, running away, joining Cirque du Soleil, finding out I had different parents but I got switched at birth, winning an Oscar, a Tony, a Grammy, the Turner, having glorious hair that does what you ask of it, being able to eat slabs of chocolate without putting on any weight, spending the rest of my life with my soul-mate. Many times, I've pictured having a total freak-out at the GIF in great detail, telling them I will never see any of them ever again, then going off and becoming a cool but wistful waitress on a Caribbean island and actually sticking to my threat. And of course I've spent countless hours dreaming about Rose.

But now all I can think about is searching Mum's inbox. That is my only dream. I think of it during tutorials, showers, as I'm eating, sleeping, oh, and trying to write my thesis.

What if there *is* something there? What if there is nothing? I wish I had a teenager's courage. I wish I could just go to my parents, yell and rage and break the way I might have done once. But instead I'm aware that other people can be just as brittle and breakable as me. Oh damn, that must be Jeremy Vine – the great voice of my conscience – again.

I'm dragged back into a memory of sitting on our porch as a teenager. Mum had come out of the house. She was wearing trousers and an Indian mirrored top. She had been in the kitchen for the last two hours doing dishes, drying, mopping, and chopping vegetables.

'Rilla, can't you take your earphones off, for once,' she said.

I was wearing lipstick the colour of an ox's blood and eyeliner so thick it could have been seen from the NASA space probe. My cropped top was halfway up my tiny breasts. I had had my belly button pierced not long before, leading to a lot of yelling from Mum (and a lot of mopping up of blood from me).

I tore off the earphones but kept them around my neck. 'What?' I said.

'Mrs Winters was saying that maybe you need to get more serious about your studies. If you want to go to university.'

I probably was going to university, I hadn't really given serious thought to any alternatives. But I didn't say that. Instead, I said, 'Maybe I don't want to go to university.'

My mother didn't pay any attention to this. 'In our family, everyone goes to university, okay? Don't get ideas in your head, it's not going to work.'

'Oh yeah, like you're doing a lot with your degree.' Deliberate intention to hurt. My mother had studied education at university in Leeds. 'I'll do that too, shall I? Get a degree, get married, have children and never do anything ever again?'

She pursed her mouth. 'Can you ever show any gratitude for anything I do? Do you even notice it?'

AMITA MURRAY

'Are we done now? Can I go now?'

'Mrs Winters says you've been bunking classes, that you never hand in assessments on time, that you rarely seem to care about what you're doing. She says you'll fail your exams if you don't work harder. She says last week she took a packet of cigarettes off you – she said you weren't smoking a cigarette, you were selling them in school.' She reached into her pocket and held up a joint. 'I found this in your room.'

I snatched it off her. 'Is there no privacy in this house? Do you know how invasive this is?'

'Stop shouting at me, I'm not your boxing bag. But you have to understand we're not like them.'

'Like who? What the hell are you talking about?' I was standing up now, pulling my backpack on, collecting my things.

'British teenagers grow up too quickly, Rilla. Drugs, sex, birth control.'

'I *am* British,' I said. 'Maybe not Dad because he wasn't born here. And maybe not you because you don't really fit. But I'm British. Get it?'

I was going to run off, I usually did, but she stopped me. 'Are you using birth control?'

My cheeks were hot. 'What is the matter with you?'

She was nervously clutching her fingers. 'You're such a teenager sometimes. Can't you grow up, show some respect? Do you know how much I do for you? Do you know I give up everything for you? Why can't you be more like—' She stopped abruptly. 'Why can't you be more like your

206

dad? He never hates me. He sees and appreciates all that I do.' Her eyes went blank. She was no longer looking at me. That lost look, that enraged me more than anything.

'That's not what you were going to say, though, Mummy, is it,' I said softly, slowly.

Then I did run off. Like I said, I usually did.

What is it between my mother and me? Another memory swims to the surface. Once, when Rose and I were little, our next-door neighbour in Balham accidentally broke one of my mother's plant pots. It was special to her, that plant pot, and she was cold to the neighbour when they came to apologize. The woman who had done it was a single mum, always looking harassed, ageing before her years.

Later, Rose said to my mum, 'She didn't do it on purpose, Mum, surely you can see that. She's just tired.'

And like I knew she would, when Rose said these words, Mum nodded slowly. 'You're right, I was mean.'

'You could just go over and say you're sorry,' I said, not wanting to be left out of the conversation.

And then Mum's chin started trembling. 'Why, because I'm so mean? Because I'm always so mean? Is that why?'

'She didn't say that.' Rose glanced nervously at me.

'That's what she's saying though. Don't you think I know how you look at me, Rilla?'

I felt numb. I should have been used to it, but I felt numb. Rose bit her lip, and Mum got up and started banging things about in the kitchen.

Oh, I don't even know why I'm picking at these memories now, or why they have the power to hurt after all these years. Do I care that Mum and I were never close? Or is the real problem this: that I know Mum has never loved me as much as she loves a fragment of her memory?

25

The Rest of the World

A few days later, I am still obsessing about the things Jharna has said to me, yet powerless to do anything about it. I'm in limbo, not happy where I am but unable to move forward. I've spent so much time in bed this morning, thinking about the potential clues hiding in Mum's email, that I am running late for the weekly seminar that the department organizes for post-grads. I hate being late for work and classes, so now I'm cursing, bumping into things, dropping cups and pens and shoes and bags and my Oyster card, sloshing tea everywhere.

To my utter distraction, my phone is also buzzing off the hook. This can only mean one thing; the GIF is having an extended WhatsApp conversation. Auntie Pinky has recently created this group. The notifications are so insistent that I am developing a nervous twitch. Did you know that you can't delete a WhatsApp group from your phone?

Well, you can't. I tried taking myself out of this one, but they keep adding me back in.

I look at the messages as I try to brush, shower, dress, eat breakfast. I can't stand them, but I can't help obsessively looking at them either.

Auntie Pinky: *You look so good in your Facebook picture, Renu. So young! What's the secret, don't keep it from the rest of us poor oldies!* *a series of emojis showing young women, older women, family groups, and horrified faces*

Mum: *Oh, stop!*

Dad: *She has to keep up with me, what! Eh?*

Auntie Pinky: *Someone should patent whatever you're doing, that's all I'm saying. You look like you're Rilla's age.*

Jharna: *If someone says you look my age, Muv, I'm going to shoot myself*

Auntie Pinky: *Try not to give me, your one and only mother, a heart attack by this talk about shooting yourself. Or anyone else.*

Jharna: *MI5 tracks WhatsApp messages and you're now on their Most Wanted list. Also because you're a brown foreigner*

Auntie Pinky: *I'm a bona fide British citizen, if anyone's listening, I was born in Leicester, down the road from a fish-and-chip shop run by a Jewish gent! I pay my taxes and if anyone talks to me on the tube, I glare at them suspiciously. You can't get more British than that! Has Rilla apologized to Simon yet or what? No one tells me anything!* *enraged face, followed by a sad face*

210

Uncle Jat: *Let's not harass these young people, Pinky*

Auntie Pinky: *I'm only asking. Not harassing. Why do you think I'm harassing?*

Mum: *Pinky is right, Simon won't wait forever, no?*

Uncle Jat: *Has she thought about pre-marriage counselling? I can set it up. I was looking at options yesterday. There are two therapists right around the corner from Lewisham, very qualified, PhDs. It is worth a shot. I can set up an appointment, I'll pay for it, goes without saying. What do you say, Manoj? Nothing ventured, nothing gained. I say, strike while the iron is hot. My wife is right for once*

Auntie Pinky: *For once?!!!! Oh man, what do you mean by that?!!!?* *enraged red-faced emoji* *Anyway, Rilla should sort it out, not wait too long, and use gram flour and turmeric on her face so Simon can't see the biological clock ticking!*

Dad: *She's only twenty-five . . .*

Jharna: *She's gorgeous*

Uncle Jat: *Definitely above average*

Mum: *She's okay. But looks don't last*

Auntie Pinky: *She's twenty-five. That's what? Five fertile years left at most?*

Me: *Will the bloody lot of you stop talking about me?*

I leave the house, burning with irritation. I pull on my coat as I hurry down the road. I'm heading to campus for a seminar called, 'Existentialist Rage: A Necessary Evil in the Fragmentation of Our Post-Modern Condition? Or Just a By-Product?' This sounds very apt.

I rush headlong into the wind that is pushing against me, pushing my blouse into my breasts, my skirt between my legs, my hair all around my head. When a man in his car calls out to me – 'Hey, sexy!' – I glare at him and show him a finger.

My phone buzzes again. I expect it to be the GIF, but it's Federico.

'What?' I bark. He hasn't done anything to deserve my anger, not really, but he gets it anyway.

'Don't chop my head off.'

'Sorry,' I mutter. 'I hate my family, I hate London.'

'Anyway, I was thinking we haven't hung out in a while. Just you and me. Do you have time to go out maybe? For a drink or something.'

I have no reason not to. And I should pay attention to his voice, to the uncharacteristic note of *something* that I can't quite identify, but I don't. 'Sure. Soon, okay? Just not now.'

'Look, *chica*, I know you feel like you've messed up—'

'Damn you, who said I felt like that?' I click the phone off, growling again.

I slope into class half an hour late and I slide into an empty chair next to Tyra. The professor, a guest in our department, is speaking. I have never seen him before. He has teeth missing, a hard-boiled head with no hair, and gunk at the corners of his eyes.

I look over at Tyra. She shrugs and I slide closer.

'I am suffering from aesthetic revulsion,' I whisper.

She snorts. She scribbles something in her notebook, tears the page off, then passes me a note. It reads: *Can't figure out more boring or more ugly???*

'What is rage?' the professor is saying. 'Meta-anger? Anger at yourself? Anger at the world?'

I raise my hand. I actually have no idea what the class has been talking about in my absence, but rage, I know a little about rage. I tell him about the man in the car who called me sexy on my way to university. When I'm done, I say triumphantly, 'I hated him! And that's rage.'

Tyra's shoulders are shaking and she is hiding her face in her book.

The professor looks confused about what to do with a real-life example. 'Quite.' He scratches his head. 'You mean you're post-symbolic?'

Tyra raises her hand.

I look over at her. 'Ms Williams?' I say, crossing my arms.

She's trying desperately not to laugh. 'Rilla's position,' she says, glancing at me, 'is maybe a humanist one. Maybe she can only understand hate if she first comes to grips with love.'

'That's deep, Miss Williams, real deep.' I pinch her arm and this makes her squeal.

I can handle – just about – Tyra's making fun of me, but now Wu Li has her hand up too. She's an undergrad but often asks permission to attend post-grad seminars.

'Maybe the ability to love, maybe it's more of a bone than a muscle. Maybe some people just don't have it.' She considers her own words. 'Because then it isn't Rilla's fault.'

Thanks, Wu Li. Thanks for always saying the thing that cuts me into shreds.

I spend three hours doing tutorials with my undergrads, then I head home, feeling a little defeated by the world. I enter the house with a firm resolve. I can work today, I can work on my thesis. I will be able to work once I've shut everyone out.

But I'm wrong, because at the flat Federico is on a mission to multi-task and he's running around everywhere, impossible to avoid. He's carving a courgette into some kind of wind instrument, trying to get some food inside Lord Basingstoke and talking to his boyfriend on the phone, all at the same time.

'Come on,' he keeps saying, 'I love you, you know that, how can you say that I don't care?'

I exhale loudly and cross my arms.

When he's finished talking to Pip, I say, '*Do* you love him? Or is it just that you can't walk away from someone who loves you?'

Federico's father has never accepted his sexuality. He grew up in a household in which his mother and father did not talk to each other about him, where he had to hide all the time, where he felt ashamed and unloved. I understand that, I see that about him. And I'm trying to get him to see it too, but the questions come out sounding harsher than I intend.

He looks seriously at me. 'Don't give me advice on my relationships, *chica*, we will get on much better.'

214

I purse my lips. 'Whatever.' Just talk to your beloved Fountain, then, and see where that gets you.

He looks funny for a moment like he's going to say something further, but then he disappears into his room.

Fine, Federico, see if I care. Now I can work. I head up to my room, settle myself down at my desk, turn on my laptop. But before I can even open my notes, I hear the doorbell. I listen for Federico but he is making no move to go downstairs to let anyone in, I can hear him on the phone again. I take an exaggerated breath and stomp all the way down the stairs. Standing outside is my cousin Sulekha with the Toddlers. Before I can blink, the boys have run upstairs and inside my flat.

'What?' I say stupidly.

Sulekha looks demented. 'You *have* to take them,' she says, her hair flying about her, her mascara running, her lips pulled down. She holds my hands briefly, makes a sympathetic face. 'I'm so sorry,' she whispers. Then she's gone before I can say Shitty Biscuits.

I walk upstairs slowly, enter my flat and stare at the Toddlers, who are running around the living room, tearing everything to shreds. What has happened to my life? It's all going to pieces. No one in their right mind would make me responsible for their children. This has never happened before in the history of my relationship with the GIF.

'Rilla, Rilla, Rilla!' one of the boys is shouting. He is running in circles around me.

215

'Rilla, where's the bathroom?' the second is yelling. 'Rilla, I need a wee-wee, Rilla, I need a wee-wee, Rilla I did a wee-wee!'

'There's wee-wee in his pants!' The third is yelling, laughing and pointing, and jumping up and down on the furniture.

'Stay off the furniture!' I scream. 'Come on!'

I drag the wee offender off to the toilet. Clean clothes have been thoughtfully provided in The Toddler Bag that goes with them everywhere, and there are two full changes of clothes for each boy. That's a lot of clothes, and this fills me with dread. It takes twenty minutes just to change the child's trousers because he keeps alternating between running around the bathroom and wrestling with me.

When I come out, there is a river of toilet paper on the floor, and the fridge, the oven, the washer, the dryer, the microwave – they are all open and all of their buttons have been pressed so that there are lights blinking everywhere. The front door is open.

'What!' I run around frantically closing doors, turning things off, trying to clean up green goop on the floor (apparently jelly has also been thoughtfully provided in The Toddler Bag).

'What is the matter with you!' I yell.

'What is the matter with you! What is the matter with you!' yell the Toddlers.

I hold my hair for a moment. I tentatively raise my palms, slowly, like I'm about to negotiate with a dangerous criminal.

'Okay,' I say, 'okay. We can figure this out. You want to play a game? Let's play a game.'

I scratch my head. The Toddlers seem to sense that I won't be able to come up with anything half decent. It's like they can read my mind.

'Let's make up songs! You, Aman. *There was once a man called Aman. He was a genuine article shaman. He . . .*'

'What's a shaman?' asked one of them.

'Hmm. Okay, let's try you first, Manush,' I say to another one, 'let's start with you instead. *There was once a boy called Manush, who . . . who loved to eat Baba Ganush. He went one day to the market, and put aubergines in his basket, then he ran all the way home to his mummy, and asked for mushy aubergines with honey!*'

This is a success. The boys are doubling over with laughter. This stuff is easy. 'You, Rahul. Let's see, what rhymes with Rahul? *There was once a boy called Rahul, he asked his daddy for a towel. He went out into the woods, to collect some berries and – and—*'

'Blood!' one of them shouts.

'Woods doesn't rhyme with blood,' I say.

'*There was once a girl called Rilla, she was a nasty, horrible killer, she had a big, long knife, she slit someone's throat with a knife . . .*'

'Okay, let's stop this game, shall we?'

'Rilla, a police is knocking at the door. We have to kill it!'

'Rilla, why is your name Kumar and ours is Burrows?'

'Rilla, why are you brown? My mummy's brown like you. But Daddy isn't.'

'Get off the bloody kitchen table, get off the bloody kitchen table!' they're shouting.

Federico comes out of his bedroom. 'They're so cute!' he says. He's dressed in a black-and-white-striped tuxedo coat, coral trousers, a shirt with frills at the collar and a top hat.

'Why are you dressed like Willy Wonka?'

His eyes look suspiciously red-rimmed, but I can't pay attention to that right now because the Toddlers are all jumping up and down in front of me, trying to see who can bop my forehead first. I clutch at Federico. 'You have to take them!' Now they're running around again. I lift one of them off the kitchen counter where he is standing and wielding a meat knife.

Federico looks bemused, and Lord Basingstoke is standing in the corner of the room, his hair on end, completely frozen in terror.

Federico goes to speak to them for a second, so I sneak into the kitchen to make myself a strong coffee. When I come back the Toddlers' faces are smeared in melted choc-olate.

'Are you crazy?' I yell at Federico. 'This stuff,' I say holding up chocolate wrappers, 'is like their meth!'

Federico shrugs. 'Don't exaggerate, Rilla. They're good as gold. I'll see you later.'

I grip his arm. 'You're *leaving*?' I shriek. 'You can't *leave*, do you hear? You can't leave!'

He pats my hand, but then he's gone.

When I turn slowly around, the Toddlers have turned

on the radio and are singing along to Sia at the top of their lungs, shouting that they don't need no money, they just apparently want to feel the beat.

An hour later I am tearing my hair out. One of the Toddlers is on top of the fridge and I have no idea how he made it up there. But he is the least of my problems. Because I am trying to stop the other two from climbing into the oven and suffocating themselves.

There is the doorbell again. 'Nobody move!' I yell. I do the Professor Grundy I'm-watching-you gesture, but it has no effect on the Toddlers. I walk down to my front door, a broken woman.

It's Simon. 'I'm here to bond with my cat,' he says, his hands stuffed in his pockets.

'Thank god!' I grip his arm.

Fifteen minutes later the Toddlers are sitting quietly, all cleaned up, hair combed, fed and watered, and Simon is reading them *Dr Seuss*. The boys are on board with this kind of rhyming apparently.

'It's easy-peasy,' Simon says, looking at me. 'Why don't you come and join us?'

I stare at him sitting there with them. He's so good at this, with his floppy hair and his nice ears and his blue eyes that crinkle when he smiles. His shirtsleeves are rolled up today, though the shirt is coming untucked, spilling ever so slightly out of his jeans. Just for a second, I reach out my hand, unthinkingly, to tuck in the shirt. Then I snap it back.

'I have so much to do. Do you mind looking after them

for an hour or two? I might go to a café and do some work.'

His face is serious for a moment. 'Rilla—'

Just for a second, I have the strongest yearning to curl up on the floor and watch him do his thing with the Toddlers. Not to join in, because that would be too much, but just watch. The yearning hits me in my stomach.

'Sorry, okay?' I say quickly. I don't look at him again, I don't turn around at the door. I have to get out of here before I do something stupid.

26

You Jest Not

A few days later, I get a call from Jharna as I am sitting cross-legged on my bed, marking papers, eating noodle soup.

'Hey, Sis. Sorry about the other day, yeah? I won't pry, of course I won't.'

It takes me a moment to realize that Jharna is apologizing for bringing up Rose. I blink foolishly. I have the strongest urge to say, 'Please, please try. Please try to find out something, anything. Please help me.' Because what Jharna is offering, I suddenly want it more than anything. The desire to know hits me in my stomach, like a punch.

The words are on the tip of my tongue. I don't care if Jharna is a spy, I don't care if the GIF has planted her, I don't care why she's really here. I need her. I grip the phone.

'Can you do something?' I mumble incoherently. At that moment a train goes by, drowning out my words.

'Wait, sorry, I can't hear anything,' Jharna says. 'Train passing.'

I frown at the phone. 'Where are you?'

'Oh, in your back garden. Where are you?'

I hang up the phone. What is Jharna doing in my back garden? I walk slowly downstairs and head outside.

This morning, I was reading Maya Angelou's writings on the travails of love. I was reading an interview in which Angelou says that most women marry other people's husbands. I think she means that most women feel lonely, impatient, insecure and they marry the first person available, instead of waiting longer, holding out for deeper contentment, holding out for the right man to come along. Most women marry other people's husbands, husbands who would be better off with someone else. These lines ring in my ears now as I walk downstairs and out into my back garden. There I see Jharna and Simon.

'Oh, hi, Rilla. We didn't know you were even at home,' Jharna calls. She finds this hilarious.

The back garden is long and narrow. There is an archway in the middle of it, overgrown with creepers. There are a few sunflowers, long, ungroomed and tangled, and the grass is wild because neither Federico or I know a thing about gardening. In this overflowing wilderness Simon is riding a unicycle, and Jharna is jumping up and down and laughing her head off. The new Jharna – the monster I've created – finds everything hilarious and the chit has an infectious, irritating laugh.

I stand on the porch and cross my arms. I am finding it hard to breathe.

'Simon is teaching me what to do at his party!' Jharna calls. 'Yaaaaa,' she goes, as Simon cycles past. 'I'll get the kids to jump up every time he cycles past, see?' She yells again. 'You want to try it?' She explains it all to me again in great detail in case I have only half a brain.

'Make sure you don't fall off the bike,' I call to Simon. 'With people yelling at you like that, you might break all the bones in your body!'

Again he cycles past and Jharna springs up from her cute crouching position. Simon is wearing a white shirt and a loose pair of yellow stripy trousers that cinch in at his ankles. He waves at me as he goes by. Jharna is wearing a short frilly skirt and spotty tights. Clearly this is a dress rehearsal.

When Simon gets off the unicycle he starts juggling. It looks like he's holding twenty pieces of fruit but I can't tell for sure because he's juggling so fast I can't count how many things he has in his hands. He changes from fruit to hoops to skittles and back to fruit again. How does he do that? The movement is a blur. Jharna keeps throwing more things at him to juggle. He's juggling the apples and bananas higher and higher and now the man is tap dancing as he juggles. This stuff is unreal. I had no idea he knew how to do any of this. It's making my head hurt. It's like seeing someone for real for the first time. Like they've been pretending to be one person and actually they are someone else altogether. And the reason they've been pretending is not to protect themselves, but to protect your feelings, in case you realize they're much more interesting than you. My eyes bore holes into Simon. Why the hell has he been lying to me all along?

I sit on the steps that lead down to the grass, or maybe I fall over unconscious. The effect is about the same.

Now Simon is showing Jharna how to hula hoop. He can do it for minutes at a time.

'Put one leg in front of the other like this,' he says to Jharna. 'And then don't go round and round. Go back and forth, like this.'

He's talking and demonstrating at the same time. I am waiting for him to put his hands on her hips to show her what to do. Her hips are luscious. She's one of those women, flat-chested, with a skinny waist and then juicy bum. God, I hate women like that. He's going to put his hands there, I just know it, and I am going to have to wash my eyes out with chlorine if he does. But there's no holding of hips and it turns out Jharna isn't going to be able to hula hoop after all. They decide this isn't a big problem because it would actually be funnier if she kept dropping the hoop. Then Jharna sits down, ready for the next bit.

Simon starts telling a story that goes with the rhythm of his hula hooping. 'A long time ago, I went to the Isle of Wight on a ferry with a jester named Bo-Bo who had just discovered a love for gooseberry jelly and cream pie. Bo-Bo only knew two emotions – very happy and very sad. Jelly and pie made him very happy. Everything else made him sad.'

Two words into this story, Jharna is giggling like mad. She is giggling so hard she's rolling around on the floor. That girl is cute even though she's not trying to be. Simon is now juggling, hula hooping and telling his story.

'When Bo-Bo and I got off the ferry we realized we were really thirsty. On the beach there was a shack where a pirate with a hook instead of an arm and only one eye sold chocolate and rhubarb milkshake. By this time, Bo-Bo had eaten all of his supply of jelly and pie, and so he looked really, really sad.'

The rest of the story went something like this.

'Have a banana,' the pirate said.

Bo-Bo shook his head.

'Have some chocolate,' the pirate said.

Bo-Bo shook his head and wiped a tear.

'Have my speciality. Chocolate and sugar-apple milk-shake. I'll throw some marshmallows in it, just for laughs. Just for you.'

The pirate offered him a series of things that the jester refused. Gradually the entire beach, and then the whole of the Isle of Wight got involved in trying to make the man smile. But no one had any gooseberry jelly or cream pie, so the jester was always sad. Simon is now unicycling and juggling and telling the story at the same time. And he's telling it faster and faster. In the end, Jharna is waiting with what looks like a cream pie and jelly. She calls, *I have it, I have it!* And of course Simon falls off the unicycle in his excitement and lands in the cream pie.

I don't know how the children will respond to these

antics, but Jharna is laughing her head off and I am wiping away tears by the end of it. I am nearly throwing up, that's how funny it is.

Then Jharna runs up to Simon and hugs him.

'I love it!' she shouts.

Simon hugs her back. Now there is cream in her hair that she is rubbing off with her fingers. And now the bitch is licking her fingers. Simon begins explaining something or other to her, and she's riveted. She is clearly finding it the most fascinating thing she has ever heard. I have stopped laughing. In fact I am deeply regretting my previous laughter. I wish I hadn't laughed at all. I wish I had sat stony-faced throughout the stupid story that doesn't even have a punch line. I could have done it better in my *nautanki*, Prince Rup could have done it better.

I picture their wedding in great detail, Simon and Jharna's. They'll have this story to tell their kids and grandkids, about how it was actually Auntie Rilla (you know Auntie Rilla who never comes to any family dos and lives all by herself with her disabled cat who she's beginning to look like, you know the auntie who smells of cat piss and wet Whiskas?) whom Simon was going to marry, but luckily Auntie Rilla got arrested on the day of the wedding, or Simon and Jharna would never have gotten together. Moral of the story: just because you think you want one thing and that thing leaves you, don't worry. You actually want her cousin!

Jharna is now on her phone. Simon is clearing up all his things from the garden, and then he comes up to me. 'What do you think?' he asks.

'Amazing. I never knew you were so funny. I thought you juggled a little bit. Guess you and Jharna have been practising a lot.'

He shrugs. 'She's a quick learner. It's new for me having someone to work with. It helps with the kids.'

'Sure, sure,' I say. Have you tried pinning her to a block of wood and practising throwing knives at her? I hear it's all the rage, that old trick. Oh, you're not that good with knives? Let me have a go. One, two, three. Oh whoops. I've sliced her head off. Shit, so sorry about that. Someone will have to tell her parents the skanky cow is dead.

'We still need to talk, you know that?' Simon is looking at me intently.

'There's nothing to talk about.' I stare at Jharna's juicy bottom. Why is it wiggling so much?

Simon gives me a hand, and I take it. I stand up and brush myself off, avoiding his eyes.

'Do you remember that time we went to Torquay?'

I clench my jaw. I don't want to be reminded of that weekend.

'We'd gone down to Babbacombe Beach on that funny cable car train thing, do you remember?' he asks.

Of course I remember it. We had gone down the cliff in Babbacombe at a crazy angle in a single-car train. The train cruised all the way down, but as far as Simon – who has vertigo – was concerned it may as well have plummeted all the way down the cliff and plunged straight into the sea. For the whole time the train was descending, I could feel him shaking as he held my hand tight. He held it so

227

tight I had nail marks on the palm of my hand when we got off the train. Later we lay on the little beach, cocooned in red cliffs that were curved in the shape of a crescent moon and covered in dense green, the sea the bluest I had ever seen it, gulls gliding and swooping around us, a tourist trinket shop selling flip-flops and ice-cream at our back, a restaurant next to it, wafts of fried fish coming our way. We lay there, holding each other close and I thought, looking at those red cliffs, that I wanted to lie there forever.

'Do you know why I went down the cliff with you in that train, even though I knew I would hate it?' he says now.

I shake my head.

'Because I'm sure that as long as you're here, everything will be okay.'

I take a shuddering breath. I remember Babbacombe. I remember the long walk back along the coast, through the trees, the brush and the craggy paths. I remember giggling and kissing and trying to have sex against a tree and falling over. I remember kneeling down in the crevices made by a circle of rocks and making love, holding our hands on each other's mouths when someone was passing nearby.

I don't want to think of that time. I don't want to think of the dawning realization I had then that I was beginning to need Simon as much as he needed me. I don't want to remember the grip of gnawing anxiety in my stomach that followed closely on the heels of that thought.

I look up at him now. 'Everything isn't okay, though. It

never was. I was pretending things were okay. I'm always pretending. Don't you see?'

'Rilla—' he moves towards me but I leap back. He holds a steadying hand out. 'We can solve it together. Whatever it is.'

I hold up my hands. 'We can't.'

Jharna, who is done with her phone call, picks up a skittle off the grass and shouts, 'I love this!' and does a funny wiggling dance.

I clench my jaw and turn back to Simon. 'We can't solve it because there's nothing to solve. I don't love you. See? That's the problem.'

For a second his face hardens. Then that look is gone and I'm not sure if it was there or if I imagined it.

He holds a hand over his eyes against the sunshine for a moment, then turns back to me and pulls something out of his jacket pocket. He holds out his closed fist, and without thinking I hold out my hand. Small, cold things fill my palm. And there is a sudden pinch of tears in my eyes when I see what they are. In my hand are the pebbles I collected that day in Bexhill when Simon said we should get married. I stand there, my hand still out.

'Why—' I say, a catch in my throat, 'why are you giving these to me?'

I feel his shrug. I don't see it because I can't look at him. 'You asked me to save these for you, so I did. If you don't love me any more, then – there's nothing more to be said, is there? They belong to you.'

229

27

No More Teenagers

When Simon leaves, I can't move. My arms and legs are numb and in my hand I am moving the pebbles around, slowly, grindingly. For a long time, I can't do anything else and I just sit there in my back garden. Maybe I forget that Jharna is still there because when she comes up to me, I jump.

She stands in front of me, making a rueful face. 'Hey, Sis, sorry again.'

I close my eyes, willing myself to breathe steadily. 'Don't worry about it.'

But she can't help it, she isn't done. 'Did you maybe get a look at your mum's email? I know you don't really want to. I just wondered—'

I shake my head mutely. I've already begged her once for help. Maybe I said it and the words were drowned out by the noise of a passing train, or maybe it was all in my head. But I can't bring myself to say it again.

'Thanks, Jharna, but no,' I say and I head back to the house, leaving her standing there alone in my back garden.

Later, I make a phone call. 'She's spending a lot of time with Federico,' I say when Uncle Jat picks up the phone. 'I'm just nervous about exams and such. I hear they want top grades for computer science.'

'Thank you for bringing this to my attention. A friend in need is a friend indeed,' Uncle Jat says seriously. 'You are quite right. Forewarned, forearmed. I will discuss it with her. You can be sure of it.'

'And look, this is nothing to worry about, I'm sure it's only a phase. But she's been smoking with Federico. You know, marijuana. I'm not even sure I should say something.'

'This is very serious indeed.'

'I'm sure she'll grow out of it.'

'You are right to tell me. Garbage in, garbage out. That's what I always say. The girl needs to grow up.'

'And also, maybe it would be better if she didn't know that I told you.'

'Yes, yes, you may be right. I will be delicate.'

Take that, Fountain. I am about to hang up but Uncle Jat says, 'Rilla, have you thought any more about what I said? I will give you a job right away, you know. There's a communications assistant job available, and I know you were always above par with your writing skills. Quite the little scribe as a child.'

'Thanks, Uncle Jat. Let me think about it.'

'There is no point crying over spilt milk,' Uncle Jat says. 'Strike while the iron is hot. You are a good sister.'

I suck in my breath. Just for a second, I think he is going to talk to me about Rose. It is totally unreasonable, but that's what I think, and then I quickly realize he's talking about Jharna. I release a shuddering breath. 'I try, Uncle Jat, I try.'

28

But How Can I Not?

As Rilke says, the biggest, the most important task we have in our lives is to learn to love. Anything else we do is mere preparation for this one task. This task is like an invitation to a person, saying: grow up, be someone, be as brave as you can be, stand up and be counted!

If that is love, then no wonder it is hard to do.

Rilla's notes

Finally, I give in. I give in and I decide to go to my parents' place. Because it's easier to get it over with than to keep on wondering *when* and *if* I'm going to do it, and what it will mean if I do (and what it will mean if I don't). I head their way simply because there is no other way to shut myself up.

En route, though, I get off the tube three times to turn back. I keep getting off and sitting on a bench on the platform, but then getting back on again. I am not doing

233

this, I keep telling myself. Just because Jharna is on a mission, just because my life seems to be unravelling, it doesn't mean I have to do this. But then I get back on the tube, and I continue this mindless journey for which I have no plan.

My parents' cul-de-sac is lined with cherry and apple blossom trees. There would be buttercups and daisies sprinkled on the grass outside all of the houses, but they have been ruthlessly mown away. The street is clean, shaved, manicured, a far cry from the graffiti and grime of Lewisham where I live. There is a neat garage on the ground floor of the house, and my father's study. On the first floor is a large open-plan living room and dining room, with French windows at the back that lead out to the sloping garden. I walk around the cul-de-sac five times before I make up my mind to ring the doorbell.

'Can I come in?' I say when my mother opens the door. My hands are stuffed in the pockets of my patchwork skirt. I am wearing a short yellow jacket, and I am planning to keep it on even though my parents' house is always boiling. I am leaving in a few minutes, I'm not going to be here long.

'Is everything all right?' my mother asks, raising her eyebrows. 'Are you ill?'

'Can't I visit my parents?' I say as I walk in. 'Or do you need to see a full doctor's report before you can let me into the house?'

Mum smiles uncertainly. I've thrown her, that's for sure. Maybe it would have been better to make a phone call first. We stand in the hallway, staring at our feet, neither one of us knowing what to say. She is wearing a floral green *salwar* with a plain dark pink tunic, the ready-made kind, no doubt from Tooting, that flattens your breasts but is too loose around your waist. Her hair is wet from her shower and her face free of make-up, making her look young and vulnerable. We look at each other awkwardly. The conservatory doors at the back are wide open. I can hear my father doing laps with the lawn mower.

'He needs the exercise,' Mum says, twisting her hanky in her hands.

'Sure.' I haven't taken my bag off my shoulder.

'He spends too much time behind his computer.'

'Sure, sure.'

Then we have nothing to say.

'I'll get you a drink.' She walks towards the kitchen. 'I want him to trim the hedge today. We take it in turns with Mrs Wang next door, but she doesn't like the way we do it.'

She comes back with a glass of Pimm's for me, with strawberries, cucumber and mint leaves floating on the top.

'They're from the garden,' Mum says, pointing out the mint leaves.

I sip it slowly, not tasting it.

Dad walks into the living room. 'Rilla, how jolly to see you!' He's covered in bits of grass and splatters of mud. He has his casual clothes on, long cargo shorts and a white cotton *kurta*, on top of which my mother has placed a stiff dirty apron for gardening. His eyebrows are slightly raised. A look passes between him and my mother, who shrugs her shoulders. He turns back to me. 'Will you stay for lunch?'

'That would be nice,' my mother says. 'Unexpected, but nice.'

'Do say you'll stay,' Dad says politely.

'Why yes, Papa and Mama,' I say ironically. 'I surely will.'

Dad pats me on the shoulder. 'Good, good. Very good. Splendid. We always enjoy your company, we say that to each other all the time.'

This is so blatantly untrue, I can't suppress a snort. I have to turn it into a cough. 'Spiffing,' I say.

Another look passes between them. Dad shakes his head slightly. I sigh. This could be a long afternoon.

Mum is bustling in the kitchen, chopping things, dehydrating the washed lettuce, timing something in the oven, making more Pimm's. I walk around the living room, stopping and staring at the familiar prints. There is a Madhubani on the wall, with elongated women frolicking around Krishna in an orchard, and some miniatures with sinuous women consorting with deer, riding elephants. There's a vibrant Gond print showing a family of intertwined peacocks on a bright yellow background: parents and two children, the perfect family. Then there is the enormous Warli print, tribal style, in earthen colours, which is my favourite. I have been trying to get it off my parents for years. The backdrop is a rough-textured chocolate terrain. All of the drawing on it is chalky white. There are feathery delicate trees, peacocks with fanned tails, pencilled pagodas, tents and houses, and throughout these there are funny stick figures with two triangles to form torso and skirt, that jest, play drums and trumpets, carry babies and pots and pans. They spiral in and in to the middle of the painting, dancing arm in arm, leading to a Pied-Piper-like central figure – the earth goddess, Palaghata. Did I say it was my favourite? I remember now as I stare at it that it had been Rose's favourite. Not mine, Rose's. She used to spend hours sitting cross-legged on the floor, trying to copy the painting on large sheets of card paper when it used to hang over the old Victorian fireplace in our living room in Balham. I turn away from the memory.

The large windows in the living room with their faux-stained glass let in the light of the sun and I stand by them for a minute, letting the rays soak into my bare arms, which suddenly feel cold. It steadies me for a second. There is a warm grassy gold smell to the sunshine, molten and liquid. I have the greatest urge to curl up on the sofa and go to sleep like I used to when I lived here, before I left for university. The need is so great that I go so far as putting my knees on it. I want Mum to put a bed sheet on me, I want her to bring me a cold glass of milk and a biscuit when I wake up. I can taste the milk and the chocolate chip. I dip the biscuit in the milk. That is the best, most comforting taste in the world, dunked biscuits. I can feel them travel slowly, sweetly down my throat, I can see the broken bits of soggy biscuit at the bottom of my glass. There is a lump in my throat. I swallow painfully.

I tear myself away from the sofa with sheer force of will.

I walk around the room. The cleaner has obviously been recently because everything is neatly tucked in, the carpet hairs all point one way, vacuumed clean, the books on the bookshelf are all vertical and there is dust only on the backs of things. I finger the ornaments on the mantle. This is the house we moved into a few short years after Rose disappeared. I grew up here and the house isn't haunted by Rose. There are no pictures of her, no old drawings, no toys that we shared. Everything like that has been thrown out or put away, some immediately after Rose left, some over the years.

So why can I hear her laugh? I stare at a bookshelf, blindly. Why is my hand reaching out to her long silky hair to give it a gentle tug? Why can I feel her pick me up and spin me around, panting for breath because though I am smaller than her, I am not *that much* smaller.

Can I smell her here?

I try desperately to recall her smell. There is a trace of it in my brain, I know it because there are smells that immediately bring her to mind. Liquorice, peppermint, Vim, Wispa, make-up, angel cake, the inside of a car, the smell of a thunderstorm. But when I think about her, I can't bring her smell to mind.

My mother brings a quiche and salad to the dining table. It is a grilled chicken salad, on a bed of lettuce leaves, green beans dressed in a delicate olive oil and lemon dressing, and the entire thing is sprinkled with shoestring onions, soaked in an egg-and-milk mixture, then coated in flour and deep fried. I crunch some in my fingers and nibble at them.

'Have you washed your hands?' Mum asks.

This is more of a statement rather than a question, so I don't bother to answer it. I bring over a pitcher of water filled with lemon and orange slices and start to lay the table with knives and forks.

'Did you talk to Simon?' my mother asks. 'Have you apologized to his parents for what you did?'

I grind my teeth. Why is it that as soon as I am around my mother, I feel like a teenager, I regress. It's not a mental thing. Oh no, that would be too easy because then I would be able to talk myself out of it. It's a physical transformation, a werewolf howling at the full moon kind of metamorphosis. My jaw clenches, my shoulders creep up, I frown, my face becomes less animated. On top of all that, the adult-me has more inhibitions than my teenage self, so my rage is fuelled by my need to suppress it.

I don't answer.

'Promilla says you're looking after a cat for her,' she prods.

I snort. I spear a potato from the salad and munch on it. 'It's not a cat, it's the spawn of Satan.'

'She says Simon wants the cat.'

I avoid her eyes. I place a spoon carefully on the table. 'I don't like being bulldozed.'

239

Mum wipes her hands on a towel. She walks around the table, correcting my cutlery placement. I have placed spoon, fork, knife all in a pile next to each plate. She places them the correct way, fork on the left side, knife on the right, spoon next to the fork. My hands tighten on my glass of water.

'Simon cares about you. He's a good boy,' she says.

I sit down at the table. 'Isn't that strange, someone who actually cares about me.'

'Yes, actually if you ask me. After the way you treat him, it is surprising he is willing to consider things.'

'Treat him?' I scowl. 'How exactly do I *treat* him?'

'You tease him all the time, make jokes about how he talks, eats, walks, works. He's nice about it, but a man doesn't like to be made to feel small. Men don't like to be emasculated.'

I grip the table. There are tears of rage in my eyes. I stare at her, correcting the way I have laid the table, so sure of herself she's not even looking at me to see the effect of her words. How dare she, how *dare* she question my relationship with Simon? My mother, who has no bloody idea about relationships. My breath is shallow, and I'm working hard not to let the tears spill out.

'All you know,' I say slowly, through the rock lodged in my throat, 'is how to cry so that Dad will give you his attention.'

Dad comes in just then, taking his boots off, his apron, his hat and the words are drowned in the commotion. My heart is thudding.

He sits at the table, and my mother comes and joins us. I don't know if she heard what I said. Dad helps himself to quiche and salad. He warily eyes me and my mother, but doesn't comment on whatever it is he sees.

I play with the salad on my plate. I put down my fork. As I do it, I knock my glass of water over. I stand up in a rush, waving at my mother to stay. I get a roll of kitchen towels and start mopping the mess.

'Look, I know you don't like what I've done. And I've been meaning to apologize for all the wasted expense.'

'We just want you to be happy,' Dad says. He reaches out for Mum's hand. 'Don't we, Renu?' he prods.

Mum doesn't say anything. Dad gives me a thin smile. He reaches over for the grater and starts grating a *mooli*, sprinkling the white droppings onto his salad. Mum and I are avoiding each other's eyes. For some minutes no one says anything, then my parents start a conversation about the garden. And that is that. We are no longer talking about Simon, the wedding fiasco, the expense, or my life.

After lunch, my mother makes tea and brings it out to the dining table. At the same time, my father's phone rings. It's his publisher. She wants to discuss the index to his book.

'Ah, sorry about this, Rilla. I'm sure you won't mind.' He disappears downstairs and into his study.

My mother starts clearing the table.

'Do you mind if I check my email?' I blurt out before I can think better of it.

'Of course not,' she says.

She walks back to the kitchen and I can see her loading the dishwasher. I sit down at the table and chair in the corner, in front of her laptop, my heart thudding. It takes me several minutes to open the screen. Of course her email account is open, it is always open. I peer round into the kitchen. Mum has put BBC Asian network on the radio and is humming along to an old Bollywood song. I look at her email.

This is the time to put a stop to this, to go back to the way things were. But then, almost like I'm doing it against my will, I start scrolling down her email. How far back do I have to go to find something? I have no idea. There may not be anything. If there is something, it could date back many years.

My mother brings me a glass of water, but then luckily walks back to the kitchen without looking too closely at what I'm doing.

I stare at the computer screen. I know most of the names that pop up in Mum's inbox. Most of the emails are from the GIF, some friends of my mother's, some colleagues going on about marking and policy and forms. There's a colleague talking interminably about a student from Thailand who is worrying him. He goes through all the possible options of what could go wrong with the student, the various options the faculty has in order to do something about it, and how the faculty could be liable if something happened and they had done nothing to prevent it. The email is the longest in the history of emails.

There is an email from someone called Janet. I wonder

if this is Janet of the cowboy hat and boots fame. She wishes Mum a happy birthday and talks about various things going on in her kids' lives and a grandchild and some horses.

There is an email from someone called Meenakshi. It's a picture of a Caribbean island and Meenakshi is describing what it's like to be a waitress there. She sounds thrilled with her life. All she talks about is the beach, sunshine, Piña Coladas, rum, a boyfriend who is always singing and has a terrible voice.

There are a few emails from a Charity Lau, talking about something Charity bought from Mum and telling Mum how it was doing. Could she be talking in code?

Then a name hits me. Gareth Jones. I have no idea why this seems significant, it's just that the name strikes a chord. Something long ago, something that is probably of no importance at all. It is a short email.

'All well here,' it says. 'I hope you are too.' That's it, nothing more. How ridiculous. Who writes an email like that? You may as well send a blank email with no message in it.

I start going further back in the list of emails. To my surprise, there is a similar email a year before, and then again, a year before that. Each is succinct to the point of rudeness. And then it hits me. The email always comes on my birthday. Rose's birthday. I was born exactly two years after Rose. My heart is now beating so fast I think I might pass out. There are synapses in my brain synapting as we speak. Who the hell is Gareth Jones?

29

But Then, How Can I?

The following afternoon, Federico is sitting on the floor, in the corner of the living room, cursing and swearing.

'What's up, Feds?' Jharna says.

She's in my flat. Has Uncle Jat spoken to her yet? Why is she here? Though if they are all in it together, then nothing I say would work anyway. I sit on my living room floor, watching Federico and Jharna.

'My model village,' Federico says. 'I don't know what's happening, all the houses keep falling down.'

I snort, turn it into a cough. Jharna bites her lip.

He's trying to glue tiny apples to his trees but the apples keep falling down, leaving long white gloopy stalactites hanging off the trees.

'This glue is shit,' Federico keeps on saying, but he keeps on squirting out more.

Jharna walks over to Federico. 'Let's just open another glue.' She's filled the new one with lube procured especially from a sex shop in Soho. I see Jharna open it and hand it to Federico.

'Use lots of it,' she urges.

She comes back and sits down next to me, trying her hardest not to collapse laughing. As she sits down and crosses her legs, my heart starts bumping hard in my chest and I have no idea why. I put my fingers on my pulse; it's booming. What is wrong with me? And then it hits me. I know why I'm terrified, because a mere fraction of a second before I say it, before I blurt it out, I know I'm going to do it. And there's no way to stop it.

'Jones.' I choke on the word.

'Bless you,' Jharna says, her shoulders still shaking as she watches Federico trying to figure out why nothing in his model village is working.

I try to take deep breaths. I know how to control this, this is how Tyra helped me manage my panic attacks. But I am starting to pant.

Then Jharna looks slowly over at me. 'Jones?'

I shake my head. 'Forget I said it,' I manage to wheeze.

She places a hand on my shoulder. 'Is it Jones?' she whispers. 'Rose Jones?'

I cough and splutter. She quickly gets up and runs into the kitchen. Federico has disappeared into his room. He is on the phone to the company that made the glue, and judging from the recorded music coming through the speaker phone he's been put on a prolonged hold. Jharna comes back and gives me a glass of water, then sits down next to me and starts rubbing my back. It takes me several minutes to get some sense of control. When my breathing starts to return to normal, I close my eyes and hide my face in my knees.

After a few moments I look up. 'It could be Jones. Or it could be a red herring. It's just I haven't found anything else.'

'Rose Jones?' she says slowly. 'Not the easiest name to track down. Or what I mean is, it's a bit too easy.'

'Sorry.'

'I'll see what I can do.' Then she's quiet for a moment. 'You're sure?'

'I'm not.'

'Okay,' she says. 'I understand.'

When Jharna leaves, all I can think is: I've done it now. I've done something I never thought possible. It's a dangerous thing to do, because in the darkest recesses of my mind, my Rose still lives. I can see her going about her day, I imagine her, her kindness, her wariness, her acute sensitivity that exhausts her. I visualize her looking out for me, in the same way as she looks out for herself, with an intensity that I don't often encounter in others. To start this quest might destroy that image forever.

But it's okay, I tell myself. Jharna is unlikely to find anything. There will be millions of Rose Joneses. Nothing will happen.

But the very next day, Jharna drops by and hands me a Post-it.

'Check out this list. They're all roughly the right age

and for one reason or another I couldn't rule them out. It may be worth a phone call. I can do it but I thought you might want to.'

I stare at Jharna's list like it's a cobra, raising its hood up, in preparation for attack. Jharna has conscientiously listed name, profession and phone number. Where she's been able to find an age, she has also written that, and only when the Rose Jones in question is roughly two years older than me. For a few she has even pasted little pictures. In one or two instances she has written notes in parenthesis. Things like, *May be able to hack email address*, or, *Might be able to arrange a meeting anonymously*, or, *Can access school records*.

I look up and stare at her. She is looking at me sympathetically and this I can't bear at all. I use every effort of will to straighten my face.

'Thanks,' I whisper, before shutting my front door, walking all the way up to my bedroom, jabbing the Post-it into a storage box and pushing it into the furthest reaches of the eaves in my room.

30

Clutching at Straws

The next day, I'm sitting in my office between tutorials and trying desperately to ignore my phone, but it keeps buzzing. I pull my sweatshirt hood over my head and half-way down my face.

Sometimes all I want to do is disappear. Disappear somewhere where people can't find me. On the day we met, when Simon asked me what my three worst things were, I could just as easily have listed Other People as one. I run from Other People, I hide from them because when Other People are around, I forget who I am. Or at least I forget some of the stories that I have constructed so carefully about myself over the years. I sometimes forget that I am very good – I have *become* very good – at pretending.

My phone won't go away. I peek at it with one eye shut. I know who it's going to be before I see the pinging WhatsApp notifications.

*

Auntie Pinky: *Hey Rilla! How are you???*

Five minutes later: *Anyone heard from Rilla? The girl is like off the map. And what about Simon? How's he doing? He's such a good, sweet boy. SHO SHWEET!!!!*

Uncle Jat: *How's the MA going, Rilla? I have a list of jobs you could apply for*

Some minutes later: *There are many benefits to being married. Tax cuts, automatic next of kin advantages, mortgages*

Auntie Pinky: *Men take you more seriously if you're married*

Jharna: *Marriage is an archaic institution to keep women in their place*

Auntie Pinky: *Who has filled your head with this nonsense?!!!!?!! Is this what we've taught you? This is the beginning of the end, Jat ji*

Dad: *She's messing with your head, Pinky*

After several minutes, in which Auntie Pinky is seemingly having a one-on-one conversation with Jharna, because they're both online, Auntie Pinky types:

More important, how are you, Rilla? Sleeping? Eating okay? Not any more frogs' legs, I hope!

Some minutes later: *Rilla?*

Uncle Jat: *How about coming out for some Chinese?*

Auntie Pinky: *I don't like Chinese*

Jharna: *You're so racist, Mummy*

Auntie Pinky: *I'm like the least racist person in the world!!!!! *horrified emoji**

Mum: *My neighbour Su Kim loves my lamb curry*

Me: *To elaborate, what Mum is trying to say is: Chinese –*
Korean = same thing
Dad: *Rilla, stop trying to give your mother an aneurysm*

'Yes, but how do you *really* think I'm doing?'

An undergraduate student is looking up at me hopefully. Everything about her is youthful. Her shiny fingernails as she scratches her cheek, her puppy-dog eyes, her rosy cheeks.

'It's not great,' I tell her about her paper on Lacan's symbolic order and the gaze in Hitchcock films. 'And this reference to Hockney, you've inserted that there just to be interesting.' She nods slowly. There are other students waiting to talk to me about their essays as I sit in my broom-cupboard office.

Professor Grundy sweeps by, and stands at my open door in her turtle-neck and olive trouser-suit, the high-waist trousers not hiding her thick midriff, looking at the large watch she wears in her inside waistcoat pocket. The undergrads, including the one in my office, evaporate as if by magic.

Professor Grundy blinks at their retreating backs. 'This seems to happen a lot,' she muses. She turns back to me and hands me a sheaf of papers to mark. 'All yours. I've looked at a few. They're so shit I had to clean my hands with disinfectant afterwards. It's like they don't care.'

'They don't,' I say.

She eyes me. 'Rilla, anything to show me? A few chapters? One?' She frowns slightly. 'We'd hate to lose you,

you know.' She doesn't sound overly distressed about it, but it's more than I would expect her to say.

'I've had a lot going on. But I'll show you something soon. Before the summer.'

'Rilla, I don't understand.' She peers closely at me. 'Why *soon*? Why not *now*? You had so much promise when you came here. What's changed?'

I shake my head quickly. 'I don't know, Professor, I really don't.'

And that is the plain truth. My life is unravelling, and it's all I can do to hold the skeins together in one tight bunch. To look at each and every individual skein and try to understand what it means – that would be too much. It's like in my heart, the love syntax has broken, and the words appear in haphazard order. That is why I can't work on my thesis.

'You realize you can't be a teaching assistant here any more if you leave the MA?' she says.

I nod. I know this. No job, no salary. But I can't seem to focus on this question either.

'Rilla, I feel like I'm not getting through about this,' she says looking into my blank face. 'You do understand that my hands would be tied, right? If you want to stay on for another year, we need a proposal for your thesis. It is about four years overdue.'

'I've only been here for three.'

'Yes, you should have given it to us as part of your application.'

'I'm working on it,' I lie.

251

'I'll believe it when I see it, Kumar,' Professor Grundy says. She gives me a my-eyes-are-on-you sign before she leaves.

Coffee, I need coffee.

Fifteen minutes later, I am standing at the coffee machine in the faculty common room, the coffee mug hanging limply in my hand, a sachet of demerara sugar in the other. No MA, no job, no Simon, no MA, no job, no Simon, that is the chorus in my head.

Tyra walks in carrying books and a bulging handbag, and gives me a one-armed hug. 'I'm going to a club at the weekend. Wanna come?' Tyra has been trying to get me to go out for weeks. 'Are you okay?' she asks sharply, seeing my face, clamping a hand on my shoulder. 'Are you getting panic attacks again?'

I shake my head dumbly.

'Rilla, sweetie, what's going on?' She is peering into my face. I shake my head and shrug. But before Tyra can say any more, two of our colleagues walk into the coffee room, and it's obvious that one of them has been crying, because her face is blotchy and red.

'Hi, Tyra, Rilla,' one of them says.

The other one, the one who has been crying, sits down heavily on a sofa. I am trying to remember her name. She is small, wears neon-green-rimmed glasses, studded with crystals, a tunic with horizontal stripes in blue, fuchsia, yellow and green. Her shoulders are hunched and she is disappearing into the leather sofa, even though, in this beige and musty room, her clothes make her stand out like a colour highlight in a black-and-white photo.

'Sarah-Lee is going through a rough time.' *Sarah-Lee! That's it.* This from the other woman, Lily, who is tall, pale and pinched-looking, like she hasn't spent any time out in the sun for years. She is holding a box of Kleenex in her hands.

I clear my throat. Lily sits down next to Sarah-Lee, then gestures to Tyra and me to join them. Tyra puts a hand on my arm and propels me along. Knowing her, this is her way of trying to make me feel better. Even though she doesn't know what I'm feeling bad about, she thinks being sociable is the answer to all ills. I sit dumbly down on the sofa next to Tyra.

'What's wrong, Sarah-Lee?' Tyra asks. She has a hand on my back.

'I don't want to bore you,' Sarah-Lee says.

'Go on,' Tyra says helpfully. 'We want to know. Don't we, Rilla? We do!' She says it cheerily, like she's talking to a golden retriever.

I take a deep breath. 'Sure,' I croak, then clear my throat. 'Yes, sure.'

'It's just my husband and I, we've been trying for a baby for so long. Two years. And it's just not happening. You know?' Sarah-Lee says.

I look slowly up at her.

'Every month I keep thinking it's happened and I keep reading every little sign.' She's crying again now. 'And I think, this is it! This is it! And it never is. It's just PMT. You know?'

253

'Sorry, that sounds really hard.' Tyra pats her hand.

'It's the worst two years of my life,' Sarah-Lee says.

'Sorry,' I mutter. 'I'm so sorry.'

It feels like too much, this reminder of how hard it is for other people. It should make me feel better about my own problems, it should give me perspective. Isn't that what hearing about someone else's sorrow should do to us? Yet, instead, Sarah-Lee's grief seems only to compound my own.

Later, back at my flat, I call Mum. I call her, but then I have no idea what to say. There's something on my mind, something that started when I was listening to Sarah-Lee.

I clear my throat. 'A story you told last time I was around for lunch,' I say awkwardly. 'I mean with Simon. I – I didn't know you and Dad had trouble having . . .' Us. Us, that is the right word to use, but I can't say it. 'A baby,' I finish lamely.

'What made you think of that?' She sounds surprised.

'Nothing. Nothing, really. Just something I heard someone say. They said it was hard for them.'

'Yes. Yes, it was. In a way that you can't imagine.'

'She, she said that it wasn't just – that it was something she thought about every day, waited for all the time.'

'Yes, yes, it takes over your life.' Mum's quiet for a moment. 'You – you will want children some day, won't you?' There is an uncharacteristic note of emotion in her voice.

'Mum, for god's sake.'

'I don't want you to end up alone, Rilla.'

I am alone, I want to say, *I have always been alone*. But I can't say it.

'What difference does it make, Mum?' I sound tired. 'Don't you see, nothing will ever make a difference.'

I can hear her breathing on the other end. Maybe, maybe she'll say something, acknowledge what I've just said. I *know* she understands exactly what I'm talking about.

'You do say some strange things,' she says at last. There is strain in her voice, but this is as good as I am going to get. 'I was going to call you today. I wanted to tell you that Marie called.'

'Who's Marie?'

Mum makes an impatient sound. 'Marie Langton. Your fiancé's mother.'

'He's not my fiancé,' I snap.

'She said the door is always open for you to come back.'

'Why did she say that?'

'I was wondering the same thing,' Mum says. 'It seems that she thinks Simon has never been happier than when he's with you.'

'He's always happy.'

'That's not what Marie said. Anyway, I thought I should tell you. It was nice of her. She was nice on the phone. I never thought they'd feel that way, to tell you the truth. They seemed a little stuck-up to me.'

And that's that. We are done talking about babies – or whatever it is that we have just been talking about.

*

The next day, on campus, Sarah-Lee walks up to the broom cupboard – it is her turn for office hours next. She is wearing Stella McCartney yoga trousers, a dark pink racer-back tank top, carrying a yoga mat on her back and drinking coconut water. Her hair is twisted into a graceful knot. I stand up and start packing up my things to get out of her way.

'Hey, Rilla,' she says sadly.

'Hey, how's it going?' The sad eyes are too much for me at the moment. I lug my bag up onto my shoulder.

But she smiles today. 'Sorry about yesterday, it gets too much at times.'

'It's okay. I know.'

She nods. 'If it doesn't work, I suppose we could always adopt.'

I look at her slowly. 'Yes. That's a really good idea.'

'I was adopted, you know.'

'Oh, I didn't know that.'

'It was the best thing that ever happened to me. I know it isn't like that for everyone. But for me, drifting as I was from foster family to foster family, it was like – well, like coming home. Suddenly I had a new family, parents, a sister. Can you imagine? It was everything I ever wanted. I mean, don't get me wrong, the early years don't leave you, they can make you – hyper-vigilant, I suppose.' She smiles. 'But I got my family in the end.'

I nodded, feeling a shudder go through me. 'I'm glad you had that.'

*

Later that day, Jharna emails me another list.

'Hey, Sis,' she writes. 'All okay? Look, I have some more names for you. Any luck with the previous list? Any promising leads? Actually, probably not, since you would have told me. Right? I'm going to keep on going. Keep the faith. Xxxx'

The first list Jharna gave me, the list in my bedroom, is a monster. I can't sleep knowing that it's there, and now there's another one. I quickly delete the email and slam my laptop shut. What is the matter with the girl? Does she have nothing better to do, exams to study for, universities to apply for?

And anyway, I tell myself, even though I've sent her on this quest, it is so unlikely that Gareth Jones even has anything to do with Rose. So it doesn't matter. Neither the list in my bedroom nor in my deleted documents folder matters. They are as good as invisible, because I'm barking up the wrong tree with Gareth Jones. I must be. But then I can't quite clear my mind of these questions: why does the man send my mother an email every year on my birthday? On Rose's birthday? Why on that date? And what does that strange, strangled email mean?

31

My Nani's House

When I was little, we used to go and stay with my nani
– my mum's mum – at her farmhouse in Sussex for
Christmas. Me, Rose, Mum and Dad, Uncle Jat and Auntie
Pinky (this was before Jharna was born), and various other
members of the family. It was more fun in the summer,
running riot in the fields, petting the sheep, teasing the
horses, picking blackberries and having berry juice permanently drying on our hands, sitting for hours in paddling
pools, but Christmas was fun too. There were fires on in
every room and Trevor, my nani's second husband – my
granddad died young and Nani had recently married Trevor,
who reared sheep – made us marshmallows and toast and
roast monkey nuts on demand.

I always think of the Christmas when I was seven and
Rose was nine as the time when things changed, when
everything went horribly wrong. Or at least that's how
I've thought of it all these years. We had been doing our

nautanki feverishly all through Diwali season and in the lead up to Christmas, and both Rose and I were exhausted, not only from the shows, but because we found ourselves at odds with each other all the time. We had argued before, of course, like any pair of siblings, but at the peak of our *nautanki* it felt like we argued all the time.

We arrived at Nani's house on a windy day, two days before Christmas Day. By the time we got there, Rose and I had had just about enough of sitting in the back of the car. We both used to get travel sick and we were restless and fidgety beyond belief. When we got to the rambling house that was Trevor and my nani's, even getting out and standing in the rain and the wind was a relief. Trevor's daughter Hannah came running out of the house, oblivious to the rain, her chestnut hair flapping about behind her. Rose and I grinned ear to ear when we saw her. Hannah was fourteen, seven years older than me, and she was great fun.

She was always up for playing hide-and-seek, What's the Time Mr Wolf, hiding things for us to find, chasing us up and down the stairs, jumping on the furniture with us. But better than anything else, she baked with us. Normally we weren't allowed in the kitchen. Mum was definitely not one of those people that thinks that cooking with children is fun. There was cooking, which was a chore, and there was playing with children. Actually that was probably a chore for her too. But Hannah would get us involved baking chocolate chip cookies and mince pies and treacle tarts and we could make as big a mess as we wanted. We were allowed to dip our fingers in the cream and lick it (my mother would have a fit when she saw us doing that), we got covered head to foot in flour, and we could experiment with recipes as much as we liked. There were no grown-up rules with Hannah.

It was always a full house at Nani's. Downstairs, there were three reception rooms and a study, all in a line leading to the back of the house, and upstairs there were five bedrooms and an attic room crammed full of boxes and furniture and old dusty things. People slept in sleeping bags, on the floor downstairs and in all of the five bedrooms, and of course the children just wanted to sleep in the dusty attic room. The house was crammed full of bags and suitcases, plastic bags of shopping, and boxes of chocolates and sweets.

All Rose and I wanted to do was run riot, as soon as we got there, but first we had to be presented to Nani. Our hair was smoothed, our hands washed, our clothes tucked in and we were sent on our way. Nani sat on the straight-backed armchair in the study at the back of the house, a tiny box room in which you could barely fit one sleeping bag. Her enormous chair took up most of the room, and she sat there regally in a pair of black tailored trousers, a white cotton shirt and a beige cardigan. She wore gold earrings and an enormous gold-and-emerald ring that engulfed her hand, but no other jewellery or make-up. She had a thin, lined face, sharp dark brown eyes that saw everything, and hair pulled severely back into a bun at the base of her head. In all the years that I knew her – she died seven years ago – I literally never saw her smile. Nani's way of talking to children was to sternly quiz them. There was a cursory kiss on both cheeks (we were presented cheeks to kiss, I mean), and then there came the inevitable question, the first of many.

'Do you know your fourteen times table?' she asked before she even said hello.

We shook our heads at our dismal lack of knowledge. 'Nope, no idea,' I said.

Then followed a litany of questions. These varied from visit to visit, though they were always set up so that you could only shrug and say no, you didn't know the answer. She would make a *hunf* sound as if to say, of course, we didn't know how to do anything. Our education was lacking, and our morals and conduct were unspeakable.

The questions were:

Did you tidy your room before you came?

What are the properties of all the planets in our solar system?

Are you top of your class in Maths and English? What do you mean you don't know?

Name the Prime Ministers we've had in this country since the Second World War.

Name all of Henry VIII's wives.

Do you help Mama with her chores?

Do you know how to cook? All girls should know how to cook, no matter what your Auntie PK says. Your mother says you don't help her. Is she right? Why do you call her Mum? Are you British?

Give me ten synonyms for flower *in Hindi. What do you mean you don't know Hindi? Less fortunate girls than you know their Hindi. They can speak, read and write it. And you with everything you have, you know nothing. Do you know how important it is to know your roots? What did you say, Rilla? You're British now? Is that what you've learned in all these years? Spoilt girls!*

There was nothing you could do right, really, not with my nani around. You were always clumsy and stupid. But luckily everyone was in the same boat.

This one fateful Christmas, my mum came into the study to say hello to Nani.

'Have you taught these girls nothing, Renu?' Nani said to her daughter severely. 'You don't even have a job, you should at least teach them something, prepare them for adult life.' Nani had been a school teacher before she retired. Now she worked with Trevor on the farm. 'Say something, Renu. Don't ignore me when I speak to you.'

I stared at my mum. She wasn't looking at us or at Nani. 'Come, on girls,' she said. 'Let's get you settled in the attic room with the other cousins. Good to see you, Mama, the farm looks good,' she said to her mother, and we left the room, Rose sneaking her hand in mine in sympathy with Mum.

Someone had come up with the idea a couple of years previously that we had to have a themed fancy dress party for Christmas Eve. This year it was Film Characters, which was a lot easier than the previous year's theme of National

Leaders. That time Rose had dressed up as Maggie Thatcher and me as Indira Gandhi. In fact, there had been five Thatchers and seven Indira Gandhis altogether. I mean, really, what else were we meant to do with that theme?

This year Rose was Belle from *Beauty and the Beast* and I would have been Captain Jack Sparrow, from my favourite film of all time, but it was three years too soon for that, so I was Rafiki. Who's Rafiki? you say. Well, that's what everyone asked me all evening too. They gushed over Rose who was wearing a yellow dress with frills on it, but they didn't get the snow-white fur that framed my face, they didn't recognize the blue eye mask, the grey top and trousers, the long stick with two coconuts hanging off it. Rafiki, damn it. I'd explain it to them, and they'd say, *Ah, the baboon!* And I would say *He's a mandrill!* Rafiki, the mandrill monkey from *The Lion King*. Seriously!

You go through this conversation twenty-five times in one evening and you kind of get tired of it. You eat a boatload of chocolate and sugar and then you start screaming. But I wasn't screaming at the people asking the questions. Of course I was screaming at Rose. Rose–Belle. Perfect Rose with her yellow dress and long dark ringlets. Rose, who everyone loved. I was fed up and I screamed at her, till our parents had to separate us.

We were both sent up to bed early on Christmas Eve – unfair on Rose, it's true. Predictably, as we left the living room, Mum told me that I had no idea how to behave and that no one would want to marry me when I grew up. Our relatives were divided: some (Nani chief amongst them) were of the opinion that this kind of behaviour was unacceptable and being sent off without dinner was too lenient, while others (like Auntie PK and Auntie Pinky) tried to intervene and say that the excitement had been too much for us and maybe we could stay up a little bit longer. But the voice of discipline prevailed; Rose was sent off to the attic room, I was sent to sleep by myself in the box room downstairs so that I could think about my behaviour.

Around one in the morning I was so hungry I decided to brave the wrath of my parents and the possibility that the place was haunted – there were rumours – to go and find some food. There had been pizza for the kids at dinner, and the smell had wafted back to the box room, that's how good melted cheese on dough smells. I did make it to the kitchen without waking any ghosts, but on the way back to my room I made the mistake of stopping outside a door where I could hear a conversation.

I can tell you that this is always a mistake. I have a lot of experience with standing outside doors listening to conversations, and I can say with some conviction that you never hear anything good about yourself. But I did it anyway.

I stopped outside the door, hopping about from foot to foot on the cold stone floor, and I overheard something that was not meant for my ears.

'Child psychologist,' were the first words I heard, in the voice of Uncle Jat. 'I can make some phone calls.'

'That's not necessary.' Dad.

'It's getting worse and worse.' Mum's voice was low. 'You know it. It would help us. It's not such a bad idea.'

'It's getting worse since they started doing their *nautanki*.' Auntie Pinky sounded firm. 'Let's call a spade a spade. Okay? There is no point beating about the bush.'

'She's right,' Mum said. 'If you two would listen . . .'

'Renu, we've been over this. You were exactly the same when I was auditioning. You were never happy with it. Let's not start this again.' Dad sounded weary. 'They enjoy it.'

There was the sound of crying, probably my mother.

'Mrs Daniels says separating them would help,' Dad said. 'Why don't we try that to start with?'

My heart started pounding at this point and I was afraid I was going to pass out, and I would be found there by the adults, with pizza sauce smeared all over my hands and face.

My class teacher Mrs Daniels knew about me, this was the worst thing that had been said. If what Dad said was true, Mrs Daniels knew that I shouted and screamed at Rose, that I argued with her.

At that age, I was pretty well behaved at school. Did Mrs Daniels know what I was really like inside then? Did she know about the secret rage that I couldn't keep bottled up? I tried to be good but maybe the evil lurking in me always showed, the evil that Mum knew was there, that she could see even if other people couldn't. Maybe I couldn't hide it any more. Maybe it was becoming stronger. Maybe Mum was right, and no one could ever love me.

I went back to the small room I had been consigned to for the night and crept into my sleeping bag, but I couldn't close my eyes, not for a second. I stared up at the ceiling. They wanted to separate us! The words rang in my ears. I was suddenly and utterly convinced that they were going to send me away, send me away from Rose. This fear was so great that I forgot to eat the pizza slice I still had in my hands.

I looked around the little room. There was a night-light there for me, but it seemed to make the shadows longer and larger. It was like the walls were closing in on me, like there were things lurking behind the narrow bookshelves. I would do better, I vowed. I wouldn't fight with Rose any more, I would be nice to her.

Now when I look back I can still feel the searing black pit of guilt in my belly that I felt then. The shame of having my worst secrets exposed, I still feel sick from it. I was terrified I was going to be sent away.

And then, when Rose disappeared, I thought that maybe they had sent her away to protect her from me.

32

On the Last Day of Christmas

On Christmas Day, I woke up late and went down to the kitchen where the population of a small country seemed to be gathered. Hannah in a floral pink-and-white dress, and Rose with multi-coloured ribbons tied all the way up one arm, were getting mince pies out of the oven. There was already the usual spread – a turkey the size of, well, Turkey, game pie, enough potatoes to fill a bathtub, roast vegetables, brandy butter, cream for a medium-size river. Baileys-and-coffee was already going around. I instantly dipped my fingers in the brandy butter and started licking myself like a cat. Rose came up to me, gave me the biggest hug and slipped a present in the pocket of my pyjamas. I grinned and kissed her ear and then clung to her for a moment, feeling terrible for screaming at her. She was everything to me. Often, I felt like she was the only one in our family who truly loved me. So why was I mean to her? I had to do better.

Auntie Dharma was busy making chicken tikka on the tandoor, paneer kofta balls and biryani. Besides the Christmas pudding and cake, there was also thick rice pudding made with heavy double cream that a Danish friend had once made for us at Christmas and it had become a staple. There were two pots of alcoholic and not-alcoholic mulled wine simmering on the oven. My mother was stirring the pots. She was wearing a plain green cotton *salwar-kameez* this morning, before she changed into something more festive. She was sweating buckets.

'Don't think I've forgotten what happened last night,' Mum hissed in my ear as I tried to sneak past. She dropped her ladles, grabbed me by the arm and marched me out of the kitchen to one of the reception rooms. 'I've had it up to here with you. Why do you have to act like you have no education? If you can't get along . . .'

I was shovelling chestnuts into my mouth. (Remember, I had been sent to bed without dinner. Also, I like chestnuts.)

'Don't look at me like that, Rilla. I'm sick of how much you fight. Sick of it, do you hear? You just have to stop or we will have to take you to a psychologist and they don't like girls that are vicious.'

I shrugged off her arm. 'They don't like mothers who are nasty to their children.'

The day passed with more food being eaten than probably gets eaten for a whole year in smaller countries. The Queen's speech was promptly put on, but the running commentary given by everyone and everyone's auntie (literally) made sure that no one actually heard a word of it. The kids spent the entire day running wildly around the house opening presents, hanging up bunting, doing and re-doing the Christmas tree, and generally getting overexcited. There was a lot of chocolate eaten.

After dinner, we were sitting in the big reception room, the lights of the Christmas tree twinkling on and off, on and off, surrounded by explosions of wrapping paper, paper hats, used glasses, Christmas cards and empty envelopes, and various discarded jumpers and cardigans as the room was boiling hot from the coal fire. Everyone looked a little bloated and red. The yearly game of *antakshiri* was going on. This is a game I have no idea how to play, and neither did any of the other kids. It involves knowing basically every Bollywood song there is to know. One team sings a song, and then the next team has to sing something starting with the last letter of the previous song. I mean, try this with songs in the English language and you'll see what I mean when I say that the game is impossible. And of course Rose and I, poorly educated as we were, didn't know any Hindi songs, but the grown-ups could keep this game up for hours. I mean, hours and hours. It probably would have gone on forever if it hadn't been interrupted. I was falling asleep on Rose's shoulder when there was a sound of breaking glass, and then raised voices. It was Mum and Dad in the kitchen.

'What's going on?' someone asked.

I was about to get up and run into the kitchen, but

Rose placed a hand on mine. I didn't have to look at her, she didn't need to say a word. I knew she meant for me to sit down and shut up.

There was more breaking of glass and then the sound of crying. Crying, then talking, crying, then talking. At first, when it started, people tried to keep on singing louder and louder, but this soon started to seem a little bit pathetic. So the TV was turned up really loud, but we could still hear. Not all the words maybe, but the tone, the crying.

'This is your fault,' we heard Mum say. 'If it hadn't been for the *nautanki*. This is your fault. Don't you see?'

'Let's talk about this,' Dad kept saying. 'It doesn't need to come to anything. It's just talk, nothing, no substance behind it.'

More crying. Lots of whispering.

'What can we do now? How can we change it now?' Mum.

'We can work this out,' Dad said. 'We can work this out.'

Uncle Jat patted my hand. He was drinking a cup of tea, with his pinky finger raised up. His soft cheeks were red and he was blowing into the cup before each sip. 'These things happen between couples. It is not a big deal. You can come and stay with us for the holidays if you like. Give your parents a break for a bit.'

He was always asking us to go and stay with them. And he didn't like it that Rose and I always chose to go to Trevor and Nani's (and Hannah's, which was the main point) instead of Uncle Jat's and Auntie Pinky's.

'Yes, yes, you must come,' Auntie Pinky said, nodding at her husband. They were looking at each other significantly, but I didn't know why. 'You can get a break from your *nautanki*.'

I was quiet. Uncle Jat looked at me. 'You don't like it? You're very good at it. I thought you enjoyed it?' I quickly shook my head. 'Why not?'

I shrugged.

'Rose?' he prodded. 'You hate it too?'

She nodded slowly. She was sitting in a vest top and tights, someone's red voile *chunni* tied around her waist like a sarong, her warm pink Christmas cardigan discarded on the floor. She was responding to Uncle Jat, but she was still listening to what was going on in the kitchen, her face pale.

'We can change it,' Uncle Jat said. 'We can make it more so that you like it. What changes can we make, do you think? Come on, tell me what you'd like to do. Does it get boring doing the same thing? We can change it.' He was talking to us in an extra loud voice, also keeping an ear out for what was happening in the kitchen.

I didn't say anything, I just shook my head. There was the sound of something breaking in the kitchen again. Rose slipped her fingers under mine and I gripped them. I wanted her to reassure me, say that it was nothing, but she looked more scared than I did.

A bit later, Dad came back from the kitchen. Perhaps he saw something in me and Rose, wedged together on the sofa, or maybe he needed this more than us, but he asked if we wanted to go for a walk. Normally we would have complained about being dragged out into the cold, but we quickly pulled on coats and boots, Rose her long dark pink quilted coat with its furry hood, me with Hannah's pea-green wool coat because mine had disappeared in a sea of coats. Hannah's was nearly all the way down to my ankles, and I pulled out some gloves from her pocket as we stepped out of the house into the frost. Rose had left her gloves inside so I gave her one of Hannah's. Rose had pulled a maroon hat over her long, dark hair and her face was white in the icy night, her nose pinched, but her eyes sparkling and her cheeks rosy in the cold air. She looked beautiful. I impulsively gave her a kiss on her nose. She giggled.

The cold hit our faces as we walked, our breath instantly visible. We walked away from the lights of the house, and through the trees of the driveway, crunching pebbles and leaves underfoot. We were nudging each other with our elbows, trying to push each other over. Rose was lifting up one side of my ear muffs and yelling into my ear. I could feel her warm breath.

'There's a famous *nautanki* about two sisters,' Dad said to us. He was wearing his quilted mittens, his parka, someone's enormous hat that had floppy bunny ears. 'Have I ever told you that one? It is about two sisters called Phool and Pyari. Flower and Sweetie. The girls both fall in love with the same man. Of course a lot of songs and comedy ensue, they fight each other, they pull each other's hair, they claw at each other's faces.'

'What happened at the end then?'

'Who got him?'

'In the end their love for each other is stronger than their feelings for this man. They decide to give him up.'

Rose sighed. The romantic one. 'That was the right thing to do.'

'It would be much funnier if they both married him,' I said. Not the romantic one.

Dad laughed, then he was quiet for a minute. 'Don't worry about anything, okay? Everything will be all right.'

'Is there something going on?' I asked.

'There is something, yes,' Dad said seriously. 'But it isn't anything you need to worry about.' His face looked tired, pulled down. 'We'll sort it out.'

'What is it about?' Rose said.

We stood for a minute under the large oak that we had decorated with bunting earlier in the day. Dad looked into the distance. It looked like he wanted to say something, but then he shook his head.

'It'll be all right. I promise.'

When we walked back to the house, Dad went inside and straight into the living room. Rose and I stood for a moment in the empty kitchen. The remains of the dinner were spread everywhere. Potatoes, vegetables, half-eaten Christmas pudding, dirty dishes and cups and cutlery. Foil was strewn around the kitchen, and someone had bundled a huge pile of Christmas-cracker detritus in one corner.

'They aren't going to get divorced, are they?' Rose looked distressed. Her imagination often ran ahead of her. I stared at her mutely. I couldn't say anything. I didn't think our parents were going to get a divorce. I had a horrible sinking feeling that that conversation in the kitchen had been about me. It had something to do with what I had heard the night before. *Am I bad*, I wanted to ask Rose, but I couldn't do it, I couldn't form the words. I couldn't ask her. I couldn't bear it if she said yes, I was bad, and I could bear it even less if she was kind to me, telling me of course I wasn't bad. I just grabbed her hands – one warm and one cold, like mine – tight in my own, screwed my eyes shut and said, 'You won't let them send me away, will you? You won't, will you?'

Rose laughed. 'You're such an idiot,' she said.

The next day I guess another thing happened of some significance but at the time I had no idea it meant anything. We were all sitting around. Everyone had eaten too much the day before, but we were still eating, in the spirit that it was too late to stop. I remember I was munching dates. I was gnawing on a hairy pit when Nani came in and whispered to Mum who was sitting next to me. She said, 'Renu, it's Gareth Jones.'

Mum looked quietly at Dad, and then they both left the room.

And that, sadly, is all I remember of this incident.

Over the years, it has occurred to me a few times that I should try to hunt for that last Christmas present Rose gave me. Every time it occurs to me, I go into a frenzy of cleaning. I look in places in my parents' house and my own things where I have already looked before many times, and I try to think of new places to look. But I've lost it. I've lost the last present she gave me. I keep thinking it'll turn up one day, in an old box in my parents' attic, in a drawer, somewhere. It hasn't yet. But I do dream of finding it though.

33

Dialling in My Sleep

For Plato, *eros* is not love of a person, but of beauty. In love, we don't just desire a person, but rather our love of a person is our quest for beauty itself. And this quest for beauty can never really be satisfied, it is never attainable. It is what Lacan might call the *objet petit a*, the sublime object, an unattainable love. A love that is always around the corner, around a corner that you can never turn.

Rilla's notes

In the middle of the night, I lie awake, staring up at the flickering fairy lights. I haven't slept in days, not since Jharna handed me that Post-it note. I've tried counting sheep, deep breathing, listening to a meditation app, I've tried wearing myself out with exercise, I've avoided caffeine and alcohol. Federico has been insistently asking me to go out for a drink, but I haven't even done that.

I do sometimes fall asleep, I haven't suddenly turned

into *The Machinist*, but just as soon as I fall asleep, I jerk awake. It's because the Post-it in my storage box makes a noise, I'm sure of it. It moves, it whispers, it calls out to me. Yesterday morning, I had woken up with sleep paralysis, my brain waking up but my body unable to move, and then I had dreamed that I got up, opened the box in the eaves, only to find that the Post-it was on fire. I was desperate to put out the fire, but I was paralysed. I couldn't move, and I could do nothing to save the list.

I look at my clock now; it's half past two in the morning. I spring out of bed. Well, fine, I don't need to sleep and if I can't sleep, I can use this time productively.

I start tidying my wardrobe. It's a mess! If Auntie Pinky saw the state of it, she would have a fit. I start tidying, but then realize that it is a much bigger job than I realized. I sweep everything out of my wardrobe and onto the floor. There, that's better! Now I can sort through everything. I glance out of my skylight. It's still dark, but dawn isn't far off. I keep on making mountains of clothes. Tops, leggings, dresses, skirts, tights, about a million pairs of jeans, cardigans, jumpers, coats, scarves (so many scarves!). I have way too many clothes. So a bin bag! That's what I need. Two would be better – one for what I need to throw away, and another for a charity shop. I also need Post-its to label the two bags so they don't get mixed up.

I fling myself down the stairs and head to the kitchen to find a bin bag. I bang doors open, I rummage, I juggle things in my hands then discard them over my shoulder. Where the hell are the bin bags? Does no one in this flat care how we live? Are we too bourgeois to have bin bags now, are we going packaging-free?

Federico's bedroom door crashes open and he springs out of his room, carrying a baseball bat in his hands, his knees bent, his eyes bleary but hyper-alert, his nightshade pulled up to his head.

'What!' he says stupidly. 'What's the matter?'

'Federico, shit, sorry.' I look at his face. He looks wild, his hair is standing up all around his head, he is glancing around him frantically like he's expecting a fire, a carbon monoxide leak, a burglar, a nuclear strike. I grimace. 'I thought I heard a noise, but I think it was just Lord Basingstoke. Sorry.' I mutter this excuse, not wanting him to see the real reason – that I was on a mission to tidy my room at four in the morning.

'Oh.' He lowers the baseball bat. 'It sounded like a herd of elephants fell down the stairs.'

Now he's awake too. I give up on the idea of tidying my wardrobe – or rather my floor, my wardrobe is actually shiny and clean now – and we sit down with several cans of Bass and listen to Rag'n'Bone Man. Neither one of us talks, but this is still the most time we've spent together in days. Or is it weeks? I know I've been absent, hiding in my room, not reaching out. I look at him guiltily. His face is kind of pale and pulled down, his eyes are red-rimmed. Since when am I so self-absorbed that I don't even notice my flatmate is depressed?

'Did you and your boyfriend break up?'

'My father died,' he says flatly.

I jerk up. 'Federico!' I whisper. 'No!'

His face is completely still for a moment, then to my horror it crumples.

'Oh, Federico!' I move closer to him, put my arms around him, and I don't know how long I hold him for but by the end of it we're both sobbing. 'Why didn't you say? Why didn't you tell me? When are you going to Mexico? Oh, Federico, I'm so, so sorry.'

Federico is trying to speak, but there is a sob caught in his throat. 'He got sick a few weeks ago. He hated me, he hated what I was,' he says finally. He talks through sobs, his voice cracked and broken. 'We used to scream at each other all the time. Or we did that half the time. The other half we would walk coldly, silently around each other, you know? When I was a teenager, he could barely stand looking at me, he was disgusted.' He sobs. 'When I left home I told him I would never go back. I can't go back.'

I hold a hand on his arm.

'Are you going to say, *You have to go back*, or, *He loved you*? Because I don't have to and he didn't. So don't say it!' He's looking at me with warning, his eyes begging me not to say it.

'No,' I shake my head, 'of course not. You should do what you want. You don't have to do anything you don't want to do.' I swallow painfully. 'Do what you want,' I repeat.

'What I want is to tell him is that he's a bigoted little bastard and I wish he'd got over himself.' He gulps down his beer. 'But I can't, can I? I'll never be able to tell him that.'

The tears are pouring again. I sit with him silently, shoulder to shoulder, listening to his tears, feeling the shudder of his body. I feel it for a long time, and then when he falls asleep on the sofa I still feel it. When his breathing is finally steady, I slowly get up so I don't disturb him, I cover him with a fleece blanket. I put a bottle of water by him and I place a couple of sturdy cushions on the floor next to him in case he rolls off the sofa in his sleep and crashes to the floor. I pick up Lord Basingstoke from the kitchen and place him in a comfortable puddle on Federico's feet. I look at them sleeping on the sofa for a few minutes, their breathing slow, both twitching a little as they dream.

Then I walk upstairs, I stand in my room staring at my eaves storage. I take a deep breath. I pull out the cardboard box, I bring out the Post-it and I dial the first number on the list.

'Could I speak to Rose, please?' I say, with not a quiver in my voice.

'This is Rose,' says the voice. It sounds impatient. I stare guiltily at the clock. It's six in the morning.

I clear my throat. 'You – uh – you're a man?'

'Yeah, and? I suppose you can't be called Rose and have a dick at the same time? Look, do you know what time I went to bed?' the man complains. 'Four. That's when.'

'I'm so sorry to bother you.'

'Call me if you need a stripper,' he says, 'but not for anything else. Get it?'

I end the call. Okay, not the most promising start. But

now the dam has broken. There is a list of Rose Joneses in my hand, and another in my deleted folder just waiting for me to retrieve it. There is nothing that is going to come in the way of my calling all of them. Every single one. My hands are working of their own volition, there is nothing I can do to stop them now, even if I wanted to. But I don't want to. It's the last thing I want to do.

A couple of hours later, with no leads, I make a few more phone calls and I say things like, 'I wanted to send Rose a birthday present. Would that be okay?' or, 'I haven't seen Rose in ages, I was in primary school with her.' Usually these questions are leading enough to tell me whether or not this person's Rose is my Rose. The person at the other end of the line tells me a birthday or an age that confirms it. At other times, I need to probe some more. These are circuitous conversations in which I try to sound convincing, and yet sometimes I still can't get the person on the other side to give me the clue that would confirm things one way or the other. But I persist. I persist until they let out some detail, anything that confirms that I don't have the right number. Not yet.

34

Lonely Wanderings

The next day I have a long line of undergraduates to get through during my office hours. I keep glancing at the clock, but time seems to have slowed to a crawl. Each student seems to want extra feedback. When I finally get through all of them, I can't get home fast enough. I walk quickly to New Cross Gate to get my train. I seethe every time it slows down on the way to Lewisham. At the other end, when I finally get there, I growl when my Oyster card takes longer than usual to register on the barriers. I practically run home.

When I'm finally, *finally* in my room, I call the next number on my list. A man called Jasper picks up the phone.

'You have a really sexy voice,' he says. 'Are you brown, black, mixed? I like women with dark skin. How about you come on over and we can have a proper chat about Rose?'

Soon after, a woman called Mabel answers and it is obvious from her voice that she has been crying.

'Are you a friend of Rose's?' she asks. 'She's so sympathetic. You sound really sympathetic too.' She tells me she has never had a boyfriend and asks me to guess her age. When I do, she says, 'No, guess again.' It takes me ten times to get all the way up to thirty-nine. 'A thirty-nine-year-old virgin,' she says. I want to give her Jasper's number. I have a feeling the two of them will have interests in common.

There is one time when the Rose on the list answers the phone herself. My heart stops as I hear her voice. The voice could belong to Rose. It is soft, taking tentative footsteps, like she doesn't want to disturb anyone, like she doesn't want to crease the air around her.

'Rose?' I say softly, chokingly. All the lines and questions I have prepared flee from my mind and I suddenly find nothing there. A blankness. I have nothing to say, nothing to ask.

'Who is it?' She says it patiently, even though I seem like a freak, calling someone and then not saying anything at all.

My heart pounds in my chest. What if this is Rose? What if this is *my* Rose? After all these years of imagining this moment, after all the hours I've spent recently trying to create it, I have no idea what to do.

'It's me, Rilla,' I say finally. What else can I say?

'Who?' she says.

There is no urgency in her voice, just a polite enquiry. It can't be my Rose. For her, the name Rilla would have the same effect as the name Rose has on me. When I hear the name Rose – even when people are just talking about roses – I can't breathe. Is it possible that she's forgotten, or that she doesn't care any more? Who knows what the years have done to her. Have the people she has lived with, grown up with, been kind to her? Has their kindness and love, perhaps even the love of another sibling, made her forget me? Or worse, has neglect or abuse been her lot in life and that has made her block everything from her other childhood, the one she was never meant to have lived? Am I the sister she was never meant to have?

'I was in primary school with you.' I clear my throat. 'I thought I'd reconnect.'

'Oh, how nice.' The voice is still polite. 'Do you mean primary school in Paris, or over here?'

Of course, the softness in her voice is the hint of a Parisian accent.

'I'm so sorry,' she says. 'If it was Paris, I have very few memories of that time. I was only five when we moved here.'

'Oh. Look, I think I may have the wrong Rose. Sorry about this.'

'Not at all. Lovely to talk to you anyway. Good luck with your search. It is a dismally common name, is it not?'

'Tell me about it.'

I hang up the phone. This Rose had sounded so sympathetic and nice. At that moment, I would have settled for a phone friendship with a stranger, that's how lonely I feel in this strange quest that I have started. Lonely. And alone.

*

Loneliness. I lie back on my bed. That's something I am intimately familiar with. So familiar that there have been times in my life that I have latched on to anything I could find just to fill the space next to me. Anything, or anyone. I wasn't lying to John Langton, Simon's father, when I said that I had been arrested before.

When I was a teenager, I was friends with a girl called Miriam. Though, the word 'friends' can have all kinds of meanings, I suppose.

Miriam was quite pretty. She had long ringlets that seemed to have a life of their own, doe eyes, narrow hands and feet. She didn't walk, she swayed, she didn't talk, she sang. It was like the air tinkled when she passed through it.

I was often in trouble at school for being defiant and starting arguments with teachers that escalated into shouting and screaming (on my part), wearing make-up, jewellery, piercings and short skirts to school, bunking classes, smoking and, on one occasion, being in possession of marijuana leaves. But Miriam took things further. She broke things and stole from the school, she was devious in ways that I could only aspire to. And then she could cry on demand, she could look at you like she was the most innocent girl in the world and you were mad to think otherwise.

I liked getting caught. Because of course what was the point of causing trouble if no one found out? I spent a lot of my time in detention and in the head teacher's office, many hours in discussion with the person I had wronged, talking it through, apologizing, shaking hands . . . My school was big on that kind of thing, reconciliation, they called it, and if that didn't work I was sent to the behaviour centre where I was counselled, warned, threatened – whatever worked. Nothing much did. I wanted to be at odds with the world, so being warned of the consequences I would incur if I did something or other was only an incentive. I was in trouble a lot more than Miriam ever was. If someone caught me, I would shrug and accept the punishment. If someone caught Miriam, she looked outraged that they would even think she was capable of whatever it was they were accusing her of. She looked so convinced of her own innocence that it was difficult not to believe her.

There was something unhinged about Miriam, I often thought, something dark, and I was definitely a poor imitation, a pretender. But she was a good partner in crime and in any case I didn't have many friends, I didn't hang out with anyone else. Once, when we had spent hours in counselling – separately – for a particular indiscretion, and we were waiting outside the counsellor's room to get some paperwork, I broke down and made the biggest mistake of my life. I told Miriam about Rose. I had never done that before. But for some reason – I have no idea why, these things are not rational, maybe because I was distraught or tired or looking for attention as usual and Miriam always used to get more than her fair share – I told her about our *nautanki*, and how our parents sent Rose away because we used to fight. I used to hit her, I told Miriam, I used to scream at her. I was horrible to her, I said.

Almost right away, Miriam started blackmailing me for money. *I'll tell everyone about your sister Rose*, she said, *I'll tell everyone that you're not an only child. I'll tell everyone you have a sister.*

I don't know why this felt like the darkest hour to me, people finding out about Rose. It was the worst possible outcome, the thing that I could not even contemplate. Rose was in my heart – there was nothing outside of that, no one knew, no one at all. In our family we didn't talk about her and she may as well have not existed. Sometimes I wondered if she was a constructed, artificial memory. Maybe I had had such a lonely childhood I'd made her up. Maybe she was an imaginary friend, my imaginary sister Rose, and my family didn't talk about her because she had never existed, because they didn't want to set me off again, pander to my delusions, take me over the edge to schizophrenia.

I couldn't bear for people to find out about Rose, to talk about her like she was someone on the news who had been arrested for something or a celebrity who had been drinking and driving. I couldn't stand the idea. So I started working weekends – gardening, doing the newspaper round, whatever I could find to do – to keep paying Miriam, to keep her quiet, to keep her from revealing the worst of me to everyone. I know Mum was worried that I was spending the money I earned on drugs, because I never seemed to have any. But no, Miriam took all of it. I gave her every last penny.

You would think that would have been the end of our

friendship. But no, I still used to hang out with her. I don't understand kids, I really don't. To be friends with someone who is blackmailing you for money, that sounds pathetic. But despite the dark secret that underpinned our friendship, Miriam and I carried on being friends. Sometimes we even managed to have fun together.

That was the year that the Bollywood actress Shilpa Shetty was on *Big Brother*, and Miriam thought it really funny to say the things that had been allegedly said to Shilpa Shetty to me. And she was pretty good at making up more things to say. The word 'Paki' was too easy for her really. She got over that one pretty quickly. *I hope you've washed your hands, Paki*, she'd say. *Before you eat. Don't want shit getting everywhere. You smell of curry, Indian girl. Have your parents found you a boy to marry, brown girl. You weren't born here, Sharmilla, so you won't understand our ways. Oh, you were born here? Then why do you talk funny, why do you look funny, why do you smell funny?* I stood all that. It filled me with rage but I didn't do anything about it. I was too ashamed to tell anyone what was going on; it meant admitting that it got to me, it meant admitting that I was different from everyone else. And anyway, if I told a teacher, then Miriam would tell them about Rose.

One day we were in the toilet. No one had complained about my make-up yet that day, so I was applying more. It was clearly too subtle. I drew a large red bow on my mouth, I spotted my cheeks with lipstick and rubbed it in, I put sparkly eye shadow on my eyelids. I was putting pins in my skirt to make it shorter, when Miriam started her usual nonsense in a sing-song voice. I never knew when she was going to do it. There was never any warning. One minute we'd be talking about this or that teacher, or doing our make-up or missing class, the next minute it would start.

You're not an only child, she started. *You had a sister. Your parents used to sell you to people and make you do shows. Your parents used to prostitute you. You're such a slag, Rilla, you enjoyed it, didn't you.*

And then she decided to go a little further. She wasn't even looking at me. She was just doing her make-up in the mirror.

And then you killed her. You killed your little sister. She's dead, Rose is dead. She's lying under a tree somewhere, totally dead. She's so dead that her face has already been eaten up by maggots. You'll never see her again.

I didn't know I was going to do it before I did it. I lunged at her, I grabbed her throat and I started to strangle her. I meant to kill her, I swear it. I can feel the rage now. I meant to kill her, I meant to choke her to death.

She looked shocked, totally and utterly shocked. Her face was going purple, her lips and eyes bulging, her ringlets wiping the bathroom floor dry.

I'll kill you if you say anything like that again, I said. *I am going to kill you, do you hear? Do you understand what I'm saying? Tell me you understand what I am saying.*

She was trying to nod her head even though she couldn't breathe.

We were found before I could choke her to death and the police were called. Of course I told no one why I had done it.

Still, Miriam never said a word to me ever again about anything. And she had bruises for weeks.

35

Digging into the Past

The problem is that now, all of a sudden, I need to know. I need to know what has happened to my sister, where she is, why she disappeared. I can't think of anything else. The wasted years are weighing on me. I can't eat and I can't sleep. When I lie in bed, I feel twitchy and restless, obsessively glancing at the time to see if it's okay to start on my list again. Why, why have I wasted all these years?

Jharna keeps giving me phone numbers, and I keep calling. I am getting obsessed with it. I sneak glances at my lists all the time, on the tube, walking along the pavement to the corner shop, during tutorials with my undergrads, and many times when I'm supposed to be reading or writing.

But after several days of trying, I'm having no luck with the lists. I need more information, Jharna needs more to go on.

I finally give in and call Jharna, and ask her to hack into

Dad's email. I am not proud of it, but I do it. She manages to hack into it almost before my conversation with her is over, that's how good the woman-child-wizard is.

I sit on my bed in the attic room, computer on my lap, feeling totally ashamed. I stare at the laptop for ages, not having the courage to go on. When I do finally look, I feel so ashamed that I look through most of his inbox with one eye shut. I really don't want to read any more than I have to. I feel worse about this than snooping through my mother's email. She leaves her inbox open, so she can't mind that much if someone sees her emails, but my father's is protected by passwords and such, and it has actually been hacked into at my decree. So yes, I feel ashamed. I feel like a worm, a Judas, a snake in the grass.

There are a lot of emails from his publisher. A lot of really boring conversations, with various different people: editors, proof-readers, cover designers, tour bookers. It is interminable. There would be less of this stuff, but for each email from his publisher there are ten back from my father, giving lengthy explanations for why things in his book should be this way and not that way, why there is a rationale for this kind of cover and not that, why the index should be presented in that way and not this, why italics should mean this, why words in bold should mean the other thing. And not only does he give his own opinion but he also cites research (with references and quotes) to explain his thinking. Predictably, there are also a lot of emails from various members of the GIF – Uncle Promod trying to get Dad to invest in what he calls 'a mind-controlled toilet flush', Auntie

PK sending him petitions to sign to make it a crime for van men to leer at women, Auntie Pinky writing several times to complain that Mum won't give her her samosa recipe, so would Dad please send it to her?

In fact, I find nothing current of any importance at all. I keep looking though, remembering that with my mother's email I had to go a fair distance back. And then something interesting jumps out from a few years ago. The emails exchanges are with a lawyer whose name is Sheila Jenkins. There are only three such emails, and they are all to discuss various dates on which there are hearings. Hearings about what? Hearings, like legal hearings? That's what it sounds like. In the emails, there is no clue as to what the hearings are about. Why do my parents have a lawyer I know nothing about? What have they done that they need this lawyer to represent and defend them? My heart beats painfully. I close my laptop. Why don't I know anything about this? Is this the lot of all snoopers: to find out things about people in your life that you had no idea about, that make you question not only who these people are, but also who you are? Knowing nothing about the people near you and close to you?

'There is a Rose Jones who poisoned her own child.' The next day, Jharna calls me again. I am alone when she calls, because after many phone conversations with his mother, Federico has now flown to Mexico. 'She put poison in the child's milk. I'm guessing that's not your Rose Jones. Then there is an author and composer, an environmental scientist, a few school teachers, a woman that bakes cakes for her church fund-raisers, but all too old. There are various obituaries of grannies.' Jharna has come up with a new list. 'It's all quite vague.'

'Where are you looking?'

'Medical records, various other lists.'

'How on earth can you get into medical records?'

'I can't all of the time,' Jharna says. 'Some are compli-cated. But – you know—'

The girl can hack into medical records. This is insane.

'Can you find out something about Sheila Jenkins? She's a lawyer.' I tell her the firm that was referenced in the emails. 'Not sure she still works there, though. It was a while ago.'

'I'll give it a go,' Jharna says.

She calls again the next day. 'Sheila Jenkins doesn't work at that firm any more. You know, the one you gave me? But they specialize in civil cases. Divorces, settlements, custody battles, that kind of thing.'

For some reason this makes my heart beat faster. This should make sense to me, but it doesn't, not completely. I have a strong feeling that Sheila Jenkins is something to do with Rose, but I can't piece it together and the effort, this groping in the dark, makes me feel faint.

Jharna gives me a couple more phone numbers for Rose Jones. 'This one is really promising, and she lives in London. Do you know why she's so promising? Because she has the same birth date as you!'

I nearly fall over. 'Really? Are you sure?'

'Yup. Dead cert.'

'Thanks, Jharna, that's really great. Same birth date. Two years older?' My heart is pounding. Surely, surely, this has to be Rose. I close my eyes tight. I want it so badly, yet I can't bear it.

'Yup.'

I haven't actually seen Jharna in person for a few days. Our conversations have been on the phone. 'So,' I say, 'how've you been?'

'Sorry I haven't popped over. I'm grounded.'

'Oh, so sorry to hear that. How come?'

'Mum and Dad found a couple of joints in my room. I mean, who does that, right? Can you imagine, searching in your daughter's room like I'm a convict or something?'

'Yeah, that's really shit. So, you're grounded for a month or two? That sucks.'

'Oh, no, just a week.'

A week? Do Uncle Jat and Auntie Pinky not care about their own child, the light of their life? This stinks. What is the world coming to?

Then as I'm sitting cross-legged on my bed, looking through Jharna's new list, I get a phone call. It's my mother. I stare guiltily at the phone, then at the list in my hands, then back at the phone again. The knowledge of what I have been doing behind my parents' back hits me. For a second, I think, *She knows!* My heart starts racing. But then I force myself to breathe. She can't know. My mum can't know what I've been doing.

'Hello,' I croak, as I finally click on the phone and take the call.

'Rilla, *beta*,' she says. She sounds unlike herself, her voice soft and tentative. For some reason, my heart starts pounding in my chest. For some reason, just for a second, I think she's going to talk about Rose.

'You – you won't end up alone, will you?' she says instead.

'Not this again, Mum.' I sigh wearily. For heaven's sake, will people stop asking this question that makes it sound like I'm dying?

'No, wait, Rilla, I just – it's just I don't want you to – even if you don't want to be with Simon – which I don't really understand – but if you don't, I hope you won't turn away from love altogether.'

I'm surprised at what she's telling me, at the tone of my mother's voice. I'm so surprised, I can't say anything. I stare blindly at the list in my hands.

'Okay,' I say finally. 'Anything else?'

'Rilla. . .' She says my name, then she says something, something that I barely hear, something whispered that seems to be stuck in her throat. I think she says, 'Is it because of me?'

I'm stunned. I can't believe what I'm hearing. I hold the phone closer to my ear, my heart pounding even harder now, and screw my eyes shut. I have so many things I can say to that. I can say, *Mum, let's talk about this*, or, *Mum, thank you for saying that*, or even, *Say more, Mum*. Actually even, *I can't believe you said that*, would do. I'm completely shaken up, because here is an opening, here is something I've been waiting for all my life that I've thought would never come my way – an opportunity to talk, to start slowly, slowly to heal. But habits sharpened over a lifetime are hard to shake off. So instead of all these things that I can say, I blurt out, 'Did Dad put you up to this?'

As soon as I say it, I know the moment is lost, and since it has taken seventeen years for my mum to say something like that, it may be that I never hear such words again. I clutch the phone, wondering what I can say now, but it's too late. My teenage self calls back the mother of my teenage self.

'Rilla, really it's like you deliberately want to hurt me.'

I growl under my breath. 'Sorry, okay? Got to run. I'll talk to you later.'

And I click off before she can say anything more.

36

Sometimes It Fails

In the *Bhagavad Gita*, love is devotion to all beings. And life is about *karma*, about knowing why you are doing something, doing it with everything you have, and not dwelling on the outcome. Doing something with love, for love, and for nothing but love. Even if the end result is failure.

Rilla's notes

A Rose Jones, whose birthday is two years before mine. The same date. That's all I can think about. The day after Jharna tells me about this woman, I walk out of my house in the morning, my shoulders squared, keys, phone, water bottle in my bag, ready to face whatever this day brings. I must do this, and I can. *I can!*

I get as far as the park across the road, and find that suddenly my feet feel like lead. I slow to a crawl, then I come to a standstill. I'm lucky that there is a handy park bench behind me, because my knees buckle and I sit heavily

298

down. I stare blankly across the street towards my flat. I crumple the piece of paper that is in the pocket of my jacket.

What if *this* is my Rose? What if this is it? What if today is the day, and there is no going back?

And what if it isn't? a treacherous voice whispers. *What if I build this up in my head, and then it isn't my Rose, after all? What if I never find her?*

As soon as this thought enters my head, I bend double and bury my face in my hands. I can't think like this. *I can't!* I can't think about any of it. I just have to keep going. There is no way I can stop this quest. Not now. It's too late for that. This flood that has started can't be stopped.

Yet the terror of discovery, of finding answers – *any* answers – the terror that has been building in my chest for days, lying there dormant and unnamed, it threatens to choke me now. I take heaving breaths, my face still in my hands, my body shaking.

'I can't do it,' I whisper. 'I can't. Please, please don't make me.' I have no idea who I'm beseeching, but I know this. No one is listening.

After many moments of sitting there, unable to move, or sense, or see anything, I finally hear a distant whir. I sit up slowly, and I see Earl in the distance, doing laps on his mobility scooter. He gives people a queenly wave as he passes, his hand twisting this way and that like a weather vane.

'Oh, Earl,' I hear myself say with a catch in my voice. Despite myself, I can't help a quivering smile at the sight of his white hair floating behind him like a banner.

I sit there for some more moments. And I know. Living in this terrible uncertainty is no longer an option.

I take a deep breath and stand up. I walk to the train station, take the train to New Cross Gate and then the overground to Dalston to find this Rose Jones.

When I get to Dalston, I walk out of the tube station and stare all around me. I can't remember the last time I've been to Dalston. It seems the place is going mad with murals, words, colour, faces, animals jumping out of seemingly every wall. I try to look at the area like this is any other day. If I were here on a normal kind of day, on an average kind of mission, I would see it, I would notice Dalston, its strange mixture of grunge and graffiti, vines and head scarves, Shoreditch and steampunk, jazz and rage, dreadlocks and performance art. I try to breathe it in.

From the train station, on the way to the address that Jharna has given me, I stop at a shop in the wall called Can Hatch that sells a million kinds of craft beer and I buy a water. For a moment, as I take a sip of the chilled sparkly drink, I just want to sit down there on the pavement, drink my water. I want to carry on pretending, for a few more moments, that this is any other day. But then, almost against my will, I start walking again. My footsteps slow as I get closer to my destination. I find myself in a residential street, narrow brown-brick period houses lined up shoulder-to-shoulder like toy soldiers, neat trees planted every few metres, covered in blossoms – white, pink, purple. Rose Jones's place has creepers crawling up the walls and a pretty yellow door. I take a deep breath, and turn my back on the house, just for a second, to steady myself.

I do a double-take.

Across the road from Rose Jones's house, there is a large brick house and there are people hanging off windows. I don't mean this as any kind of euphemism, they are actually hanging off the wall of their house. I tell myself it can't be real people, it must be mannequins. But they *are* real! What are they doing? Is it performance art? Or is this just the Dalston way to socialize with neighbours? I blink, wondering if all the sleepless nights are catching up on me and I'm finally losing it.

I shake my head, feeling a little disorientated having seen this strange installation of people. It's like I've stepped through the looking glass. I turn back around and stare at the yellow door again. I stand there for fifteen minutes before I can bring myself to ring the doorbell. A black woman stands there. She is wearing a floral dress, a belt around her comfortable waist, her hair is in neat curls and she is wearing a blue hat with a hairnet. She is on her way out.

'I'm sorry to disturb you. I'm a friend of Rose's from primary school,' I say, trying to steady my shaking lips. 'My name is Rilla.' I've said the words so many times now, I sound like a zombie when I say it. It is the least convincing thing I've ever said in my life.

And in front of my eyes the woman starts crying. She

doesn't make a sound when she cries. There are two streams of tears coursing down her face. She stabs at them with her handkerchief but they just keep on coming.

'I'm sorry to tell you this,' she says in a soft Jamaican accent. 'Rose passed away. It would have meant a lot to her to know that you were looking for her.'

I freeze, I'm numb, I can't feel anything at all, faced as I am with this woman's grief. This isn't my Rose, this can't be my Rose. I know it, because I know she is alive. I would know if she were dead, I'm sure of it. I stare at the woman, the tears running down her cheeks.

Then my brain tells me something else, adding to my conviction. Rose wasn't adopted by a black family. So this can't be Rose's family. But then suddenly I panic, I search my mind frantically for *why* I imagine I know this. How do I know that Gareth Jones – if I am right and he had something to do with Rose – is white? I realize that there is nothing, no kernel of knowledge in my head, there is no evidence. I have assumed Gareth Jones is white, but for all I know he could be black. And how the hell do I even know that Rose was actually adopted or if this is a story I've made up for myself?

'I'm sorry.' My voice is steadier now because I can't feel anything about this news. Because this can't be my Rose. I have my life to sort out, and the only way I can sort it out is if I resolve what has happened to Rose. How – how can I do that if she's dead? My voice is steady but my breath is shallow.

A man joins the woman in the doorway. He puts an arm around her.

'You said you knew our daughter?' There is hope in his voice, hope that I somehow, at some point, knew Rose, and it is as heartbreaking as the woman's grief. Like the woman he is dressed smartly: a striped shirt, neatly pleated trousers, a tie, shining shoes, and a hemp hat that makes him look like he's going on a safari. He is white, tall and bulky, his shoulders stooped, heavy pouches around his eyes. His accent is Scottish. And on his shirt pocket there is a 'J' embroidered.

'My wife and I were just going to visit Rose's grave – we would be honoured if you would come with us.'

'No.' I say it abruptly, almost like the word flies out of my mouth before I can stop it. But when it does come out it sounds no more than a whimper. 'No,' I say again.

I stare at the couple. I can't do this, I can't visit their Rose's grave.

'I'm sorry.' I turn around, start to walk away. I have to get away, as fast as I can.

But the man calls from behind me. 'It must be a shock. Please.'

I stop and slowly turn around.

There are tears in the man's eyes. 'Please,' he says again. 'It would mean a lot to us.'

I clutch my skirt. The plea in his voice, it's impossible to ignore, to walk away from. I nod mutely.

The three of us start walking. The graveyard is nearby and we are there in a few minutes. When we get there I realize I have no recollection of the journey, no memory of turns, road names, signs, the weather, shops, nothing. For all I know, I have walked there through a vacuum. It is a mild morning, but I can't stop shivering.

The graveyard is pristine, the grass neatly trimmed, the flowers staying safely inside their neat enclosures. There are gravestones of all kinds, plain ones, ones that are in the shape of angels, others that look like a plinth, one has a skull on it and I notice with shock that the person who lies beneath it was just a child when they died. From not noticing anything at all, now I can see, hear and feel everything. There is a dry crispness to the air, the sound of a car driving by, with loud house music playing. A squirrel stands on two feet, beats its tiny hands, looks at us, twitches, then bounds off. There are two robins tweeting on a gravestone, there are flowers everywhere. Rose's mother bends down once or twice and pulls out weeds that she drops into a plastic bag that she is carrying. And then we are there.

I stand by the grave. It is a simple stone. *Rose Jones*, it reads. *Beloved sister*, it says. It says her birth date, my birth date but two years before mine, and it says the day she died. Just three months ago. I have missed her by three months. *No*, my mind says, *no, this is not my Rose*. I have to stop thinking like it is.

I watch Mrs Jones clearing the gravestone. Mr Jones walks around it, brushing a hand here, dusting with a hanky there.

A panic is growing in my stomach and a realization is beginning to hit me.

I understand now that I have always known I will never see her again. I have always known that, deep down.

Of course she is dead. There was never any question of seeing Rose again. Never a chance that we could be sisters again.

For a second, just for a second, I'm relieved. My shoulders slump, I take a shuddering breath. I'm relieved. Only for a second, but it's there. Because if she died all those years ago, then it wasn't because of me that she was sent away. It isn't that I was horrible to her, that I resented her, that I was jealous of how beautiful and perfect she was, and how imperfect I was. The *nautanki* hadn't come between us. Something else had happened.

But then I shake my head. I shake my head hard. This Rose died three months ago. I can't have it both ways. She can't have died when she was nine, and died three months ago, at age twenty-seven. I stare at the couple.

Mrs Jones has placed her bunch of tulips on the grave and she is moving around it, pulling away the grass that is trying to creep closer. 'She was a gift from heaven,' she says.

Now Mr Jones starts to cry, not like the woman, not with silent streams down his face, but with great wracking sobs. He sits down at the foot of the grave and his body shakes uncontrollably.

'She came to us when she was so young, so pure, her hair in a long plait. We promised each other then that we would treat her like a gift, like a miracle. And we did, didn't we?' the woman says. 'We did.'

She crouches down next to her husband. In the face of her husband's grief, the woman's tears have stopped. She places a hand on her husband's back.

She came to us when she was so young.

'She was adopted?' I whisper.

'Yes,' Mrs Jones says. 'But she was ours.' She looks at me with eyes that are soft brown velvet. 'We knew it the moment we saw her. She gave us the courage to adopt again. We have one daughter left now.'

'What was she like?' I ask. 'When she came to you?'

'She was gentle,' Rose's mother says. 'Gentle as a rosebud. She looked like she could see things that others couldn't. She couldn't bear to hurt anyone. She couldn't bear it if anyone got hurt. It was like it hurt *her*, you know, it was painful for her.'

And I screw my eyes shut. No one who knew my Rose could fail to see that about her. It was the one defining thing about her. She couldn't bear other people's pain.

'She is in heaven, a better place,' the woman says. Mr Jones is quiet now, and they both sit there hand in hand.

'Do you remember the time Amelie broke your vase?' the man says. 'And Rose kept saying it was her?'

The woman smiles. 'Even though it was clear to everyone that it was Amelie.'

They tell me more stories, but I don't respond because I can't hear them clearly, I can't let them in, these people and their stories.

'You said you knew her?' the man asks me finally.

I nod. I can't say who she is. The words are stuck in

my throat. I can't bring them up. Sister is a word that will forever make me choke.

'She looked just like me,' the woman says. 'Don't you think?' she asks.

I look at her uncertainly, I don't know what she means.

'Rose?' the woman says, inclining her head towards the grave. 'Her personality was different from mine though. I shout and yell when someone crosses me, Rose would never have done that. She would hide in the cupboard when I yelled. She was tall and long, not short like me, but she was the one that used to hide!'

I shake my head. This doesn't sound like my Rose. She was nervous in one way, but she wasn't someone who hid in closets. Then I hear myself, the words going slowly through my brain. This isn't the thing I should be focusing on, that Rose hid in closets. This isn't the thing. But there is something else. There is something I should be focusing on, something that has been said, but I can't call it to mind. But then there it is. *She looked just like me, don't you think?* I shake my head to try and clear the numbness. I look at the woman. 'She looked like you?' I say stupidly.

'Well, no,' the woman says. 'Her hair was long and wavy. Not like mine. And she was tall. But her eyes were just the same as mine.'

I stare at the woman's eyes. 'If she was adopted,' I say, my voice sounding strange and unnatural, like it is coming from far away, through a tunnel, 'how – how could she look like you?'

'She was my sister's child,' the woman says. 'She looked

so much like my sister, and my sister looks a little like me. Don't you think, Germaine?'

The couple stay for a while, saying nothing, not crying now, calm in the moments they spend with their daughter, but finally they leave. They make me promise that I will visit them. I watch them leave, all the way through the gravestones, all the way out of the gate, walking slowly, supporting each other.

I sit by Rose Jones's grave. It starts to rain, slowly, hesitantly. I see the fat drops on the stone first, then I feel them on my head, making their way down my face. There is a blue jay not far away, looking for worms, stopping, looking up, hopping again. It is April, it is spring, but there is a quietness in the air, the kind you have when it snows. Everything resting, subdued, the world unnaturally still.

I have had to carve a life for myself without my sister. Why have I had to do that? Why has there always been a hole where my Rose should have been? Why did we get seven years together, why do that to us just to take it away? It makes no sense. I would have done better as an only child from the beginning, I would have had a chance. I wouldn't have raged at everything. I wouldn't have felt this loss, an emptiness next to me where there should have been something. Where there should have been Rose.

I have this memory. No, it isn't a memory. It probably happened so many times that it isn't one memory, but a feeling, a bodily remembrance. A memory of sleeping, with another person next to me, curled around me, behind my back that is curved like a comma. I remember a feeling of utter safety when Rose was there, sleeping on our double bed next to me. And I would wake up sometimes and she would have slid further away, just by a few inches, and I would panic. *Where is she, where is she?* I would think. For some seconds, in the darkness, I wouldn't be able to see her. But then shadowy outlines would become clearer and I would see that she was there, not far, just further up the bed. And I would roll closer, nearly pushing her off the bed, I would fit my back into her tummy and she would put her arm around me in her sleep and I would know that as long as she was there nothing bad could ever happen. The memory is as clear now as the stone that I am sitting next to. Actually it is clearer because I can feel it in my bones. The stone is hazy. And I have a yearning so sharp, so clear, to be back there, to be entwined and entwinned. I would do anything to be back there, in the place where I was whole. I lie down next to the stone. I curl up into a ball and I squeeze my eyes shut.

When I finally sit up, when there is some feeling in my fingers, I dial a number. Whatever it is he hears in my voice, Simon reacts to it. He is with me in twenty-five minutes, it's some kind of record. No one can get anywhere in London in that time. It takes longer to walk to the corner store. I see him walking through the gate, walking quickly to me. He is wearing brown cords, a shirt, and I realize that he must have been at work. But I can't say sorry, I can't say anything at all. I just look at him.

He sits down next to me, he doesn't say a word, his shoulder pressed to mine.

'I had a sister,' I say. 'And I have no idea where she is.'

And I cry. I cry like I've never cried before, like I've never allowed myself to cry at the loss of Rose. He holds me and he doesn't ask questions. And I tell him everything.

Two hours later I am standing outside my parents' house. When my father opens the door, I utter the words I should have been allowed to say years ago.

'Dad,' I say, 'where the hell is Rose?'

37

Maybe I Don't Want to Know

I felt guilty as a child and that has stayed with me as an adult. I know the feeling so well, it's almost a being-Rilla feeling. Without the guilt, there is only emptiness. And with emptiness comes panic.

And the guilt. You already know about the guilt.

I feel terrible for every time I was mean to Rose, and there are lots of those times. I feel sick about it. Sick and hopeless. I feel even worse about what happened with my mother soon after Rose disappeared. Dad's words creep into my mind when I think about that time, and I keep trying to shut them down. *You know what nearly happened, don't you, Rilla, you understand? You and me, we have to be careful now. Very careful, you know that, don't you?*

I try my best to shut my mind every time I remember that. I try to think of something else, I tell myself I'll think about it later.

*

311

I stand outside my parents' house, alone now. At the train station, in Dalston, I had said goodbye to Simon. And being Simon, he hadn't argued. He hadn't said, *You can't be alone right now, Rilla, you need me.* He hadn't even asked me to call later and tell him what happened with my parents. And I hadn't made any promises either.

I take a shuddering breath and knock.

My father lets me in. He has been listening to Radio 4, while doing something on his laptop, checking something else on his desktop and watching an old episode of *Silent Witness* on the television. He is in his shirt and tie.

'Going somewhere?' I ask.

'Meeting. With my editor.' He is eyeing me warily. 'Rilla, I can't do this. You know that.' His voice is gentle, but not in a kind way, more in the way of someone trying to prevent a missile attack.

I nod slowly. My hands are stuffed in the pockets of my skirt. 'Yes, Dad. You made that very clear to me.' I had checked with him before I came here, made sure that Mum wasn't home. 'But I'm not leaving till you tell me, do you see that? I want to know where Rose is. You can either tell me now, when Mum isn't home, or we can wait and I can ask her.'

His face changes. It pulls inwards, his cheeks go hollow. He smoothens his hair, fiddles with the collar of his shirt, his oblong face looks a little lost. He glances about him for a second like he doesn't know where he is and I feel a pang of guilt, but I stuff it down. I stuff it down because this isn't the time for it. And I've let that guilt lead me by the nose for too many years.

'You have to ask them,' Simon had said as we sat at a stranger's grave. 'You have to ask.'

'Rilla, you know I can't,' Dad says again.

'No!' I feel the rising panic. I can't let him talk me out of this, not like he did all those years ago, I can't let him shut me up. 'I need you to tell me where she is. I want to talk to her, I want to see her. I want us all to stop acting like she's dead. Or that she never was. That's how you two do it, you know that? You act like she never existed!'

Just for a second, my brain says, what if this is the real truth – that she never existed and there is something irreparably wrong with me, something that makes me invent things that weren't there? I can imagine a self that would conjure up a sister like Rose, a sister that would make me less lonely.

I shake my head violently. 'I need to know.'

'It isn't that simple, Rilla—'

'I don't give a shit.'

'Language, Rilla. There's no need—'

'There is a need! And it's right now. Tell me right now.' And then the tears that started at a stranger's grave start pouring again. This is what I have been afraid of all my life, that once the tears start I won't know how to turn them off. 'Please,' I say, 'you have to tell me.'

Now that I've asked, it's like I can't wait a moment longer. I have to know right now. And the fear that my father might still not tell me, that he might say or do something that makes me shut up again, is choking me. Through my tears I tell him about the Rose Jones whose grave I visited.

Now Dad is crying too. I have never seen him cry. We are both standing in the living room crying, not touching each other, not reaching our hands out. Just standing alone, each in our own circle of memories, a hopeless bubble, and we are crying.

'How do you know her name is Jones?' he asks finally, wiping his face.

'Something someone said. I can't remember who,' I blurt out.

I can see him thinking, I can see his mind working away. He looks smaller suddenly. His shoulders look thin, there is so much grey in his hair, and the skin on his cheeks is hanging down, pulled as if by weights that are permanently attached.

I can't bear to be still, it's like I am going to burst. I pace the living room.

Dad finally seems to make up his mind. He shrugs and something changes in his face. I know now that he will talk, he will tell me. I'm not sure how much, but he will tell me something.

'Okay, I'll do this. I'll give your details to them and we'll ask them if they'll give them to Rose. And we'll have to take it from there. But you have to promise me, not a word to your mother? Unless you promise me, I won't do this, do you understand?'

I nod. It's more than I expected.

'The thing is,' he says, 'they moved to the States a few years ago. That's something you should know.'

'Okay. Okay.'

Now I have nothing to say. I feel deflated. My tears have stopped and there is just emptiness.

'Gus-Gus,' I say suddenly. 'Where did Gus-Gus go?'

'With Rose,' Dad says. 'He went with Rose. We thought – we thought it would help her.'

My shoulders slump. I'm relieved, glad that Rose had Gus-Gus. I'm glad, more than I can express, and I'm filled with gratitude – to hear that Rose is alive.

38

Not the One I Want

A common theme in *nautanki* is of a princess who is kidnapped or who gets lost as a child and is raised by a farmer or a villager. Inevitably the child will grow up and through overcoming many obstacles they will be restored to their proper place. No matter if you are raised a pauper, if you were born a princess, then that is who you really are. The idea is that you always go back to the beginning – you go back to the place where you started.

Manoj Kumar's book, *Nautanki and Other North Indian Curiosities* (working title)

As I leave my parents' house and head south on the train to my flat, my heart is slowly beginning to fill with something, something that I can't immediately recognize. Hope, perhaps it is hope, but the feeling is so alien that I have trouble naming it. Gus-Gus went with Rose, yes, that's good. That's what I have always thought and hoped for, I realize now. Rose had Gus-Gus. And I – I have a chance with Rose. A smidgen of one perhaps, but for the first time in all these years, it's there.

I wait and I wait. Every time my phone beeps my heart starts racing. I think it is Rose, I think it will be a message from her. Every morning I wake up and I think today will be the day I hear from her. I walk around campus, half dead to the world, incessantly checking my phone. My undergraduates have to prod me sometimes, in the middle of a meeting, because I have lost my train of thought. I can feel Tyra watching me, eyeing me. I can see her wondering if I am completely losing it. Every night I lie in bed tossing and turning, troubled by dreams, convinced that now I've taken this big step and set things in motion, she won't want to know me any more, she won't care.

But then one day, when I'm sitting on my bed, unable to read my notes, to focus on my work, unable to see anything, there is a message. All it says is, *Hi. Dad gave me your number. If you want to meet me, I'll be at the Wild Food café at Neal's Yard tomorrow at noon. R.* It's from an English mobile, not an American number.

I run into the bathroom and throw up. I sit on the floor of the loo for what feels like hours. I've left my phone in the bedroom, I can't bear to look at that message. It takes me a long time to come out. I sit next to the phone for ages – or maybe it's a lifetime – wondering how I am going to get through the day, survive until tomorrow. I have no idea how to face this, I have no idea what to do. I find myself thinking odd thoughts, wishing for strange inconsequential things – that I'd had a haircut recently, that I had lost the two pounds I promised myself I'd lose after Christmas, even that I had made more progress in my MA so that I could tell Rose about it.

I shake myself. What difference does it make how I look or what I can tell her! Will she even be interested? Will she care?

But I know what it is. It isn't about how I look, about what I have done. The truth is I want to do better this time. I don't want to push her away and lose her again. I want to *be* better. I want to be a better version of myself.

Or maybe – maybe what I want is to be a completely different person.

The next day I can't breathe as I sit in the café. I'm there at eleven. It is a miracle that I managed to wait that long before going there. I keep asking for lemon and ginger tea. I must look like I'm dying because the server looks sympathetic.

I have no idea what this will be like. I've imagined this scene a hundred, a thousand, a million times. In my dreams, we sit together and we cry. We hug and we can't let go. We can't speak for hours, days, weeks, all we can do is hold hands. Because what can we possibly say to each other that will be enough? I miss her like a limb, I miss her like there's only half of me left without her.

Finally, ten minutes after twelve, when I'm getting ready to burn the place to the ground, the door to the café opens.

And it's Rose. Exactly as I've pictured her. Long black hair, dewy skin, and those sad, slanting eyes. She's wearing a long white skirt, down to her ankles, and a turquoise tank top. There's a necklace around her neck, made of a series of threads in different colours, twined around a cord with a plain round stone pendant hanging from it. I swallow painfully. I'm ready to cry, hug, not talk, whatever it is sisters do when they have been torn apart. She slowly walks in, she looks around the café with a hesitant look that I recognize so well it takes my breath away. And then she spots me.

There's a pause, just for a second, as she is silhouetted against the door. Then she slowly walks towards me. I stand on the spot, paralysed, yet my heart thudding at full speed like a race horse. She clutches her skirt in her hand for a second.

'Rilla?' she says softly.

For a moment she stands in front of me, looking at me. But suddenly after the initial recognition, I have no idea how to read her eyes. I used to know every nuance but now, somehow, I realize I've no idea what she is thinking.

Then strangely, like in a slow, repetitive dream, she holds out a hand to me. I stare at it. I think I jerk my head quickly, suddenly, but I'm not sure. I have no idea what to do with Rose's hand. It is as if it is disconnected from her body. It's as if my brain and body are not coordinated. Then some automatic part of me reaches out and touches it briefly. It's so brief my body has no imprint of the touch of her hand. The sister I haven't seen for seventeen years wants to shake hands with me.

'How lovely of you to contact me.' Rose's voice is soft, so soft, I almost can't hear it. I want to lean closer, but her eyes are so distant that I can't. Her eyes are someone else's eyes.

'This is civilized,' she says as we sit at the table. She sits there for a few moments, clutching and unclutching her hands. She looks at me uncertainly. I still can't say anything. She gives me an awkward, tight smile, she busies herself, moves things around on the table. She moves her bag an inch, puts her denim jacket straighter on the chair, she settles herself like a cat, little steps, little movements. For a second, I think she has forgotten I'm there. 'It was nice of you to contact me. Dad said you wanted to get in touch and he said I could decide what I wanted to do.'

Dad. She means her dad, not mine, not ours.

'Dad said you'd moved to the States,' I say finally. It comes out like a croak. I try to clear my throat. It's a painful sound. I glance at Rose to see if she has noticed, but I can't tell.

She orders a blackcurrant *chai* with almond milk, and a salad. 'Dad and I moved there a few years ago. We live in San Diego.' She gives me a tight smile, a little crease in her lips. 'I'm in London for a little while.'

'Why?' I blurt out. This sounds stupid, an odd question to ask, but I can't elaborate, I can't make it sound like a sensible question.

She doesn't say anything for a few moments. The waiter brings her tea and salad, but she doesn't touch either. She looks down at her food, but I don't know if she can see it.

'Maybe for old times' sake,' she says finally. 'But mainly for work.'

'Work?'

She smiles nervously. 'How strange this is.' She shakes her head quickly, a little gesture aimed at something in her head, nothing to do with me. It occurs to me suddenly that it's like I'm not here, it's like she's following a script. 'I'm an assistant for a documentary filmmaker – Talia. She moved to London recently.' She stops for a few moments, finally takes a sip of her tea. 'You? What do you do?'

I blink slowly. 'I'm not really sure.' I clear my throat again but I can't make my voice sound normal. 'I'm doing an MA. I guess.'

She picks up a sliver of carrot and nibbles at it. 'How nice.'

Thankfully she doesn't ask me to explain, because these hollow croaks, this is all I have.

'What's your documentary about?' I ask.

'About old British families that have royal blood. You know, the kinds of lives they live.' She stops abruptly. Now she is struggling for words too, she's playing with her salad. I am torn because all I want is to get away from her, I don't want to see and hear her, I don't want to hear the things she is talking about. I don't want this Rose. But at the same time, I can't bear to let her go. She looks at her phone in one of those moves that people make when they are about to say goodbye. If I don't stop her, she will leave.

AMITA MURRAY

I can't think of anything to say that will keep her here. I search frantically. Finally, I ask her about the man she calls Dad.

I want to say to her, *Why were you adopted? How is it possible? It makes no sense, no sense at all.* I want to say to her that her life doesn't make sense. I want to scream that my life doesn't make sense. But I don't.

'What is he like?' That's all I can manage.

'Oh.' She looks a little surprised. 'He's nice. He lost his wife a while ago. He was single for a long time but he has a girlfriend now. She works in a human rights charity, wears her hair in long braids and dances to James Brown every evening with a glass of merlot in her hands. Zoya, that's her name.'

She says it all like a list. I stare at her. Perhaps the indifference isn't as real as it looks. She's playing with the sachets of sweetener on the table. She looks up at me from under her eyelashes, just for a second, then down again.

At least it isn't as bad as I have sometimes imagined. In the odd moments that I've wondered about Rose being adopted, I've thought, has her new family been nice to her? I can't bear to listen to stories about abusive parents because in every story I find Rose. I see her in every tale of parents that neglect their children, beat them, shout at them, bully and abuse them. I've dreamt of Rose locked up in a basement, seen her in my mind left on her own in a house, alone and afraid, imagined her falling asleep by herself, hugging a teddy to her, crying into its fur. I

322

should be glad, I should be glad she seems to care about her father.

'Gus-Gus,' I say suddenly.

She flinches like I've slapped her, she clutches at her arm. There's the little jerk of the head again.

'He died a while ago,' she says finally. She doesn't elaborate, she doesn't say anything more. She is not looking at me. 'Could I possibly have a refill of my tea?' she calls suddenly.

She waits patiently for the waiter to clear her teapot, cup, strainer, plate of barely-eaten salad. She waits for him to bring her another pot of tea. She touches her hair, looks up at him with those dewy eyes of hers, she laughs with him. He blushes.

She doesn't say anything for a bit when he's gone. Then, 'I hope he doesn't think I was flirting with him.' She says it not lightly, but with a degree of discomfort. I lean a millimetre closer, I study her face.

I remember this now, all of a sudden, this thing about Rose. Her way of checking in with me when she's unsure of something she's done. She used to do it as a child. What will this teacher say of something Rose did in class? What must Auntie Dharma think of Rose's remark on something or the other? I would tell her not to be silly, and she would feel better. But right now I have nothing to offer. I don't want to make her feel better. But I am watching her like a hawk now, after that innocent question. I'm staring at her, every contour of her face, the way her hair sways in a wave about her face and then falls down her back. I'm looking for more signs of the old Rose.

'Do you have a boyfriend?' she asks.

I hesitate, then shake my head. 'You?'

She shrugs. And then I see something in her eyes, another little something that reminds me of the old Rose. A glimpse of something. But then I realize with a jolt it doesn't remind me of the old Rose, it reminds me of me. That little flicker around the eyes, the uncertainty. She seems confident in the things she says, but her eyes, they watch, they are forever watchful.

Someone had used a phrase in conversation not long ago, someone on campus. Hyper-vigilant, they had said. It was Sarah-Lee. And I see it all of a sudden in Rose. She's talking, smiling, she is good at making small talk with the waiter, better than she realizes. But she is watching, protecting herself. She notices the door open, she notices who is in the café, she notices the people that walk by and look in, she sees every move I make, she looks carefully at people to see how they will react to her. Will they stay or will they leave, will they be kind or will they hurt her? And I realize that when you have lost someone the fear of loss becomes a part of you. You are always waiting for people to leave. And this is as much a part of Rose as it is of me.

For the first time since I've seen her, this – this watch-fulness in her eyes – it gives me the shivers, but it also gives me hope.

39

Isn't It Ironic

In theatre, there is a surplus of signifiers. Not only do you get words, story, and emotional drama, but you also get costumes, masks, make-up, props and sound-effects, to overwhelm your senses, immerse you in the experience so that what you witness is not real life but so much more than that. In *nautanki*, one of the biggest accessories is music. Music makes *nautanki* what it is. It is the *shahnai* (like an oboe), the *dholak* and *nagara* drums, and the loud, high-pitched singing that tell the audience how to experience a scene, an emotion, a character, it gives the audience room to laugh and cry, yell and scream, cringe and cry again.

Manoj Kumar's book, *Nautanki and Other North Indian Curiosities* (working title)

The next morning I wake up in my bed, and everything is the same as it always was: the room, the bed, the park across the street. Yet everything is different.

Sometimes there is no going back, there is no undoing. There are some things you cannot and should not unravel because on the other side lies madness. I now know that I have lost the last seventeen years forever. I don't know why I've always imagined that we would pick up where we left off, Rose and I. I don't why I have always thought that she would have the same feelings about me as I have about her.

Yesterday I walked back from the café, took the tube, then walked again through the streets of Lewisham knowing that, although I had found her, I had finally found her, my sister was a stranger. I entered the flat in a daze, ignoring the missed calls from my dad. I lay on my bed, awake for hours, but hardly moving, not tossing and turning, but unable to move, feel or think. I had to pinch myself to make sure this wasn't a nightmare.

But over the next few days, I find a new resolve. I have to take things slowly. The reunion I have imagined all my life isn't going to be mine, but my Rose is in there somewhere, I've seen her. She didn't want me to but I saw her in there.

So I have to pace myself. We have all the time in the world to get reacquainted. There is no reason to rush or to push, to get a reaction out of her that would make me feel better. For once, I have to make it about her, not about me. Just for once, I have to let her breathe.

Because I am wrong to think that I don't want this Rose. The truth is I want any Rose that I can have.

*

We're walking in the grounds of the Horniman Museum in Forest Hill and Rose is singing along to Madonna's 'Like a Virgin'. There are children and families everywhere, doing treasure hunts, eating at the farmers' market, getting faces painted. They're banging on outdoor glockenspiels and reaching out to hairy alpacas. From my memory, I pull up a Bangles number, in response to Rose.

When we were little we had two wigs. Mine was long, red and curly, Rose's was short and yellow with a fringe. We used to put them on, along with long strings of fake pearls in white and pink and grey beads, white dresses and pointy shoes, and we'd jump up and down on our beds and sing, holding the insides of toilet rolls as microphones. We are re-enacting this now, as we walk together, minus the wigs and the paraphernalia.

'Wait, wait, wait, what was that one? "All That She Wants", how did it start?'

Now we're both screwing up our faces, trying to remember. But in the end we can't.

'Like a tra-a-a-in on your wedding day, it's sweet lice when you're already dead . . .'

This is what I have resolved to do, remind her of the good times. And there are moments when it feels like it is working, where I see that we can reconnect, we can form some kind of relationship. The moments come and go, they vanish quickly, but they are there, briefly.

We've eaten hot dogs in the farmers' market, drunk hot chocolate and now we're nibbling on a rocky road between us. We are milling through the crowd, walking down the twisty bends, past the football pitch under the trees.

Would we be here if we had grown up together? What would we be doing right now? Where would we be? How often would we see each other? Who would I be? Would I be doing an MA in philosophy? Are our parallel selves in a different life, in a life where we have grown up together, walking this same walk in the grounds of this particular museum? Do I see our ghosts? Would my hair be the same, would Rose be wearing a red skirt and a white blouse, the many tinkling bangles on her arm punctuating every move? Would there be a tiny foot with yellow nail polish on its tiny toes in the pocket of my blue cotton skirt, from one of the women in Federico's model village?

'Do you remember that time when we went to Brighton and this giraffe you had—'

'Fell over the pier and into the water!' I screech.

'You were ready to jump in after it,' Rose says.

'You grabbed my knickers so I wouldn't jump off!'

'And they came off!'

'One of my less graceful moments. Anyway, they didn't come off, they tore off. I had no underwear on for the rest of the day. I was so mad at you, I nearly scratched your hair out.' I shake my head at the memory. If I close my eyes, I can still hear the squawks of the seagulls.

'I actually did scratch you on your cheek,' Rose says.

'No, you didn't,' I say quickly.

'Yes, I did, you had the marks for a week.'

It's funny, but I don't remember that bit. I try to think

back to that day. I can feel the salty sea breeze, I can see my giraffe, Harold, so clearly, soft and big and spotty and orange and brown and white with soft pointy ears and stubbly legs. He smelt like my bed. I was running down the pier, holding him over the edge, pretending he was water-skiing behind me, cascading over the waves. I was screaming and laughing. And I remember the exact moment he went over. I remember thinking for a long time that all I needed to do was retreat one moment, go one second back into the past, and I could hold on to him and not let him go. I remember nearly going into the water after him and I remember the feel of Rose's fists in my hair. But I have no memory of the nail marks on my cheeks.

'Are you sure?' I frown.

'Oh, yes. Remember that time I bit you on your thigh? Because you'd coloured my doll's hair pink and blue and purple? No, wait! You'd cut it and *then* coloured it pink and blue and purple! And I screamed at you and bit you? You howled and howled.'

I can't remember this. 'No, no memory of that at all. I remember the doll though. Sophia, long blonde ringlets, big blue eyes. It used to wear a pinafore. Gingham.'

'Yes!'

In the crispness of this beautiful day, we lie down on the grass. There are so many memories, I think to myself. No, I tell myself, there are far too few. And even the ones we have, we have different versions. I remember Rose as the one who was kind. I was the mean one, I was always the mean one, but she reminds me of things that I can't recall, things that fall into place, missing pieces of my jigsaw that curl a ribbon around the two of us that reads 'Sisters'.

Before heading to the museum we had stopped for a moment in the studio flat that Rose was renting in Sydenham to pick up a light wrap. It was an attic room like mine, and this thing we had in common – though fleeting and completely coincidental – had given me a moment of secret joy. Of course she would have an attic room!

She had disappeared into the bathroom for a few minutes and I had walked around the small room – a living area and kitchen rolled into one – reverently touching things, standing in front of Rose's things that she had carefully placed around the room, making it her own space even though it was temporary. I had felt intensely grateful for being allowed in, for this glimpse into her life, small and brief as it was. So far we had only met in cafés, outdoors, in safe anonymous spaces. But now, I felt as I walked around her flat, I had this. Even if only for a few stolen moments.

There was a deep green sofa-bed, a work chair, a desk with a desktop computer (I like desktops too, better than laptops, I thought). There were pages marked in yellow and pink highlighter stacked neatly, a series of colourful pens, Post-its in many shapes. Stubbly rounded cane chairs dotted the room, cushions in Indian block print, and prints on the wall: a Klimt, a Vettriano, a Brontë sisters set. I had stared at the Brontë sisters. Three silhouettes of women, with shadows of their main works embossed on them – *Jane Eyre*, *Wuthering Heights* and *Agnes Grey*. Oh, Rose, I had thought as I stood there, of course it *would* be the Brontë sisters!

There were cacti everywhere. One had three large leaves with curvy striations. There was a skinny thorny one with large pink flowers exploding along its length. And a cluster of five, each with a thick phallic stalk, with floral fingers emerging from the top – coral, fuchsia, a green entwined globule, a purple, a snow-white.

Just a few moments more, I had thought when she came out of the bathroom, just give me a few more minutes here.

Lying on our backs in the grounds of the museum, we talk for I don't know how long. The things we chat about, the memories we dwell on, are safe. We have not yet mentioned the *nautanki*. That one doesn't feel like a safe memory. It happened in the last year of Rose being with us, when we were together. But we have not talked about that year at all.

'I used to hate that bloody *nautanki*,' I finally blurt out. My heart beats painfully, I don't know why. Aren't these just some more memories? What is wrapped up in the *nautanki* that makes us avoid it like the plague? I honestly have no idea. But I can feel the familiar knot of anxiety in the pit of my stomach.

'I know, but I could never understand why. You were a natural at it,' Rose says.

We're both on our backs, staring up at the sky. I am tracing the clouds with my fingers.

'Prince Rup. You were so good. I used to think you'd grow up to be an actress.'

'I remember thinking that the first couple of times.' I squint my eyes. 'But *nothing* would make me go on stage again. Can't stand the idea.'

'You were hilarious, I was so jealous.'

I turn onto my side and I stare at her. '*You* were jealous of me? That's a ridiculous thing to say, and you know it.'

She turns onto her side too. Mirror images, almost. Propped up on our arms, legs slightly curved, mine mostly bare in my short cotton skirt, hers covered in a skirt that goes all the way down to her ankles. Black hair, mine in rough waves down to my shoulders, hers straight and almost down to her hips, with a natural ripple and shine to it. Skin tone slightly different, hers cream, mine honey. Her limbs bony and long, mine shorter, broader. The same slanting dark eyes.

'That's just a lie,' I say. 'You were never jealous of me, I was madly jealous of you! You were so beautiful, you were all anyone could talk about. The family was always going on about how beautiful you were, how tall and fair. And you are, I get it, so why wouldn't they? But man, I had had enough of listening to it. You in your sparkling clothes, and that tiara of fake roses that someone had made for us. Who was it? Auntie Dharma?'

'I think it was Hannah actually. I was madly jealous of you, Rilla. You were the one with the lines, the funny ideas, you made people laugh so much, tears came out of their eyes the minute you started talking. I used to have to try so hard not to laugh, watching you doing your antics on stage. I would have done anything to swap roles with you.'

I shake my head. This is crazy, these are not my memories, this is not my version of the truth. My picture doesn't look like this. How can the me of today reconcile with these images Rose is giving me? How can I slot in these memories that change the shape of mine, and yet be me?

'I can't imagine a world in which you are jealous of me,' I say. That is the plain truth. I eye the remains of the rocky road, sitting on a white paper bag. I pick at the cashew in it.

'You were such a brat. You were always running off,' she says.

'You were always following me. It was the most annoying thing in the world.' I take a nibble of the cashew.

'Oh, please,' Rose says. 'You wouldn't have made it back from half of your stupid adventures if I hadn't dragged you back.'

'I know that. Annoying all the same.' I automatically, without thinking, hand her half the nut. Then I suck in my breath. It was what I used to do as a child. She takes it, not so automatically. I know she remembers too.

'It wasn't just that,' she says quietly. She nibbles slowly at the cashew. I remember that too, that she could nibble at a little morsel for an hour, if there was no one to rush her. 'I was taking care of you, but it was something else too. I hated being without you. That's why I followed you.'

I swallow. I've never, not once, thought of it that way. But somehow her saying it now, now when everything is so fragile, is more than I can bear.

'How come I never took care of you?' I say quickly.

'You did. Not in the same way. You'd stick up for me with Mum and Dad.'

I remembered that. You could always count on me to shout and scream when the occasion called for it. Even when the occasion didn't call for it, come to that. If Rose was in a fight with Mum and Dad, she would go quiet, her chin would tremble, she would start shaking and I'd be the screamer and turn their wrath on to me. That was usually the way.

'I don't know that I was taking care of you. Sounds like I was just trying to get all the attention.'

Then I realize it. She said Mum and Dad. That's the first time she's said it. She is tracing circles in the grass with her finger. I can't tell if she realizes what she said. I don't know what to do about it, what to say. The day I saw Rose for the first time in the café, Dad had called me later on and we'd had the most stilted conversation in the history of conversations.

'All right?' Dad had said.

'All good.'

'Everything good?' I heard him clearing his throat.

'Yup. Fab.'

'Rilla . . .' he started. He paused, coughed. 'How are things?'

'Fine, Dad, really, fine.'

'That's good. Very good. Okay, then.' He waited the space of a few heartbeats that I couldn't fill with words, not for the life of me. 'Take care, *beta*.'

'You too, Dad.'

What do I do now? Do I talk about them or do I avoid the subject? This is so precarious, I have to take things slow, I have to be careful not to say the wrong thing. I am trying to take tentative footsteps. When we talk of safe topics, I see her. I see my Rose. She is there, inside, behind the slight American accent, underneath the polite smiley-ness that is Rose Jones. Rose Kumar is in there somewhere. If I can steer clear . . .

'How are they?' she says.

I take a deep breath. 'You know how they are. Mum cries at everything.'

Rose nods slowly.

'Dad is working on his book on Indian street theatre. He has a publisher.' There's a little flicker in her eyes when I mention the book, but she isn't looking at me so I can't be sure. Rose doesn't know about the book. The Dad I know, the one After-Rose, is not the same as the one During-Rose. The Dad she knows wasn't a writer, a chronicler.

'He kind of disappeared after . . .' I say, 'he kind of disappeared. I didn't see a lot of him growing up. He was working on this book on *nautanki*. You know all the research he used to collect? It's taken ages, years. And it had become a bit of a family joke. *Manoj is working on his book*, everyone used to say, with lots of significant looks. But he's made something of it. An academic publisher is going to publish it. Mum – she kind of disappeared for a while, too, actually.'

It wasn't the same way Dad disappeared, not into the study. She disappeared in a different way, but I can't tell Rose. I want to, but the words will choke me so I don't say them. Instead I take a leaf from her book. I stick to something safe.

'Mum teaches Life in the UK. She tells people chicken tikka masala is the national dish. They don't believe her and they think she only says that because she's Indian. She tells them that the scientist Christopher Merret invented champagne in 1662, that Ian Fleming called Bond 007 because of a Canterbury bus route, and that the Ghost Research Foundation says that York is the most haunted city in the world.' I pull grass out of the ground. 'Do you want to see them?' I ask.

She shakes her head quickly, she doesn't even think about it. I don't blame her. If my parents had given me away, I wouldn't want to see them either. I wouldn't forget and I wouldn't forgive. And if my parents had given my sister away? I wouldn't forget that either.

I tell her about Auntie PK and Auntie Dharma, Uncle Jat and Auntie Pinky, Auntie Menaka and Uncle Promod. I tell her about Jharna. I tell her I speak now and again on Skype to Hannah who lives in New Zealand and works with local women to make Kiwi handicrafts.

'She wears a long dress and a pendant that hangs down to her belly button.'

Rose smiles. 'That sounds like Hannah.'

I ask her again about her 'Dad'. She tells me about their life. They live not far from the sea in San Diego where Rose went to university and studied film-making. She has recently helped make a documentary about old Spanish houses in California. They lived in Bristol before then, she tells me. It's strange to think of Rose in Bristol. Not that far, really, all those years, but yet so far away that it may as well have been another world. She tells me about Gareth's girlfriend Zoya some more, about Gareth, who does interior design.

'He's quite good. He's good at gleaning the history of a place. He uses historical design, even myths and legends, to design houses. It's quite interesting. He's clever.'

Was he nice to you? I want to ask. Did he care about you? Did he play with you, read to you, spend time with you, take you out, buy you birthday presents, know what you liked and what you hated? Did he hear you when you told him things? Did he remember what you said the other day? Did he *see* you for who you are?

Yet I don't want to know. She sounds like she cares about him and this hurts. I don't want Rose's childhood to have been lonely, I don't want her to have suffered, I want her to have felt loved, secure, like she belonged. But this easy way she has of talking about Gareth, I can't stand that either. How can she have a father that I don't know? How can she have a father that I don't share? Memories that are no part of me, memories of which I am no part. It isn't right. It isn't fair.

40

A Million Reasons to Die

The next morning Jharna drops by. She's wearing a 1950s-style red polka dot Rockabilly hairband in her hair, denim shorts and a knotted white shirt.

'I'm not staying,' she says to me. She's standing awkwardly at the door, she doesn't want to come inside. She hands me a square of garlic chocolate. 'I found some, since you wanted to try it.'

'Sounds totally disgusting,' I say. 'Have you tasted it?'

She doesn't say anything. 'It's just. . .' She's avoiding my eyes. This is unusual for her.

I reach out and lightly touch her chin.

'The thing is,' she says, 'now that you've found Rose, well, the thing is this. I was wondering if I can still come around.'

I incline my head. 'What?'

'It's just you have Rose now. I get that. But you're the closest thing I have to a sister. It's cool if you don't have the time—'

I place a hand on her shoulder. 'Listen, Fountain, stop being such a sap. Come around Monday after your exam. I have plans for the model village. And when I say plans, I mean *plans*.' I look at her significantly.

She grins. 'I'll be there.'

'And do well in your exam, or Uncle Jat will kill me.'

She shrugs. 'Obviously I will.'

As I'm standing on the porch, watching Jharna disappear towards the bus stop, Earl sweeps past the house.

'Hey, Earl!' I call.

He waves. 'You look happier than I've seen you in a while, Rilla!'

I smile, shake my head. 'You know how I am.'

His hair is flowing in the breeze, he is wearing a brown check shirt, black billowy trousers, braces and a deerstalker hat.

'I'm courting a lady today!' he tells me.

'No way!'

'Yes, way! Life is empty without a partner, Rilla. You know that!'

I shake my head. 'I'm no good at that sort of thing, Earl.' I lean on the porch railing.

'You don't have to be, Rilla. You just have to put one foot in front of the other.'

I need to take Simon to meet Rose. I don't explain it to him, because what can I say about something for which there is no explanation? I just need him to meet her.

Because the truth is I can't imagine how anyone would prefer me to Rose. I can't imagine that anyone, once they've seen Rose, could ever want me. So I need to get this over with. This thing, this impending moment that I have always dreaded. This core belief that everyone, anyone would love Rose more than they could ever love me.

So I take him to meet her. He doesn't ask me questions. This is the thing about Simon. He doesn't say, *Oh, why are you taking me to meet your sister, we aren't even together.* Or, *Does this mean we're back together, you're giving me mixed signals.* He's Simon, he never says things like that.

We meet at a café in Kensington. I watch them like a hawk the entire time they talk. Rose is being her sweet self, with that polite veneer I'm already getting to know, and Simon is making jokes about something or other. They're talking about Brexit, they're talking about Trump and they're talking about the news. Simon shows us a funny video on YouTube. There are cats doing funny things, a monkey riding a cat, a toddler climbing over two baby gates and making his escape. Rose is laughing. Simon is telling her about Lord Basingstoke.

'He's starting to walk in arcs, isn't he?' he says to me. 'We're making progress. You just have to nudge him a little bit now and he can actually almost pee in the litter tray.'

Does he notice her tall willowy-ness, her long black hair, the way she looks up at him from under her eyelashes? The way she has of being hyper-conscious of her surroundings, yet at the same time the knack she has of hiding it, of pretending that she is easy everywhere, that she belongs anywhere? How can any man prefer me? Anyone with their head screwed on right would immediately want to hold her and protect her and want to keep on doing that for the rest of their life. As they talk, I watch their every move.

Eventually Simon has to leave. He is about to bend down to kiss me, but then he remembers that we aren't together. I see it in his eyes.

'Later,' he says. 'Good to meet you,' he says to Rose.

Rose and I walk out of the café after he's gone. We walk over to Kensington Gardens and we sit on a park bench. There is something about sisters that makes them end up on park benches. People whizz past us on Boris bikes, others run with their dogs, speed-walk after their runaway children, talk into hands-free sets. It's a breezy afternoon. I shiver slightly and pull my jacket closer around me.

'Let's go away somewhere,' I say suddenly. 'You know, like a trip. We could go to Paris or Bruges or Barcelona! Have you been to Barcelona? I really want to go. Or Corfu! Let's do that. Maybe we'll spot dolphins!'

She doesn't say anything for a while. 'I'm leaving, Rilla.'

'What do you mean?'

'I'm going back to the States.'

'For how long?' I'm disappointed. I want to see her every day, I want her to move into my flat, I never want her to be out of my sight ever again. But I can work around this. 'How about after?'

'I'm not coming back.'

My heart stops. I make a strange jerky motion with my head. 'I don't understand.'

She isn't looking at me, she's looking down at her hands. 'The thing is, I don't know why I came back. My boss was coming here, but I didn't have to. There were other projects in the States I could have done. I came because I had this idea, of going back to my childhood—'

'You told me.'

She shakes her head. She's quiet for a bit. 'I wanted to reconnect with you and it was the right thing to do. And now we've done it, so I can go back.'

'Why?' I say stupidly. I shake my head. 'I don't understand. Why? You don't need to move back. You'd get a job here. I don't get it.'

'I just – I'm going back, Rilla. That's all there is to it.'

'That's all there is to it?' I stand up, in front of the bench. 'Actually you're wrong! There's a bloody lot more to it than that. There's a shitload more, I'd say. You come here and you talk to me like we're basically strangers, with that fucking polite smile of yours and that American accent, and you talk like we were friends at school. Do you remember this, and do you remember that? And we walk in the park and we sing songs. And there are moments when I think – when I think we can go back to who we were, and then those moments are gone and I keep feeling like I have to tiptoe around you so that you won't disappear. But you know what, Rose *Jones*, we weren't friends at school. I was willing to play your little game, but don't tell me you're leaving. This is total, utter rubbish!'

She's quiet, she hates conflict.

'Don't go quiet on me. You're not moving back. We have so much – we have so much to catch up on.'

She shakes her head. 'There are some things that can't just be mended because you need some kind of closure.'

'Closure!' I practically scream the word. I startle a pigeon that has been clacking about around our feet and it flitters a few feet away. 'I don't want *closure*!'

'Well, that's what I want,' she says quietly, gracefully, ignoring that I am ready to tear myself to pieces. She stands up, she looks at me, though I can see she doesn't want to. 'That's what I wanted and I have it. It was great to see you. You look really well. You're gorgeous.' She gives me a strained smile.

I can't speak, I have nothing to say that won't result in my utter collapse. I have nothing to say that won't result in me trying to throttle her.

'You can't do this. You just can't. Don't you care?'

'Of course I care,' she says. 'How could I not? But – you have no idea how it was for me.'

'I can imagine it.'

'No – no, actually you can't. Nothing much changed for you. I get it, you lost me. But other than that nothing changed. I was sent away, not you. *I* was sent away.'

'I know—'

'No, you don't. Because you can't.' She is staring into the distance, not looking at me. 'I was sent away. I was sent to live with someone who I had never met before. You don't know what that was like. You can't know. He

343

was kind to me, don't get me wrong. He was grieving his wife and he was kind.' She's quiet. She's struggling with herself to keep her composure.

'I don't want you to imagine that he was horrible to me, because he wasn't. He – he didn't have much of an idea what to do with a child though, he didn't have a family around, only a sister who lives in Sydney. That's where his parents – my grandparents – are too. Think about how it was for me. I was surrounded by people all the time with you, and then – there was no one, just Gareth. A new school where people already had friends, a new town. And when I came back home I had hours and hours every day when I was on my own. Gareth was at work, so I had a baby-sitter looking after me. She was this teen-ager who used Gareth's phone to call people all the time. Lindsay, that was her name. I clung to her. She was the only one who spent time with me. She used to do my fingernails and she used to put make-up on us, and we used to get dressed up. Gareth would come home from work later in the evening and we would sit in front of the TV and eat dinner. Quietly, never saying a word to each other, completely silent. It was like living in a tomb.' She stares at her fingernails for a long time, clipped and plain like mine. 'Don't get me wrong, I know people have it worse. I'm not sorry for myself.'

I couldn't breathe. It was like Rose to say that it was okay, it was fine. But it wasn't. It was the opposite of fine.

'Dad – Gareth thought it might be better if we had a fresh start. He decided to move to the States, but I had

344

an even worse time there. I wanted to kill myself. When I was a teenager, I did try to kill myself. I used to cut myself on my arms, my thighs. It's to cope, it's to manage anxiety, my school counsellor said. She's doing it as a coping mechanism. But the truth is I couldn't cope, I wasn't coping at all. I was just too much of a coward to cut deep, that was all. How can you possibly understand?'

I want to tell her about how it was for me when I was a teenager. Fighting everyone and everything, wanting to destroy things, hurt people, at war with the world. But now is not the time. And perhaps it never will be.

She looks pale and pinched. I want to reach out, touch her, hold her, anything she'll let me do, but there's a wall there. She's telling me things I don't want to hear, she's giving me memories that I don't want to have. But there's still a wall. If I reach out and touch her, the wall will harden and she will retreat behind it further.

She shakes her head again. 'I took care of Gareth. He needed me, he had no one. And he was heartbroken after his wife died, she was so young. He was so young.' She works the fringe on her bag.

'There should have been someone taking care of you.'

She shrugs. 'All I'm saying is, I can't go back. I've learned to cope now. I'm better at it than I've ever been and I'm not going back. Not to this fractured existence where you can't reconcile anything because no two threads can be entwined together.'

A fractured existence where you can't reconcile anything. She has described me so perfectly I want to write it down.

'I'm fractured without you, though, that's the problem,' I say softly.

She shakes her head. 'This will help, our spending some time together. And we'll write and email. It won't be like before, there won't be a complete void. We'll have that. Maybe, in time. But I can't do more. Please understand. I know it's hard for you to understand, but I have to take care of myself. I can't go back to who I was. I can't, do you see?'

There's a look of desperation in her face, she wants me to understand, but I can't. I can't understand, I can't give her this. I can't give her anything.

41

One Reason to Live

When we were four, a teacher at school asked our class to walk over to a bunch of dolls and pick the one that looked like us. It was a progressive school and the dolls were all manner of colours, ranging from vanilla white to the darkest of browns. And there were ones with short hair, long hair, curly hair, one that wore dungarees, carried tools, and so forth. I mean, they'd gone to town with their doll selections. Rose picked one that had creamy white skin and long brown hair. I picked a perfect blonde doll with blue eyes. In my mind, I suppose I picked Rose, the fair-skinned tall one who was always good and kind to people. Rose isn't blonde of course, but in my mind she was perfect, and everyone else saw her as perfect too. I suppose I picked the one I wanted to be like.

'She's leaving, she's going back.' I can't even cry when I say it. I can't look at anyone or anything. I sit slumped on a chair in my parents' living room. I'm numb, I can't feel anything at all.

'Maybe it's for the best,' Dad says. When I called to say I was coming over, he told me that he had spoken to my mother this morning, he had told her that I had met Rose.

Now they are sitting side by side on the sofa. My mother's hands are folded on her stomach, over her paisley top. My father has placed his hand next to Mum on the sofa, not touching, but in touching distance. What does he think she will do? And so quickly that he might not be able to reach her? I resent this, this protectiveness that has defined my life, this minding of my mum's feelings that has silenced me for most of my life.

'How?' I snap. 'How is it for the best? You did this. You did this to me, you did this to us. I don't understand how you could have done this! Why, why did you do it?'

'Gareth Jones is Rose's father, Rilla,' Dad says quietly.

I take a shuddering breath. I rub my face for a second. 'She isn't my real sister, is she.'

And I realize that I do know this. I haven't known it till recently, but my brain has been piecing things together, things that I haven't wanted to admit, even to myself.

'We had a rough few years after we got married,' Dad says.

I am waiting for Mum to pull out her hanky but she's doing nothing at all. She is staring at the ground. There is a lost look on her face that I can't bear, that is horribly familiar, so I look away. I look resolutely at my father.

'The family was at us to have children. There was a lot

of pressure. A lot of spoken and unspoken censure that we hadn't conceived.'

'But you were so young. What was the big deal? It was none of their business.'

'They don't see it that way. In their eyes, it is exclusively their business. We got married, even though the family wasn't sure of me,' Dad says. 'I wanted to be an actor, as you know. It was a stupid sort of thing to want to be. They tried to talk your mother out of the marriage, for a long time. There was one thing in my favour, though. Unlike Renu, I was born in India. So it was a good thing, sort of a going back to the roots for her, they liked that. But they got on our case once we were married. Why weren't we having a baby? Didn't we want a baby? Were we using birth control? Why, what were we waiting for?'

I shake my head, but I can totally imagine it. It sounds exactly like the GIF.

'I'd done everything by the book up until that point,' Mum blurts out. I am so startled by the sound of her voice that it makes me jump. I can't help glancing at my father, who glances back at me, and the connection in this look we share is so familiar that it is like we have been doing it all my life. 'I'd finished school with straight As, I'd gone to uni. I'd got married. I planned to have two children, hopefully a boy and a girl. I spoke Hindi, though not all Indian girls of my generation did. I knew how to do henna patterns on my hands, and not many Indian girls could boast that. I'd even taken Hindustani classical music lessons as a child. I learned to play the harmonium, like a good little Indian girl.'

I have a sudden flashback to our *nautanki*, to Mum playing the harmonium in one of our performances.

'You were terrible at it,' I say. 'It sounded so awful, it was totally out of tune.'

My mother smiles uncomfortably. 'It was a success, it made people cry laughing.'

'Except Rose and I were laughing so hard we had to be taken off stage.' I frown at the memory. I have not thought about this for years.

'*Never again*, I said.' Mum is twiddling her hanky in her hands.

'That was me,' Dad says. 'I said, *Never again*.'

They are silent for a few moments.

'Then what happened?' I prod.

Dad lets out a long breath. Mum is staring at her hands. 'Then we made a mistake,' he says.

My heart is beating painfully. 'What mistake?'

'I left your father,' Mum says. 'It wasn't even his fault. The pressure to have a child, it was coming from my family. It was coming from both of us, because we really wanted a child. It wasn't your dad's fault. But I didn't want to be married any more. It was too much. I wanted to be single, I didn't want to feel like a big fat failure. I didn't want to feel the shame of not being able to have a child, so I left him. I rented a studio flat in Clapham.'

I stare at them. 'You separated? For how long?'

'A couple of years,' Mum says.

'You didn't want to be with him any more?' I ask slowly. My brain can't make sense of this. 'Did you go after her?' I ask Dad.

He shakes his head. 'She's not my property. She said she wanted space, so I let her have space. What is the point going mad about things you can't change?'

'Wow, it's like we're not related,' I say. 'Mum might have liked it if you acted a little bit possessive.'

'Your father is obsessively rational about things like this. I asked for space, so I got it.'

'Then?' I realize I'm holding my breath.

Dad is searching for words, I can see it in his face. Whatever needs to be said, there are no good words for it.

He finally speaks. 'A cousin of your mother's – his daughter Priya, she was fifteen at the time – she had had a baby when she was fourteen.'

They look at each other. My mother's jaw jumps for a second. Just for a second, like she's in pain, but she doesn't say anything. She sits there, staring at her hands, hunched forward, her shoulders thin.

Dad continues with the story. 'Uncle Jat and Auntie Pinky had been trying to get things patched up between us all along. They'd been trying to talk to us, get us to see sense, trying to get Mum to move back in with me. They wanted us to adopt in case that helped us, helped heal our relationship.'

'But I couldn't stand the thought of all the paperwork, the questions, the invasion into our life,' Mum says. 'In those years – and maybe now as well – agencies like to match parents' ethnicities with the baby's. We had talked to an adoption agency and they had said not to get our hopes up because there were hardly any Indian babies given up for adoption and we were very unlikely to be matched up with babies that weren't Indian – even though I was born and raised in London! I couldn't bear to go through years of that, of more hope and disappointment.'

'Uncle Jat told us about Priya's baby,' Dad says. 'He invited us both to go to their house for dinner.'

'Rose is Priya's daughter?' I ask.

'She wanted nothing to do with the baby,' Dad tells me. 'She was so young when she had it. Apparently, she had wanted to get an abortion, but it had been too late. She hadn't told anyone till she was over six months pregnant. Anyway, she had had the baby. And then the family had wanted nothing to do with it. So she – the baby – was being passed around between uncles and aunties and relatives.'

I want to cry. No one had wanted Rose. This makes no sense to me. I can't bear to imagine her as an unwanted baby that had been passed around from relative to relative. I can't bear to imagine her lying in her cot waiting to be picked up. I see the uncertain look in her eyes that is so much a part of her that I have never even questioned it. I can't bear to think now of how she got that look.

'Jat was the answer to their prayers,' Dad says. 'He said he'd take the baby off their hands immediately, no questions asked, no health tests, nothing. Rose was about a year old at the time.'

'So you adopted the baby – Rose?'

They look at each other and I can see the tiredness.

'We did,' Dad says. 'And we should have been more thorough, we should have found out everything. Priya had told her family that the father, a boy in her school, didn't want the baby, didn't want to be with her, that he was not in the picture. And we made the biggest mistake of our life. We didn't insist that they sign papers. We didn't get them to sign anything. We were handed a baby, a beautiful baby.'

'You don't have any paperwork?' I'm shocked.

'We were so young and we were so very stupid. We took their word for it. Paperwork is a big deal now, it wasn't like that back then. And the thing is Priya had disappeared by that point.'

'How do you mean, disappeared?'

'Not sure exactly,' Dad says. 'She had had the baby the previous year. And then she disappeared. The family said they had no idea where she was.'

I frown. 'Do you believe that?'

'Yes,' Dad nods slowly. 'I do. At the time she had actually disappeared. She just took off with some money and some clothes. We know that she came back after a few years, but at that time, she had actually taken off. They didn't know where she was. That's what I think. The thing is, this was fine with us. We were never going to bump into them, or Priya. It was exactly how we wanted it. We would have agreed to the kind of adoption where the parent wants to stay involved if we had to, but this is what we really wanted. We desperately wanted the baby. As soon as we heard about it, it had started to heal us. Renu moved back in. For the first time in years there was hope. The baby was already ours before she was put into our arms.'

'Why didn't you make it legal?'

Neither one of them says anything for a few moments. I can hear the click-clock, click-clock of the wall clock. In the background I can hear the radio that is on in the kitchen.

'The baby's parents were not in the picture and her family didn't want any paperwork. They just wanted us to have the baby and no one to say anything about it ever again. They were happy to be rid of it, they wanted it never to be mentioned again. They thought of it as Priya's failure, the family's failure. They couldn't bear the thought of what it would do to her reputation, the chances of her getting married. They wanted no paperwork, no paper trail, and even more importantly they wanted no delay. They wanted us to take the baby and they didn't want to ever see us again.'

'But they're related to us.'

'Yes, Priya's father is my cousin, from my father's side,' Mum says. 'But we never really knew that side of the family. My father died when I was a child, you know that. Jat tried to keep in touch with them, you know how he is about family. They're not as well off, and he tried over the years to offer them money, take care of them, offer jobs. But they didn't want that.'

'And Gareth Jones was the father?'

My parents nod. 'He knew nothing about the baby, it turned out.'

'How did he find out?'

'Of all the unlikely things that could happen, he saw a picture of the two of you doing your *nautanki*,' Dad says. 'And it made him look twice.'

'That's how striking it is? The resemblance?'

'He had met Jat at Priya's house a few times,' Dad says. 'He recognized Jat in the picture, so he read the article. He made nothing of it at the time, except that he thought the resemblance between Rose and his own sister was odd, uncanny. But then a few days later he went back to the article. The article mentions your ages. I guess it got him thinking. He called Priya's house and was told that she had disappeared. He told us later on that he had taken a punt. He said, *And where is Priya's daughter?* or something. And it worked. He said he thought it was a total shot in the dark. Anyway that led him to us.' He shook his head. 'To tell you the truth, I still can't believe that he managed to work it out. He could so easily have missed it. So easily.'

Mum briefly touches Dad's hand and says softly, 'He had recently lost his wife when he saw the picture. He was looking for something to help with his grief, anything at all. He was about twenty-five at the time. Very young.'

'Then he came to visit us.' Dad rubs his forehead.

'That Christmas?'

Dad nods. 'You remember that? Yes, that was it. Once

Gareth realized she was really his, he was desperate to have Rose.'

'Why did you let her go?' I'm so tired all of a sudden, I can't even be angry. I'm just sad, I'm lost. I want the last seventeen years to be different. I want to physically go back and change them. I feel desperate. 'It wasn't just your decision to make. It should have been ours too. Rose's and mine. How could you decide for us?'

'We fought with everything we had, Rilla,' Dad says softly. 'We didn't just let her go, we fought with everything we had.'

I look at him and I know that they had. With the help of Sheila Jenkins, their custody lawyer, they had fought for years.

'She was our daughter. You have to understand that. It made no difference that she was technically a distant relation,' Dad says.

I totally understand it, it doesn't need to be said. Rose was my sister. She still is.

'We fought and fought. But Gareth fought harder. Or he had a better case. Or – well, it came out that Jat had been paying money to Priya's family. This really went against us. We didn't talk to Jat for ages after it all happened. We blamed him for everything that had gone wrong. All of it. And he blamed himself, he still does. We went to court over it, we fought, but we had no documents, nothing, we had no proof. The judge said Jat had bribed the family, he'd practically bought Rose off them, he had taken advantage of their financial difficulties. Priya wasn't around to say anything at all. There was no trace of her. She had taken off, disappeared. She hadn't told Gareth she was pregnant, he hadn't been consulted. And here he was, he was Rose's biological father and he wanted his daughter back. In a way, it was his right, but we fought it anyway. We argued that it wasn't right for Rose to be separated from us, from you. Gareth argued that we were using his daughter for financial gain.'

'The *nautanki*?' I frowned.

'Yes, but I don't know if that was even what did it in the end, swayed things in his favour. He was Rose's biolog-ical father and the legal system doesn't like it when you haven't gone about something the right way. If we wanted to adopt Rose, we should have done it right. But it was more than that, perhaps. It was that Rose was half white too. The judge – he asked us how we were planning to raise a white child.' Dad shakes his head.

'I'll never forgive us,' Mum says. She takes a long shaky breath. Her face is pale, the skin around her eyes pulled, shrunken somehow.

'Gareth called us every day after Christmas. He cried on the phone, he begged, he pleaded, he threatened us. In the end, he won. Your mother went and stayed near her in Bristol for a few months. I don't know if you remember,' Dad says.

How can I forget anything about that time? I hadn't mentioned it to Rose the other day, but of course I remem-bered it. A few weeks after Rose left, Mum left too. She left for some time. I thought that she was with Rose, I thought she was never coming back. Auntie Dharma and Auntie PK moved in and looked after me when she was gone. I have tried not to think about that time, or perhaps I blocked it out, but now, all of a sudden I remember it like it was yesterday. All of a sudden, it is hitting me. And I feel the panic, the panic I used to feel each night when I went to bed in the months after Rose left. I developed a strange cough. Not like a proper cough. Just a short, pulsing, fast, exhaling sound that would go on and on. Auntie Dharma and Auntie PK used to discuss it. At first they couldn't figure out where it was coming from. Then when they realized it was me, they discussed the possibility that I had TB. They took me to the doctor to do blood tests. Finally, Mum came back, and that was when I started screaming at her.

For days and weeks I screamed at her. 'Tell me, tell me where she is. You – you've done something to her, you've killed her! Where is she? Where is she?'

And every time I did that, Mum cried. She cried, she broke down, she sobbed. 'Leave me be, Rilla, please, please stop. Leave me alone, please just leave me alone.'

This went on for weeks. Until one day, my mother took the car, and she drove away and we didn't hear anything from her for hours. When the police knocked at the door, asked Dad to go to the hospital with them, I stayed at home with the aunties. Later, Dad called and said Mum was okay, she had been in an accident, but that she would be in hospital for a few days, and he would stay with her. Whilst they were in the hospital I wasn't allowed to visit. It was for the best if I stayed away, Dad told me.

When they finally came home, my mother disappeared into her bedroom and stayed there for – I don't actually know how long it was. Days, weeks? I don't know. Her face was broken up, her ribs cracked, but it was her spirit that was dead. The day after they came back, my father told me she had been in a coma, that the doctors hadn't been certain she would pull through. He told me we couldn't talk about Rose.

'Do you see what could have happened, Rilla? Do you see what can still happen? She won't be able to tolerate talking about it. You see that, don't you? Promise me, promise me, Rilla.' His voice shook as he told me. He looked like he had had the shock of his life. And he couldn't cope with it, just then, not any of it.

And this, this is the memory I have tried so hard all my life to run from. The details, the words, the terror of it. I have tried so hard to suppress it, to undo it somehow. And I have been successful. More or less. Until now.

And I had nodded. The police hadn't known, had thought it was an accident, but Dad and I knew that Mum had driven the car into a standing truck on purpose. And I also knew that it was my fault, I had driven her to it.

Mum speaks now, and so lost am I in that time that I'm startled by the sound of her voice.

'I thought it would be easier on all of us if Rose didn't have to be cut off – I thought if I went and lived near her in Bristol, it would be easier for us all. But the one meeting we tried – Rose, me, Gareth – Rose was distraught. She screamed and cried.' I can't bear this. I don't want to hear it. 'And Gareth said there was to be no more contact, not till Rose was reconciled, settled. They met with a counsellor who told them the same thing. Gareth told us that – how the counsellor said it was important for Rose to accept her new life, her new reality, for us not to confuse her.'

No one can speak. For many moments, we sit silently. I pore over everything they've told me. I can't get the picture out of my mind of Rose as a baby that no one wanted.

'I can't understand it. I can't understand how Priya and her family didn't want her. Why was she passed around?'

'She suffered for it,' Dad says. 'She was a nervous little thing when she came to us.'

I nod slowly. 'She always was, she still is. It's like she's always looking to get hurt.' I swallow painfully.

'The first time she started to feel more at home with us was when you came along, a year later, on her second birthday. That was when she started to feel more settled.'

There are tears running down my cheeks now. And then she was taken away again, she was sent away again, to yet another family.

'I'm so sorry, I'm so very sorry,' Mum is saying.

'It wasn't your fault,' Dad says quickly. He places a hand on hers. And somehow I can't bear that little touch, that automatic protective gesture.

'You – did you love me when I was a child?' I say suddenly. I don't know that I'm going to say it, but then I do. I say it.

'We love you more than anything.' Dad says this, but I am not looking at him and my mother knows it. She is looking down at her hands, holding them in her lap. My father is giving me a warning look, but I am ignoring him.

'You weren't – you weren't nice to me when I was a child. It was like you – hated me.'

My mother shakes her head. 'Of course I loved you.' The tears are flowing. 'When Rose came to us, I thought I had everything. I wanted for nothing. I will never want anything again, that is what I thought. She was a magical baby, I loved her more than I could have ever imagined loving anything.'

My breath is stuck in my throat.

'When I found out I was pregnant, just a few short months later, I was terrified.'

I search her face.

'I was terrified of two things. I was terrified that I couldn't possibly love the new baby as much as I loved my first. And I was scared out of my mind that you were my biological daughter and I would love you more and forget all about Rose – or at least not be able to love Rose as much.'

My heart is beating painfully. 'And?'

She shrugs. 'And nothing. Neither one of those things is true, but the fears stayed with me. That is all I can say. I love you, of course I love you. I did my best for you.'

I am sorry for her, I really am, but I shake my head. 'No, Mum, you didn't.'

*

After a long time, Dad clears his throat. 'How was it – seeing her?'

It's a while before I can speak again. 'It's funny. When we were kids and we were out, no one used to think we were together, much less that we were sisters. Like if we got on a train together, and we both sat down with you, people would assume Rose was with the white family next to us, that she couldn't possibly be with us. All our relatives were always going on about how tall and fair she was too. This one time, she and I were messing about on a railway platform. It was with one of the aunties, I can't even remember who it was and we were racing each other. Who can get to the pole first, who can touch the security guard, and stuff like that. We raced each other to see who could find a seat in the waiting room. We ran in through two different doors. There was only one seat available and Rose got to it first, she was standing right by it. But I distracted her or something and somehow sat down first. Rose nicely stepped out of the way. I had won fair and square. And this white gentleman on the next seat made a big thing of standing up and offering Rose his seat. And he said to Rose, *Don't mind these foreigners and their children.* And he muttered something about British manners.'

'You have more in common than you know,' Dad says.

It's the nicest thing he could say to me right now. We sit quietly for a long time.

'Do you want to see her?' I ask my parents.

'Has she asked?' Mum's chin is shaking uncontrollably. I shake my head.

'Then no,' Dad says. He holds my mother's hand. 'She's our daughter, you know. Not by blood maybe, but she is our daughter. But she has to choose for herself. We let her down. I don't blame her for not wanting anything to do with us.'

Mum is crying. 'It is her decision.'

We sit silently for a long time. Finally, Mum gets up and goes to the kitchen. For a while all we hear is the tap running. There is no other sound, and neither Dad nor I look towards the kitchen. We resolutely keep our eyes away. Finally the tap stops and I hear Mum put the kettle on.

'Rilla,' Dad says, 'you know about the shoplifting – now, don't get mad – I just want to know what that was about. I mean, is this something we need to think about? We could hire a counsellor, we could talk with them, all of us, if it helps.'

I sigh. 'I don't know what happened. I don't know, okay? One minute I was about to have a panic attack about the wedding, the next I was running out of the store with a six-pack of a sport drink and Stevia. It was a really shitty drink as well and I don't even eat Stevia.'

Mum walks over with mugs of tea. She hands me mine, and I warm my hands on it.

'They didn't catch you at the time?' Dad asks.

I shake my head. 'I ducked into the underground. They didn't catch me.'

'Then how did the police find out it was you? CCTV?' Dad frowns, blows into his tea, then he takes a large slurping sip.

I don't meet their eyes. 'It wasn't CCTV.' I clear my throat. 'I called them and confessed.'

'Oh!' Dad looks surprised for a moment, then nods slowly. 'Yes, yes, that was a good thing to do. When did you do that? Right away?'

'When I was waiting for you to come and get me from the back room at Bloomington House,' I say guiltily. 'At the wedding.'

'Rilla!' Mum looks shocked. She sits down again. She is holding a tea towel around her tea.

'There was a number to call for missing persons on the notice board. I called it and told them I wanted to confess. And there was this woman on the other end of the line. She said, *And is this related to a missing person?* No, I said. *And have you spotted a missing person?* I said, No. *Are you a missing person, is anyone you know a missing person, have you abducted a missing person?* I assured her, No. She was going to hang up but I told her I'd just keep calling her unless she transferred me to someone relevant. In the end she gave me the number of the nearest police station.' I grimace. 'Sorry.'

Dad is shaking his head. 'Maybe it was the stress of the wedding,' he mumbles, trying to make sense of this picture I am painting of his daughter.

'I don't know. I think it was more to do with Rose.' But I have more questions. I frown. 'What did Mrs Daniels mean about wanting to separate us?'

'What?'

It takes me a couple of minutes to explain this to my parents. They have no memory of my teacher Mrs Daniels.

'Oh,' Dad says finally, 'what a strange question. I remember though. She said that during your breaks you always played together. You'd always been like that and it had never been a big problem, but apparently you were beginning to fight a lot.'

'Because of the *nautanki*, we thought. It put a lot of stress on you. On everyone,' Mum says.

Dad doesn't say anything.

'Anyway, she suggested that they would try to separate you more, help you make other friends so there was less fighting. Why do you ask?'

I shake my head. 'No reason at all,' I say and finally, after seventeen years, I can lay that ghost to rest. Maybe I can't change who I am and the niggling feeling that I've done something terrible will always be there, but maybe I don't have to let it define me. Maybe.

'Why?' I ask. 'Why didn't you tell me all this? You should have told me.'

'We didn't want to make your whole life about this,' Dad says.

'What do you think my whole life has been about?' I ask.

42

I Cry

As Maya Angelou says, when someone you've loved, and then lost, comes tip-toeing into the cubby-holes of your mind, calling to you and beckoning, they show you all the days you've lost. They call to mind the jewel of a stolen touch and the whisper of a secret word. And when they do that, all you can do in turn is cry . . .

Rilla's notes

I sleep half the day. When I wake up, I remember suddenly that Rose is leaving, that I'm losing her again. In fact, the truth is, I've already lost her. This knowledge hits me square in the chest. I lie there, staring up at my ceiling, tracing with my eyes the cracks that are forming there, and the old cracks that have always been there. Of course, it was better that I saw her again, of course it was, I tell myself. Even if I'm now finding it unbearable, of course it was better.

Tyra calls me. 'Where are you? Are you going to come out with me or what? Today, tomorrow? Give me a date, babe!'

I take a deep breath. 'I will soon, Tyra. Just not yet.'

'I have the phone number of this guy you'd really like.'

'No, Tyra. Thanks, but no.'

'Are you okay, sweetie? It's just you've seemed really low these last few weeks. And I barely see you.'

I swallow. 'No, I'm not okay. But I will be.'

I walk slowly out of my room and make my way downstairs in my PJs and slippers. Federico is crying in the kitchen. He's been in Mexico for two weeks. He missed his father's funeral, but he spent some time with his mother. And now, back from Mexico, his boyfriend Pip has broken up with him. There are dark circles under his eyes. Last night, I could hear him crying in his room but he didn't open the door when I knocked. There's the smell of burnt toast in the kitchen, an explosion of cranberry granola on the counter, an oaty milk leaking in the middle of the debris. Lord Basingstoke is trying to lick the trails of milk that are making their way off the counter, and all the way down the dishwasher to the floor. He is mostly just bumping his head again and again on the dishwasher and mewling. I take margarine out of the fridge and dab the cat's paws with it. He sits down and licks contentedly. I walk over to Federico and give him a hug, and now we are both crying. I pull away from him, dab my eyes and nose on my sleeve.

'It's okay, Federico.'

367

'It's okay, Rilla.'

We cry for all the things we've lost.

'Federico.' I look at him. 'Why do you let Jharna give you advice about your relationships and not me?'

He sighs. 'It's like . . .' he thinks about it ' . . . you make me feel stubborn. You know everything about me, you see too much. I have nothing to fight back with. I feel – what is the word? Exposed.'

'That's crazy.'

'Also, you are pretty shit at relationships.'

I slap him in the face and threaten to drop the large pumpkin he is carving for his vegetable orchestra out of the window. He hugs me again, but pushes the large hollowed-out squash on which he has carved four small holes safely out of reach.

'You were right, I should reveal myself more. Pip should know more about me. But it's like – that's not who I am.' He half-heartedly dips a piece of granola in the milk on the counter and eats it. 'It's like no matter what I do, my father is always in my head, telling me I'm no good.'

I nod. Yes, it's difficult to escape the essence of who you are, he's right about that.

Federico leaves for university for an afternoon lecture and I walk upstairs, take a long shower that leaves me scalded and pruny. I dress in a turquoise t-shirt and a cotton skirt that is the colour of a sunset and has pockets in it. I like skirts that have pockets, but that's not why I wear this one today. I wear it because appliquéd on the waistband is a large rose in full blossom. As gestures go, it is small and insignificant and there's no one here to see it.

I hear the doorbell. I want to ignore it, but it's hard because it just keeps on going. It's easier to open it than to listen to the din for a moment longer and get permanent tinnitus.

Simon is standing outside the front door in a dark blue t-shirt that matches his eyes and in his brown cords, my favourite ones. I grab the door for support, because I'm afraid I'm going to collapse entirely. I can't catch my breath.

'You were right,' he says. 'We rushed into it. You were right. You tried to tell me but I was too scared to listen. I'm listening now.'

He's here. He's here with me, even though I don't deserve it.

'Simon.' My voice cracks. 'If – if you're mad at me, it's okay. If you think I'm too much work, if you want someone easier—'

'Rilla, listen to what I'm saying,' he says, his voice steady. 'I've never wanted anyone else.'

And then I'm in his arms. I don't know how I end up there, but I never want to let go. He's holding me so tight I can't breathe. He's going to crack ribs and I'm going to start bursting blood vessels. When he kisses me, I hold on to him for dear life.

I pull back my head and look at him. 'The thing is, I don't want to get married.'

He nods. 'Okay. I can wait, I'm not going anywhere.'

'You would fight for me?' I don't know exactly what I

mean by this. 'If I left you, you wouldn't just let me go? You would fight for me?'

'I haven't been fighting for you at all, I really want that mental cat. Where is it? Let me take it away, then I never have to see you again.'

I lunge at him, kiss him, the feel of his lips, his face in my hands, the way he smells so familiar that I can feel the sharp relief deep in my stomach.

When he finally puts me down, I say, 'You don't want Jharna instead? Would you prefer her to me?'

He looks at me like I'm crazy. 'She's ten. She's a child. I'm thinking of adopting her.'

'And Rose? You wouldn't rather be with Rose?'

'She seems sweet.'

'That's all?'

He shrugs. 'She seems nice? I guess?'

'Okay. That's okay then.'

'This isn't the last time you're going to ask me this sort of thing, is it? You're pretty much always going to be a paranoid freak?'

I nod slowly. 'That could be true.'

He clears his throat. I wonder what he's going to say. It looks like something important or he wouldn't look this serious. He finally comes out with it.

'Do we have to take that cat with us? There's something really wrong with it.'

'Federico wants it. We're off the hook.'

'Phew,' Simon says. 'I can stop plotting parabolas.'

*

Simon has to leave for a party he's doing.

'Do you have to go?' I murmur.

'I could cancel everything and stay,' he says softly. He presses his lips to my forehead. 'It's only a fourth birthday party. The child will probably get over it by the time she's twenty. With a bit of timely therapy.'

He's joking, but I can see in his eyes how much he wants to stay. It's physically painful for me to push him out of the door. 'Come back later, okay?'

'Wild horses wouldn't keep me away,' he murmurs.

He turns to leave, but I pull him back and I hand him a fistful of pebbles.

'I asked you to keep those for me, Langton.'

When he's gone, I sit down on the porch with my laptop. I open an email that I have been ignoring for many days. My colleague Sarah-Lee had sent me a job posting for an assistant editor for an arts and humanities publisher. Some days ago, when I had seen it, I had closed the email quickly, not having any room in my life, in my head or my heart really to think about the rest of my life. I could only see as far as the next day, another day with Rose.

It occurs to me now as I look at it, read the ad more carefully, that it was a thoughtful thing for Sarah-Lee to have done.

'It sounds perfect for you!' she had written in the email, with five kisses to follow.

I write a quick email back. 'Thanks for thinking of me. You're right, it sounds cool. Coffee some time?'

I send it before I can think better of this strange sociable impulse. I tap my fingers on my laptop. Then I do what I have known I have to do – it's time. I have to acknowledge that I'm not doing what I need to do for my MA. I have to say goodbye to it. I write to Professor Grundy to tell her that I have decided to quit the MA programme, I tell her about the job I'm thinking of applying for. When I've sent the email, I sit back on the swing not knowing exactly what I feel. I don't know if the hollow feeling in my stomach is relief or panic. It's decisive, that's for sure.

My phone rings. It's Professor Grundy. This is so unprecedented I stare at her name dumbfounded. I pick up and say a tentative hello, almost sure that her phone has picked a random name and dialled my number by mistake.

'Rilla, I'll write you a reference,' Professor Grundy says without preamble. 'Take the job. But listen to me, do the MA part-time, finish it. You've done so much work on it already.'

I take a shuddering breath. 'I don't know much about love, Prof.'

'But you know about being different.'

I frown. 'What do you mean?'

There's silence at the other end like she's thinking. 'You're quite private, I see that, and I'm not one to probe into private lives. To be honest, I don't want to know. But love – well, love is about accepting how you're different. Maybe. And you do know about that.'

I shake my head. I pull the phone away from my ear. I have never heard Professor Grundy talk like that.

She clears her throat like she's realizing this herself. 'Finish the MA. Make it about you – connect yourself to it and it will become easier. If you want to go part-time, we can probably cook up a bit more flexibility for you. And anyway, I'm not marking all these papers by myself!'

A joke! 'Are you all right, Prof?' I ask cautiously.

'Just think about what I've said.'

I stare into the distance. For some reason, at her words, the hollow feeling in my stomach dissipates a little. It's still there, but maybe it shrinks just a smidge. 'Okay, Prof. I will.'

And she's gone.

I put the phone down. Love is about accepting how you're different. I shake my head. A tall order, Prof, a tall order.

I have to get used to this, somehow or the other, all over again. I have had years to get used to it, this void in my life, but in the years since Rose disappeared there was always the hope – even if it was fleeting – that I'd find her and we would be sisters again. Now I have nothing, no sister, no hope and I have to get used to it all over again. I can email her, I tell myself, we can talk on the phone, I will sometimes see her, perhaps. Yes, I nod, yes, that has to be okay, that has to be enough. It's better than nothing.

Earl rides past. I give him a sad wave.

'Say something, Earl,' I call. 'You always have important things to say.'

He shakes his head at me. 'What can I say, Rilla?' he

calls. 'Make your own choices. Don't let anyone else decide for you.'

I'm flicking television channels, wondering what to do with myself, when the doorbell goes again. I sigh and walk slowly downstairs. My parents, Uncle Jat, Auntie Pinky, Jharna and various other aunties are standing there. Then I'm surrounded by them, they are hugging me, and suddenly I am crying because my heart is breaking.

'It's okay, *beta*, it'll be all right,' Dad is saying.

Mum is clinging to me. I hug her back, hold her tight for a moment. She surreptitiously wipes a tear as she pulls away, and I realize with a jolt that it isn't for Rose, it's for me. The others are standing about on my porch, sniffing and wiping tears.

Then I draw back. 'Why, why did we let her go? We've let her go again. Why?'

They all shake their heads.

'It was a mistake,' Mum says. 'The biggest of my life.'

'We should have done it right the first time,' Dad is saying.

'It's my fault,' Uncle Jat says as Auntie Pinky wipes tears.

'We shouldn't have let her go,' I say slowly. Then I stare at them. I look at my phone. 'We can't make the same mistake. She must be on her way to the airport now. We have to go after her. Don't you see? I have to go after her.'

Of course, as soon as the words are out of my mouth, before my poor brain has even registered what I have just

said, everyone is galvanized into action. This is the thing
with the GIF, there's not a whole lot of standing about,
doing nothing. In a matter of seconds, the tears have been
wiped, tissues tucked away, jackets that were halfway
down the arms firmly back on and buttoned up. Sad frowns
are being smudged away like on a dry-wipe magnetic board
and quickly replaced with expressions of dogged determi-
nation. Phones are out and routes are being mapped. I
look at them, feeling a little bemused. What have I just
started?

Everyone wants to go to the airport. They're already
plotting it, acting like I'm not even there, but then it turns
out that there is only one car – some members of the GIF
having taken public transport to get to my flat. They can't
all go to the airport. There is now a fierce debate about
who gets a place in the car.

'Of course Renu and I must go,' Dad says.

'Without a shadow of a doubt, *ji*, without a shadow of
a doubt,' Uncle Jat says.

'It may be too emotional for you,' Auntie PK says firmly,
looking at my mother. 'If I go, I can help diffuse the situation.'

'Try and keep me away, Parminder,' my mum says, a
militant look in her eye, softened only by the trembling
chin.

'It's okay, Renu, it's okay,' Dad says, patting Mum on
the back.

'Well, I'm definitely going,' Auntie Pinky says. 'You can't
manage without me.'

'Look, there is a simple way to solve this problem. Who has passports?' Uncle Jat holds up his own.

Everyone holds up their passports.

'Why do you all have your passports?' I stare at them.

'Just in case they came in handy today, that's all I'm saying.' Uncle Jat taps his nose.

'You're all crazy.' I stare from one to another. 'You realize that?' I blink a few times, hoping that it will clear my head. 'Listen, there are too many of you and there's only one car.'

Okay, I'm getting a grip on this. I try to stare them down.

'Come on, we don't have much time. Her flight time is five p.m.! How about just I go?' I say it hopefully, like I'm offering a neat solution to the problem.

No one pays any attention to me.

I shake myself, there is no point arguing, there isn't time. I run upstairs, quickly drag some shoes on, grab my phone and keys and run downstairs again. Uncle Jat is patiently explaining to Auntie PK, Auntie Dharma and Jharna that there is simply no room in the car and the three of them need to stay put.

'Get some lunch ready or something,' he says, and gets a glare from Auntie PK in return. 'Send us updates on traffic and the status of the flight,' he says to Jharna, avoiding Auntie PK's eye.

'Whatevs,' Jharna says. 'Peace.'

Uncle Jat and Auntie Pinky get into the front seats of their BMW, my parents and me at the back. Just as we are about to drive off, Auntie Dharma jumps in as well, and before I know what's happening, I'm sitting in her lap, my neck twisted sideways, my cheek squashed up and stuck to the top of the car.

'You need me,' she says, 'the moon is in your fourth house. You need a mother figure.'

Auntie Pinky turns around and glares at her. She is wearing leggings, a big t-shirt with a peacock on it and trainers, and she even has a sweatband around her wrist. She has come prepared.

'Oye, what do you think I am?'

'Go, go, go!' Dad says. He is wiping his hand on a hanky, his eyes are on the road. He looks bigger today and I swear there is less grey in his hair.

'We don't have a moment to lose! Do your talking later!' Uncle Jat pulls away, tyres burning, accelerating fast. 'A miss is as good as a mile!'

The ride to the airport is better forgotten. There are several near collisions, many red lights skipped, quite a lot of unnecessary tyre screeches. Uncle Jat does U-turns and changes lanes to avoid traffic more times than I can count. It takes us two hours of cursing and swearing to get to Heathrow, and another half hour to find parking. By the time we do, I am seething, in a frenzy. We pop out of the car like burnt toast pinging out of a toaster, everyone trying to stretch and unravel. My neck is throbbing and it's unlikely I'll ever be able to straighten it again. By the time we get inside, there are no passengers in the American

Airlines check-in line. Rose has cleared check-in and security. It's an hour before her departure time.

'We have to go in,' Dad says in his best English to the
woman at check-in. 'You don't understand, it's of the
utmost importance. We don't really have time to explain,
but if you knew the story, you would understand.' He taps
his forehead.

'Sorry, sir,' the woman says. 'I have tickets you can buy.
But that is the only way you're going in. Only business
class though. There's nothing left in economy.' She types
industriously, not once looking at her hands, only scanning
her screen. After five minutes of furious clickety-clacking,
she pauses. 'No,' she says, 'there's nothing. Oh, wait . . .'
More clacking. 'No, nothing. Sorry, only business class.' She
smooths her hands over her blue jacket. She pats her hair
even though it is impeccable, not a blonde strand out of
place.

'That's fine, we only need one ticket.' I look beseechingly
at Uncle Jat. As if there's a chance of convincing him not
to part with money that he doesn't need to spend. He is
already pulling out various gold-plated cards.

'We want,' he turns around and counts, 'six.'

'Why *do* you all have your passports with you?' I say.

'It is best to be prepared,' Dad says.

'Mars is in my ninth house,' Auntie Dharma says, 'it's
best to be ready to travel at the drop of a hat.'

The woman checks our passports and then our visas.

'Why on earth do you have visas?' I shriek.

Simon and I had got visas because we were supposed

to go to Hawaii for our honeymoon, and the GIF, they tell me, all have visas because they were going to surprise us there after two weeks. (Surprise! Oh, how lovely to see you . . . I am so excited that you came to our honeymoon. This is my happy face, it really is.)

'Seriously,' I say, flagging, 'we only need one ticket . . .'

'We need six,' Uncle Jat says. 'A stitch in time saves nine. Six stitches, fifty-four.'

Armed with business class tickets we make a dash for it across the airport, Auntie Dharma with her flimsy flip-flops in her hands, trying to keep her *chunni* around her neck.

The woman at the counter had said there was no way we would make it in time before the gates closed for take-off, our gate being at the other end of the airport.

'No way,' she had said, looking at her screen. 'Wait, wait . . . No, no way. It's just too far.'

But then she had suddenly got into fifth gear and took off across the airport, holding on to her mobile phone, running on her high heels, her blazer flap-flap-flapping.

'Go, go, go!' she said when she started running. Now every few seconds she turns her head around, and without breaking stride, shouts at us, 'Come on, what are you, pussies?!' She doesn't actually say that bit, but she may as well. We're all sweating and panting and hyperventilating and not one of her hairs has escaped the ruthless doughnut on top of her head.

We run through security, fuming at the slowness of the bag checking and the body scans. We run all the way across the hundred or so gates to our gate, an airport trolley beeping next to us all the way, egging us on. And then we're finally there.

'Just in time!' Uncle Jat says. 'Come on, they're already boarding first class. It's us next!'

Dad reminds him we're not actually going. He turns to Superwoman to thank her, and probably to slip her a little something. Dad loves to slip people a little something and the woman will probably strap handcuffs on him. But then I forget about the lot of them, because there is Rose, sitting in the lounge waiting to board the flight. She is staring at me. I slowly walk up to her.

'Rose?' I whisper.

'What on earth are you doing here?' She stands up. She looks around. People are looking at us curiously. Rose doesn't like that, she hates being the centre of attention, it scares her. I want to protect her from that, but at the moment, I know I am living on borrowed time. I only have a few minutes before I lose her again. She looks cool in her long pink skirt, bordered with purple elephants, her white tank top. I have sweat moons expanding around my armpits.

'You're all here.' She looks behind me. I watch as the tentative look on her face sets to something else, perhaps to a kind of resolve not to let me – us – in again.

'No.' I slowly shake my head. 'This is all we could get in the car. This definitely isn't all the people that wanted to come.'

'It won't change anything, Rilla. You – you can't just

force people to do something they don't want to do.' She says it kindly, like to a simple child.

'You have to stay here.' I take a deep breath. 'You don't understand.'

She shakes her head.

I hold out my hands. 'Please, don't shake your head yet. Listen to what I have to say.'

'I – I came because I thought we could go back – that we might have a chance. But we don't. It's too late. Rilla.'

'Rubbish,' I say sharply. 'Of course we have a chance. The thing is, I have no idea who I am without you. And I get into all kinds of shit when you're not here. Rose, please, I can't go back to it – the emptiness, that constant feeling that something is missing. Don't you see? You can't – *you can't* give us a few moments together and then take it all away again. Please, you have to stay. I need you!'

She shakes her head, her face tight. 'Do you? You never liked me trying to take care of you.'

'I'll probably hate it now too, but you have to do it anyway. And you – you need me too. As much as I need you. I know you do. I want to take care of you. I want to do it better this time. Please give me the chance.'

I see her taking a deep breath. She is quiet for a few moments. I can see she's trying to decide if she should say something. I know her like the back of my hand. Better.

'Go on,' I say softy. 'Say it.'

'You let me go, Rilla.'

I suck in my breath. She's staring at me. It's hurting her to say this, but I know this is what she actually thinks.

'You shouldn't have let me go. You should have burnt the house down to get me back.'

I close my eyes for a second. This is why she's leaving.

'You – I thought you wouldn't let them do it. I thought you'd fight every inch of the way to get me back. I waited and waited for you to come and get me.'

A tear tries to run its way down my cheek. I wipe it savagely away.

'I thought you'd been sent away for your own protection – from me,' I splutter. 'Don't you see? I thought they were trying to keep you safe.'

And I was scared of losing Mum. I was scared that she would die, that after losing Rose, I would lose her too. And it would be because I couldn't think of anyone but myself. But I don't say this, this isn't the time for it.

'I thought they wanted to get you away from me.'

She looks incredulous. 'What are you talking about?'

'They said they were going to separate us because I was always hurting you, screaming at you, hitting you.'

She frowns, shakes her head. 'I did those things to you.'

'I didn't know what I might have done to you. How far I'd gone. I didn't know. I thought maybe it was something I'd blocked out. I tried to strangle someone when I was a teenager.' I tell her the story, quickly and concisely, knowing that I'm on borrowed time.

'If someone had said that to me about you, I would have killed them.' Her eyes are big and black. 'I used to fight with you just as much as you did with me.'

I shake my head. 'I don't remember it like that. You

382

were always the good one. I thought they were going to send me away. When they sent you away I thought maybe whoever had taken you didn't want me. I thought they chose the nicer sister.'

She looks at me for a long time. 'You are so incredibly stupid,' she says softly.

'Not as stupid as you.' I look at her with I don't know what in my face. A begging look, because begging is what I'm doing. Begging for my life. I take a deep breath. 'Are you coming with us or what?'

There is an announcement. They are letting business class passengers board now, and families with little kids. I am getting a sinking feeling we're going to have to get on this flight. That we're all going to California.

'Rose?'

She bends down, picks up her bag. I have nothing now, I have nothing left. I am feeling desperate, but I can think of nothing else to say to convince my sister to stay.

'You looked after me,' I say desperately. 'How can you leave me now? I need you.'

'You have Simon,' she says.

'And you – you have me.'

She shakes her head.

'They fought for you, you know. They fought, Mum and Dad. They kept on trying to get you back. We – we nearly lost Mum.' I say it and I watch her face, the flicker around her eyes.

She is staring at me. 'I didn't know that.'

'They were stupid, it's true. They didn't do it right the

first time. They thought – they thought that it would all be okay. Your mother – your biological mother – she said that was how she wanted things and they believed her. They were desperate to have you. They wanted you so much they didn't think about doing it the right way in case it slowed things down. They tried for years to get you back.'

There are more announcements. I look desperately at the shrinking queue of people. I look at Rose, she is biting her lips. For the first time, she is hesitating. I can see what I have said has taken her by surprise.

'They should have done it right.'

I nod frantically. 'Yes, it was very stupid. I know that and they know it too. I know – I know you can't forgive us.'

'I'm just not sure it's going to work, Rilla. Sometimes the time is gone. The time when something could have been done, the time when there was the chance of going back.'

'Please,' I say urgently. 'Please. You have to stay. I swear it, I'll burn down this airport, I'll throw things, I'll scream. I swear it and it'll be on your head.'

They are making final boarding announcements. Rose looks over to the gate, then she looks at me.

'Do it then,' she says.

'What?'

She puts down her bag. 'Scream. Then I'll stay.'

'What are you, mad? They'll arrest me.'

I stare at her. She looks back at me, she raises her

eyebrows. She's not going to back down. I sigh. If they did arrest me, I guess it wouldn't be the first time. I take a deep breath and I start screaming. Like I said before, I'm pretty good at it.

I scream and scream and scream. I go wild. I start clawing at my hair. I take my hoody off, the next thing is my t-shirt. I am screaming my head off and my clothes are coming off. I'm quickly regretting the clothes because none of the GIF is trying to stop me. There were frantic whispers at first, when I started screaming, admonitions, furious barked instructions to stop. But now they've turned around and are pretending they don't know me. They're looking at their passports and tickets, they're shaking their heads at this scene created by some crazy mad bitch who's taking all her clothes off. Police officers are running up to me shouting something or other, and now my hands are behind my back and I'm being pinned to the floor – I'm being pinned to the floor in my bra and knickers. This is a new low for me. They put me in handcuffs, they lift me off the floor and stand me up. A policeman places a coat around my shoulders.

Rose says, 'Sorry, Officer, sorry about all that. It's just we need to leave now. Thanks for your help.' She smiles and nods reassuringly at them.

'Sorry, miss,' the man says, 'she's coming with us.'

'Then I'm coming too,' Rose says. She picks up her bag again, places it demurely on her shoulder.

'No, miss,' the officer says, 'she's under arrest, she's coming with us. You're staying here. Family can visit later.'

That's when Rose drops her bag on the policeman's foot and starts screaming.

When Rose and I are finally released from custody (negotiated by Gudrun, the Rottweiler hired by John Langton), we walk outside. I remember the lecture Gudrun gave me last time I was in this situation – not that long ago, come to think of it. I wait for it. Her mouth is pursed, she is frowning, no, growling at me, the two little buns at the back of her head are standing to attention, but the lecture doesn't come. She hands me her business card instead.

'Don't flash police officers,' she says mildly. Then she takes the card back for a second and writes something on it. I look at it, it's her mobile number. 'See you soon,' she says before she walks away, clearly thinking that I'm too far gone and will need her again before too long.

The GIF is waiting for us, to take us home. Mum is there, looking at the ground. Not only is the airport contingent there, but Auntie PK and Jharna have joined them, as have the Toddlers. They are tearing around the sides of the BMW in a frantic mad dash and each of them is in imminent danger of crashing onto the ground or into the car at any moment. Or falling into the path of other cars. Their parents, Sulekha and Benji, are snoring in their car.

Rose is standing completely still. She's staring at Mum. Suddenly I feel like I can't get enough breath into my lungs. Mum walks slowly over to her, she holds out her hand to Rose's cheek. I can't watch this. I don't look at them, I look at the ground. There are some things you don't want the memory of, there are some things that are too painful to bear witness to. When I do look up, Rose has her smile on, the polite one, the I'm-not-letting-you-hurt-me one.

'How are you?' I hear her say. I hear nothing in return. It'll be a while before Mum can say anything.

'Come now,' Dad says gently, 'let's get you some luncheon.'

'Least said, soonest mended,' says Uncle Jat.

'Least said, my foot,' Auntie PK says. 'You think this is the way women of this family behave? Like shrieking banshees? I can't believe the stories you're telling me!'

'Oh, I don't know,' Dad says, 'it worked, didn't it? They had to do something.'

'Punch someone in the face then, show them what's what. Why the screaming, that's what I want to know? Have you learnt nothing?' Her short hair is spiky, and she is wearing a beige tunic, jeans and hemp shoes.

'Cool to meet you, Sis,' Jharna says to Rose. She makes the peace sign.

'Auntie Rose, Auntie Rose, Auntie Rose,' the Toddlers shout. 'Auntie Rilla, what are you doing? Auntie Rilla, why were you arrested? Auntie Rilla, why do you keep saying fuck?'

'Shit,' I say.

'Who're they?' Rose looks at the boys. 'They're cute!'

'Run now before it's too late,' I say. 'They're the devil's children. And if you think there aren't going to be lectures about the airport incident, I'll say you don't know a thing.'

Rose sneaks her hand into mine. 'Don't worry. I'll say it was my idea.'

'It was your idea,' I say crossly, snatching my hand away. 'That's my necklace you're wearing around your neck, by the way. I want it back, thief.'

She's wearing the necklace she gave me a long time ago for Christmas, the necklace I thought I had lost, the necklace that says 'RILLA'. As gestures go, it's quite significant, and I am here to see it.

I reach for her hand again, and we get into Dad's car. 'Where are we going?' he says. 'Ours? Maybe everyone can come back to ours, all have dinner, we can call Simon, maybe even the Langtons, you can stay the night! I'm thinking—'

'No way,' Rose and I say.

A few hours ago, we were sitting in a small room in the police station, waiting for Gudrun to make an appearance. I walked over to the blackened glass on one of the walls and stuck my tongue out, lifting my t-shirt up to show my bra. Rose came up and stood beside me, and there we were in the glass. Me, small, brown, bushy hair down to my shoulders. Rose, taller, lighter-skinned, long hair down to her tailbone. Both with eyes that slanted and looked out uncertainly at the world.

'You know there's no one there, right?' Rose said, eyeing the glass. 'They only do that for hardened criminals.'

'I am a hardened criminal. I have a police record and I tried to strangle someone.'

She hesitated. 'I'm still not sure how this will go, Rilla, you have to understand that. I'm making no promises. We just have to see how it goes, okay?' She said it softly.

'I know.'

Her eyes sought out my own in the glass and I looked calmly back at her. For the first time since I had found her again, I saw her eyes lose that searching look. Just for a second, but it was there. She slipped her hand in mine and I gripped it with the gentlest touch I could manage.

Acknowledgements

Please note that these acknowledgements are full of nause-ating sentimentality, and oh, there may also be an overuse of adjectives. My eternal gratitude goes to you wonderful people.

Charlotte Brabbin, my gorgeous editor. I don't know how I got so lucky. I'm in awe of your insight, and your ability to step back and look at the bigger picture of a book. Thank you for so generously listening to my crazy ideas (you know which I'm talking about), for giving me support and guidance when I need it, but also trusting me when I want to run with things. This book owes much clarity and heart to your vision. Please don't leave me. (No, seriously, please don't.)

The HarperCollins team, you're amazing. Thank you Kate Bradley, Lynne Drew, Charlotte Ledger and all the other brilliant editors, the marketing, copy-editing, produc-tion and design teams. I'm humbled by your knowledge and skills, and in love with your love for books. (If you're giving away any more books, you know where to find me.)

Samar Hammam, my superwoman agent. You trusted my writing before I gave you this book and you know how to get the deals. I cherish your integrity, your desire to champion good writing even when you don't know where it'll lead, and your ability to cut to the heart of the matter. Thanks for letting me be one of those annoying, grumpy writer types.

The SI Leeds Literary Prize team: Fiona Goh, Irenosen Okojie, Kadija George, Bernadine Evaristo, the Ilkley Literature Festival, Peepal Tree Press, The Literary Consultancy and everyone else associated with the prize. I'll never forget that you got me started on this journey. I'm grateful for your championing of writers, your passion, commitment and conviction. Without you, and the tireless work you do, the publishing industry would be the poorer.

Leverhulme, for the Artist-in-Residence grant that gave me the space and courage to write *Marmite and Mango Chutney*, and for giving me much needed validation. You brought some very important people into my life: Tariq Jazeel, Claire Dwyer, Nazneen Ahmed, Caroline Bressey and everyone else at University College London. Go Room 108!

Over the years, the support of many people has meant a lot to me. These include Keshini Naidoo, a woman of heart and substance. Teachers: Bill Roorbach, Eric Fredin and Priya Srinivasan. Friends: Andreas Otte, Charlotte Hennessy, Ananda Breed, Jamilah Ahmed. People and organisations that have supported my writing in various ways: Paul Vlitos, Billy Clark, Sabine Sorgel, Plymouth

University, Literature Works, the Cambridge Institute for Continuing Education, and the literary magazines that have published me.

Anisha, what can I say? Thank you for saving me, for reading everything I throw at you, for saying you love some of it, for going unnervingly quiet when you don't like some of it, for your sunny and passionate self.

Thank you to friends and family for giving me the courage to do this, and for putting up with my crazy ideas and neurotic longings.

In the meantime, I would recommend reading *Grounds for Play* by Kathryn Hansen, to find out more about *nautanki*.